Loyalty and Honour

By

Michael J May

Contents.

Intro.

Welcome to Loyalty and Honour! My first step into the historical/spy/was/thriller genre.
This is a work of fiction; Historical accuracy is very much secondary to story line. There is some historical fact in the story, but it is mostly a work of fiction. Please view it as such, and enjoy.

1. The Hospital.

Sound was the first sense to come back. Distant sounds became ever clearer, though he still struggled to identify them. He could hear shuffling, coughing, and birdsong. Next came smell, it smelled medicinal, clinical. Where was he? He focused on opening his eyes. It was a struggle. A small amount of light filtered in; bright. Very bright. Shapes moved around, out of focus. Damn. Why was it so bright? Slowly but surely, his vision returned to normal. He was lying on his back in bed. Behind him was a large open window, which explained the birdsong. A gentle breeze blew onto his face. He lifted his head and looked around; he was in a large, narrow hall, lined on two sides with beds. All the beds were occupied by men. Wounded men. Was he in a hospital? Where? And, perhaps more importantly... Why?

A shape stopped at the foot of his bed; a nurse.

"Ah, nice to see you are finally awake Rottenführer Deckman"

Deckman? Yes. That was my name! Joseph Deckman, Corporal in the Waffen SS.

I cleared my throat "Where am I?"

"You are in the Hohenlychen Sanatorium" she said.

Where? Wait. I had heard of it. An SS Hospital, near... Near... Shit. Where was it? Berlin! Of course. But why was I here? I felt a dull pain in my leg, and tried to sit up to see what it was. Tried, but failed.

A searing pain in my leg prevented me sitting up fully and I fell back in frustration. "Aaah! Sheiße"

"Your leg" the nurse said, sensing my anxiety "Don't worry, it's still there"

I let out a loud sigh of relief.

"They all do that you know" she said "Check for amputations"

"It's still there" I said.

"Yes, it is" she said "You're lucky, a bit higher and *you* wouldn't be here"

"What?" I couldn't remember what had happened.

"The bullet. It missed the artery and lodged in the thigh bone"

"I was shot?" I was shot??? What? Where? When? How?

I remembered nothing.

"I presume so, hence the bullet" she smiled "You'll be fine tough. Your memory will return in time. A week or so, and you'll be out of here"

"How long have I been here?" I asked.

"Three days, not long" she signed the sheet on the clipboard and went to walk away, but stopped. "Oh, I forget. You have a visitor, he's been waiting to see you for two days"

"A visitor?" A visitor? Here? Who? Could it be my parents? No, wait, they were in... In... Dammit. Austria! Yes, they lived in Austria.

"Yes, a Hauptsturmführer Wiezinge"

A Captain? Waiting for me? What was going on? I couldn't recall ever meeting a Captain Wiezinge.

"I don't know who that is" I said.

"Well, he seems to know who you are. Maybe seeing him will help with your memory?"

"Perhaps"

"If you are up to seeing him, I can fetch him for you now?" she asked. I nodded, and arranged my bed and pyjamas as she walked out of the ward.

What had happened for me to end up in here? I couldn't remember.

I heard him long before I saw him, his boots sounding loudly on the stone floor, echoing around the tiled ward. The sound grew louder and louder until he turned the corner and walked into the ward. His crisp, grey uniform gave an aura of importance and style. How smart he looked.

A memory flashed into my mind; I remembered why I had wanted to join the SS; the uniform. I had visited Berlin with my parents in 1936, and had seen one of the many parades. There were hundreds of black clad soldiers of the Leibstandarte SS Adolf Hitler marching in unison, their hobnailed boots stomping loudly on the cobbled street. What a sight it had been!

I knew right then that I wanted to be one of them. Against the wishes of my parents, I had joined the SS Standarte Der Führer as soon as I could. It had been hard work, and the selection process intense, but I had been accepted.

There were questions about my mother, of course, but she had taken German citizenship after her marriage to my father.

Still, the doubt was obvious in their faces. Regardless, I had gotten in! I had taken part in the invasion of Poland, and then… And then? Grrr! I couldn't remember. How had I ended up here? If only my memory would work! The loud footsteps ended abruptly as the Captain found my bed. He snapped his heels together sharply and his right arm shot up in salute. "Heil Hitler!" I stiffened up, and returned his salute as best I could "Hauptsturmführer" I did not recognise the man.

"At ease Rottenführer" he said. He removed his peaked cap, placed his black gloves inside it, and set it down on the bed. He opened a briefcase, and removed several objects; some letters, two envelopes, and a case. Medals. For me? Why? He picked up a piece of paper, cleared his throat, and read loudly: "Rottenführer Deckman, it is with honour and pride that I present on behalf of the Führer Adolf Hitler, and a grateful German people, the Verwundetenabzeichen Schwartz for being wounded in combat" he took the badge from is package, and placed it on the bed next to me. Wound badge. I should have expected it; it was presented to all wounded soldiers. You had to have been wounded twice; this was my second time. I had been wounded during the invasion of Poland a few years earlier. Yes! I remember now! Shrapnel wound to the right shoulder. He picked up another piece of paper, and repeated the ritual; "Rottenführer Deckman, it is with honour and pride that I present on behalf of the Führer Adolf Hitler, and a grateful German people, the Allgemeine Sturmabzeichen Silber for showing exceptional bravery in combat" Again, he placed the badge on the bed next to me. The Assault badge in Silver? What had I done to deserve that? He picked up another piece of paper, smiled, and read again "Rottenführer Deckman, it is with honour and pride that I present on behalf of the Führer Adolf Hitler, and a grateful German people, the Ritterkreuz".

He beamed with pride as he pinned the heavy Knights Cross to my pyjama top. He promptly snapped off another salute, accompanied by applause from those capable of doing so in the ward.

He shook my hand "Congratulations Deckman. It is a great honour to receive the Knights Cross"

"Thank you sir" The Knights Cross???

"Would you permit me to read out your commanding officers commendation?" he asked.

"Not at all" Please do, I thought. I can't remember a thing.

He unfolded yet another piece of paper, cleared his throat, and spoke loudly once more:

"From: Obersturmführer Rotmann II/SSDF to: SS Command; Commendation for Rottenführer Deckman.

Rottenführer Deckman was part of the raiding party led by Hauptsturmführer Kuttel that crossed the Ijssel River on May 10th 1941, to capture Fort Westervoort. Under intense enemy machine-gun fire, they crossed the river, when sadly, Hauptsturmfürer Kuttel was killed.

Still under intense enemy fire, Rottenführer Deckman rallied and led the remaining men to the opposite bank, where they successfully neutralised the enemy positions, allowing the remainder of the Division to cross in safety. Rottenführer Deckman personally took out 3 of 5 enemy machine gun positions using grenades, despite being wounded during the crossing. His conduct under fire is an example to us all. Heil Hitler. Signed: Rotmann."

There was silence in the ward, which was broken moments later by another round of applause from the other injured men, and from the captain.

"You are a shining example of an SS man" Wiezinge said whilst applauding.

"Thank you sir" I didn't really know what to say to that. Flashes of memories returning; the whizzing of bullets, the acrid smell of cordite, the screams of dying men, the coldness of the water. Kuttel was dead. He had been my commanding officer for over a year, and I liked him a lot. His loss saddened me.

"One final piece of paper" Wiezinge said smiling "If you permit"

"Of course Hauptsturmführer"

"It is my honour to inform you of your promotion to Oberscharführer, by order of the Reichsführer SS himself, effective immediately"

He handed me the promotion letter, and a small package containing the requisite collar and shoulder insignia. The letter was signed by Himmler himself.

"You honour me, Hauptsturmführer" I said.

"You honour us all Deckman" he smiled, and shook my hand "Congratulations"

"Thank you sir"

He placed the commendation letters on my bedside table, and sat.

"You know, you will get a choice of posting, it comes with the Ritterkreuz"

"I do?"

"Indeed. Think carefully Deckman. This could be your ticket out of the front lines."

"But, I couldn't leave my comrades sir" I couldn't remember my brothers in the division, but I'm sure I had some. And I sure as hell didn't want to abandon them.

He leaned towards me, looked around, and then whispered "Consider your choices Deckman. You want to carry on being cannon fodder? Our casualties are severe, especially in the lower ranks. This is your chance to get out of the firing line"

"Thank you sir, I will think about it"

"Good man" he said, standing. He picked up his cap, and put his gloves back on.

"I wish you all the best Oberscharführer Deckman" he saluted, and turned to leave the ward. He stopped and thought for a moment, then turned to me "By the way, if you are considering taking the officer route, let me know, I will recommend you to the Jünckerschule in Bad Tolz.

I'll give you my number, call if you are interested" He scribbled a number on a slip of paper and handed it to me. "Get well soon soldier" he said, smiled, and then left.

As I sat there thinking about what had just happened, I could hear his loud footsteps in the hall diminishing slowly.

The Knights Cross? OberScharführer? Officer school? Wow. What had just happened? Was it a dream? A hallucination?

Moments later, the nurse returned with a tray. "Congratulations Sergeant Deckman, I brought you some coffee and a piece of strudel to celebrate"

"That's very kind of you" I said, gathering the sheets of paper and folding them up. "News spreads fast"

"Difficult not to overhear" she smiled "His voice echoed all around the hospital. I'm pretty sure he wanted everyone to hear"

"I guess he did."

"How are you feeling?"

I considered this for a moment. I was feeling ok, like a bit of a fraud in fact.

I should be back with my unit, fighting alongside my comrades.

But I just said "I'm feeling better, can I get out of bed yet? I'm dying to go for a walk"

"No, you must rest your leg" she said sternly, shaking her head.

Reluctantly, I agreed to do so, but was determined to get out of this bed as soon as I could.

"I have other patients to see, congratulations again Sergeant"

"Thank you"

And with that, she was gone. The ward fell silent once more.

There was the occasional moan from one of the beds opposite, but silent otherwise.

I wondered where my comrades were right now. Still in Holland? Had we been successful? I scolded myself for not asking the Hauptsturmführer. Idiot. I felt guilty for laying here whilst they were out there fighting for our Fatherland. I picked up my new shoulder patches with the two pips. How on earth had I deserved this? When I returned to my unit I would be a squad leader, with a whole new set of responsibilities. I had some idea of what the job entailed, having been in the same unit as OberScharführer Kahn for almost two years now, and had assisted him with the running of the squad.

Would I actually go back to the same unit? I had no idea. I had not received any orders that I was aware of. I looked around; there was no sign of my uniform, and my bedside cabinet was empty.

I lay back and thought about the raid. It had been intense, and I was extremely lucky I hadn't been killed.

A few of the boats had been sunk by gunfire, and I had dragged all of the men to the shore, with bullets whizzing around my head.

Some of the men had been dead when I dragged them ashore, but I didn't stop to check. We were being shot at, and I wanted to get my comrades to safety.

Did I really want to go back to the front line? Part of me said no, you've done enough. Wounded twice.

Three years of constant combat. I had only been home once in that time, and much to my parent's dismay, I had spent most of it asleep.

Sleep. God, sleep was a luxury on the lines. I has slept in wet trenches, in abandoned buildings, in a chicken coup, anywhere I could. I was permanently tired, but I suppose you don't really feel it much when your life is under constant threat.

A doctor woke me from my daydream.

"Ah, OberScharführer, how are you feeling?"

"Better, feeling good enough to get up and try my leg" I said.

"Hmm, let's give that another day or so shall we."

"May I ask a question?" I asked.

"You may, though I am not sure if I would be able to answer"

"My unit. Do you know anything about what happened?"

"During combat in the Netherlands? I know nothing, sorry. However, I can tell you that your orders came in a few days ago. You will be going to the eastern front as soon as we've patched you up"

I was silent. The eastern front. It meant almost certainly death.

"Not the best news, I know" he said.

"No, it's not. But, we go where we are ordered"

He leaned in, and whispered "Between you and me, OberScharführer, I hear the casualty rates on the eastern front have been catastrophic, especially in our Waffen SS units"

"I've heard the same" I said. I had. The Leibstandarte Adolf Hitler had been in the east for a few years now, and their numbers had been decimated.

One of my childhood friends, Oskar, had been lucky enough to join the elite LAH unit; it had been the proudest day of his life.

Then, two weeks after finishing his basic training in Berlin, his unit had been shipped out to the Ukraine.

He had been killed the day after they had arrived; shot by a sniper whilst walking to the latrine. I didn't want to go to the east, it was cold out there, really cold.

I was tired of being cold. And the Russians were barbarians.

They tortured and mutilated captured Waffen SS soldiers.

"I'll come back and check on you in the morning, try to sleep" he said, and went off to see to his next patient.

I put thoughts of the east out of my mind. But, it wasn't easy; the thought of going to Russia terrified me. I lay for a long time, just staring at the ceiling, thinking about what I should do. Eventually, I lost the battle and fell into a deep sleep.

"Good morning Oberscharführer"

I woke with a start. "What!?" My shout echoed around the room. I looked around, and calmed.

I was still in the hospital. My dreams had been haunted by gruesome images of combat and comrades falling all around me.

"You slept well I hope?" It was the nurse from yesterday, doing her morning rounds.

"Yes, yes I did" I said, focusing on the girl in front of me, instead of the images of broken bodies in my mind. She was beautiful. My god, she was beautiful.

"Good. How is the leg feeling?"

I moved my leg without thinking, and a searing pain shot up my left side. "Aaaah! Verdammt!" I shouted.

"Try not to move it!" she said, hurrying to my side "You're leg hasn't healed yet. It needs rest"

I remembered the constant indoctrination during our basic training: "Pain is in the brain". We were trained to think pain didn't exist; that the Waffen SS man didn't feel pain, that he should fight on, regardless of injury. Hmm, this pain was definitely NOT in the brain; it was very real indeed.

"I suppose so" I laughed. "You have a moment to sit?"

"I can spare a war hero five minutes" she said, and sat.

"Can I ask you something?"

"Of course"

"First off, my name is Joseph, not Oberscharführer"

"Gisela, not nurse" she replied.

"What a beautiful name. Pleased to meet you Gisela" Just speaking her name out loud made me feel happy. What an effect his woman was having on me.

She blushed "Thank you. Pleased to meet you too. Your question?"

"My question" I paused "Oh, yes, my question"

"Yes?"

"I've been offered a choice of posting after I get out of here"

"That's great" she smiled "You deserve it"

"I'm not sure about that, but, the Captain mentioned transferring to a non-combat role"

"Seems like sound advice" she said.

"Yes it does. However, leaving my comrades behind would feel like betrayal"

"I can understand that" she said "However, consider your position; would you want to end up back here again? Or worse?"

"It is what I signed up for, what I trained for. I would not dishonour myself or my parents"

"Ach, you men with your honour. You have a Knights Cross, how much more honour do you want? I'm sure your parents would prefer to be proud of their living son, rather than honouring a dead one"

"Are you always so forward in your answers?" I asked.

"Forgive me, I didn't mean to offend or be presumptuous" She hung her head.

"I was joking" I smiled "You give sound, honest advice, and I thank you for it"

"Do you know where your next posting is?" she asked, her smile returning.

"Eastern front"

The smile disappeared instantly. "Oh"

"I know" I said.

"I hear nothing but terrible things about the east, the losses are incredibly high"

"I hear the same. But, should I let my comrades fight alone?"

"You have a choice" she said.

"Yes, I do"

"Seems like an obvious choice to me"

"How so? You think I should abandon my comrades?"

"The losses are so high, what difference would one man make?"

"Who knows? Maybe all the difference"

"Or maybe none. Many brave men die out there every day, you don't need to be one of them" she said.

I laughed "People die everywhere, what difference would it make where I am?"

She was not amused "Do you want to die?" She looked angry, and it made me feel bad.

"Of course not. But my comrades..." I protested.

She cut me off "Your comrades will do just as well without you. Don't be a fool"

"You wouldn't know what I mean" I said, and turned away dismissively. This angered her.

"Oh really? And why not? You think I don't see the broken men they send here from the front every day? The hospital is full of men with the most horrendous injuries" she took a breath, then continued. "I'm surrounded by death and suffering. You think the parents of the dead are happy that their sons died for our country? No, they are devastated that the boy they spent years raising and nurturing is gone."

"I'm sorry" I said "I didn't mean to offend" I clearly had, and I had clearly upset her.

She breathed deeply "No, it is I who is sorry, I shouldn't have snapped at you. I just see so much suffering" she started crying.

My god man, look at what you've done. I scolded myself. Fool.

She was right; what difference would one man make? Did I really want to die? Did I want to break my mother's heart?

"Snow isn't really my thing" I said.

"What?" she looked up.

"I don't do well in the cold" I added.

"You have decided then?" she asked, wiping her eyes.

"I have"

A beautiful smile spread across her face.

"Where will you go?" she asked.

"I have an idea" I said, and reached for the slip of paper "I will need a telephone"

2. Bad Tolz

And so it was that, two weeks later, I found myself reporting in at the SS officer school in Bad Tolz. It suited me for a couple of reasons; it would be good for my career, and I would be close to my parents. I could visit them on weekends. My first day was mostly administrative; I was assigned to training group 2, allocated a bunk, issued with my kit, and shown around the school with the rest of the new entries. During breaks, I was approached by a lot of the lads, asking about my Ritterkreuz, which I wore proudly on my uniform. I must admit, I took a small amount of guilty pleasure in regaling them with my tale of heroism. They lapped it up like hungry kittens. Don't get me wrong, I'm no boaster; I just gave them what they wanted. The training consisted of military leadership training, and corporate operations training. This was in order to create adaptable officers who could be utilised in any part of the greater SS organisation, be it combat, political, policing, or (God forbid) concentration camps. The latter was not part of my plan, I did not want any part of that. I had joined the SS to fight for Germany against Bolshevism, not to imprison defenceless people. As much as I received training on Nazi ideology, I did not believe in it. I kept that to myself of course, and was as engaged as anyone during the lectures. Some of the lads on the course were fiercely anti-Semitic, and loved all the ideology lessons. I had to be careful not to show signs of doubt; we were monitored constantly for our ideological reliability. The slightest sign of doubt meant intense questioning by SS political officers, followed by hours of additional instruction, or worse still; expulsion. I was fortunate enough to be extremely convincing, so was spared this torture. The training took 16 months in total, and included small-unit tactics, focusing on raids, patrols, and ambushes. Additionally, there were standard military units, such as map reading, tactics, maneuvers, weapon training, physical education, combat engineering, and automotive mechanics.
I have already mentioned the political aspects; indoctrination, propaganda movies, and speeches.
We were also offered additional units, based on our future specialisation.

I had always had an interest in the law, so took units in law, policing, and intelligence. In my leisure time, I took the opportunity to join the SS fencing club, and mountaineering class.

I enjoyed physical activity, and had long held a passion for fencing. I also enjoyed shooting, and took part in as many competitions as I could during my time at Bad Tolz. We were issued with our P08 pistol on our first day, and the 98 model rifle.
Many of the lads were disappointed to be issued with the P08 rather than the newer P38. The P38 was a modern weapon, and they viewed the old P08 as a bit of a relic of the past. I, however, was happy with the P08; it was a fine weapon, and I was very good at shooting it. I had a chance a year or so later to exchange my P08 for a P38, but declined.

Seeing my parents whenever I could was a blessing. They were proud to parade their Knights Cross hero son to all their friends and acquaintances. I didn't mind of course, they were allowed their pride. During this time, I also corresponded with Gisela. Sadly, I didn't have any opportunities to visit her in Lychen, as it was too far away.
My free time was limited, and our budding relationship suffered as a result. Her letters were always welcome, and I was sure to check the post every morning. I hoped I wasn't boring her to death with my tales of fencing, climbing, and visiting my parents. She seemed ok with it, and certainly never complained, she looked forward to my letters as much as I did to hers. She had sent me a photograph of herself, which was one of my most treasured possessions. In return, all I could offer was the usual formal military portraits the school offered; serious, stiff looking character in uniform. If she had doubts or concerns about my SS affiliation, she never mentioned it. Which was a good thing, as our letters were screened by the SS political office. We were not permitted to mention anything about our military life.
Sports were allowed, so I spoke mostly about my love of fencing.
My parents presented me with a beautiful Leon Paul foil upon my graduation. It is a gift I treasured for the rest of my life. The months passed by in a blur, and before I knew it, graduation had crept up on me.

Monday, 22 January 1942 was a beautiful day. My class was lined up in the parade ground, in our dress uniforms. Our parents were sat among a crowd of dignitaries and high ranking SS officials.

We were called up one by one by the commanding officer, who congratulated us, handed over our certificate, and saluted us.

I scanned the crowd as I walked up the steps to the podium, and found my parents.

My mother had tears in her eyes, and my father looked like he was about to cry also. I searched for Gisela, but couldn't find her. She had told me she would try to attend, but couldn't guarantee it.

"Congratulations Untersturmführer Decker, may you serve our Führer loyally until death" he said as he handed over my new officer's insignia. I smiled broadly, looking at my three pips.

He shook my hand, and I said "Thank you sir, Meine Ehre heißt Treue" *My Honour is Loyalty*. I received my certificate, and took my place with my fellow officers in line. There was a speech by the chief political officer, and then we were free. We were officers.

I congratulated all my smiling, happy comrades, and went to see my parents. I was an officer in the Waffen SS, a second Lieutenant! I was proud of myself, but not as proud as my parents were. We talked enthusiastically as we stood in line for the portrait photographer.

I was an only child, so you can imagine the emotions my parents felt. They were proud of my service, but quietly wishing or hoping, that I would choose a non-combat role. They didn't want their only child to die in some far off place. Gisela's words resonated in my mind.

I was hoping to get a position in the general administrative arm, as it would mean being based in Berlin. Close to Gisela. My heart ached for her.

After we had our official portrait taken, I bade my parents farewell; I had to sign my kit back in, and pack. I would be joining them tomorrow, catching the morning train to Salzburg.

As I walked towards my barrack, I was approached by a Sturmbannführer. He looked very young to have reached such a rank I thought.

"Untersturmführer Decker?" he said, as he approached.

"Yes Sturmbannführer?" I stopped and saluted.

"At ease Lieutenant" he said "I was hoping to steal some of your time if I may?"

"Of course sir" I said, and he led me to a bench under the shade of some tall oak trees.

"I am Major Stauffman" he said, holding out his hand.

"Pleased to meet you Major" I said, shaking his hand.

"You mind if I call you Joseph?" he asked, lighting a cigarette.

"Not at all sir"

"Good" he smiled "Please call me Joachim"

"As you like sir" I said, and corrected myself "As you like Joachim"

He smiled. "I like you Joseph, you seem like an honest, genuine character"

"I hope so sir" I said.

"What are your career thoughts Joseph?" he asked, taking a long drag from his cigarette.

"I was hoping to join the Administrative arm" I said.

He made a dismissive gesture "Admin? Pah! Boring!"

"You have another suggestion?" I asked.

"Yes as it happens, I do" he exhaled a cloud of smoke, fortunately carried away by the wind. I was not a smoker, nor did I like smoking. He was, however, a superior officer, so I wasn't going to say anything. He gave me a questioning look. Reading my mind, he held up the cigarette, and dropped it on the floor, crunching it under his boot.

"Bad habit, apologies" he said "I have read your file Joseph, as I have read the files of all your class mates. You took a unit in Intelligence work?"

"Yes, I did"

"You have an interest in intelligence work?"

"I do sir." I corrected myself "Joachim. If you permit?" he nodded "I have always enjoyed reading crime and espionage novels"

He laughed "Me too Joseph. We will get along nicely you and I"

He showed me his left sleeve "You know what this means?" he asked, indicating the SD patch sewn onto his sleeve.

"Sicherheits Dienst" I said "SS Intelligence".

"Correct. We take our work very seriously Joseph, and we are always on the lookout for potential candidates to join us. You are an educated lad, and your political profile is impeccable. Tell me, do you speak any foreign languages?"

Was this a test? Surely he would know this if he'd read my file. "Yes sir, English, Dutch, and some French"

"Excellent. Which would you say are your strongest languages?"

"English and Dutch"

"You speak both without foreign accent?"

"Yes sir. My father is a financial lawyer who has been based in both these countries. I have lived in both London and Leiden for extended periods, and went to both English and Dutch schools"

He smiled broadly "Superb. Now tell me, Joseph, would you consider a position in the SD rather than boring old SS Admin?"

I laughed "Yes sir, I would"

He clapped his hands together "Most excellent" He turned serious. "One question though, if I may?"

"Of course sir"

"You are half English, are you not?"

"Yes sir, my mother is English"

"I only need one guarantee from you Joseph"

"Sir?"

"Tell me that isn't going to be an issue for you, or for me"

He meant tell me you're not going to stab me in the back and spy for the British government.

"You have my word of honour" I said, rather reluctantly. It must have been obvious, because he asked "Are you sure?"

I half nodded. I wasn't sure of course. I wanted to be, but I just wasn't. If he knew, he didn't let on.

"Good. Don't disappoint me. Here" he said taking a letter from his pocket "Your transfer orders"

My transfer orders? He knew I would join? I was both flattered and scared all at once.

"Thank you sir, I won't let you down"

He regarded me for a moment "I know you won't." he said "Take a few days to be with your family, then report in Berlin on the first of October"

"Thank you sir" I shook his hand.

He stood "I predict a bright future for you Lieutenant. See you shortly"

"Yes sir"

I sat and watched as he walked away towards the main building, his boots crunching in the gravel. What had just happened? Why were all these things happening to me? Just because of this medal? I was nothing special, or so I thought at least. My ignorance perhaps. I was fluent in two languages, of course that was a valuable asset in intelligence.

What would I be doing though? Would I be posted to the occupied territories? Would I be posted to England? A spy on foreign soil? So many questions. I sat on the bench for a while, trying to make sense of it all. I had just graduated, and had been recruited into SS intelligence on the same day. Surely he had spoken to others also? Surely I wasn't the only graduate he had approached today? I was likely at the bottom of his list.

I was ready to leave the Waffen SS and transfer to the regular SS, I had made that decision last year with Gisela. The SD though? Spies? Was I ready for that? Bur, on the other hand, what have I got to lose? It meant going to Berlin, which meant being close to Gisela. A bonus indeed.

I couldn't tell her of course, as such communication was forbidden. I would go see her at the hospital a soon as I could. In the meantime, I had packing to do and kit to return. I had booked a room in a hostel, and was looking forward to a decent meal, and perhaps a beer or two.

3. Berlin.

After spending a most agreeable week with my parents, it was time to report for duty. I alighted the train at Berlin Anhalter Bahnhof, and asked one of the Reichsbahn officers for directions to the Bendlerstrasse, where the SD office was located. I was not at all familiar with the topography of the capital, and it would take me some time to get it grips with it. When I eventually arrived at the office, after asking a few more people for directions, I stood outside for a moment to admire the imposing, classical architecture of the building. It was beautiful. I couldn't wait to work from here.

With a smile on my face, I approached the receptionist, and presented her with my orders. All my enthusiasm quickly disappeared; "Take a seat Untersturmführer" she said, pointing to a bench in the lobby. She didn't even bother to look up. I turned around, and saw six other Untersturmführers sat there already.

Oh no. Was this some kind of test? Would there be a selection process for the job? Doubt entered my mind. As I waited, the other Lieutenants disappeared one by one, until after almost an hour, I was left sitting on my own. I stood, and walked to the receptionist "Excuse me Fräulein, I just wanted to check I was in the correct place"

She looked up from behind her typewriter, which had been clacking away incessantly since I got there. "Untersturmführer..." She looked at me questioningly.

"Deckman" I added.

"Ah, of course. One moment please" she picked up the phone and dialed a number. She had a brief discussion, then dialed off.

"Apologies Untersturmführer, Sturmbannführer Stauffman has been delayed, and begs your patience; he will be here as soon as he can." she looked past me, towards the bench. I got the point; sit and wait.

"Thank you Fräulein" I said and returned to the bench. This was not a great start to my new career in intelligence. I sat and waited for the Major to arrive. I was almost at my wits end when, approximately 40 minutes later, he walked in. Much to my relief.

"Deckman! Apologies old chap, I got held up by Reinhard, he's really on one today" he rushed over, his hand outstretched. I was about to snap a salute, but seeing is hand, I changed my mind.

I relaxed and shook his hand.

"No apologies needed Sturmbannführer" Reinhard? Reinhard Heydrich? Obergruppenführer Heydrich? A dizzying thought.

"Come, follow me. Let's get some coffee. You have eaten?"

"No Sturmbannführer"

He stopped abruptly, I almost walked right into him. "Listen here Deckman, we're going to get on famously if you just stop calling me Sturmbannführer. It's Joachim, or Stauffman if you prefer"

"Yes sir" I said.

"Fantastic. Now, let's eat, I'm famished"

We walked into the canteen, which was about half full of men in various uniforms; SD, Luftwaffe, Wehrmacht, Kriegsmarine.

They were all here. What a melting pot of military life! My eyes fell on a table in a far corner, where 3 men sat, in long black trench coats and black hats. Stauffman noticed me staring. "Be mindful of them" he said with derision in his voice "Gestapo".

We sat at a table far away from them. A steward came over immediately, and Stauffman ordered for both of us. Boiled eggs and buttered bread. Eggs. Eggs! I hadn't had a real egg for almost two years.

The steward returned a minute or so later with a tray containing a pot of coffee, milk, sugar, and cups. Again, I hadn't had milk for some time. What a dream this was!

I instantly felt guilty for my happiness; out there, somewhere, my comrades were dying. And here I was getting excited over eggs and milk. Shame on you Deckman!

"You ok Deckman?" Stauffman asked.

"Yes, of course"

"You were thinking how lucky you were to be having eggs and milk, whilst your old comrades are dying on the Russian front?"

"How..." He made a dismissive gesture "Ach, it is obvious ja? I know how bad rations are on the front. It's natural to think that way. But you shouldn't feel guilty about it. You'll be on the front line before you know it" he winked.

"I will?" I asked. Just then, another steward appeared and served up breakfast. I stared at the plate for a moment. Eggs. I hesitated.

"Hmm, eat, before it gets cold" Stauffman said.

I obeyed, and ate greedily. He laughed.

"Oh, my apologies, I meant no offence by laughing" he said.

"It's ok Sturmbannführer, I would likely laugh at me also" I smiled.

"Don't worry about it too much Deckman, like I said, you'll be out on the front before you know it. And please; drop the Sturmbannführer"

"Of course. Apologies. I'll be out on the front?"

"Yes, of course. A man with your skills is wasted here in Berlin, I have plans for you my friend. You will have to complete some training first of course. But, before that, eat. Please. Before it gets cold. We can talk after"

We ate, and I drank 3 cups of coffee. It was Ersatz coffee, but coffee nevertheless. He told me about life in Berlin, how things were changing as the war progressed, and how the SD had an important job to do in defending the Reich from foreign spies.

"The SD?" I asked "I thought foreign espionage was under the control of the Abwehr?"

"Ach! The Abwehr! Pah!" he was disgusted. "Those amateurs. They will be the end of us yet."

"You don't think they are doing a good job?" My naiveté was showing; I knew next to nothing of the political differences between the Abwehr and the SD.

"Canaris is up to something, mark my words" he said in a hushed tone, then added "Heydrich distrusts him"

"I thought the two were friends?"

"That's what they want the world to think, but secretly, they hate each other's guts"

"I have a lot to learn it seems" I said.

"We all have a lot to learn" he said with a smile. "You'll find most of us different from the regular SS men, more relaxed if you like"

"I can only speak from a Waffen SS perspective sir, where obedience and loyalty are valued above all other virtues"

"Thank god we saved you from that eh?" he laughed, and patted my shoulder.

"Yes sir, I am grateful"

A young Stabsscharführer walked into the canteen, looking for Stauffman. "Ah, there you are sir" he said "I have Oberst Junckers on the telephone for you, he says it's urgent"

"Ah! No rest for the wicked, eh Deckman! He thinks everything is urgent, but, duty calls. Come, I will take you up to the office"

I got up and followed him up the wide marble staircase to a large office on the second floor.

"Have a seat here, I'll be back momentarily" he indicated a chair at an empty desk, then walked into one of the two private offices at the far end of the open space. I sat and waited. The Stabsscharführer that had sought out Stauffman came over "You must be Untersturmführer Deckman, welcome to the section sir"
"Thank you, Stabsscharführer…?"
"Apologies" he said, holding out his hand "Spitz, Wilhelm Spitz"
"Nice to meet you Wilhelm, please call me Joseph" I said, shaking his hand. "My apologies, I am still trying to get used to the relaxed formality"
"Ah yes, it takes a while. You are from the Waffen SS I hear?"
"Yes, SS Standarte Der Führer"
"You have seen action" he said, pointing out the Knights Cross.
"Yes, Poland and the Netherlands." I said, then laughed and added "Wounded both times unfortunately"
"Oh, nothing too serious I hope?" he said, with concern.
"No, no, nothing that won't heal with time" I reassured him.
"You were very lucky to be selected for combat" he said, then added with a look of disappointment "I myself was not. Sadly"
"Getting shot is most overrated" I winked. We laughed.
"What's so funny?" Stauffman said, reappearing.
"Oh, I was just telling Spitz here that being shot at is nothing worthy of envy"
"Indeed Willie, it is not." he said.
I pointed to his wound badge "You have been wounded in combat also sir?"
"Yes, Poland and the Ukraine, nothing too serious though thankfully"
"Amen to that sir" I said. He had the Eastern Front campaign ribbon on his uniform, indicating he had indeed seen combat on the Eastern Front.
"My unit was posted to the Eastern Front after I transferred" I said, mournfully.
"You should thank the heavens that you were spared *that*" Stauffman said quietly "It's a terrible place" he looked away, focusing on some far away object and seemed momentarily lost "Terrible" he repeated.

"Yes sir. You were going to show me around?" I said, trying to change the subject.

"What? Oh yes. Yes, of course" he cheered instantly, and slapped his thighs. "Come Deckman, I'll show you our little empire"

I stood, and followed him around as he showed me around and introduced me to the rest of the team. I say rest of the team; there were only two others; Stabsscharführer Kolk and Stabsscharführer Heitzinge.

"It would appear the section is run by just yourself and three administrator's sir" I commented to Stauffman.

"Yes, well, we are a new unit, and I am still actively recruiting new people. You are the first operative recruit"

"Operative?" That sounded exciting.

"I intend to have you out in the field Deckman, spying for the good of the Reich" he smiled.

"Spying? Treading on the toes of the Abwehr"

"Don't you worry about the Abwehr, I'll keep them in check. Come, I'll introduce you to the big boss"

We walked up two flights of stairs to the fourth floor, and stopped at a door. The sign said "Standartenführer Von Harten". Stauffman knocked.

"Enter" a voice said from within. Stauffman opened the door, and we entered. Inside the small office, a man sat behind a desk, surrounded by paperwork. There was a bust of the Führer being used as a paperweight, and two swastika flags hanging on posts behind him.

"Morning Stauffman" the man said "Who do we have here?" He was a tall man, seemed in his forties perhaps, pleasant demeanour.

"This is Untersturmführer Deckman, our new operative recruit" Stauffman said, introducing me.

I saluted the colonel "Standartenführer"

He half-heartedly returned the salute "Please, at ease Deckman. We don't stand on such formalities here." he said, holding out his hand.

I shook it. "Unless the Gruppenführer is around of course" he added laughing.

"Yes sir"

"You'll have to forgive the erratic nature of our section Deckman, you are our first recruit, and we are still finding our feet, so to speak"

"Of course sir"

His phone rang. He looked at it, hoping it would stop, but it kept ringing. "Apologies, I will come down to see you later?" he said, and answered the phone "Yes?"

We turned and walked out, closing the door behind us.

"He likes you, that's good" Stauffman said.

"I'm glad" I said, unsure what else I could add. We walked back down to the main office, and Stauffman pointed at the other empty office on the far side.

"That'll be your new home whilst you're here" he said "Please make yourself at home. If you need anything, please let Willie know and he'll do his best to help you out. I have a meeting to attend, but will be back in a couple of hours. We'll discuss your training when I return"

"Yes sir, thank you" I walked into my new office. It was small, square, with a desk, filing cabinet, and a small window. I looked out of the window, and was met with a rather splendid view of the gardens where the old palace used to be. I sat at the desk, and looked through the drawers; they were all empty. What kind of stuff was I going to need? I wasn't sure. Pencils? Notepads? I got up and opened up the filing cabinet. Inside was a small supply of stationary items, which seemed to include everything I thought I would need. I stood by the window, and contemplated my situation.

Outside, Berliners were going about their day with a blissful ignorance of the horrors their compatriots were enduring on the front. I thought of my unit. How would they be getting on? I had an idea, and walked out to find Willie. He was sat at a desk, typing a letter.

"Excuse me, Willie?"

"Yes sir?" he said, stopping his click clacking.

"Would you be able to find out where my old unit is stationed?" I asked.

"The SS Standarte Der Führer, correct?" he asked.

"Yes. You think it would be possible?"

He made a note. "Let me finish typing out this letter for the boss, then I'll go see what I can find out for you sir"

"Excellent, thank you"

"Not a problem"

I walked back to my office, and plopped back into my chair. Willie had resumed his furious typing, with renewed vigour it appeared. I guess the new assignment I had given him had spurred him on to finish and do something new and exciting. I hoped my comrades were doing well. I felt so very guilty, sitting here in my cosy office, eating eggs, drinking milk whilst they were being shot at and bombarded.

There was a knock at my door, even though I had left it open. It was Stabsscharführer Heitzinge.

"Pardon me sir, I have some files for you to read, related to your upcoming posting. Thought you might want to fill your time until the Major gets back"

"Thank you" I said, my relief apparent. "I was wondering what it is I should be doing"

"I wouldn't worry sir. From what I hear, you'll be departing for the training establishment within a few days"

"Training establishment?"

"Yes, the Abwehr training facility at Quenzsee, near Brandenburg"

"The *Abwehr* training facility?"

"Yes, although we are rival agencies, officially we are one unit. They train our SD operatives"

"Oh, I see. Well, that should make for an interesting trip" I smiled.

"I hear the course is quite intense" he commented.

"All the better, make the time pass quicker" It would, but a busy course meant no free time. Also, Quenzsee was not close to Lychen, so my chances of seeing Gisela were slim. Disappointing.

"I'm sure you'll do fine sir. I'll leave you to your reading"

"Thank you" He returned to his desk, and I was left alone once more. I looked at the file. It was labeled Secret, and was pretty thick. Curious, I opened it and started reading.

Ah, I would be posted back to the Netherlands, Fliegerhorst Twente in the east of the country. Not an area I was familiar with, but it appeared to be a good place to be posted. The Luftwaffe had night fighters stationed there, and their role was crucial in preventing enemy bombers reaching their German targets. There was a small SS contingent stationed on the base, consisting of an Oberscharführer and two Rottenführers. I would be the new intelligence officer, managing the team.

Our main task would be the monitoring of resistance activity in the area, and general oversight of the Luftwaffe and Wehrmacht personnel stationed there, which numbered around 1500. I assumed that general oversight meant spying. There was also an Abwehr/SD presence in the nearby town of Enschede, with whom we would have regular meetings to "Share intelligence".

Accommodation had been allocated on the base, and there were some entertainment facilities there too. Though, it seemed a lot of the officers spent time in nearby towns. This was something worth observing, I thought. Going off-base was always a risk; apart from drunken conversations, the men were also easy targets for local resistance attacks.

I was looking forward to this, it sounded like an exciting posting.

As I finished reading, my stomach rumbled loudly, indicating lunch was required. The clock on the wall confirmed this; it was just after twelve.

I walked out into the main office, and asked Willie "Where do I find the head steward? I need to register for the canteen victualing"

"Of course" he said standing "Follow me sir, I'll take you to him"

I followed Willie down the stairs, and into a small office just outside the canteen. "Afternoon Herr Zucker, this is Untersturmführer Deckman, he started today, and needs to register for the canteen"

The man stood and extended his hand, which I shook "Welcome Untersturmführer, please to meet you. I have my ledger here, let's get you registered so you can eat" he winked. I liked him instantly.

Willie said "I'll leave you to it sir"

"Thank you Willie, I appreciate it" I said, and he left to go back upstairs.

I sat with Herr Zucker for a few minutes, giving him my service number and various other details required for registration. Zucker wrote as I spoke, and I just had to sign my name when he had finished.

"There" he said after I'd signed "All done. I bet you'd like to go enjoy lunch now" he smiled broadly.

"Yes sir, I am very hungry"

He laughed "Please enjoy. And if you ever need anything, please don't hesitate to ask"

We stood and shook hands again "I will, thank you very much for your assistance" I said.

"My pleasure, nice to meet you"

"And you" I said, returning his smile.

I made my way to the canteen, signed in, and found a table by one of the windows. I was a great lover of daylight, so always sought out a window seat wherever I went. The luncheon menu was as expected; cold meats, sausages, cheese. A steward soon came over to take my order. I ordered the cold meats and buttered bread. He nodded, and informed me he'd return with my order in a few minutes. I thanked him, and walked over to the bar to get a glass of cold water. I stood for a moment, observing the room. It was getting busier; small groups here and there.

It was a typical army canteen scene, though slightly odd in my mind because of the mix of all the different branches of the German forces. They each tended to stick with their own, I couldn't see any mixed groups. I also couldn't see any other SS.

Were we the only SS in the building? It would make sense, this being the Abwehr headquarters.

I made a mental note to ask Stauffman later. Speaking of which, where was he? Not that it was really important, but it would be nice to talk about the posting before I left for the day.

I had a leisurely lunch, and enjoyed a nice coffee afterwards, served with cinnamon biscuits. I found myself thinking of my comrades in the unit again. Poor guys. Then I remembered I'd asked Willie for information. I wonder if he had a chance to look into it for me yet. I finished up, thanked the head steward on my way out, and went back up to the office.

Willie wasn't there, he must have gone out for lunch.

"Ah, there you are" Stauffman called from his office "Do you have a moment?"

"Of course sir" I went in and sat at his desk.

"How have you been getting on?" he asked, peeling an orange.

"Just fine thank you sir. I got a file to read from Stabsscharführer Heitzinge"

"Ah yes, to your liking I hope?" he ate a wedge of orange.

"Yes sir, very much so. I enjoyed my time in the Netherlands"

"I assume you are talking about your childhood time, not recent experiences" he joked.

I laughed "No sir, not recent experiences"

"You are aware of your training posting?" he wiped a bit of stray orange juice from his chin. I wondered how long it had been since I last had an orange.

"Yes sir, Quenzsee, training with the Abwehr"

"Indeed. I have spoken to the Commandant, Oberst Steiner, he's an old friend. He has a specialised course for you, so you don't have to go through the entire operatives training"

"Thank you sir. How long?"

"Two weeks" he finished the last piece of his orange "Then you may have a day's leave before departing for the Netherlands"

A day's leave! That was great news. It meant I could visit Gisela before I left. I had no idea how long I would be away for, so any time spent with her before I left would be excellent. Stauffman obviously read my mood.

"You will visit with your parents?" he asked.

"No sir, I will be visiting a nurse at the SS hospital in Lychen"

"Nurse eh? Good for you Joseph. Whilst you're there, have your leg checked. I'll write you a note, so you have the correct travel documents"

"Thank you sir"

"Young love eh Joseph!" he smiled "I remember it well. Make the most of it, you'll be old before you know it"

"Oh I will sir, thank you."

"Oh" he said sticking up a finger "I almost forgot" he took a letter from his briefcase. "I was summoned to the office of Von Harten upon my arrival this afternoon. He was not best pleased that I was sending an Untersturmführer out into the field"

"Sir?" I asked, curious, and worried. My heart sank. Would my career be over before it had even begun?

"Don't worry Joseph, it is good news" he said, smiling. Relief washed over me.

"He has promoted you to Obersturmführer"

"He has?" I asked incredulously.

"Yes, now you can go to your death as a full Lieutenant at least"

I was silent.

"I jest Joseph" he laughed, and held out his hand "Congratulations"
I shook his hand "Thank you sir, I don't know what to say" I didn't.
I was speechless. I'd gone from a Corporal to a First Lieutenant in a
year. I couldn't believe it. I told him as much.
"We have faith in you, and expect great things Joseph" he said
earnestly. "And we couldn't put you in charge of a unit unless you
outranked everyone there now could we?"
"I suppose not sir"
"I wish you well Deckman, enjoy your time at the training
establishment. Pay attention to your instructors; they will teach you
valuable skills that may one day save your life"
"I won't let you down sir" I said saluting him.
To my surprise, he returned my salute. I was expecting to be scolded
for being overly formal.
"Take care Deckman, look after yourself. And trust no-one."
"I won't sir" I said, and turned to walk out.
"Oh, Joseph" he said.
I turned "Yes sir?"
"See the quartermaster, get yourself a couple of new uniforms before
you leave. May as well whilst you still can"
"Yes sir"
I walked back to my office, put the thick file in my briefcase, and went
off to find the quartermasters office. Willie walked in as I was about
to leave.
"Ah, glad I caught you sir" he said.
"You have news?" I asked hopeful.
"Yes sir. Though, not perhaps the best news I'm afraid"
"Tell me" My heart was pounding in my chest.
"Up until last week, they were located outside of Moscow,
spearheading the attack"
"Moscow?" I said "I can't believe it" They made it all the way to
Moscow?? How I yearned to be with my friends.
"Yes, I must tell you though that they suffered an extremely high
casualty rate" he said.
"How high?"
"94 percent" he looked away in embarrassment.
I almost fell to the floor.
"Sir!" he yelled, and rushed to support me.

"I can't believe it" I said "There must be some mistake"
"I'm afraid not sir, I checked twice, and the figures are correct.
A request for reinforcements was sent out three weeks ago"
Stauffman came out of his office "What's going on here?" He asked,
seeing me half on the floor, supported by Willie.
"My unit" I said quietly "My unit"
He looked at Willie, who gave him a sad look. "Oh, I see. I'm sorry
Joseph" he said, helping me stand.
"All my comrades. Gone" I was in a daze.
He turned to Willie "Willie, get the Lieutenants measurements, and
requisition three new uniforms, have them sent to his quarters."
"Yes sir" he replied.
"Go to the canteen Joseph, toast your fallen comrades. There is
nothing else for you to do today"
"Thank you sir"
"Kolk?" he yelled, and he came running over.
"Sir?"
"Make sure the Lieutenant gets to the canteen; instruct the steward
to look after him"
"Yes sir"
Slowly, I walked to the canteen, Kolk in tow. When we got there, he
exchanged words with a steward, who immediately went and poured
me a glass of cognac. I stumbled to a table, and sat down heavily.
The steward set the glass on the table, and left. I drank it in one go.
The liquid burned all the way down to my stomach. Instantly, the
steward reappeared and exchanged my glass for a full one. This time I
savoured the cognac rather than downing it. I was heartbroken.
The men I had trained with, my friends. All gone. Gisela's words
echoed in my mind *"The losses are so high, what difference would
one man make?"* The words whirled around my mind like a hurricane.
Would it have made a difference if I were with them? Could I have
saved even just one of them? I felt insanely guilty. What could I have
done? Likely very little, I would have been killed along with the rest of
the men.
Self-pity didn't suit me, and I wasn't very good at it. The cognac
helped to focus my mind, and I decided that my being there wouldn't
have changed a thing, and that I would just be another name on a
casualty list.

Yet, I couldn't shake the feeling of guilt. I finished my drink, thanked the steward, and went out for a walk to clear my mind.

The air was cold, and there was a threat of rain in the air, you could feel it. The streets were busy, government officials and men in uniform everywhere. I wandered around for what must have been hours. This was the centre of the web, and out here on the streets it was likely just as busy as in each of these impressive looking buildings. That one over there, I thought, Himmler is probably inside. And that one, Goebbels likely, he had the eyes of the devil. The big names of the Nazi war machine were all here. The air ministry; that fat slob Göering.

They all disgusted me, sitting there in their ivory towers, whilst thousands of young boys were dying in the name of an ideology they were peddling. An ideology I had bought into. I was angry with myself for haven done so.

I found a café near the Tiergarten, and had a coffee. The place was about half full, probably because the weather wasn't great. There were civilian couples, Off-duty soldiers with their sweethearts, and me. Alone. I didn't want to be alone. However, at this precise moment in time, there was nothing I could do about that. Tomorrow I would be off to Quenzsee, and then I would get to visit Gisela.

We had exchanged letter of course, but I hadn't seen here in some time. But soon, I would. This lifted my mood. I had grieved for my brothers, and would never forget them, but that was the past. I had a future to focus on. I finished my coffee, and returned to my quarters.

My new uniform was hanging on the wardrobe door when I got back, and my transfer orders were on the bedside table. I was to report to Quenzsee by 14.00 tomorrow. That meant I could have breakfast here, then take a leisurely stroll to the station.

I looked at my uniform, it had my new rank flashes on it, and perhaps more importantly, the SD patch indicating I was now no longer part of the Waffen SS, but of the Sicherheits Dienst. I was no longer a soldier; I was an intelligence officer.

I spent the time before dinner writing to my parents and to Gisela. My mother would be happy with the news, as would Gisela. I was safe. Or, as safe as could be I suppose. Danger was everywhere, even in the capital.

4. Quenzsee.

The following morning, I packed my things, and went downstairs for breakfast in the canteen. A steward showed me to a table in the window, and brought me coffee. I ordered eggs and toast from the steward, and ate in silence. I didn't see anyone I knew, but wasn't expecting to; it was almost 09.00, and past normal breakfast time. It suited me, I enjoyed my own company. The eggs were delicious, and the coffee was still real. Later, I would have to get used to the taste of the rather disgusting Ersatz coffee, but for now, I savoured the taste of the real thing. I finished up, thanked the steward, collected my things, and left.

Even though I took a leisurely stroll to the station, I still found myself walking along the platform towards the train at just after 10 o'clock. I was going to be reporting in early. I didn't care. I just wanted to get it over with so I could visit Gisela. I found a seat in a third class carriage, and sat staring out of the window. The train shook into life, and slowly built up speed, soon leaving the hornets' nest behind. The countryside was a welcome change to big city life; fields, trees, lakes flashed by. The ticket collector asked for my ticket and travel documents, I handed him both. He checked them, smiled, and left. I was alone once more. I opened the window a bit to let some fresh air in. On the seat opposite was a newspaper, I picked it up; it was today's paper. I had a quick read, but found nothing but the usual Nazi propaganda about how we were beating back the Bolshevist monster and how victorious our troops were. But at what cost? Was it really worth it? I threw the paper back on the seat, and shrugged off the negativity as the train pulled into the station. I alighted, and walked over to a Reichsbahn official on the platform. He gave me directions to the training establishment, which was about 4 kilometers away. There were no taxis, so I walked. I had time.

I got to the front gate about an hour later, and presented my orders. The duty guard let me in, and directed me to the administration building. When I got there, I repeated the process. The receptionist made a call, and asked me to wait.

Seems familiar, I thought. Hopefully I wouldn't have to sit here as long this time! I need not have worried; within five minutes a Feldwebel appeared.

"Obersturmführer Deckman" he saluted, Army salute.

"Yes" I returned his salute in the same manner. Adapt and overcome.

"Please follow me sir" he said, picking up my suitcase.

I followed him to what looked like a school building, where we stopped.

"This is where you will need to report first sir" he said "Your first class starts at 14.00"

"Thank you" I said, looking at my watch; it was just after one o'clock.

He continued on, and we eventually entered an accommodation block. "This is the Officers' accommodation block" he said as we entered. We stopped at the reception, and he introduced me. "This is Obersturmführer Deckman"

"Ah, welcome Obersturmführer, here is your room key." He handed me a key. "Please sign here" he turned a ledger, and I signed where indicated.

"Your room is on the second floor, number 37. Please let me know if there is anything you need"

"Thank you" I said, and picked up my case.

"Sir?" the Feldwebel said, wondering if he should help me or not.

"I can take it from here, thank you for your assistance"

He smiled "You are welcome sir" He saluted, and left.

I found the stairs, and walked up to the second floor. My room was at the far end of the corridor, on the right. I unlocked and opened the door. The interior was rather Spartan as expected. However, it was clean, and the bed looked comfortable. I'd walked past the bathrooms half way down the corridor, and he desperately wanted to freshen up after the walk to the base.

After unpacking my case and hanging my clothes, I went to the bathroom and washed. The place was spotless, taps gleamed, tiles shined. I felt bad about splashing water over the clean surfaces. However, I had no choice. I washed my hands and face, then stared at myself in the mirror.

What I saw shocked me. I hadn't seen my reflection for a while. The face in the mirror looked haunted, scared, unsure, hollow. Wow. Is this what I had become?

The only good thing I could see was my smart new uniform. I stepped back and admired it. It was not quite as awe-inspiring as the black uniform of old; the grey uniform was hard to distinguish from the Wehrmacht uniform, except for the collar and shoulder flashes.
I missed the black uniform; it set us apart, and just looked better.
I sighed, and returned to my room. The clock on the wall told me I had twenty minutes until I had to report. Sitting at the desk, I stared out of the window onto the parade square below.
There were people milling about, all Wehrmacht. I felt out of place, and extremely conspicuous in my SS uniform. I removed the file from my briefcase and spent the time I had re-reading some of the pages. When I next checked the time, it was almost five minutes to two. Verdammt! I jumped up, and ran to the school building, where I managed to check in with only one minute to spare. The receptionist laughed and directed my to the class room. When I entered, I expected to see a room filled with students, but it was empty, except for the instructor.
"Ah, Lieutenant Deckman" he saluted smartly.
I returned his salute "Apologies for my tardiness Herr Hauptmann"
Whilst it may seem odd that a captain saluted a Lieutenant, it should be remembered that recipients of the Knights Cross were saluted by even superior officers. It was something I was still not used to.
I was careful to remember that the Hauptmann was my superior, and was suitably subordinate.
"It is your first day Deckman, let's forget about it. Please, sit" he motioned for me to sit at a desk. I chose a desk front and centre.
"Now then, let's begin by going through the course content. It has been especially put together for you, as requested by Standartenführer Von Harten." he started writing a list on the blackboard. My course was to consist of the following:

Communications (Sub-headings; Radio, Morse, Enigma, Coding/Decoding)
Explosives
Weapon handling
Lock-picking
Photography (Subheadings; Use of miniature camera, developing film)
Close combat

"It is a lot to fit into two weeks" the Hauptmann commented "But, we'll do our best"

And so, my training started.

I was already a formidable shot, so the weapon handling was enjoyable, and straightforward. I had also had previous experience with explosives, but not to the extent of what I was being taught. It was however, enjoyable.

The explosive devices I had to master were time delay grenades, and improvised explosive devices. I basically had to assemble an explosive device from materials provided.

Lock-picking was new to me, it was particularly difficult. We covered picking of mortice locks and various pad locks. By the time I had finished the course, I was good at it, but not great. It would prove to be a valuable skill though.

I had some experience with photography, but not with the miniature camera and film I was to use in the field. I had never seen anything like it, it was like something alien to me. Developing was even harder; the film was so small, it was difficult to handle in the darkroom.

But in the end, I managed.

The two weeks flew by; the course was intense, but highly enjoyable. On my last day, I had just finished my close combat course when Hauptmann Ost (I learned his name from one of the instructors) approached me.

"Deckman" he said, handing me a towel to wipe the sweat from my face.

"Thank you sir"

"No rest for you I'm afraid" he said "You are to report at Fliegerhorst Berlin-Gatow, your flight will depart Tuesday morning at 07.00 sharp. Don't be late" He handed me the envelope with my transfer order and travel papers in it.

"Yes sir" I said.

He held out his hand, I shook it.

"Best of luck Deckman, whatever it is you're destined for. You know, for an SS man, you're a decent human being" he said, kindly.

"I am grateful for your assistance and training Herr Hauptmann. And, for an Army man, you're not bad sir"

He smiled "I hope the training is of use to you."

"It will be" I saluted, and he walked away. I turned to find that my instructor had disappeared, leaving me alone on the training field.
I shrugged, and made my way back to the accommodation to shower. Hurriedly, I threw my stuff in my suitcase, grabbed my briefcase, and ran out to catch a transport to the station. It was only two in the afternoon, and I calculated I could be in Lychen by nightfall.
The transport rattled across the cobbled parade ground, and out of the gates. I watched from the back as the camp slowly disappeared from view.
I was going to miss it.

5. Lychen

My calculations were correct; I stepped off the train at Lychen at half past seven. It was starting to get dark, and I was fortunate to find a transport to the hospital outside the station. The rickety old truck slowly wound its way down the bumpy streets towards the hospital. It was dark by the time I arrived at the hospital, the lights inside were glowing, and a gentle rain was falling from the black skies above.
I walked inside, and spoke to the receptionist. She sat behind a tall tidy desk, and greeted me with a smile.
"Good evening Obersturmführer, how can I be of assistance?"
"Good evening, I have to report here for physiotherapy on my leg" I handed her the paperwork I had got from Stauffman.
"Ah, I see. Well, welcome. You have been here before?"
"Yes, I was in a ward here some months ago"
"Well, this time you won't have to stay on a ward" she smiled "You have a private room on the top floor"
"Excellent" I said, grateful not to be on the ward with the wounded men.
"The stairway is over there" she pointed to a door on my right, turn left at the top, and your room is on the left side"
"Thank you. Tell me, is nurse Gisela on duty tonight?" I asked.
She sniggered "Ah, you are *that* Joseph"
"Yes" I said uncertainly.
"Gisela is a good friend of mine, she has told me all about you"
"Ah" I said. "Not sure if that's a good or a bad thing"
"She isn't here yet I'm afraid. Her shift starts at 05.30 tomorrow morning."
The look of disappointment was obvious. "Sorry, she's been away to Berlin to see her uncle, she won't be getting back until later this evening. I'm really sorry."
"No, its fine" I lied. "Would you keep my arrival a secret? I want to surprise her"
"Of course" she smiled "She will be so very happy to see you"
"I hope so" I took the room key, and picked up my case "Thank you for your help"

"Your secret is safe with me" she smiled.

I made my way up the stairs, and to my room. It was a small, but comfortable space.

The room had a depressing view of a road and the rear of the building. I sighed, lay down on the bed, and thought about how I could surprise Gisela tomorrow. I did have a physiotherapy appointment at ten o'clock, which is how I was able to stay overnight.

There was a knock at the door, I sat up on the end of the bed.

"Come in"

An old lady entered and asked if I wanted any dinner. I took some buttered bread and cheese, and a tall glass of water. "Thank you"

"You are welcome" she smiled, and left. I could hear her trolley moving down the corridor, and she knocked on another four doors before I assumed she left the floor.

I ate my dinner, then read more of the file until I fell asleep.

A knock on the door woke me with a start. "Yes?" I kind of yelled.

The same lady opened the door "Pardon me, but would you like some breakfast?"

"My apologies, I was asleep. Just some coffee and toast please if possible." She smiled and told me she'd return in about ten minutes.

I rubbed my eyes. Papers covered the bed. I cursed myself for falling asleep with all this sensitive information lying around. It took me a couple of minutes to tidy up, and I had made it to the bathroom and back before the lady returned with my breakfast.

"I got you a pot of coffee, just in case" she smiled.

"I am extremely grateful, thank you" She smiled again, and left me to eat. I poured myself a cup of coffee. It was Ersatz coffee, which tasted like muck. I hadn't had real coffee in almost two years. I'd forgotten what it tasted like.

I devoured the toast, drank two cups of coffee, then got dressed.

It was just after eight, so I was hopeful of finding Gisela down on the ward.

With a spring in my step, I made my way down to reception.

There was a different girl there this morning, and I her asked if Gisela was on duty. She was indeed, on the ward, doing her morning rounds. I thanked her and made my way quietly to the ward.

Looking through the door window, I could see her half way down the ward, clipboard in hand, talking to a wounded man.

How beautiful she looked. Her long blonde hair tied up in a bun, her beautiful smile instantly cheering even the most depressed of men.

I took off my boots, gently opened the door, and crept up towards her. This elicited some strange looks from the men in the ward, but I continued.

I made it all the way up to where she was stood without her noticing. Standing right behind her, I put on a voice and asked "Excuse me nurse, can you empty my chamber pot please?"

She turned and shrieked "Joseph!" she flew into my arms.

I held her tight "Gisela, I am so happy to see you"

"And I you" she said "What are you doing here? Are you hurt?" she let go, stepped back, and looked me up and down.

"No, nothing like that. I have a physiotherapy appointment at ten"

"And you've been promoted? Again?" she said, indicating my collar flashes.

"Erm, yes it would appear so"

"Oh, but look at you" she said with concern, stroking my face "You look so tired"

"I've had a challenging couple of weeks" I offered.

"Poor thing. You need rest"

"I'll be fine. I don't have time to rest"

"You look very handsome in your uniform"

"I do?"

"Yes, very much so. Your pistol is a bit old fashioned, but you look very dapper"

"Well, I will take your word for that. Old fashioned pistol?"

"My uncle always says the Luger is an old fashioned weapon, worn only by professional officers"

"That makes me a professional officer?

She laughed "Yes, I guess so"

"Well, in that case, thank you very much, I accept the compliment"

"How long are you here for?"

"I have to leave for Berlin tonight, I have to be back there before seven in the morning."

Her face dropped "Oh, that's not long. And I'm on duty until five"

"I'm sorry. I have to leave for my new posting"

"Tell me it's somewhere safe?" she said, hope in her eyes.

"Is there anywhere left that is safe?" I joked.

"It's not a joke!" she said angrily.

"I'm sorry, I know. You know I can't tell you where I'm going"

"At least tell me you're not going east"

"West" I said.

"Oh, thank god." immeasurable relief was evident in her eyes.

A loud coughing noise at the far end of the ward brought us back to reality.

"You should probably finish your rounds" I said "I'll be reading out in the garden until my appointment, find me if you have a break"

"I will" she kissed me on the cheek, and went back to the realities of everyday life. I smiled, and walked back to my room to retrieve my briefcase.

I passed a man dressed in a black suit on the stairwell, he smiled amiably. I returned his smile, and carried on to my room.

When I entered, I found utter chaos. Someone had searched my room! The man! I turned and raced back to the stairwell, but he was nowhere to be seen. I ran to a window, and saw him getting into a car and then he drove away. My leg was protesting madly at the sudden abuse.

Dammit. I limped back to my room and tidied it. The contents of my briefcase were scattered on the bed. He'd read everything. How could I have been so stupid? From now on, the briefcase would never leave my side. Too late perhaps, but better late than never.

I cursed myself over and over again.

Whomever he was, he knew everything about my new mission.

Who would possibly be interested in what a new, low level agent was up to in the Netherlands? What benefit would there be in possessing this information? It wasn't top level espionage, just a standard local resistance observation assignment. It didn't matter. I was angry. More with myself than anyone else. Who was the man in black? Abwehr? Gestapo? Who knows? I would likely never find out.

My room back in order, I tried hard to put the whole thing behind me. I picked a book from the small collection of books on a bookshelf in the corridor. There was nothing inspirational, just government approved literature.

I didn't care; I just needed to pass the time until my appointment. With a sigh, I went downstairs, and walked outside to find a nice spot in the sun.

I found a quiet corner in the garden, under a cherry tree, and started reading. The book was dull, and uninspiring. I put it down and lay back against the tree. Soon, I'd drifted off to sleep.

Nightmare like imaginations of my comrades falling in action haunted the world behind my eyelids. My sleep was disturbed, the images upsetting.

"Joseph" a gentle voice cut through the darkness. I tuned in slowly. "Joseph" it repeated. I realised it was not part of my dream, but reality. I opened my eyes, and saw Gisela hunched down in front of me.

"Gisela" I smiled.

"You looked distressed. Were your dreams so bad?" she asked, looking sad.

"I have a lot of tragedy feeding my imagination" I said.

She put her hand on my cheek "Poor man. This war is just terrible" The sensation of her hand on my cheek calmed me; I enjoyed the feeling of her skin on mine.

"It should be over within a year" I assured her.

"You really think so?"

"No. No, I don't"

"Oh, the war is just so futile. Is it really worth the cost?" she said.

"You doubt the Führer?" I asked.

She took a moment to weigh me up, the SS flashes on my collar likely influenced what she said next "No, no, of course not. Our Führer will guide us to victory" She sounded sincere.

"We need to watch what we say" I said, looking around.

"Why? Who's going to report us?" she said, voice filled with anger.

"Anyone. Trust nobody. It's sound advice that I was given recently. You never know who might hear" I said.

She lowered her head "What? Even here...?"

"Even here, anyone could overhear and report us"

She lowered her voice "This world is just so crazy, I don't know who to trust, who to believe. It's madness"

"I don't disagree, you just need to be careful, ok?"

"Yes, ok"

"Good, come" I said standing, and holding out my hand "You can show me to the physiotherapy section"

She took my hand and led the way.

We walked through the maze of corridors, and eventually she knocked on a door. The sign on the door informed me that a Doctor Ernst Weitz resided within.

"Come in" a kindly voice said from the other side of the door.

"I'll leave you" she said, kissed my cheek, and walked off.

I entered and sat through an hour and a half of pure pain. I should obviously have added that my leg still hurts, depending on what I do. The session was pure torture. And Doctor Weitz did it all with a smile.

"Repeat these exercises once a day until no pain is felt" he advised when he'd finished.

"Everyday?" I asked unsure.

He chuckled "It will get less painful each time, I promise"

"Very well, every day. Thank you Doctor Weitz"

"You are welcome Joseph, please take care of yourself won't you?"

"I will" I smiled, shook his hands, and left.

My leg still smarted as I walked back to the reception. Or tried to at least. I must have taken at least three wrong turns. Frustrated, I eventually ended up back at the reception desk. Gisela's friend was back on duty. She smiled "Oh hi, how was your appointment? Did you find Gisela yesterday?"

I returned her smile "Hi. It was painful, but good for me apparently. Yes, I found her. Do you know where she is now? I was hoping to take her for lunch"

"I'm here" Gisela said, walking up behind me.

"Fantastic" I smiled "Do you have time for lunch?"

"Yes, but not here. Take me away from here" she said.

"Ok, I don't mind, but you'll have to tell me where we can go"

"There is a bus into the village, let's take it. There's a place there we can eat outside in the sun"

"The bus is still running?" I asked.

"Yes, it's how most of us get here"

I liked the sound of taking her away from here, the hospital environment was not exactly conducive to romantic overtures.

The thought made me blush.

"You ok?" she asked.

"Yes, I'm fine. I'll follow you"

We walked out into the sun, and waited at the bus stop.

I picked a wild flower for her, and she wore it in her hair.

How beautiful she was. What were my intentions? I suddenly became insecure. What was I going to do? Was I going to ask her out? Did I need to? My experiences with the opposite sex had been extremely limited, and I didn't really know what I should do. Or not do.

The bus saved me from my thoughts. After a short, bumpy ride up into the village, Gisela led me to a small guest house overlooking the forest.

We found a table outside and ate a wonderful lunch. We talked about our childhoods, our work (to a limited extent), and she asked me why I had joined the Waffen SS in particular, not the Army. I told her about the parade we'd seen in Berlin, and how enchanted I was. She was likely trying to gauge my loyalty and dedication to the national socialist ideology.

"I'm no fanatic, don't worry. It was all about the uniform, and being part of an elite. Nothing to do with the government, or the Nazi's"

"Fanatic? I thought the Waffen SS were loyal to our Führer and personified the Aryan race. You should be proud" She responded.

Her response was slightly curious and confusing, and it made me question whether she fully trusted me. Had my words to her earlier been so harsh?

All too soon, it was time for her to return to work. Sadly, she would not finish until after I needed to depart for Berlin, so I told her I'd escort her back to the hospital, and then make my way to Berlin early.

"When will I see you again?" she asked after we got off the bus.

"I don't know. I may be gone for some time" I said. It did not please me, and I could see it did not please her either.

I gathered all my courage and said "Gisela?"

When she turned, I kissed her. I expected her to push me away, but to my surprise found her returning the kiss. It was only brief, but it told me all I needed to know.

"Please come back to me" she said.

"I will"

"Promise?"

"I promise" It was an empty promise, we both knew it, but we both needed the re-assurance, however meaningless.

We hugged, and she quickly disappeared off to the ladies bathroom before I could see her tears.

I felt sad. Empty. Like something was missing. Is that what love feels like? Was I in love?

Downhearted, I fetched my case and managed to catch a ride to the station. From there, the train journey to Berlin passed in a haze. My thoughts were elsewhere, somewhere in that hospital. Nurse Gisela. I missed her already, and wondered how long it would be before I saw her again.

I had no idea. I was due to fly to my new posting in a few hours' time, and would be flying into the unknown. The idea both scared and excited me. The excitement of a new job, and the fears that came with the unknown.

I caught a tram from the station to the airport, and found my plane standing on the hard stand, ready for take-off. I climbed aboard, and was shown to a seat by one of the ground staff. Ten minutes later, we were high above the Fatherland, heading towards a new start.

6. Fliegerhorst Twente

The flight from Berlin to my destination took longer than it should have, the weather was fine, so I can only assume it was due to either enemy aircraft or some form of standard safety procedure.
I didn't care. I looked out the window, and saw greater Germany below me. It did not look like a country at war from up here. It all looked very normal, but I knew the reality was very different.
Eventually, we descended through a cloud towards what looked like a collection of farm buildings. The airfield had been cleverly disguised, I was impressed. Gripping my seat hard, I prayed for a safe landing.
The landing was bumpy, and slightly concerning for a non-flyer like myself. As soon as the aircraft came to a full stop, I was at the door, waiting to get out. The Luftwaffe Corporal looking after me laughed "Not a flyer sir?"
I shook my head vigorously "No!"
He laughed some more and opened the door. As I climbed down onto the ground, he was still laughing. He handed down my case, I took it and walked over to the SS men lined up to welcome me. I double checked that I had my briefcase. Safe.
"Obersturmführer!" the young, idealistic looking Oberscharführer snapped off a sharp salute. The two Rottenführers by his side followed his example.
I returned their salute "At ease gentlemen". Thankfully, they relaxed. Well, the two Corporals did. The Sergeant maintained his stiff posture. "Welcome to Fliegerhorst Twente sir" he said "Please follow me and I'll show you to your quarters"
"Thank you" I said, and followed him as the two Corporals disappeared off to wherever they had come from.
There were building sites everywhere, the airfield was undergoing a substantial expansion.
"We have a lot of local workers on site" he said, noticing my gaze.
"Ah, it looks very well camouflaged from the air" I noted.
"They are using local building styles, to ensure all buildings look like they are part of a farm" he informed me.
"It is certainly effective"

"This is the officers' mess" he said, pointing to a newly constructed building on our right, it had stepped gables, and looked like it had been there for a long time.

"And here are the officers' quarters"

The quarters were close to the mess, which was good. It was getting late, and would soon be dinner time. The building was of a similar style, but with a pitched roof.

"I will collect you at seven tomorrow morning sir" he said, quickly adding "If that suits"

"Perfect, thank you Sergeant"

He nodded, and snapped off another salute "Heil Hitler!"

I returned his salute without saying anything, and he turned sharply and marched away. Inside, I found the staff officer and signed in.

He then showed me to my room. I thanked him, and closed the door. I fell doen onto my bed, exhausted. Mostly from the flight, and also because I hadn't slept well last night. I was clutching my briefcase. Paranoia.

Thinking about dinner, I freshened up in the bathroom, checked my uniform, and went to the mess.

Heads turned as I walked in, and I noticed most of those present looking at me with thinly veiled disgust. I couldn't blame them. However; I needed to assert myself. If I didn't, they would walk all over me. "Good evening" I said loudly, so they could all hear. One by one, they all stood and saluted. I returned the salute, being careful to use the army salute, not the SS salute. This put most of them at ease. I did not outrank some of them, but they were duty bound to salute anyone wearing the Knights Cross, regardless of rank. There were some twenty air force officers present, and they all returned to their meals as I made my way to an empty table. A steward approached after I had sat down, and handed me a menu. "Would you like a drink from the bar before dinner sir?"

"Cognac, if you have any. Please"

"Very good sir" he smiled, and walked over to the bar, where he poured me a generous measure of cognac.

He held out the tray, and I took the glass. I swilled the liquid around a bit, then took a sip. "Excellent, thank you" I said to him. He nodded, and left. I meant it, it really was excellent.

I was surprised that such good cognac was still obtainable.

I looked around the room; there were about 20 people sat around in little groups. All Luftwaffe, no Wehrmacht, no SS, no Gestapo. I took a breath, and told myself it seemed like a good place to be. Although, here, I was the one everyone feared and was quiet around. That was both an advantage and disadvantage.

Personally, I was not like that at all, I'd love nothing better that to be friends with everyone, and have a good time. Professionally, it was my job to do the opposite.

I ordered my dinner, and picked up one of the newspapers from the stand by the bar. I sat quietly, reading the paper, trying not to appear like a fanatical SS troublemaker. The Volkischer Beobachter was full of the usual propaganda; our heroic troops were battling for the Fatherland, victory after victory ensured our fight against Bolshevism continued. More nonsense filled the pages. It was difficult to read without getting angry. 94% was all I was thinking about as I read.

94 out of 100 of my comrades lay dead on their precious battlefields. I wondered if I knew any of the survivors. I had not known all of the men in my unit of course. Well, I knew them, but not necessarily in any great depth. Still. I wonder if any of them blamed me.

"Your dinner sir"

The steward woke me from my daydream. "Hmm? Ah, yes, of course. Thank you."

He set down the plates of food, and asked if there was anything else I needed. I thanked him, and said there wasn't. He nodded and left.

I looked at my food; half of a roast chicken, potatoes, carrots, cabbage, gravy. I wondered if the local population got to eat as well as this. Not that it made a difference. Did it? I put the thought out of my mind and ate.

I was enjoying a coffee after my dinner, browsing the newspaper, when a Luftwaffe officer approached.

"Good evening Lieutenant. Mind if I join you for coffee?"

I stood and saluted; he was an air force Major. He returned my salute, and introduced himself.

"I am Major Adolf Edler von Graeve, commander of this glorious airfield" he held out his hand.

"Lieutenant Joseph Deckman" I said, shaking his hand.

I gestured for him to sit, and called the steward over. "Coffee for the Major please".

We sat, and he asked "You mind if I ask what brings you here Lieutenant?" he asked. His voice was warm and friendly.

I waited for the steward to finish pouring the Major's coffee, and replied. "Local resistance groups"

"Ah yes, the infamous resistance. We haven't had much trouble from them here thankfully"

He then gestured towards the remainder of the officers in the room "You see the fear in their faces? They all think you're here to spy on them, to ensure they are loyal to the Führer"

"Are they?" I asked, taking a sip of coffee.

He smiled "Of course, we wouldn't be here otherwise, would we?"

"Indeed" I returned his smile "I am not here to spy on your men Herr Major, they may rest easy"

"That is good news". He turned to the room, and spoke loudly "You hear that? The Lieutenant is not here to spy on you"

The mood in the room relaxed in an instant, and chatter got louder and more animated as a result.

"I didn't realise my being here would have such an effect" I said truthfully. I didn't. Why did they fear me? Because I was SD?

"They see SD, and instantly think the worst, it's a natural reaction" he said.

"I can only apologise for such a reputation Herr Major. I shall do my best not to live up to it"

He laughed "I like you Lieutenant. Would you join me in the morning for a tour of the base? I'd be more than happy to show you around"

"That would be great, thank you Herr Major"

"Splendid. Shall we say 07.00? I'll have a car collect you from your quarters" he stood. The meeting was over. I rose and stood at attention.

"You have seen combat" he said, referring to the medals on my uniform.

"Yes sir, Poland and here in the Netherlands"

"A Knights Cross, admirable indeed. Not just a pencil pusher then eh Deckman" he winked "Good"

After he walked out of the mess, I sat and took a deep breath.

I had not planned on seeing the Kommandant until tomorrow, and so was not prepared. Perhaps it was for the best; the meeting had gone quite well after all. Hadn't it? I hoped so. I thanked the steward and went back to my quarters. I slept well that night.

I woke the following morning to a knock on my door "Your wakeup call Obersturmführer"

"Thank you" I checked my watch, it was six o'clock. After stretching out, I got out of bed with a spring in my step. I had a shower, dressed, and had breakfast at the mess. At 06.59, I was stood outside my quarters, and a staff car approached.

It was a crisp winter morning, the sun was out, and the sky was blue. The car had its top down, and I sat in the back. We drove for a few minutes, then pulled up outside a rather plain looking house. A few seconds later, the Major appeared from the house, and walked up to the car. I jumped out, and held the door open for him.

"Good morning sir" I saluted.

"Morning Lieutenant, beautiful day"

"Yes sir" I said, and sat next to him. He motioned for the driver to go, and we set off on our tour of the base.

We drove for almost an hour, and I got a good handle on the layout of the base. The Major showed me all the main buildings, and I saw some of the planes also. The ME 110 looked quite alien with their antenna arrays on the front, like nothing I had seen before. These were the night fighters.

From what I understood, they used radio direction finding and ground radar stations to locate their prey and destroy them. It was all very impressive. I told him as such.

"Thank you, it's been quite the journey. We had almost 6000 locals working on the project" he said smiling, then hastily added "All voluntarily of course, the government pays them well. No forced labour here. The airfield was pitiful when we got here. They had ploughed through the runways, and blown up the hangars. A futile gesture, of course"

"Of course" I agreed.

"We have expanded the airfield to 1600 hectares, which meant we had to raise some 71 farms and 22 houses. They were all generously compensated, naturally, but we needed the land."

I nodded in agreement "How many personnel are stationed here Major?" I asked.

"It varies of course, but about 1500 at the moment" he replied.

"It's a great airfield Herr Major, I must congratulate you"

"Thank you Lieutenant" he smiled. The man was obviously proud of what had been achieved here in such a short timescale.

On completion of the tour, he asked if I wanted dropping back at my quarters, or my office.

"At my office please, if convenient"

"It is not a problem, I'm quite enjoying the fresh air"

What an amiable, likeable man this was, none of the superiority that was usually evident in Luftwaffe officers. I liked him instantly.

The car drew up at a small building in the main part of the base; my office. I thanked the Major again, and bade him farewell.

Before he left, he said "Lieutenant?"

"Yes sir?"

"If you ever desire a cup of actual coffee, come see me in my office. I have a small supply for special occasions" he winked.

"That is very generous sir, I will be certain to take advantage" Real coffee? The mess served Ersatz coffee, which was not to my liking at all. I planned to take the Major up on his kind offer.

As the car drove off, I stood and observed my new office. A small building, but then I wasn't expecting anything spectacular.

It was charming, and looked like a traditional Dutch farm building, with its distinctive orange roof tiles and colourful window shutters.

I walked inside, and found my team in what I assumed was the main office.

All three immediately jumped up and saluted "Heil Hitler". It was overly loud, and not necessary.

I frowned "At ease gentlemen, please" I said "You will find that I am quite a relaxed as far as saluting goes. Unless someone important is visiting of course. A simple good morning will suffice in future"

Smiles all round, though I noted the Sergeant looked like he didn't really appreciate a drop in discipline. He would have to live with it; I was in charge after all.

He approached me and asked "What would you like to do today sir?"

"I would like to visit the SD headquarters in Enschede, in order to get a feel for the resistance activity in the area"

"Very good sir, I can drive you there whenever you need"

"We have a vehicle?" I asked.

"Yes sir, we are allocated two kübelwagens, one for your private use, and one for general use"

"Excellent. I may be relying on a driver for the time being, until I get my bearings"

"Of course sir"

"Would you be so kind as to show me my desk?" I asked, unsure as to where it was located.

"It is this way sir" he gestured for me to follow, which I did.

We walked up to the first floor, where my private office was located at the front of the building, overlooking the airfield. The other rooms on this floor were either used for storage, or were empty. I had the whole floor to myself.

"Thank you Sergeant" I said "I'll be down in ten minutes or so if that suits?"

He was obviously not accustomed to officers being so polite, so I tried to put him at ease. "Like I said, I'm not a strict disciplinarian. That doesn't mean I won't run a tight ship though Sergeant"

"Of course not sir" he relaxed a little. I hoped he would relax more, and not become a thorn in my side. But somehow, I doubted that.

He left me to it, and I took a moment to take in my new office. It was quite large, and smelled like it had been only recently finished and furnished. A simple desk stood in the bay window, and the room was bright and cheerful; quite unlike a military room.

A large map of the area dominated the wall opposite my desk. It was very detailed, and I looked forward to adding my own detail as I got to know the area. I had a few more minutes, so tried to call Gisela at the hospital. Unfortunately, I got no further than the receptionist; Gisela was not in today, she had a day off so was visiting with family in Berlin. Disheartened, I went down to see if the Sergeant was ready. Of course he was.

We went out, and he held the car door open for me; I jumped in the back, and he drove off.

7. Enschede

The drive into the town was pleasant enough; farmers' fields, the odd rows of houses, sunshine, fresh winter air. Perfect.

We passed only minimal traffic until we reached the outskirts of the town, where fields gave way to factories and houses. The Sergeant was giving me a running commentary as we drove, apparently the city was famed for its textile factories. We drove past a few of them as we went along. The streets were busy with bicycles and German army vehicles.

"SD headquarters is just up this street" the Sergeant said from the front as we turned into a street in an affluent looking area. Before the war it likely was. Now, most of the larger houses were requisitioned by the Ortskommandant for military use. We pulled up outside a grand looking villa; our destination.

"Would you like me to wait sir?" the Sergeant asked.

"No, it's fine. I'll call you when I'm done, let me have your number" I wrote the office phone number in a notebook, and he drove off.

A few ambulances drove by as I stood in front of the impressive looking villa. I took a breath, and went inside.

"Can I help you?" A rather stern looking Corporal asked without looking up. He was sitting behind a small desk in what I supposed used to be the parlour.

I stiffened and said angrily "I beg your pardon Rottenführer?"

He jumped up and snapped to attention with a loud click of his heels "Apologies Obersturmführer!"

"Who is in charge here?" I asked, maintaining my fake anger.

To my surprise, I was actually quite enjoying this.

"Obersturmbannführer Ecke sir"

"Fine, take me to him" I said, waving my glove.

"Yes sir" he almost fell over, trying to get around the desk in the cramped space. "Please, follow me sir"

He led me up to what likely used to be the master bedroom, and knocked on the door.

"Come!" came a loud voice from within. He opened the door, and led me in.

"Obersturmbannführer" he saluted. The man behind the desk gave a limp return. "This is Obersturmführer..." he looked to me for help.
"Deckman" I said.
"Deckman?" the Lieutenant Colonel asked sternly, and motioned for the Corporal to leave, which he did, closing the door behind him.
"Yes sir, Deckman" I said, wondering what was going on.
He looked pensive "Deckman? Deckman?" pause, then "Ah! Yes, of course. The new man from Berlin" he rose, and shook my hand.
"Welcome to the madness. Forgive me, my mind is all over the place. Can't show weakness in front of the staff though eh?" he laughed.
He obviously meant the Corporal.
"Of course not sir" I smiled.
"Sit, please" He gestured towards a chair. I did as commanded.
"So, you've been sent to root out the local resistance eh? Good man. We don't have a lot of trouble with them, but trouble enough to warrant someone being sent to deal with it, or so it appears."
"Sir, my brief is barely existent; I was simply told to investigate the local resistance"
"Well" he said, looking at the clock "No time like the present" he rose, and took his cap from a coat hook.
Sir?" I asked, confused.
"Come Deckman, I'll take you for lunch" he said.
I followed him down, and outside, where we walked towards what I guess is the town centre. More ambulances rolled past.
"A lot of ambulances" I noted.
"Yes, there are a couple of Kriegslazerets dotted around the city, we're far enough behind the lines for this to be considered a safe area"
Made sense, and I immediately wondered if Gisela could get a transfer to one of these hospitals.
The town centre was lovely; old brick streets, shops, café's, restaurants, busy with people going about their daily business.
The war seemed distant, far away from here. In the very centre was an old church, set in the middle of a market square.
The square was ringed by restaurants and bars. We sat outside one of these, called De Graaf. A waiter came out and took our food and drink order.

"You want to speak to the local resistance?" the Lieutenant Colonel said.

"That is possible?" I asked.

"Sure, they're over there" he pointed to a water fountain, where a group of men were stood talking.

"That is the resistance?" I asked.

"Yes, they're there every day" he said.

"Why don't you arrest and interrogate them?" I asked.

"Lieutenant, do not mistake me for one of those fanatical SS or Gestapo monsters." he sat back, swilling his brandy around his glass

"You know what I did before the war Joseph?" he asked.

"No sir"

"I was a lawyer. That's the only reason I have these" he said, flicking his collar flashes. He took a sip of his brandy, and continued "I'm not a soldier Joseph, I'm an administrator. That's why I'm here. I don't arrest and torture, I leave that to the animals"

"Like me?" I asked.

He looked at me for a moment, as if he were sizing up his prey, then asked "Are you a monster Joseph?"

"No sir, I am not"

"I didn't think so. You were Waffen SS correct?"

"Yes sir"

"Not one of those Einsatzgruppen monsters I hope?"

"No sir, standard infantry"

"Good. Last thing I need is a fanatic running around pumping people full of scopolamine"

"I wouldn't know how to sir" I laughed.

"I'm glad to hear it" There was a look of relief in his eyes, like I had passed some kind of test.

"Do you have much in the way of resistance troubles sir?" I asked.

He waved his hand dismissively "Ach, minor things, nothing we can't deal with"

I could see there was something on his mind, but I was still being assessed for trustworthiness.

Or not. I wasn't sure, maybe it was nothing. I hardly knew the man, after all.

Yet... I couldn't shake the feeling that this man wanted to confide in me. I made a mental note to do my utmost to earn his trust.

"Tell me about yourself Joseph" he said, interrupting my thoughts.

"Me?" I asked.

"Yes, I am always interested in people's stories. Tell me yours"

"Well, I liver, or lived, in Austria, my father is a financial lawyer, so I have lived abroad a lot. England and the Netherlands"

"You lived around here?" he interrupted.

"No sir, in Leiden"

"Ah, forgive me, continue, please"

"I was of a mind-set to follow my father into a career in law..." I continued, then paused.

"Until the war started" he said.

I nodded "Until the war started. My father took us to Berlin to see some of the parades. That's what I believed at the time, but now I think they were likely ordered to Berlin as my mother is English."

"Your mother is English?" he asked, a look of surprise on his face.

"Yes sir, she was born in Stratford"

"Stratford upon Avon? I have been there" he leaned in and said in a quiet voice "I love the works of Shakespeare. Before the war, I traveled to London quite often on business, and took the opportunity to travel to some of the historic places. It was thoroughly enjoyable"

I smiled. I liked this man. His unpretentious personality appealed to me. Previous experience of higher ranking SS officers had proven them to be sticklers for rules, fanatical followers, zealots even.

This man gave me a different impression. I hoped I was right, and he wasn't playing me. He seemed genuine, but I warned myself to remain on guard.

"How did you come to join the Waffen SS?" he asked.

"Like I said, the parades in Berlin. I don't know why, but they just inspired me to want to be one of them. The imposing black uniforms, the discipline. They looked like gods"

He chuckled "The propaganda worked I see"

"Yes, I suppose so. If you think about it that way, they were marching to inspire youngsters to join up" I reflected. He was right. Was I that gullible?

"Don't beat yourself up over it, you are only one of the millions that followed suit" he said sympathetically.

"Hmmm, thank you. I fell for it. Oh well, can't change it now I suppose"

"Are you a party member Joseph?"

What a strange question. "Of course sir, we have to be" Was that a test?

He looked around, then shook his head slowly "No, I know you are. What I meant was are you an active member? Do you believe in all that National Socialism nonsense?"

Alarm bells rang in my head. What was going on here? Do I say yes, then find myself alienated? Do I say no, and find myself thrown into a cell? He could obviously see the conflict on my face.

"You don't have to answer, I know what you're thinking."

He thought for a moment, then continued "It is a dangerous world that we live in Joseph, you are right not to trust anyone. You don't know me, so are right not to answer. Like I said earlier, I am not a soldier, just a lawyer playing his part. In the beginning, I believed in the cause, they offered hope, a new, stronger Germany. That is what I wanted. I joined the SS, and they sent me to Tolz, then through a myriad of administrative jobs until I ended up here."

"It is not a bad place to be" I remarked.

"No" he chuckled "No, it is not" He looked around again, then said "I can tell that you are a trustworthy person Joseph, so in an act of good faith, I will confide in you"

"Sir?"

He lowered his voice "I don't believe in the Nazi vision. A thousand year Reich? Ha! Nonsense.

As for the uniform; there are many out there that held mundane posts before the war; teachers, farmers.

They put on this uniform and turn into tyrants, fanatical idiots, Jew haters. That's not me Joseph. And I hope it's not you." he held up his hand "Again, no answer required"

He finished his brandy, and we ate our lunch talking about the local area and the town itself. It was pleasant, and I enjoyed his company very much.

Sadly, it was over all too soon; a Corporal approached, saluted, and handed him a note. His face dropped.

"You'll have to excuse me Lieutenant, I have urgent business to attend to" he said, rising from his chair. I stood at attention. Best not give the Corporal anything to gossip about.

"Sir" I said, saluting.

He returned my salute, and left with the Corporal.

I sat back down with a loud sigh. Wow. What a story! I didn't know whether to trust him or not. No. I reminded myself to remain on guard. I finished my lunch, and walked around the town centre for a bit, familiarising myself with the layout. Ahead of me, a young Wehrmacht soldier was walking on the side of the road. To his right, a group of children noticed him, and started yelling at him. The poor lad didn't understand what they were saying, and kept walking.

This enraged them, and they started crowding around him, calling him names, knocking his cap off his head. I sensed an escalation was imminent, so ran over.

"Hey!" I shouted "What is going on here!" they fell silent. Not only shocked at the appearance of an SS officer, but also because he spoke their language.

"You lot. Leave him alone. Go on, go home" A woman appeared next to me.

"He's German scum, he shouldn't be here" one of the boys said, obviously the leader of the gang. "Vieze moffen!" he shouted. *Filthy krauts*.

"Watch your tongue child!" she shouted "Go on, go home" she insisted.

"They don't belong here!" he shouted defiantly.

"You think he wants to be here?" she asked him angrily "He's a young boy, just doing what he's told to do. Leave him alone"

"They're all the same" he maintained.

"I would listen to her and go home. Before I arrest you all" I said sternly.

The others looked unsure, scared, and wavered. "Maybe we should go Marko" said one.

The lad thought for a moment, weighing up the odds. The woman leaned down, and put her hand on his shoulder "Go home Marko, you don't want to get into trouble, your mother needs you"

He looked at her, then at me, then turned and ran away, the rest of his gang following suit.

The young soldier turned to me and saluted "Thank you sir"

He was wearing an eyepatch over his left eye. Poor kid.

He looked about 16 years old, and he had lost an eye in combat already.

He should be at home, spending time with his friends, having fun. Not this.

"Look after yourself soldier" I said sympathetically.

He nodded, and continued on his way.

I turned to thank the woman, but she was already walking away.

"Excuse me madam" I said, hurrying after her.

She turned, a look of shock in her eyes. She was stunning. Her long red hair matching her apparent fiery personality. Her green eyes sparkled like emeralds in the afternoon sun as they met mine. For a moment, I was lost, and had to try hard to focus.

"I just wanted to thank you" I said, trying to reassure her.

"Thank me?" she looked confused "I was trying to save them from *you*" she regarded me as one would a monster.

"Me?" I asked "Oh, that. I had no intention of arresting them, merely tried to scare them. The poor lad has obviously been through enough without being terrorised in the street"

The look of confusion persisted. "Jij bent SS" she said. *You're SS.*

I looked down at my uniform "So I am!" I laughed.

Her stern expression remained unchanged.

"Well, I just wanted to say thank you" I said "Good day to you" I smiled, and walked off in the direction of the SD headquarters. Or so I hoped.

I turned to see her still standing there, looking confused. To me, she looked beautiful.

When I eventually made it back to the villa on the Rembrandtlaan, I went to see the staff officer. He was an amiable man, and I asked him if there was an office available here.

"Well, there are two empty rooms sir, but room allocation is up to the Obersturmbannführer"

"Ok, thank you. If I put in a request, could you see to it that he sees it please?"

"Of course sir" he handed me the requisite form, and I filled it out.

"Could I use your telephone please?" I asked after I handed the form back.

"Yes sir" he hand me the phone. I retrieved my notebook from my pocket, and found the Sergeants number at the airbase.

He picked up after two rings "Oberscharführer Mencke speaking"

"Sergeant, it is Lieutenant Deckman. Would it be convenient for you to pick me up?"

"Of course sir, right way. I'll be there in 20 minutes"

"Thank you Sergeant"

"Of course sir" he repeated, and hung up.

Twenty minutes. That gave me enough time to walk around the park I saw around the corner. Splendid. I took a moment to ask the Corporal what the park was called.

"Volkspark sir" he responded.

I thanked him and set off. It was a beautiful park, with a hotel/restaurant set in the grounds. There were no flowers, and the trees had long lost all their leaves, adding its own special charm to the surroundings. As a child, I remembered gathering the fallen leaves into big piles with my friends, then taking turns jumping into them. The innocence of youth. How far we have fallen. There were benches dotted around the park, on most of which couples sat talking.

It seemed like there was no war going on, like everything was normal. For a while, I forgot about the war myself. Until I saw the looks I got as I walked past them. It was a look of both fear and disgust.

I couldn't blame them; I'd feel the same way if it were me sat there. We were invaders. Worse, we were killers. It saddened me to know that many locals had been sent to Germany to forced labour camps. Jews were also being identified, likely for deportation.

However, they would likely be doing the same if they were the invaders in Germany, I thought. Wouldn't they? The words the woman had spoken earlier came to mind: *"You think he wants to be here? He's a young boy, just doing what he's told to do."*

It summed most of us up. We were all young men, doing what we were told to do. Our duty.

Slightly disheartened, I found myself walking back towards the SD villa. As I turned into the street, I saw the car parked up outside.

The Sergeant appeared from the front door as I approached. "Ah, there you are sir. Ready when you are"

At least he's not snapping off a salute, I thought. Maybe he's not so bad after all.

"Thank you Sergeant, sorry to keep you waiting"

"Not a problem sir, it is a beautiful day" he smiled, and opened the car door for me.

"It is indeed" I agreed as I climbed onto the back seat.

We drove back to the airfield in silence, which suited me. The Sergeant seemed happier and more relaxed than when I had first met him, which in turn relaxed me. I was enjoying the surroundings, taking it all in as we drove. My mind was, however, fixed on the beautiful redhead I had met earlier. She fascinated me. Not in a romantic way like Gisela, but she fascinated me nevertheless. There was something about her...

8. The Office.

I spent the rest of the day going through the issues identified by the team. The problems varied from minor theft to deliberate sabotage. It was all very boring and I was only half listening, getting very tired in the process. Thankfully, a phone call saved me from further torture. It rang, and one of the Corporals answered. He held the receiver out to me "Obersturmbannführer Ecke on the telephone for you sir".
"Deckman" I said taking the phone.
"Ah Joseph, Ecke here. I saw your request for an office just now. You sure you want to be stationed here?"
"Yes sir, I think it would be beneficial" I said. And get me closer to the mystery redhead.
"Approved. You may move in tomorrow. Come see me after for a coffee won't you?"
"Of course sir, thank you" It was more of an order than a request.
I replaced the receiver, and handed the phone back to the Corporal. I could feel all three of them looking at me expectantly. Should I tell them? Of course I should.
"Gentlemen, I have secured an office in the SD headquarters, so I will be working from there from tomorrow"
The relief was obvious; they had their little empire back.
"I will remain victualled on the base, and will take one of the vehicles for my own use. I will check in a few times a week, just in case I'm required for anything" I didn't really want to, but I *was* the leading security officer on the base after all.
I checked the time, it was almost six. "To celebrate your regained freedom, I thought we may have a few Schnapps" I said, pulling a bottle from my briefcase.
There was some nervous laughter, but they soon loosened up, and we spent a pleasant hour drinking and exchanging stories.
They weren't a bad lot really.

I woke the following morning with a slight headache, but in a superb mood. Moving office would mean I could take more time to explore the town, and I would be in the hub of SD activity in the area.

The hot water system was still experiencing teething problems, so my shower was lukewarm at best.

I didn't mind though, my mood was too good to be messed up by a malfunctioning boiler.

Breakfast in the mess was excellent; my eggs were boiled the way I liked them, and even the fake coffee wasn't too bad today. Well, ok, it was terrible.

I drove to the town, and decided to take a drive around the ring road, or Singel as the locals called it. The roads were quiet, save for the occasional ambulance. Given that it was a Monday, I thought that odd. I liked the look of this town, it had many factories just outside the centre, but inside the ring road, it was very pleasant indeed.

The road eventually brought me to the Volkspark, and I took the turn into the Rembrandtlaan. I parked next door to the impressive looking villa, picked up my briefcase, and went inside.

"Good morning Obersturmführer" The same staff officer as yesterday, good.

"Good morning, I trust my approved request made it back to you?"

"Yes sir, I had the room cleaned last night, it is ready for you. Please, follow me"

I followed the sub-Lieutenant up the stairs, and then up another set of stairs into the roof space. There were two room up here; one used for storage, and the other was my office. I feared the worst. I needn't have worried however, as the room we walked into was bright, clean, and airy. There was a large window looking out towards the park, and it was spotless.

"I hope it suits your needs sir" the staff officer said.

"More than adequate" I smiled "Thank you"

"I'll be on duty downstairs all day. If you need anything, just pick up the telephone, it's on an exchange"

"Thank you"

After he had left, I sat in the comfortable leather chair, which swiveled.

I turned and put my feet up on the window ledge. This, I liked. This, I loved. It was perfect. Private, clean, and it had everything I needed, including a small safe.

I picked up the phone, and the young sub-Lieutenant answered "Staff officer"

"It's Obersturmführer Deckman"

"Yes sir, how can I help?"

"I'm to have coffee with the Sturmbannführer today, could you see when he is available please?"

"Of course sir, I will call back"

"Thank you"

I hung up. I wondered what the old man really wanted. Not that I was worried, lunch yesterday had been thoroughly enjoyable, so I imagined it wouldn't be anything bad. Hopefully.

Ten minutes or so later, the phone rang. I picked up "Deckman"

"The Sturmbannführer will be available at two o'clock"

"Excellent, thank you" I hung up. Two eh? That gave me some time to walk around the town centre, and find somewhere for lunch. I locked my briefcase away, and set off for my walk.

It was a slightly more overcast day today, but it was dry at least.

I wandered the streets of the town centre, and found only a few places I could go either for a drink or for something to eat. The war was taking its toll on food availability, and I couldn't help but feel guilty. The German war machine was draining resources wherever it went. Our troops needed food, and if that meant the occupied territories went without, so be it. Didn't make me feel any better, but like I said, I'm sure they would do the same to us if roles were reversed.

I passed a school, where noisy youngsters were playing in the playground. I stood for a moment, enjoying the innocence of it all, and remembering my own school days. I was about to walk away when I spotted her; the redhead. She was clapping along with a group of girls who were watching two girls jumping in a rather large skip rope. She looked up and saw me.

She stopped clapping, and the smile disappeared. It made me feel uncomfortable, so I just gave a quick wave before moving along. The way she had looked at me. Such hatred. Was I imagining it? Was she just surprised to see me again? Did she think I was following her? All these thoughts jostled for position as I hurried away. I was so wrapped up in them that I didn't register her first shout.

I heard the second one though: "Hey! Wacht even!" *Wait a moment.*
I stopped dead, and turned around. She was walking towards me,
looking around to make sure nobody saw. She gestured towards a
small alleyway, so I went in. She followed me in, and immediately said
"Volgt u mij?" *Are you following me?*
"What? No, I was just having a walk around before lunch, and
happened to see you is all"
She fixed me with a distrustful stare. Either she had judged my
character correctly, or was simply unafraid of insulting an SS officer.
I hoped it was the first, as the last would likely get her shot one day.
"Waarom?" *Why?*
"Why was I walking?"
"No, why were you watching me?"
"I wasn't"
"I saw you"
"Ach, I was just lost in the moment, watching the children playing.
It reminded me of my own school days. This is allowed, yes? I didn't
see you until you looked at me"
She considered this for a moment, then asked "Why are you not like
the others?"
"Others?"
"The other SS and SD men"
"They are not like me?" I asked. Stupid, of course. I knew full well that
the SS and SD had a reputation for being violent monsters.
"You're different" she commented through squinted eyes.
"I hope so" I said truthfully.
"What do you mean?"
"I hope I'm not a monster like some of them" I said.
"Those boys yesterday, why didn't you beat them?"
The thought hadn't even crossed my mind.
"What? Why would I have done that? They were just boys being boys,
they were harmless. I would have done the same were I in their
shoes" I said.
She looked me in the eyes for a few seconds, then turned and left
without saying another word.
Those beautiful green eyes. A man could lose himself in those.
I waited a minute or so, then left the alley. There was no sign of her.

Slightly shaken by the encounter, I made my way back towards the office; I was no longer in the mood for lunch.

Who was she? A teacher? Possibly. But, who was she? What was her story? She seemed to ooze confidence, and seemed unafraid to speak her mind. Though she did take precautions not to be seen talking to me. I decided to ask the Sturmbannführer. I wouldn't mention seeing her today, but would recount yesterday's events. Maybe she was known to the SD. Worth a try.

I sat in my office, trying to focus on intelligence reports, but failing. She was on my mind. More so than Gisela. I felt guilty about that, but there was just something about this girl. My interest in her was not romantic at all, I was just intrigued by her. Or was it romantic? Fortunately, two o'clock came soon enough, and it was time for my coffee with Ecke. I put my reports away, and walked down to his office.

"Ah Obersturmführer Deckman, please, enter" he said, waving me in. He was talking to another Lieutenant, and handed him a stack of papers, saying "That will do for today Heinz"

"Yes sir" he said, and left.

"I thought we could go out for coffee, if you don't mind"

"Of course not sir" I said, happy for any opportunity to get out.

"Splendid, come" He picked up his hat, and led me out.

We walked outside, and turned the corner towards the town centre.

"Have you had a chance to look around Joseph?" he asked.

"Yes sir, I went for a walk this morning"

"Ah! Good. What do you think?"

"I like it here" I said "It's a charming place"

"Certainly different from Germany" he chuckled.

"Yes sir, it is"

"Where are we going sir?" I asked, noting we weren't going to the same place as yesterday.

"Just up here" he said, taking me down a side street. Ahead, on the left was a café. We entered, and sat at the bar.

The place was deserted, except for an old bartender, who was busying himself cleaning glasses. He didn't even look up when we came in.

"We're not having coffee?" I asked.

"Very observant Joseph" he joked. "No, I can't really drink too much of that Ersatz rubbish"

"Understood sir" I said.

"Have you tried the local Jenever yet?" he asked.

"No sir, what is it?"

"It's a gin, but far more traditional"

I had tried gin before of course, but wasn't a big spirit drinker.

He held up two fingers, and the bartender put two small fluted glasses on the bar and filled them with a clear liquor from what looked like a clay bottle. He then came around the bar, and slid the bolt across the front door, locking us in. "Relax Joseph" Ecke said, noting my alarm.

"Sir?" I asked uneasy.

"Now we can talk" he said.

"Talk?"

"Yes, talk" he smiled. "Tell me, how is your mother? I haven't seen Mary for a few years"

"My mo….." I was completely stunned. How did he know my mother? What was going on here?

"Don't worry" he said "We're old friends"

"But?" I paused "You know my mother?"

"Yes, I have known Mary for some 15 years"

"She's called Maria now" I offered.

"Ach, of course. But she will always be Mary to me."

He observed me for a moment. "I have been waiting for this moment for some time Joseph, ever since Stauffman told me you had accepted"

"You know the Sturmbannführer?"

"Yes, and Hauptmann Ost, and Hauptsturmführer Wiezinge"

"I…." I was stunned. That's what I wanted to say, but the words didn't come out.

"Did you notice anything about the three men?"

I thought for a moment, and said the first thing that sprang to mind "They were all very informal"

He clasped his hands together loudly "Ha! I knew you would get it. Well done Joseph. Now, tell me, do you know why that is?"

This was some kind of test. If it was, I didn't want to fail.

"They do not agree with Nazi ideology….they flaunt discipline…."

"Yes?" he said encouragingly.

Something he had said yesterday. What was it? Ah! *"I'm not a soldier Joseph"*. He had said it more than once. Of course! "They're not military"

"Exactly"

"But, the uniforms?" I was slightly confused.

"Remember what I told you about the uniform yesterday?"

Of course I did. He'd told me he'd been given a high rank based on his civilian occupation. "All four of you are the same?" I asked.

"To a degree, we all held educated positions before joining. Stauffman; a lawyer like myself, Wiezinge; foreign ministry, Ost; European sales manager for Krupp. Now, tell me what else we have in common?"

Lawyers, foreign ministry, European sales. Travel. Yes, but where specifically? Ah… of course.

"You've all been in England for extended periods of time before the war"

"Bravo Joseph" he applauded "They said you were sharp, and they weren't mistaken"

"You work for the English?" I asked.

"In a roundabout way"

This was a stunning revelation. How to react? I thought quickly.

"Can I ask something sir?"

"Of course"

"How do you know you can trust me?"

"Judith"

"Who is Judith?" I shouted.

"Calm yourself Joseph. She is part of our little group"

"Who…? The girl in the school?"

"Yes, the girl in the school"

"The whole thing had been arranged?"

"Joseph" he said, fixing me with a serious stare.

"Sir"

"Yes, it was arranged, she was actively looking to meeting you of course. She was asked to monitor you, listen to what you said, who you spoke to. It's all fairly standard stuff."

"Judith?" I asked, still confused.

"Yes, you know, the redhead?"

"What?"

"The whole incident with the young Wehrmacht boy yesterday? All staged to gauge your reaction. Did you wonder why she ran after you this morning?"

I did actually, it seemed out of character for a local girl to be chasing an SS officer down the street.

"She asked if you were *different,* yes?"

"Yes, she did"

"Your responses were genuine, that is what she was ascertaining"

"He is genuine"

I turned in shock, she was stood behind the bar.

"You!"

"Me" she said, smiling.

"Who are you?"

"She's my daughter" the bar tender replied.

My head was spinning. I steadied myself on the bar. "This whole thing has been a setup from the outset?"

"Ever since you joined up" he said.

"Since I *joined up*?" I said angrily. "That long?"

"Yes. Tell me, who knows you better than anyone in the world?"

"My mother" I said instantly.

"Exactly. She knows you, she knows you don't buy in to that Nazi nonsense. She knew you were drawn by the glamour, the uniforms, the brotherhood"

"She did?"

"Of course. Are you a Jew hater?"

"What?" the question threw me off balance.

"Do you hate the Jews? They are responsible for all evil in the world are they not?"

I was confused. "No. No, my best friends were Jews, I worked in a Jewish bakery before the war"

This made no sense. What was going on here?

"Wait, wait" I said, trying to make sense of it all. "Why do you want to know that?"

"Because we need to be sure" Ecke said evenly.

"You need to explain to me exactly who you people are, and what it is you do" I said "It's the only way any of this is going to make sense"

"Drink Joseph" Ecke said "I will try to explain as best I can"
I drank my Jenever in one go. This was obviously not the thing to do as I broke out into a violent coughing fit, which caused the bartender to laugh loudly.
"Easy" Judith said "It's quite potent"
"Yes" I gasped "I gathered as much"
"Sip" the bartender said, re-filling my glass.
That sounded like good advice. I turned back to Ecke.
"You need to start talking sir, before I drink myself stupid"
"We are all English spies" he said abruptly "In a roundabout way"
"My mother?" I asked.
He nodded. Unbelievable. My mother was an English agent?
"There are 21 of us, spread across Germany and the occupied territories. We do what we can to feed back intelligence without arousing suspicion. But that is only a small part of what we do, what our purpose is"
"What is your purpose?"
"We help allied airmen get back to England, we help Jews to escape to safe countries, we liaise with local resistance groups, that sort of thing"
"That sounds like a lot for only 21 people" I remarked.
"22 now actually" he smiled. He meant me of course.
"22 people" I corrected.
"Yes, it is. We are separate from SOE and other agencies, far more specialised if you like."
"You have managed to infiltrate the SS and SD. How?"
"We are all chosen very carefully Joseph, with specific objectives in mind. For me, it was to get here. For the others, likewise. Joining the SS was not difficult; we fit the racial profile, and have nothing suspicious in our pasts"
"You've all been to England though"
"Ach" he waved a dismissive hand "Who hasn't? Before this war started we were all free to travel were we not? It is not unusual, and raised only a minor eyebrow during the selection process."
He had a point of course. Travel was not unusual, and certainly not prohibited in the earlier days before the war. A sudden realisation came to me.
"You have all been involved in this for a very long time"

"Yes. Yes we have. I joined the SS in 1936. It took me a long time to get the relevant experience to ensure I got posted here."

"Wiezinge, Ost, Stauffman?"

"The same. We all joined in 36, and have spent our time apart, working towards our set objectives"

"Objectives? Set by whom?" I asked.

"I'm afraid I can't tell you that"

"You can tell me all that other stuff, but you can't give me a name?"

"No, I'm afraid not. Not because I don't want to, but for your own safety"

I could see his point. Having such information could prove catastrophic if I was captured.

"My mother?"

"Your mother recruited all of us" he said.

I could barely believe what I was hearing. My mother? Recruiting spies? It all sounded very fantastical, and I could scarcely believe it.

"It's true" Judith chimed in "She recruited me also"

"You're *not* with the resistance?" I asked, confused.

"Oh I am, but they know who I really am. Embedding myself in the resistance was my objective"

I was silent for a moment, then said "You will all forgive me if I'm finding all this is a little hard to believe"

Ecke put his hand on my arm "It will take time Joseph, but you're one of us now"

"And what is my objective?" I asked.

"That" he sighed "I do not know"

"But how will I find out?"

"You will be told soon enough, we had to gain your trust and admit you to the circle first" he said.

My head was spinning like mad. How could this be? Was it all true? Was it really happening?

"I think I'm going to be sick" I said.

"That way" the bartender said, pointing to a door at the back of the bar.

I ran out and just made it to the toilet in time.

What a mess. I took a few moments to clean myself up, and stared at my reflection in the mirror.

Who was that staring back at me? I didn't recognise myself. I was a soldier, a fighter, not a spy. I don't belong in this world, I should be out there, with my comrades. A wave of guilt hit me.

There was a knock on the door.

"You ok in there?" It was Judith.

"Yes, I am fine" I replied "Just coming"

I gathered myself and opened the door. She was stood there waiting for me.

"It's a lot to take in" she said. She sounded warm, caring, and friendly. Polar opposite to how she'd been before.

I nodded "Yes, it is"

"You are doubting yourself" It was a statement, not a question.

"Yes" Though I was doubting them more.

"We all go through that phase, though I wager it is much harder for you"

"I don't belong here" I said.

She put her hand on my shoulder. The sensation was like being hit by a bolt of lightning.

"None of us belong here. I should be teaching, Ecke should be practicing law, yet here we are. We are victims of circumstance."

"The war isn't a circumstance" I noted.

"No, it is not. It is terrible, and we are all trying to end it in our own small ways. There are different kinds of fight Joseph. You are used to violence, battlefields, combat.

We are not. We do things differently. But we still win battles. What we do is equally as important"

I knew she was making sense, but the guilt was still there. Gisela's words came to mind; *what difference would one man make* On the battlefield? Very little. In this business? Apparently a lot. "One man could make a lot of difference" I said out loud.

"What? Yes, of course he can" Judith said "You could make a difference here, does that not mean something?"

"Yes" I nodded slowly "Yes, it does. I can ensure my comrades did not die in vain"

"Exactly. You have to have faith Joseph. We really do make a difference. I don't know what it is they have planned for you, but you can safely assume it is something big. They wouldn't have gone through all this trouble to get you here if it wasn't"

Dammit. She was making sense. Why would they have gone through all this if not for an important reason? I sighed.

"Ok, let's go" I said.

She smiled, and followed me into the bar.

"Everything ok?" Ecke asked as I walked back in.

There was a sense of expectancy, I looked at Judith, who smiled warmly.

"Yes, everything is ok" I said.

"Splendid" Ecke smiled, relieved.

"I have a few questions though, if I may sir"

"There are no formalities needed in this group Joseph" he said "But, please, ask your questions"

"Very well. My first question is this" I said, touching my Knights Cross.

"That was nothing to do with us" he said "You were read the commendation?"

"Yes, I was"

"You have reason to doubt it?"

"No, it all happened as written"

"There is your answer."

"Second question. My promotion?" I said.

He shook his head again. "Well, to a point" he conceded.

"I know nothing of your initial promotion upon being awarded the Knights Cross, though I am led to believe it was ordered by Himmler himself"

"It was, I saw the letter" I confirmed.

"Your latest promotion was merely a suggestion. It was considered, and your entire career was backtracked and evaluated to ensure you were ready. Just like for any other promotion. The result speaks for itself"

It took a bit of the shine off my promotion, but not much more. It was still based on merit, which was important to me.

"Any more?" he asked.

"Why here?"

"Here?" he asked

"The Netherlands" I clarified.

He shook his head. "I don't know. Like I said, we were all set objectives, and are awaiting orders on how we proceed"

"Fine" I took a deep breath. "What do I do now?"

"You do your job Lieutenant" he said "Investigate the resistance, compile reports, make arrests if needed. Just follow orders"

"I should just carry on as normal?"

He laughed. "Normal? What is normal? We are part of the German war machine Joseph, we carry on doing our bit for the Reich"

"Was my move to the SD headquarters a mistake?" I asked.

"I don't think so. You are still staying at the airfield, and need to ensure you make periodic visits to the office there"

"Can I trust the men there?"

"In your office? No. Not at all. Especially the Sergeant. As for the airfield staff, I don't know. I have met the Kommandant, but don't profess to know him well."

"Major Von Graeve seems a likeable character" I said "He offered me real coffee"

Ecke's eyebrows rose "Real coffee? Oh! What I wouldn't give for a cup of real coffee"

I smiled. "I will be sure to let you know how it was"

"Keep your eyes on him, evaluate him for me."

I nodded "Of course"

He clapped his hands together. The gesture seemed incredibly loud and unnecessary in the small bar. "Right, we should probably get back to work."

We all stood, and I followed Ecke out of the café. Judith touched my shoulder as I passed her. Again, it was like a bolt of lightning. Feelings stirred deep inside of me. It was irrational, I loved Gisela. Judith meant nothing to me. Didn't she?

There wasn't much in the way of conversation on our walk back to the villa. Ecke showed me the train station, where the trains that supplied the airfield came from. The line had been re-opened for that very purpose, and had been an important undertaking.

As we walked through the front door of the villa, he suddenly said "I'll expect that report on my desk tomorrow morning Obersturmführer"

"Yes sir" I played along. He went to his office, and I went to mine.

I closed the door behind me, leaned against the door, and breathed deep. I need to stop thinking about this new group I seemed to belong to. I needed to focus on my job in order to not arouse suspicion in any way.

But, the events of today still whirred around my mind.

So much had happened, and I appeared to be part of something I had no idea about. These people trusted me? I barely knew them, nor did they know me. But, my mother had recommended me to them, which is probably why their trust was so easily gained.

I was never going to betray them of course, their beliefs and ideas matched my own. Still, it was a dangerous situation, and a needed to be careful.

I decided to do some fire arms training tomorrow, keep my mind occupied. There was a firing range at the Fliegerhorst, and I hadn't fired my pistol for some time. I took it from my holster, stripped, and re-assembled it. It was a beautiful weapon, so elegant.

I had once again been offered a P38 recently, but had turned it down; I was not giving up my P08. I put the weapon back in my holster, and went through some of the reports on resistance activity that I had requested earlier in the day.

9. The Ranges and Sabotage.

A few hours later, I was driving back to the airfield in the dark.
The drive took longer than usual, as I had very little in the way of illumination, but that suited me. I was not in a rush. The guard at the main gate scrutinised my papers, then let me through. "Have a good evening Obersturmführer"
"Thank you" I said, and drove on. I reached my accommodation, and locked my briefcase away before heading to the gymnasium. It had been some time since I had done any physical activity, and my body was starting to let me know as much. One of the sports leaders put me through my paces, and it felt great, if not a little painful. An hour later, I was stood under a lukewarm shower. The boiler had obviously not been fixed yet, but that suited me; I needed to cool down before dinner.
I dressed, arranged my laundry, and walked over to the mess. Inside, it was busy. I scanned the room, but couldn't see anyone I knew. The usual thing happened; people rose and saluted me. Not something I could ever get used to. I returned the salute awkwardly, feeling rather conspicuous.
I found a free seat at the bar, and sat there whilst I waited for a table to become available. The brandy I ordered warmed my throat.
Not the best I'd had, but one couldn't complain when at war.
A steward came over and informed me he had a table available for me. I followed him and sat. The table was in the furthest corner of the mess, and allowed me to observe everyone in the room. Even though the Commandant had put the men at ease, I still detected a hint of distrust in the room. I could understand why; these were dangerous times. There were always people looking to denounce others for personal gain, or just because they were utter fanatics.
You couldn't really ever trust anyone, and had to constantly mind what you said. It was a sad state of affairs really, and it went totally against the German military spirit of pride and friendship.
Dinner was served, and I ate greedily. Still not used to having regular meals, I ate when the opportunity arose.
It was a habit I would never lose.

On a table to my left, four young pilots were sat talking about a recent mission. They had apparently been able to shoot down two enemy Halifax bombers each, which is what they were celebrating. I wondered what difference eight less bombers in a formation of one hundred would make. Eight plane loads of bombs not falling on a German city, that's what.

Somewhere, a family would never know how lucky they had been that their home had been missed, and how much they owed to men such as these. How I admired them, making a difference like that. I had to stop and remind myself that I too, was making a difference. Or, would be rather. At the moment I wasn't doing much of anything really.

At another table, sat, I assume, two supply officers. They were bemoaning the late delivery of something or other, and blamed the resistance for sabotaging the railway line yet again. This piqued my interest, and I made a note to check on this in the morning.

After dinner, I took a brief stroll around the base. In the distance, I could hear the engines of the ME 110's running, and I silently wished them the best of luck. I was stopped twice by guardsmen whilst walking, apparently it wasn't really the done thing. One of the guards told me about the officers casino, which was located somewhere called the Usseler Es. I wasn't a gambler, so it didn't really interest me. There was also a brothel somewhere, which again, did not interest me. I would make a point of continuing my evening walks, the guards would just have to get used to it.

I could still feel the odd twinge in my leg, but it was getting better. The exercises shown to me by Doctor Weitz, combined with my frequent walks were really helping my recovery. After my walk, I returned to my quarters, and wrote a letter to Gisela.

My feelings for her were mixed at the moment, following my meeting Judith. That made me angry at myself.

Stop being a fool. Gisela is the woman I am in love with.

I needed to see her, I missed her dearly, and yearned to be in her arms. That is love is it not? I put the sealed envelope on the dresser for posting tomorrow, and went to bed. As far as Judith was concerned, my feelings were entirely unclear.

I woke the following morning in good spirits. The sun was shining low in the sky, and peeking through my curtains. I got up, pulled them aside, and opened the window. It was a beautiful, crisp winter day. I filled my lungs with the cold fresh air, and let out a long sigh of contentment. Apart from the sound of birds chirping, there was the intermittent rattling of machine gun fire. It sounded like a heave calibre gun, and I was curious as to what it was. I washed and dressed, and went off to find the source of the gunfire.

I asked a guard as I wandered, and he told me they were calibrating the gun sights on the ME 110's today. He was good enough to point me in the direction of the range. Full of childish excitement, I hurried off in the direction indicated. The gunfire was getting louder, as was the smell of cordite, indicating I was getting closer. I turned a corner and found what I had been looking for; the aircraft firing range. An ME 110 had its tail propped up to make the aircraft level, and technicians were busy making fine adjustments to the guns.

"Try it now!" one of them shouted. Another gave a thumbs up, and blew a whistle. A few second later, he held up a red flag, and everyone cleared the range. "Fire!" he shouted. The pilot in the cockpit fired a short burst of the two 30mm Mk 108 canons. My god! The noise it made! I hastily covered my ears. When the smoke had cleared, the pilot shouted "Sicher!" *Safe*. And the red flag was replaced by a green one. I sat away to the right side of the aircraft, and observed the scene. The target was checked, and results brought back to the technicians. They seemed happy, and spoke to the pilot. The technicians replaced the cowling on the canons, and moved to the double 20mm MG151 mounted in the underside of the nose. After removing the cowling and changing the target, the signal man repeated the process, and soon enough both MG-151 were fired. The noise! I had heard plenty of gunfire in combat, but nothing like this. Even our MG-39 was nothing compared to these monsters.

I managed to have a few moments with the pilot afterwards, and he told me more about his aircraft.

"It is a good airframe" he commented "But slow as hell. We have the oldest airframes, with the rubbish engines"

He told me how the radar intercept worked, and about tactics they had developed for sneaking up on the various types of allied bombers. I found it all extremely fascinating.

My spirits were still extremely high when I walked into the mess for breakfast. I ordered coffee, toast, and boiled eggs. A familiar face entered the mess, and came over to me. "Good morning Obersturmführer, how are you on this fine day?"

It was Major Von Graeve. I stood at attention, and responded "Most excellent Herr Major, most excellent"

"Good" he said, smiling "You mind if I join you?"

"Of course not, I would be honoured" I said, pulling out a chair for him. He sat, and ordered breakfast from the steward.

"Tell, me" he said "What puts you in such a good mood today?"

"I went to watch the aircraft at the firing range" I said with a broad grin.

"Ah yes, I heard it from my quarters. You enjoyed the spectacle?"

"Very much so" I said enthusiastically.

"Ah, I remember the first time I saw it too, very loud no?" he laughed.

"Very loud" I smiled.

"I can arrange a flight in one for you if you like" he said.

I held my hands up "I'm no flyer Herr Major, thank you for the offer"

"It's not for everyone, but me, I love it. Just you and the machine, complete freedom"

"You have flown one?" I asked.

"The 110? No, I flew in the interwar years, nothing quite as glamorous I'm afraid. I was a test pilot for Messerschmitt, and flew many hours in the 109"

He didn't look old enough to have flown in the Great War, and wore no decorations like some of the other older officers. The ME 109 was our best fighter, and I envied him.

"It must be quite amazing flying an aircraft like the 109" I said, still in awe.

"It had its problems" he expanded "I've never liked the undercarriage, it's too weak"

He told me about various crashes he'd been I involved in, most of which seemed to have occurred due to the undercarriage breaking.

"Don't get me wrong, it's a beautiful bird, and a joy to fly"

"I bet it is" I smiled

He took a sip of his coffee "Oh, dear. This really is dreadful"

"Yes, it is" I agreed "I've never really gotten used to the taste"

"Come see me after lunch, I'll have some real coffee brewed" he said.

"I would like that very much" I replied.

"I have another matter I wish to discuss with you" he looked around "But best not in here eh?"

"Of course sir, shall I come at one?

"Yes, I'll let my adjutant know to expect you"

"Thank you sir"

He spoke some more of his days flying for Messerschmitt whilst we finished our breakfast, then excused himself and left.

Well, I thought, Ecke asked me to profile the man, and here's my opportunity. This was working out well. I checked my watch; twenty minutes until I was due at the range. I finished my coffee, and asked a very young looking Luftwaffe Leutnant for directions. Fortunately, it was only a ten minute walk away.

I made it to the range with a few minutes to spare. I signed in with the Feldwebel in charge, and asked for 100 rounds of ammunition. He went off, and came back holding a box of the 9mm rounds I requested.

"Through there sir" he said indicating a door behind me "Enjoy"

"Thank you Sergeant" I said.

I picked up ear protection, and checked my weapon was not loaded before entering. Inside, I chose the range furthest from the door to minimise interference traffic behind me. A young Gefreiter went through the rules, and set up a fresh target for me.

I used the two magazines I carried first, in order to use up the older ammunition. My aim was good. I had not lost my touch with the pistol. The airman complimented me on my accuracy, and asked why I was not using the P38 like most of the other officers. I explained I preferred the P08, and lauded its elegance. He had never fired the weapon before, having trained on the P38 only. I offered the weapon to him, and encouraged him to fire a couple of magazines. An offer he gratefully accepted.

He put up a fresh target and fired a few rounds. They all met their target, but were a bit low. I advised him that the balance of the pistol was slightly different to the P38, and to over-aim slightly.

He took my advice, and proved an excellent shot.

He wore a crossed sword Shützen Abzeichen (Marksman Badge) with two acorns on his uniform, indicating he had won the award seven times.

As officers, we were not permitted to wear this decoration, and sadly had nothing at all for achieving marksmanship or weapon proficiency.

"Good shooting" I smiled

"Thank you sir" he said, handing my weapon back.

"How did you like the P08?"

"I prefer the P38 I'm afraid, but you are right sir; it is a far more elegant pistol"

I fired off a few more magazines, ensured both mine were reloaded, and thanked the airman for his help. He expressed his gratitude again for letting him fire my weapon.

Right. That was all the fun over with, time to go to the office. I found my way there after asking for directions only once on the way.

When I entered, the Sergeant was on the phone, and the two Corporals were nowhere to be seen.

I took off my hat and gloves before sitting at one of the Corporals desks to wait for the Sergeant to finish his phone call. After he did so, he sprang to attention and saluted "Good morning Obersturmführer"

"Good morning Sergeant, please, at ease." He relaxed somewhat, and sat back down. "I hear rumours of sabotage of the train tracks between here and Enschede, is this correct?"

He looked surprised at my knowing, but quickly recovered "Yes sir, I sent Rottenführer Bach to investigate"

"Excellent, I would like to see his report and any photographs before my meeting with the Kommandant at one o'clock"

"Of course sir. Would you like to visit the scene yourself? I can drive you there now if convenient?"

"That would be excellent, thank you."

He retrieved the keys from a small locker, and we got in the car and drove off.

The drive to the scene did not take long, as the line had been sabotaged just north of the village of Lonneker which was only a few kilometers from the airfield. We parked a few hundred meters away, and walked through the trees to where the Corporal was busy taking photographs of the damaged line.

"Good morning Corporal, what do we have here?" I said, as we walked towards the scene. The Corporal turned and saluted "Good morning sir. Sabotage. The resistance have removed a length of line on the one side" he said, pointing at the rail bed. "No explosives were used, they had the tooling to remove the section of rail"

"Quite so" I said, leaning down to see for myself. "Any witnesses?" It was a mute question; I knew there would be none.

"None sir" he replied as expected.

"Fine. Go to the village, round up fourteen men for questioning"

"Which men sir?" he asked uncertain.

"Any men" I said "Pick them at random"

The Sergeant looked confused "What good would that do Sir, if you don't mind me asking"

"If we do nothing, we look weak. Select the men, question them, then send them away for work in the Fatherland"

"Sir?"

"You have trouble understanding?" I asked calmly.

"No sir" Was it just me, or was there a glint of happiness in his eyes?

"Good. Make it so" I turned and walked back to the vehicle.

My heart was pounding in my chest. What had I just done? I have condemned fourteen men to hard labour in German factories. I felt sick. But, I couldn't show weakness in front of these men. They were not to be trusted after all.

That didn't make me feel better. Could I have done something different? No. Well, yes, I could have. I could have had them all shot to set an example. I wanted to cry, but gathered myself, just before the Sergeant appeared at my side.

"My apologies for questioning you Sir" he said.

"Please don't do that again OberScharführer, or you'll find yourself manning a sentry post on the Eastern Front" I said evenly.

"Understood sir"

Did I detect a sense of admiration in his voice? Gratitude? My actions had obviously met with his approval, which both pleased and worried me. Had I set an example now? What next? Executions? The mere thought made me feel sick again.

"You ok sir?" he asked, noting my discomfort.

"Too many eggs for breakfast" I joked

He laughed "We've all been there sir".

I desperately needed some privacy to gather my thoughts.
"Would you like me to drop you to your quarters sir?" he asked.
"Yes, please" I said, and sat back in my seat as he drove us back towards the Fliegerhorst.

Once back in my room, I closed the door and fell onto the bed. Oh my god, what had I just done?? I was I a near panic, and needed to speak to Ecke, to explain.
He'd be furious no doubt. And Judith? She would probably be furious and never want to speak to me again.
I took an hour or so to compose myself, then went to the mess for lunch. I was a bit early, but the steward was very accommodating.
I did not want much, so ordered a glass of water, and a few slices of buttered bread.
It was only just before twelve, which meant I had some time to kill before my meeting with the Kommandant. I spent most of it reading the newspapers. Again, they were full of the latest Nazi propaganda, praising our heroic troops in Russia, our pilots, and U-Boot crews.
There were no local or general Dutch newspapers, so I asked the chief steward if he could order them in for me. It wasn't a problem, and he would have them available for me from tomorrow. I thanked him, and took a slow walk to the Kommandants office.
Despite the slow walk, I still arrived ten minutes early. His adjutant asked me to sit and wait, and assured me the Kommandant was expecting me.

10. Major Von Graeve's Office.

At exactly one o'clock, the Major opened his office door "Ah Deckman! Come in"

I did as ordered, and went inside. He sat, and I followed suit.

"I hear you went out to check the sabotaged rail line" he said

"Yes sir, and I had a request, if I may?"

"Of course"

"Would it be possible to patrol the line during the night?"

He thought for a moment. "I will have to discuss with the commander of the guard, but it shouldn't be an issue"

"Thank you sir"

"Think nothing of it, we must stop this sabotage nonsense." he picked up his phone receiver "Karl, coffee for myself and the Obersturmführer"

"Thank you sir" I said.

"I also hear you have ordered the detention and deportation of some locals?" he said sternly.

"Yes sir" I said, not at all sure of myself.

"Regrettable. But, a good call considering the circumstances"

"It seemed the right thing to do" I offered in my defence.

"Ach, relax Deckman. I judged you correctly, any other SS officer would have rounded them up and shot them in the village square. You, however, are different"

"Is that a good or bad thing?"

"It is a good thing Joseph. I despise those SS animals. I am relieved you are not one of them"

"So am I sir. So am I"

The adjutant knocked and entered with a tray. I could smell it before I saw it; real coffee.

"Excellent, thank you Karl. Be so good as to collect my laundry would you?"

Karl nodded "Right away sir" and left the room. We heard him walk down the stairs, and out the front door.

When he was sure we were alone, he poured the coffee. "Smell that Joseph" I did. It smelled fantastical.

I was stupidly excited with the prospect of tasting real coffee for the first time in about two years.

"Help yourself to sugar or milk" he said, doing so himself.

I followed his example; milk only. I held the cup under my nose and inhaled the scent. My god it smelled good. I closed my eyes and took a small sip. It was like heaven in my mouth, I felt the hairs on my arms stand on end.

"It is fantastic Herr Major, thank you" I said.

"Just watching you savour it makes it all worthwhile, and shows I chose the right person to share it with" he smiled.

We both took a moment to savour the hot coffee, after which he broke the silence with an unexpected question.

"You're new here Joseph, tell me, have you noticed anything unusual?"

"Unusual sir?" I asked. What was he alluding to? I was immediately on guard.

"Ecke, tell me what you think of him?"

I needed to tread carefully. "He seems committed sir, a conscientious man"

He waved his hand in dismissal "Yes, yes, I know all that. I get a different feeling from him though. Don't get me wrong, I have only had a few dealings with him, but he just seems different somehow"

"In what way sir?" I asked, skirting the issue.

"He seems to be a lot like you" he said, fixing me with a stare.

Scheiße. Had my cover been blown? Did he know? How? It took all my effort to stop my hand from shaking as I put my cup down onto the desk.

"In what way sir?" I asked, still not committing.

He sighed. "Tell me, how did you feel after issuing your detention order?"

I could feel my heart pounding in my chest. "I felt sick"

"Exactly!" he exclaimed. "That's *exactly* what I mean. You have a conscience Deckman, not something usually found in SS men"

"Is that a good thing?" I asked, still uncertain.

"Of course it is. Why did you not choose to send them to Mauthausen?"

Oh no. This wasn't good.

"I'll answer for you" he said.

"You don't believe in these places, these *labour* camps"

I looked him in the eyes "No sir, I don't"

"Good" he said gently. "Nor do I. Or in any of that NSDAP nonsense"

I swallowed hard, but remained silent.

"Have you ever met Göering?" he asked.

"No sir"

"Arrogant bastard. Top class pilot, but look at him now; fat useless swine, parading around in his fancy uniforms. He makes me sick"

"Yes sir" I had seen photographs of Göering, and his uniforms were getting more and more extravagant. As was his waistline.

"He promises and promises, but delivers nothing. Where are our aircraft? My men are flying around in those under powered crates, and we have no fighters here at all."

"The pilot I spoke to this morning said as much" I agreed.

"Look here, I know you are SS, and I need to watch my tongue, but it's getting harder and harder to follow that jumped up Austrian Corporal in Berlin. Why start a war against the Russians? Is he mad? We don't stand a chance"

"But we are doing well sir" I said.

"Well? Have you seen the casualty numbers? Over 300.000 so far. Just you wait till the winter sets in. You ever been to Russia in the winter Joseph?"

I confessed I had not.

"Awful place. Cold like you've never experienced before. Our men have no winter uniforms, our aircraft are not designed for those kind of temperatures."

I thought immediately of my comrades on the front, freezing to death.

"It's madness Joseph, madness. Our best chance would be to secure peace with the western allies."

He looked at me for a moment "Forgive my ranting, it is difficult to find someone I can confide in"

"It is fine sir" I said, still not committing.

"Do you have a family?" he asked.

"My parents" I said

"No family of your own? I guess you're a little young"

"Yes sir"

"I have a family Joseph, my wife and my three daughters"

He picked up a framed photograph and handed it to me.

"Beautiful sir" I said earnestly, and handed it back. He placed it back on his desk with great reverence. "I haven't seen them for almost two years"

"I'm sorry to hear that sir"

"Would you do something for me Joseph?" he asked.

"Of course sir"

"I want you to gauge Ecke for me, spend time in his company, gain his trust."

"Sir?" This was an odd request; I did not take orders from Luftwaffe officers.

"I need to know if I can trust him" he said, then added "With my life"

"Ah, I see. Yes sir, of course. I have an office there, so can arrange frequent meetings with the Obersturmbannführer"

"Meetings will not be enough Joseph, I need you to get to know him personally, otherwise how will you gauge his trustworthiness?"

"That will be difficult to do sir, I'm sure the Obersturmbannführer has better things to do than spend time with a mere Lieutenant"

"I could recommend you for promotion" he said, "Easily done"

"Not what I was insinuating sir, I was merely thinking that the Lieutenant Colonel is a busy man"

"You have a way with people Joseph, look at the two of us sat here"

"Yes sir"

"I will write your promotion recommendation anyway, as a show of faith. Present it to Ecke, and gain his trust."

"The letter will not be necessary sir, I can speak to the Obersturmbannführer on your behalf without it"

"Yes, I know, but I want to show you how much this means to me" he said, staring at the photograph on his desk. "I'll have it delivered to your mail slot in the mess"

There was no point arguing, so I conceded "Thank you sir"

"Think nothing of it, I rarely get to do anything I consider worthwhile around here. More coffee?"

I wasn't going to refuse. "Yes please sir"

We sat and drank our coffee, him telling me more about his time spent flying before the war. I was spellbound.

When I eventually made it back to the office, I went straight upstairs.
"Report and photographs on your desk sir" the Sergeant said as I walked past.
"Thank you Sergeant, good work."
"Oh, and sir?"
I stopped "Yes?"
"One of the men we picked up confessed to the sabotage"
"What?" I couldn't believe it.
"Yes sir, incredible luck I'd say" he said proudly.
I'd say so too. "Indeed, well done Sergeant"
"Thank you sir, he is to appear in court tomorrow for sentencing" he said, with a knowing smile on his face. We both knew what that meant; summary execution.
"Excellent" I lied, and went upstairs.
I closed the door, and sat at my desk staring at the report in front of me. The report I had sentenced seven men to hard labour for, and one of which most likely to death. It weighed heavy on my mind. Much heavier than my discussion with the Kommandant.
I spent the remainder of the afternoon reading through the report, and making notes in the margins. By four o'clock, I needed to get out. Even though the room was not small, it seemed claustrophobic.
I would work from Enschede tomorrow, so I packed the documents I would need into my briefcase, and left. The Sergeant bade me a good evening as I walked down into their office.
"Thank you Sergeant, you too. And thank the Corporal for an excellent report"
"I will sir, thank you"
I was sure he wouldn't, and would end up taking all the credit himself. I would write a letter of commendation for the Corporal in the morning to be sure that didn't happen.
The drive back to my quarters was pleasant enough, some of the guards started recognising me, and smiling as they saluted.
I parked up, and locked the briefcase in the cabinet in my quarters.
I was just closing the door, when I remembered the letter I'd written to Gisela, and went back in to pick it up for posting.
It wasn't there. I looked around. Maybe it had fallen on the floor.
I searched, but couldn't find it.
I'm sure I left it right here on the dresser.

I know I did. It was gone. Instantly, a chill spread through my body. Someone had been in my room. Who? Gestapo? The Sergeant?

I wasn't too concerned about the content of the letter, it was just general chat, nothing work related, so nothing incriminating. But all the same, I felt afraid and angry. Someone had stolen my private letter. I called the Kommandant's office immediately, but was told he had already left for the day. Damn.

I checked the room, and found nothing else missing. Everything had been disturbed, but nothing else taken. I was angry. Very angry.

I needed to vent my anger, if not to the Kommandant, then in some other way.

I headed to the gymnasium, hoping hard exercise would help me forget. Even if just for a moment.

11. The Resistance

I did not sleep well. My head was awash with thoughts of what had happened. Who could have done it? I didn't think the Sergeant had it in him. Besides, he would draw too much attention trying to get into the Officers' Quarters. Who then? One of the Kommandants men? But why? What did he stand to gain? He had spilled his guts out to me, revealing his true feelings. No, he was in a precarious position right now, and could not afford to cross me. Gestapo? I thought of how my room had been searched in Lychen, and the man I had passed in the stairwell, dressed all in black. Was he Gestapo? I needed to speak to Ecke about it.

I went to the mess for my usual breakfast of eggs and bread.
The steward came over with an envelope whilst I ate. "This arrived for you sir" he said, handing it to me.
"Thank you" I said. It was addressed to me, but I knew it was meant for Ecke, so I put it in my inside pocket to keep it safe.
It was a bit overcast today, so I pulled up the collapsible roof on the car, double checked I had the letter and my briefcase, and then drove to Enschede.
I spoke to the staff officer upon my arrival, and asked him to arrange a meeting with the Obersturmbannführer regarding the sabotage.
I settled into my routine, and read the reports left on my desk.
The staff officer called about fifteen minutes later, saying the Obersturmbannführer would not be available until after lunch. I made an appointment for two o'clock, and hung up. Two o'clock was a long time off, so I finished reading the reports and went out for a walk.
I needed to speak to someone, and I knew exactly who.

It took a while, but I eventually spotted her when the children ran out into the playground for a break. I caught her eye, and indicated I needed to speak to her.
She shook her head, and I mouthed "NOW". Reluctantly, she spoke to one of the other teachers, and went inside.
I walked into the alley and waited.

She appeared a minute or so later, and wasn't at all happy.

"What the hell are you doing?" she said angrily "I can't be seen with you"

"I'm sorry. I just needed to speak to someone"

"After what you did? You sentenced a man to death"

"No, no, that's not how it happened" I said, trying to defend myself.

"Oh really? Please explain how a man ended up dead then"

"Wait. He's dead?"

"He was executed earlier this morning"

"But he was due in court today"

"He was shot whilst trying to escape"

"Escape? From where?" I asked.

"He was being transported to the court, and apparently tried to escape."

"This is the first I've heard of this. Who shot him?"

"OberScharführer Mencke."

"Mencke?" This made no sense.

This wouldn't have happened if it wasn't for your order" she said angrily.

"But I had nothing to do with the shooting" I protested.

"You ordered the men rounded up"

"Yes, random men, to be questioned and for some to be sent to work in Germany"

"Random men? Seems you conveniently chose the right one"

"Me? I didn't choose anyone, the Sergeant..."

She cut me off "And why would you send them to work in your German factories? Why round them up at all?"

"You know how the SS works" I said "Anyone other than me would have rounded up twenty men and had them all shot as an example. I made what I considered, and still do, the right decision. If I hadn't it would have aroused suspicion amongst my men, and they would have reported me."

She considered this, then said in a less angry tone "Doesn't make it right"

"I know it doesn't. But what choice did I have? I'm part of this group now remember? How could I jeopardise that?"

"I'm still angry with you" she said, crossing her arms over her chest.

"I'm sorry. And I'm sorry for the gentleman, I didn't think they'd pick up the actual perpetrator"

"It was stupid luck" she agreed.

Or was it? Did the Sergeant know exactly who to pick up? I asked her as much.

"I don't know, I can find out if he was known to him though." she responded.

"Can you please pass back to the Resistance that I had nothing to do with this?"

She looked over my shoulder, and her face dropped "You're about to get the chance to do that yourself" she said, and then the world went dark.

Slowly, I came to. My hands were tied, tight. Painfully tight. The world was still dark, but I could hear voices.

"Wat doen we met hem?" *What do we do with him?*

"Doodmaken!" *Kill him!*

Nee joh, dat kan niet" *No, we can't do that.*

"Wat? Tuurlijk wel" *What? Of course we can.*

I didn't recognise the voices, but understood only too well what was being said; kill him.

"Ophouden met die onzin!" Judith. Telling them to stop this nonsense.

"Hij had er niets mee te maken" she said. *He had nothing to do with it.*

"Hoezo niet? Hij heft dat bevel gegeven" one of the unknown voices said. *He gave the order.*

"Laat hem uitleggen" she pleaded. *Let him explain.*

It was silent for a moment, then brightness. They pulled the hood off my head, and a light was shining directly into my face. I shielded my eyes, until I they became accustomed to the light.

"Who are you people?" I asked in Dutch. I knew of course, but wanted to hear them say it.

There was silence again. They were probably shocked that I could speak their language.

"None of your fucking concern" one of them shouted at me.

"Let's just kill him" Another said.

"Stop!" Judith shouted. "Stop it. Let him speak"

They all obeyed, and she looked at me "Tell them what you told me"
I repeated what I had said to Judith in the alley, and asked if they
knew the Sergeant.
"Mencke? De flikker? Die klootzak is hier verantwoordelijk voor?" one
of them said. *Mencke? That bastard is responsible for this?* They knew
him, this was good for my defence. Or so I hoped. One word stood
out; flikker. I struggled to remember what it meant.
"Yes" I said. "I asked him to select random people, seems he knew
exactly who to pick up, and then he conveniently tried to escape"
They talked among themselves for a few minutes, weighing up my
story. Eventually, they conceded. Although it wasn't directly my fault,
they still held me partially responsible because I had given the order.
They understood my position, which was the only reason I was still
alive.
I didn't know what to say, so remained silent out of fear of saying the
wrong thing.
One of them said "Weg met hem" *Get him out*. The hood went back
on, and the world went dark again. Eventually, I came to, propped up
against the wall in the alley by the school. I'd survived.
I checked my watch; "Verdammt!" it was almost two o'clock. I got up
and ran back to the villa.
Out of breath and almost 3 minutes late, Ecke's adjutant knocked on
the door to let me into the office. We entered, I was sweating, and
feeling extremely embarrassed.
I saluted sharply "Obersturmbannführer"
"At ease Deckman, at ease. You have your report?"
I held up the briefcase that I had retrieved from my office after
running all the way back.
"Good, come" I sat down, and the adjutant left the room quietly.
"Good god Joseph, look at the state of you. Whatever have you been
doing?"
I held up my hand "Permit me, please may I remove my tunic?" I
asked, still breathing heavily.
"Of course" he said
I took off my tunic, and hung it on the back of my chair. "I was
kidnapped by the resistance"
"What? How? Why?"

"Because of the order I gave this morning, regarding the sabotage of the railway line"

"Ah yes, I heard about that. That must have been difficult for you"

"Extremely. I felt sick afterwards"

"What did the resistance want with you?"

"Oh, they wanted to kill me. And they would have if it wasn't for Judith"

"Judith was there also?"

"I was talking to her when it happened"

"She was involved in your kidnapping?"

I shook my head "No, I don't believe she was"

He thought for a moment "But they released you. What did she say to change their minds?"

"She convinced them to let me speak. When I was taken, I had just finished explaining to her why I had given the order, and that I didn't know that the guilty person was picked up.

I reasoned that he must have been known to Oberscharführer Mencke, because I ordered him to pick up fourteen random men."

"But how would your Sergeant know who the guilty party was?"

The question stopped me in my tracks. He was right. How would he know? If the man was a known criminal, why hadn't Mencke come forward earlier? Why did he need my order to pick him up? Why shoot him? Something stirred in the back of my mind, but I couldn't focus on it.

"I don't know. Can you find out more about the guilty man?" I asked. "Maybe that will give us an idea as to the motive"

"I'll see what I can do" Ecke said.

"Thank you." He looked a little out of sorts himself, so I asked him if there was something on his mind.

"Yes there is" he replied "This" he handed me an envelope

"What is it?" I asked.

"A letter from the Reichskommissar, bad news I'm afraid"

I read the letter.

It was indeed bad news.

Terrible news in fact.

"Oh my god" I managed.

From: Reichssicherheitshauptamt (RSHA).
To: Reichskommissar Seyss-Inquart.

The deportation of Jews from the Netherlands is to accelerate with immediate effect. All known Jews, and Jewish Council members are to be detained and deported at once to the following locations:

Western Sector: Flossenbürg.
Northern Sector: Auschwitz, Neuengamme.
Eastern Sector: Mauthausen.
Southern Sector: Natzweiler.

All responsible SD area commanders to report progress directly to me on a weekly basis.

Heil Hitler.

Signed: Heydrich.

"Effective immediately. I have had to send out squads to arrest local Jews for deportation"
I didn't know what to say. If I felt bad about giving the order this morning, how must *he* be feeling?
"I'm so sorry" was all I could muster.
"You see? We do what we have to Joseph, even if we don't agree with it. We can't risk exposure"
"There must be something we can do? I hear bad things about Mauthausen. The other places, I haven't heard of."
"Me neither. I have requested a meeting with Judith and the local resistance leader to accelerate the smuggling out of Jews. It is all we *can* do. We are due to meet him at five o'clock. Why don't you come along?"
Anything to see Judith again "Yes, ok, I'd like that" I said.
"Good, now go back to your normal routine Joseph, don't arouse suspicion"

"Yes sir" I stood and put on my tunic. "Oh, I almost forgot" I handed him the letter from my inside pocket "A letter for you from Major Von Graeve"

"You have spoken to him?" He asked, raising an eyebrow.

"Yes sir, I had coffee with him this afternoon. It was very enlightening"

There was a knock at the door, and the adjutant came in.

"You'll have to fill me in some other time I'm afraid Obersturmführer, I have an appointment with the Ortskommandant"

"Yes sir" I said, and snapped off a salute "Heil Hitler"

"Heil Hitler" he said, and I went back up to my office.

I sat at my desk, my head spinning. There was so much going on, and I was struggling to keep up. I took a breath. I needed to stay on top of things, stay focused. Ok, let's start with Mencke. Something buzzed away at the back of my lazy brain. What was it?? Something someone had said... Flikker! The man had referred to Mencke as "De flikker" not *Die* flikker, but *De* flikker. *The* homosexual, not *that* homosexual. He meant it literally, not as a swearword. Mencke was a homosexual? In the SS? If I could prove it, I'd have him cold, and he'd be executed. The dead man had been his lover? Threatening to expose him? Is that why Mencke picked him up, and shot him when he conveniently tried to escape?

Did the man actually confess like Mencke said he had? I had to think carefully about how to proceed, whatever I planned to do had to be perfect. There was no room for error; Mencke was no fool.

I must have spent quite a long time thinking about the Mencke situation, because before I knew it, there was a knock at the door.

It was Ecke's adjutant "The Obersturmbannführer is waiting in his car sir"

"Sheiße!" I exclaimed "I'm coming" I grabbed my stuff and ran down to the waiting car.

"Apologies Obersturmbannführer" He was alone in the car. I was apparently his driver.

"Tardiness will not do Hauptsturmführer" he said sternly.

"No sir" I said, and rushed into the driver seat. Wait.

"Hauptsturmführer?"

"The letter, it was a good recommendation" he handed me a small package containing the required shoulder and collar flashes.
"The confirmation went off to Berlin this morning"
"Thank you sir" I was speechless. It had slipped my mind completely. I'm a Captain now?
"We take what we can, whilst we can Joseph" His way of telling me not to question it.
"Yes sir" A Captain? Me? Corporal Deckman?
I shook my head, and started the car. "Where to sir?"
Ecke directed me onto the Singel, and we followed it until he told me to turn right towards the small village of Haaksbergen. We drove for about five minutes, when he told me to turn left into the woods. I did so, and turned onto the dirt road, and we disappeared into the forest. Approximately one kilometer further, he pointed out a small lumber shack set in a clearing on our right "Over there"
I parked the car, and we got out.
"Let me do the talking Joseph, unless they ask you a specific question"
"Yes sir" I said, and followed him to the shack. He knocked on the door three times, then two times, then another three times. The door opened, and a man armed with an MP40 appeared. He looked at me, then back at Ecke "He's with me. He's one of us" he said to the man.
"I know exactly who he is" he said through gritted teeth, and reluctantly stepped aside to let us in.
Inside the small cabin, at a small table, sat a man I didn't recognise, and Judith. If she was pleased to see me, she didn't let it show.
Her face remained impassive.
"Good evening" Ecke said.
The man nodded.
"Right, well, we all know why we're here" Ecke said "We have to ramp up our smuggling operation"
The man replied "I have already sent out messengers to tell everyone. I'm not sure we'll be able to manage the numbers mentioned, but every life saved is a blessing."
"I just wanted to re-iterate how sickening this whole affair is to me" Ecke said "We need to do as much as we can to save these people"
"I understand your position Ecke, I do" he said sympathetically "We will do what we can"

"Thank you. Will you speak to the Jewish Council?"

"I will." the man said, then he paused. "There is another matter I wish to discuss"

"Oh?" Ecke raised an eyebrow.

The man nodded to me "Him"

Judith cut in "I've already told you he had nothing to do with what happened to Kees"

"Kees?" I said. Ecke shot me a look. "Tell me, was the man a homosexual?" I continued.

"Joseph!" Ecke exclaimed.

"I'm serious. Your man earlier referred to Sergeant Mencke as De Flikker, the homosexual"

The man nodded. "Kees was indeed a homosexual, as you call him"

"Do you know if he had relations with Mencke?"

"That, I don't know, but I can find out" the man said. "You think your Sergeant took the opportunity to kill a man who could expose him?"

"Yes, I do" I said. "But we need to tread carefully; Mencke is no fool. We'll need solid evidence to expose him."

"And then?" the man asked.

"And then I'll have him hanged" I said.

He nodded, apparently satisfied. "Ok. Let me see what I can find out"

"Thank you"

"I suggest we reconvene here at the same time tomorrow" he said, and stood to leave.

The meeting was over. I looked at Judith, and was hoping to get a moment to speak to her, but Ecke intervened. "Come Joseph, we have to get back, I don't want to get stopped by the night patrols"

He had a point. Reluctantly, I left with him, without even uttering a word to Judith.

We drove back in silence, he was likely thinking about his Jew smuggling, and I about Mencke. When we got back to the villa, he bade me goodnight, and walked off up the road towards his quarters. I got into my own vehicle and drove back to the Fliegerhorst.

I sat on my bed, changing the insignia on all my uniforms, thinking about what had happened today. I'd been kidnapped, almost killed, promoted, and had exposed my Sergeant as a homosexual.

I'd need to approach it carefully, but how?

His Corporals seemed to act strangely when he was around, perhaps they knew something? That one who wrote the report. I could speak to him, maybe with the promise of promotion?

The idea had merit. I finished my uniforms, and went to bed. Sleep did not come easily however.

One name flew around my tormented brain:

Mencke.

12. Oberscharführer Mencke.

The following morning, I did as recommended by Ecke; I stuck to my normal routine. I got up, and had my usual breakfast in the mess, followed by coffee, and a read through the papers. These now included some of the Dutch papers, in which I read about how great the German occupation force was, and how they were helping the people of the Netherlands eradicate the threat of the Jew. Not what I had expected.

After breakfast, I washed up, and made my way to the office in the car. I parked outside and got out. There was no sign of the pool car. Inside, I found the two Corporals, but no Mencke.

"Hauptsturmführer" they both snapped to.

"Morning gentlemen, at ease. Sergeant Mencke is out?"

"He drove to Enschede first thing sir"

"Hmm, ok. Well, I'll be in my office for a short time before heading over there myself."

"Yes sir" the one who wrote the report said.

I started up the stairs, then stopped and turned back to them

"Rottenführer...?" I said, looking at him.

"Zielinge sir"

"You wrote the report on the sabotaged rail line yes?"

"Yes sir"

"In my office" I said, motioning for him to come up.

"Yes sir" He looked uneasily at his comrade who shrugged and smiled. He did the same, then followed me up. I sat at my desk, and asked him to close the door and sit. He did as ordered.

"Tell me Corporal, how long have you worked here?"

"Sir? About six months sir" He said cautiously

"You like it here?"

He hesitated. "Speak freely Corporal" I said encouragingly.

"No sir, I don't"

"And why is that?"

"The Sergeant..." he stopped himself.

"The Sergeant?" I asked. "He seems strict"

"Very strict" he added.

"Hmm, and the other Corporal…?"

"Lohmann"

"Corporal Lohmann, how is he finding it?"

"He's different" he stopped himself again.

"He's a homosexual?" I ventured. All chips were on the table.

He sat upright "I didn't say that!"

"No, you didn't. I did. Nod your head if I am correct"

More hesitation, then a barely perceptible nod of the head.

"Good. Glad we agree on the facts. Now then Zielinge, tell me, where would you rather be posted?"

"Sir?"

"If you had a choice"

"Fürstenfeldbruck"

I did not know where that was. "Where is that?"

"Bavaria sir, I am from a village near there"

"Ah! Super. Well, Zielinge, I can help you"

"You can?"

"Of course, but first, you'll need to help me."

His face dropped. "You want me to report Lohmann"

"No, that isn't what I had in mind. Tell me, do Mencke and Lohmann have relations?"

"You mean…." he pulled a face, full of disgust.

"Yes, that"

He thought "I couldn't say for sure sir"

"Very well. Can you tell me if there are occasions when they both disappear together?"

"Yes sir. Every Thursday at six. They take the vehicle and drive off somewhere"

"You wouldn't happen to know where?"

"No sir, I don't. But its off-base, and they leave through the south gate"

"Thank you Rottenführer Zielinge, you may go"

The relief was obvious. "Yes sir" he jumped up and walked out.

Yes! I had him! I just needed to find out where they went on their Thursday evening outing.

But, I also needed to protect Zielinge. Thinking quickly, I picked up his report and went downstairs.

"Here, erm, Rottenführer…?"

"Zielinge sir"

"Of course." I passed him the report "I made some notes in the margins, a few suggestions for improvement perhaps"

"Thank you sir"

"Good work Corporal" I picked up my briefcase "Right. I'm off for lunch, I hear there's chicken. Good day gentlemen"

They both sprang up and saluted "Heil Hitler"

I hoped that was a convincing enough performance for Lohmann. Quietly, I stood at the closed door and listened for a moment. Lohmann was busy mimicking my voice "Good work Corporal! Hahahaha! Come on Hans, pull your head out of the old man's arse, and let's go get lunch ourselves, I'm hungry, and there's nobody left to boss us around"

Quietly, I walked away. Job done.

I spotted the car driving towards the office as I walked towards the mess, and flagged it down.

"Afternoon Sergeant, all well?"

"Yes sir" he said, looking at my new shoulder flashes.

"Just out tying up some loose ends on the saboteur case I hear. Good work. Have a pleasant day Sergeant" I smiled.

"You too sir" he smiled back, and drove off.

Tomorrow, Mencke.

You're mine.

I smiled to myself, and went straight to the mess for a large brandy before lunch. I took my glass into the reading room, where I wrote a letter to Gisela. But not necessarily *to* Gisela.

I filled the letter with false information, telling her how desperately unhappy I was here, how I was accomplishing nothing, and other such nonsense. Hopefully it would make good reading for whomever.

There was indeed chicken for lunch, lucky guess. It was delicious, and I ate generously. My stomach full, it was time to go to the villa and debrief Ecke. I called ahead and arranged a meeting with his adjutant for half past one. That gave me thirty minutes to drive over, just enough.

I thanked the head steward, and got in the car.

Despite the overcast skies, I put the top down to enjoy the fresh air. As I drove, a formation of ten ME 110 flew over, and landed on the field. They looked brand new, and I hoped they were the new model with the upgraded engines the pilots had been talking about.

I made it to the Rembrandtlaan with five minutes to spare. I quietly congratulated myself, and went inside. Ecke looked worse than ever. This deportation order was taking its toll on the man. I felt sorry for him.

"Obersturmbannführer" I saluted.

"At ease Captain, please sit."

I closed the door behind me and sat opposite him. "You look terrible sir"

"I feel terrible. Eastern sector consists of Overijssel, Gelderland, and Drente. So far, in total, we have detained over 2700 Jews. They will be shipped by rail to Mauthausen tomorrow, in cattle carts"

2700 men, women, and children. In cattle carts. My spirit sank. What had we become? I didn't want to mention my own journey to the Polish front, it had also been in cattle carts, and had been a very demoralising experience. But we were able to get off whenever the train stopped, and had a field kitchen traveling with us. I doubted they would receive the same treatment.

"I'll be glad when this is all behind us" he said.

"Me too sir"

"You said you had news?"

"Yes sir, I do" I proceeded to brief him about my meeting with Rottenführer Zielinge, the disappearing letter, and the man in black.

"That's quite a tale" he said when I'd finished. "This man in black, Gestapo?"

"I suspect so sir, but I can't think why"

"Probably because of your heritage"

That made sense. In that case, I really had nothing to worry about. I put that problem to the back of my mind, and pulled Mencke to the front.

"What will you do about Mencke?"

"He knows me" I said "If I attempt to follow him, he will spot me straight away"

"Who then?"

"I was thinking the resistance could help us out. He leaves by the south gate. They could post a series of lookouts to follow him in stages. That way he won't suspect."

"Ok, we'll put it to them this evening"

"Thank you sir. And hopefully they'll have thought of a way to smuggle more Jewish families out"

"Let's hope so"

"You're doing your best sir" I assured him.

"I'm afraid my best isn't good enough Joseph"

"It's all we can do sir, our best"

I left him to his thoughts, and went out for a walk. Subconsciously, I found myself walking towards the school. It was near to letting out time, and I may catch a glimpse of her.

Sitting on a step, out of sight, I waited. Eventually, the bell rang, and lots of screaming happy kids burst out through the door.

Ten minutes or so later, I saw her. Despite being dressed quite plainly, she managed to look absolutely beautiful. She walked off in the opposite direction, turned a corner, and was gone.

I stood, and with hope and a spring in my step, I took a long walk back to the villa.

13. Planning and The Man in Black.

I was a bit early for our rendezvous with the resistance, so I ordered some coffee from the small mess at the villa, and sat at a table in the back garden. I had what I considered a fool proof plan of trapping Mencke, so I was feeling quite pleased with myself. This evening he would be mine. I would see him hang. Sipping my coffee, I reflected on my meteoric rise through the ranks to take my mind of the Mencke problem. Had it all been on merit? Just over a year ago, I was a Corporal, on the front line. I remembered the first time I killed a man. I had been assigned guard duty with a good friend, and we were to patrol the northern perimeter of our camp. We were walking through the woods, talking about how lucky we were to be in the elite of the German fighting force, and he was just about to tell me about his girl at home when we heard voices. Polish voices. "Sssh Olaf" I whispered "Listen". He heard them too. Carefully, we crept forward. Through a gap in a bush, we spotted them. There were three of them sat around drinking what smelled like tea. "We should go back and report it" Olaf whispered. "No, we can take them" I had replied. "I'll take the one on the right, you take the one on the left, then we both take the middle" He nodded reluctantly. "Safety off" we both checked our K98 rifles; safety was off. "One, two, three, go!" We jumped up and fired almost simultaneously, both our targets fell to the ground. The remaining Pole jumped up with a look of surprise on his face, desperately trying to cock his rifle. He was too slow. Olaf got the first shot off, and the man fell to his knees, crying, then fell forward onto his face. Slowly, we walked into their little encampment, and checked the lifeless bodies for any sort of paperwork or maps.

We found only identity cards. We did however, also find a large cache of hand grenades in cases hidden under a pile of leaves.

Behind us, there was the sound of men running through the woods towards us.

Seconds later, our comrades burst into the clearing "What happened here?" My Scharführer demanded.

Olaf explained to him that I had led the attack, and we had uncovered a large cache of grenades.

All my comrades cheered for me, and the Sergeant shook my hand. "Good work Deckman". That was also how I got my first promotion from Shütze to Sturmmann. I smiled at Olaf, and thanked him.

"We're brothers" he said. We went back to our camp and enjoyed a schnapps together to celebrate.

Sadly, only 24 hours later, I would be sat not far from where we stood, his bullet ridden body in my arms, desperately trying to stop the bleeding. It was in vain; he died in my arms. I had killed my first man, but had lost my first friend. My brother. It changed me.

"Sir?"

"Hmmm?" the steward brought me back to the present.

"Your coffee is cold sir, would you like me to get you a fresh pot?"

I tasted the coffee, it was indeed cold. "Oh, yes please, if you wouldn't mind"

He took the cold coffee away and returned with a fresh pot.

"Thank you" I smiled.

He also placed a small plate of butter biscuits on the table. "You look like you might need them sir" he said kindly, then left me to my daydreams.

I checked the time, it was half past four. Not long to go.

Breaking one of the biscuits in half, I dunked it into my coffee and ate it. A ritual that always made me smile. It was a habit I picked up from my mother, though she would always drink tea. My father always looked on with disgust, which just made me want to do it more, much to my mother's delight.

"Something you picked up from your mother eh Joseph" Ecke said, walking over to my table.

"Yes sir" I said, mouthful of biscuit.

"Quirky English habits" he laughed.

We still had a few minutes before we needed to leave, so I offered him coffee.

"Yes, I think we have time. Thank you"

I poured his coffee.

"Your mother is a remarkable woman Joseph" he reflected.

"Yes sir, she is"

"Someday, when we have more time, I will tell you more about her"

"I look forward to it sir"

"Now" he said, placing his cup on the table "Tell me about your plan for Mencke"

I laid out my plan from memory, omitting no detail.

"If it works, you'll have him" he said.

"If it works" I repeated. "Let's hope so, for Zielinge's sake"

Ten minutes later, we were driving down the same forest road as yesterday, and pulled up outside the lumber shack. Ecke repeated the same knocking pattern, and the same man appeared, pointing the MP40 at me.

Again, reluctantly, he let me in. The same man was sat at the same table, but no Judith this time. "Judith?" I asked.

"She's busy this evening"" the man said.

"Sorry, can I get a name for you? In my mind I keep referring to you as *the man*."

"You don't need to know names" the man with the MP40 spat.

"It's ok, he deserves a name. You can call me Herman" the man said.

"That's not your real name, but it's better than *the man*" I said.

He smiled "I like you Deckman". This drew a sneer and a growl from guard man. "Why don't you go check the perimeter" Herman snapped at him. The man hung his head and left.

"Apologies, he still doesn't trust you" Herman said.

"I can't blame him really, I would feel the same"

"So, shall we get to business? Have you spoken to the Council?" Ecke asked.

"I have, and they have provided us with more money to pay for increased traffic. It pales into insignificance next to the numbers being deported though sadly" Herman said.

"Regrettably" I added.

"If we save just one life, it is worth it" Ecke said.

"We will save hundreds of lives my friend" Herman reassured him.

"And the council itself?" I asked.

"They have gone into hiding. Sigmund hopes you are comfortable enough in his house"

"Sigmund?" I asked.

"Menko, the owner of the villa you've taken over"

"Apologies, I didn't know" I said awkwardly.

"Do not worry Herman" Ecke said "We are taking good care of his home"

"I know you are" he smiled.

What a curious situation, I thought. The very home we were stationed in belongs to the very people we are hunting.

"Here" Ecke said, handing him a stack of signed travel papers "You'll need these"

"Ah, thank you. And the stamp?"

Ecke dug into his briefcase and retrieved the official stamp he used to authorise documents.

"Are you mad?" I said "It will be missed, and an investigation launched"

"Yes, I know" he said. "You'll be leading the investigation. In the direction of Mencke"

"You really have thought of everything" I said, in awe of the man.

"We have to Joseph, it's the only way we will survive"

"You have no idea how much this will help" Herman said, looking at the stamp.

"Oh, I think I do" Ecke said "I only wish we could do more"

"You do enough old friend" Herman said. "Right, tell us about your plan Joseph" he said, turning to me.

As with Ecke earlier, I laid out my plan, to the finest detail.

"Ok, it can be done" he said "I will post a series of sentries on bicycles along the south road to the camp. We'll find out where he goes"

"Is there anything else you need from us?" I asked.

"Well, weapons are always handy" he smiled.

"Weapons I can't supply, you know that" Ecke said.

"I could give you the details of our next supply run" I said. "The Fliegerhorst receives a re-supply every month, it gets transported by truck from the station in Oldenzaal to the base. You'd have to take the risk of hitting the convoy"

"I'll think it over" he said "That's a big risk"

"Agreed, the convoy is well guarded" Ecke said.

"It's not that" Herman said, shaking his head "It's the reprisals that concern me the most"

I hadn't thought of that. Nobody spoke for a long moment.

"Right" he said, breaking the silence "I think we are done. Thank you again for the supplies"

He patted the bag containing the forms and the stamp. "With a bit of luck, we'll meet again Friday after a successful hunt"

"Let's hope so" I added.

"Good luck my friend" he said, shaking my hand.

"And to you Herman"

He left, and by the time we had stood and walked out to the car, there was no sign of either of the resistance men.

I drove Ecke back to the villa, and carried on back to the airfield. I was keen to see if the letter I had left in my quarters had disappeared again.

I saw the Corporal on duty in the officers' quarters I was billeted in, and asked if anyone unusual had been in today. He told me he had only been on duty for two hours, and had seen nobody. But, he would phone his comrade he relieved to find out if he had noticed anyone.

I thanked him and went up to my room. As expected, the letter was gone. I was neither shocked nor surprised. I was glad. It gave me a strange sense of pleasure, knowing I was misleading whomever it was that was taking them. Whoever they were.

After I had taken a shower, in hot water this time, I dressed for dinner.

"Sir?" the Corporal said as I was about to head out the door.

"Yes?"

"I telephoned my comrade, and he did indeed see someone exiting the building as he returned from the toilet."

"Was he dressed all in black?" I asked

"Yes sir, how did you know?"

"Lucky guess" I smiled "Thank you Corporal"

"Of course sir"

So, the mysterious man in black was here. Excellent. Smiling, I walked into the mess, and was invited to sit with a group of pilots I had grown to know since my arrival.

I never tired of listening to their adventures in the air. I only wished that I could share my stories with them.

They were in high spirits; the aircraft I had seen were indeed the upgraded engine variant.

I ordered a bottle of schnapps to celebrate, which was received with a loud cheer, and we spent a rather boisterous evening together.

Feeling rather merry, and a bit unsteady on my feet, I walked back to my accommodation. A car pulled up next to me as I walked, and accelerated away, only to pull up in front of me, blocking my path. Instinctively, I reached for my pistol.

"That will not be necessary Herr Deckman" the man in black said to me, climbing out of the car.

"Let's go for a drive" he held open the passenger door, and motioned for me to get in.

I stood there, not moving.

"I am unarmed and mean you no harm Hauptsturmführer"

"Who are you?" I asked, still a bit shaken, and definitely unsteady on my feet.

"Get in, and I'll tell you all" he said with a smile. My hand twitched again.

"As I said, I am unarmed" he held open his jacket for me to see. There was no sign of a weapon.

Against my better judgement, and likely due to my slight impairment, I got in the car. He shut the door, and got in behind the wheel.

We set off towards the South Gate, and got waved through after showing our identity papers.

"Who are you?" I asked. He had credentials, so must be official, I reasoned.

"My name is Otto Müller" he said "Gestapo"

I knew exactly what he was going to say, but my stomach still dropped.

"Gestapo? Is this because of my mother?"

"Indeed it is Herr Deckman" he replied, pulling into the driveway of a derelict looking house.

"Come Joseph, let's have a chat" he said in prefect English.

I was stunned. "What?"

"Inside. Come, let's talk" he said, again in perfect English. Was this a trick? Some Gestapo ruse to get me to talk?

He got out of the car, and walked into the house. I sat for a moment, wondering if I should just run. I knew it would be pointless, he would find me again. Full of trepidation, I got out of the car and followed him in.

He was sat at a table in the kitchen, and pulled a hip flask and two short glasses out of his jacket. "Sit" he smiled, pointing at the chair across from him. No more German, he had switched to English. I sat. "Whiskey?" he offered the flask. I hesitated. He poured a bit of the liquor into a glass, and drank it down. He then poured us each a measure, and swapped his glass for mine. "No tricks, no poison, just a drink" he said.

I picked up the glass and smelled the liquid inside, no poison, just the smell of a fine scotch whiskey.

"To your good health" he said, raising his glass.

I slowly raised my own, and downed the drink in one go. My god it was good. I had had some experience with whiskey before I enlisted, my mother had introduced me to some fine single malts.

"Single malt" I said.

"You know your whiskey" he smiled. "You get that from your mother"

"Who are you?" I asked "Gestapo? Trying to get me drunk? For what reason?

"You know who I am" he said and looked into my eyes intently.

"Yes" I said "I think I do"

"Tell me" he said, sitting back.

"You're the leader" I said.

"Bravo Joseph" he smiled "If you can call it that, then yes, I suppose I am the leader"

"I know you" I said.

"Yes, you do"

"I remember you from my childhood in England"

"Yes, you do"

I relaxed. He had confirmed my suspicions. I thought I recognised him when he jumped out of the car. It had taken me this time to remember. He had been a frequent visitor to our house in London. One of mum's friends, she used to refer to him as my "Uncle Marcus". Only now I knew he wasn't a friend; he was her boss. He was the leader of the 22. The man who determined the objectives.

"Why did you take my letters Marcus?" I asked.

"You *do* remember!" he smiled "I needed to be sure you weren't telling your sweetheart about us" he said "I like the change of tack in the last letter by the way. Clever ploy, you knew they were being read."

"Glad it amused you"

He held up his hands "I apologise Joseph, it had to be done"

He reached into his pocket and handed me both letters back.

"My hospital room?" I asked

"We needed to be sure of you Joseph, we took a big risk enlisting you. We had to be sure you weren't one of those SS fanatics" he said waving his hand dismissively.

Made sense.

"Are you really Gestapo?" I asked.

"Yes, I am. Small fry though, low down in the pecking order. An insignificant cog in the greater machine. Just enough to get me into anywhere I need to go"

Again, this made sense. The leader was Gestapo; he could get into any military or civilian installation, anywhere, without question. It was truly genius how this group was set up.

"Why tonight?"

"Because you are about to do something which might compromise our organisation"

"Mencke?"

He nodded. "You plan to follow him, and catch him in the act, so to speak"

"Yes"

"I'm afraid I can't let you do that" he said.

"What? Why? It is all arranged"

"I un-arranged it" he said plainly.

My head spun, and it wasn't just the drink. "What do you mean?"

"Joseph, I can't let you be involved in this entrapment, it is too dangerous. Mencke is extremely clever. More so than you think"

"But the plan..."

"The plan would have failed. He would spot the resistance men following him."

"But..." I didn't know what to say.

"Why do you think we're here?" he said, gesturing around the room.

"You brought me here" I said.

"Come, come Joseph. Think about it"

What? What was there to...? Wait. Realisation struck. "*This* is where he comes" I said.

"Bravo" he clapped "You really are as good as they say"

"All the better, I'll just wait for him here!" I said, excitedly.

"No"

"What?"

"No. You won't be"

I didn't understand.

"You think I'd risk having you exposed?" he said.

"Exposed? How?"

"Like I said, he is cleverer than you give him credit for"

My mind raced. What could he possibly know? I hadn't seen him anywhere, nor had he seen me, except on the base.

"He came to see me, you know, Mencke"

"What?" I said, dumbstruck "When?"

"This morning"

That's what he was doing in Enschede. That explained the smile on his face. Dammit. I cursed myself for being so blind. But what could he possibly know?

Marcus must have read my mind, because he said "He suspects that you are in league with the resistance"

"How could he possibly know that?" I exclaimed.

"One of the teachers reported to him that you had met with Judith on a few occasions" he said. "She also denounced Judith as a member of the resistance"

The words spoken by Stauffman and Ecke echoed in my mind *"Trust no one"*

"Like I said, he is far cleverer than you think. He has a network of informants in the area"

How could I have been so stupid? I had completely underestimated the man, and played right into his hands.

"Nobody is infallible Joseph" he said "That's why we work as a group, not as individuals like SOE"

"But Mencke?"

"Don't you worry about him, he'll still be exposed as per your plan, but not by you"

"By whom then?"

"By us" he said "the Gestapo"

"By you?" I asked.

He shook his head.

"No, no. Like I said, I'm a small cog in the machine Joseph. I informed my superior of Mencke's inclinations, and he will lead the team"

"But he might talk! What if he denounces me? Judith?"

He shook his head "You don't understand the Gestapo, Joseph. This is not an arrest team. This is an *execution* team."

"But what if they fail?"

He laughed. "They will not fail. If there's one thing the Gestapo do well, its executions."

"I don't share your faith" I said.

"I don't need you to. I just need you to act normally, follow your routine, and stay out of the way. Have breakfast, and spend the day in the villa. Have dinner with Ecke, return to your quarters at nine. I will be there."

"You have it all planned out"

"This is what we do Joseph. This is why we have survived this far. Trust me."

The problem was that I *did* trust him, I just wanted to be involved. Being forced to take a back-seat didn't sit well with me, but I suppose I had no choice in the matter.

"Fine" I said "I'll stay out of the way"

"Good man. Come, I'll get you back to your quarters."

We drove back to the accommodation in silence. Not because I didn't want to speak, but because my mind was too busy processing what was happening. I think Marcus knew this, as he made no attempt to engage me in conversation.

As we pulled up outside my block, he spoke. "Go rest Joseph, this time tomorrow it will all be over"

I nodded, and got out of the car. I watched as the red lights on the car grew dimmer and dimmer, until they disappeared from sight. I had so many questions for him.

With a sigh, I went upstairs, to bed.

14. The Reckoning.

I did not sleep well at all. The events of the previous night had played on my mind all night. I was worried they would fail. If they failed, I would be exposed. I took a long, thankfully hot, shower to calm my nerves. Again, I stuck to my routine; I had the usual breakfast in the mess, read the papers, and drove to the villa in Enschede.

Despite appearances, I would be a bag of nerves all day, I thought. When I got there, I asked the adjutant if I could see Ecke, but was informed that the Obersturmbannführer was at a meeting with the Ortskommandant, and wouldn't be back until after lunch. Dejected, I went up to my office. I needed to keep busy. There was the usual stack of reports on my desk, but I wasn't in the mood to read them at the moment. I needed to do something useful. Zielinge. Of course. I picked up the phone.

"Staff officer"

"Deckman here, I need some blank transfer papers, could you bring me some please"

"Of course Hauptsturmführer"

"Thank you"

I would do something for the man who had helped me. There was a knock at the door, and the staff officer appeared with a small stack of papers. "The transfer order sheets you requested sir" he said, placing them on my desk.

"Thank you" I smiled.

I took one of the forms, put it in my typewriter, and wrote out Zielinge's transfer to Fürstenfeldbruck. Assignment? I didn't know what he wanted to do, so I typed "Assignment of Unterscharführer Zielinge's choosing". I signed and stamped the document. It was official. He had the posting of his choice. Now all I needed to do was to promote the lad. As a Captain, I had that authority. I picked up the phone again.

"Staff officer"

"Deckman again, apologies, I need promotion papers also if you would be so kind"

"Of course sir."

"Oh, and I will need four sets of Unterscharführer insignia also"
"Not a problem sir"
Half an hour later, I signed and stamped his promotion to Sergeant.
I put the letter and insignia in a large envelope, ready to hand to him tomorrow, after it was all over.
I would need to write a request for replacement personnel, but that could be done another time. Right now, I just needed to get out and stretch my legs. On my way out, I handed the staff officer a copy of both his promotion and transfer papers to be sent to SS headquarters in Berlin, though that was merely a formality.

It felt good to be outside. The air was cold, and the skies were grey, but it still felt good to be out. I walked around the Volkspark, and around the town centre, careful to avoid the school. Judith didn't seem in the mood to talk to me, so I thought it best to just avoid her altogether. Thirsty and cold, I found a small coffee house, and went inside to have a coffee. Ersatz, but at least it was hot.
The proprietor was insisting that the coffee was with his compliments, but I insisted on paying. I was not about to exploit these people because of the uniform I was wearing. It left me with a sour taste in my mouth. Even more so than the coffee itself. I left, and made a note never to return.
I had wasted a good few hours walking around, but now found myself wondering what to do next. I could go for a walk in the park again, or explore further afield. There was so much of this town that I had not yet seen. Maybe not. Maybe that wasn't safe.Maybe some other time. At present, the best thing, safest thing, would be to return to my office in the villa. As I walked up the Rembrandtlaan, Ecke's staff car passed me, and stopped outside. He got out and walked inside without looking at me. When I went in, the staff officer handed me an envelope "From the Obersturmbannführer sir"
"Thank you" I took the envelope and went up to my office.
Why was he communicating via notes? I thought. Strange. But I had no time to consider the why's. I opened the envelope, and took out the small note inside.

Short, and to the point, and it read as follows:

Joseph,

Apologies for the radio silence, but I thought it best we stayed out of each other's way today. As it turns out, I have meetings with the top brass all day, so am not free to meet. It has been suggested to me that we meet for dinner. Therefore, please meet me outside at five.

Ecke.

Five? I had three hours to kill. I was not in the mood to read the reports today, and had already been out for a long walk. I decided to make myself comfortable in the armchair and have a nap.
I had no idea how long I had been asleep, but I was woken by the staff officer.
"Apologies Hauptsturmführer" he said, shaking me gently.
I opened my eyes, and panicked "Verdammt. Am I late again?" I said, bolting upright.
"No sir, you have ten minutes. I hadn't heard movement for some time, so guessed you were sleeping, and thought I'd wake you"
"Thank you Oskar" I said "You are a lifesaver"
"Just doing my job sir" he smiled, and disappeared back downstairs.
I was thankful. I had time to pack what I needed into my briefcase, and lock the rest away. Once I'd done this, I went outside and waited for Ecke to appear. He came out at five sharp, and I saluted sharply "Obersturmbannführer"
He returned my salute "Hauptsturmführer, on time today I see"
"Yes sir" I opened the passenger door for him, and he got in. I went around, got in, and drove away from the villa.
"Where are we going for dinner sir?" I asked.
"Gronau" he said.
"Germany?" I said, surprised.
"Yes, unless it has moved. There's a small restaurant there where they are still serving decent meals. I'll direct you"
"Yes sir" I said smiling.
The drive to Gronau took us about forty minutes, as we were delayed at the border whilst our papers were checked.

Eventually, we arrived at the restaurant, and I was delighted to find the lights were on, and there were cheerful noises emanating from within.

"Come Joseph, let's have a decent meal for once" he smiled, and we went inside.

"Ah Obersturmbannführer! Good evening!" the host rushed over, and took our hats and overcoats. "I have your table ready for you" he said, guiding us over to a table by the window.

"Thank you Heinz" Ecke said "Something smells good"

"Ah, yes, I managed to secure some of your favourite sausage" he beamed "And I still have a bottle of wine put back for you"

"Sounds splendid, thank you Heinz"

"My pleasure Karl" he smiled "It is good to see you again my friend"

"And you Heinz"

He left to fetch the wine, leaving me time to ask "Karl?"

"Yes" he replied "Is it so strange that I should have a first name?"

"No, not at all. I've been calling you sir or Obersturmbannführer this whole time. It seems odd to hear your name is all"

He laughed "I had never considered it"

"You know Heinz?" I asked.

"Yes, I met him some years before the war. He had a café in Berlin at the time. We developed a friendship."

"Ah, I see"

Heinz returned with the wine, and poured for us, leaving the bottle on the table.

"Thank you Heinz" Ecke said. Heinz smiled and went out to the kitchen.

"To your good health" he said, holding up his glass.

"To a successful outcome" I said, clinking my glass against his.

"Indeed" he smiled.

"Tell me" I said, sipping my wine "Do you know Marcus?"

"Marcus?" he asked.

"Marcus. The leader of your, our, group?"

"Ah, apologies. I do, but I only know him as Commander Miller"

"Commander Miller? Royal Navy?"

"Sharp as a knife" he winked "Yes, Royal Navy, though on special assignment"

"I see"

"You have met him?" he asked.

"You didn't know?"

He shook his head "No, I was merely asked to take you out for dinner tonight, far away from the Fliegerhorst"

"You know what he has planned?"

"Yes, he informed us of the change of plan"

I was silent.

"You have your doubts?" he asked.

"I have a fear of failure" I said "We will be in a lot of trouble if this goes wrong"

"Have faith Joseph, he knows what he's doing"

"He said as much too"

"Have faith. Now…" he said rubbing his hands "Let's eat" He held up his hand, and Heinz appeared at his side "I think we're ready to eat now my friend"

"Excellent" Heinz said, and went off to fetch our food. He appeared a minute or so later with two plates of sauerkraut and two huge sausages each.

My stomach groaned loudly at the sight of the incredible looking meal.

"Thank you Heinz" Ecke said with a big smile "This looks delicious"

"Enjoy" Heinz laughed, and left us to eat.

Conversation during dinner was light-hearted, Ecke told me all about his time in Berlin before the war. One thing was for sure; the man had led an incredible life.

By the time we had finished our meal and wine, it was almost half past seven.

"Hmm" Ecke said "I think we should be thinking about getting you back"

"I think I am too full to move" I joked, rubbing my very full stomach. "That was delicious, thank you"

He laughed "My pleasure"

Heinz refused to accept payment for the meal, insisting that "Your money is no good here my friend". There was no point in arguing, so Ecke graciously accepted, and hugged his old friend goodbye.

"Don't be a stranger Karl" he smiled.

"I won't, I promise"

I drove Ecke back to the villa, where I transferred into my own vehicle, after remembering to pick up my briefcase. We shook hands, and went our separate ways. I drove at speed to the Fliegerhorst. I don't know why; I had plenty of time. I guess I was just keen to find out how it went, and anxious for a successful outcome. Once I got there, I paced up and down inside my room until there was a gentle knock at my door at just after nine. I opened the door; it was Marcus.

"Well?" I asked anxiously.

"Relax Joseph, it all went as planned. Both Mencke and Lohmann are dead"

"Did he say anything?"

"Only that he was loyal to the Führer. The subsequent bullet through his forehead meant he didn't get a chance to say anything else."

"Oh thank god" I laughed. I laughed hard. I was so incredibly relieved.

"Like I said Joseph; the Gestapo are incredibly good at executions"

"Yes. Yes, you did"

"How was your dinner in Gronau?" he asked "I do hope Heinz is in good health"

"Dinner was fantastic, and Heinz is very well indeed" I said, still stupidly happy.

"Good" he chuckled. "Let's sit Joseph, I have another matter to discuss with you"

"You do?"

"Yes, I do. I have your objective"

I sobered in an instant.

15. My Objective

"My objective?" I said, uneasy. I was terribly nervous, excited, and anxious, all at once.

"Yes. I think it's about time you knew"

"Ok..."

"How have you been getting on with Major Von Graeve?" he asked. Curious question. "Erm, well I think"

"You think?"

"I know"

"Better. Tell me about your relationship"

"Our relationship? Well, it started off well enough I suppose. He approached me in the mess and introduced himself. The following morning, he gave me a personal tour of the Fliegerhorst"

"You didn't find it at all odd that a Major would give a personal tour to an SS Lieutenant?"

"When you put it that way, yes. But, at the time I thought he was just being friendly, and showing off his new airfield"

"Fair enough. Please, continue"

"After the tour, he told me if I ever wanted real coffee, to come see him sometime"

"And you did?"

"And I did. It was extremely nice coffee."

"Splendid. Did you talk about anything in particular?"

"He asked if I had noticed anything unusual in my time here"

"In what way?"

"He asked about Ecke in particular, saying he was a lot like me. Then he asked how I had felt after giving the order to round up the locals for deportation. He got excited when I told him I'd felt sick. He said I had a conscience, not like other SS men"

"Interesting, and then?"

"Then he asked why I hadn't chosen to send them to Mauthausen. He answered for me, saying I didn't believe in the concentration camps. I told him I didn't"

"That was a risk"

"Yes, it was, but I could see the desperation in his eyes. He asked if I'd ever met Göering, then proceeded to call him a fat useless swine, who promised him aircraft but delivered nothing. He then told me how he didn't agree with the NSDAP philosophies, and that he had lost faith in that little Austrian Corporal in Berlin, and questioned the offensive in the east, calling it madness"

"I see. Did he talk of his family?"

"Yes, he showed me a photograph of his wife and daughters, and told me how much he missed them, and hadn't seen them for almost two years.

"Good"

"Then, he asked me something quite bizarre"

"What?"

"He asked me to evaluate Ecke for him, saying he needed to know if he could be trusted. Even with his life."

"Splendid! Tell me, did he talk about what he did before the war?"

"Yes, he said he was a test pilot for Messerschmitt, and had been part of the team testing the ME109. He said the undercarriage was too weak for the airframe"

"Yes, that is a well-known fact these days, but something they tried to keep secret at the time"

He stood and paced around the room, like he was processing what he'd just been told. I decided to remain silent and leave him to think. I was dying to shout out "What is my objective!?", and fought hard to keep it inside.

He stopped pacing suddenly, and sat back down.

"What you have told me is encouraging Joseph, very encouraging"

"It is?"

"Yes. You were requested by Ecke to evaluate Von Graeve, correct?"

"Yes, he asked me to do so"

"Did you not question why?"

"No, I thought he just wanted to know the character of the man as he didn't know him"

"Yes, that is exactly what he wanted, though not for that particular reason"

"Oh?" I said.

"And that brings me neatly to your objective Joseph"

"Yes, please tell me" I said, and instantly regretted my boyish enthusiasm.

"As you know, Major Von Graeve worked for the Messerschmitt Company before the war, and was actually the military liaison there before his posting here. We believe he has in his possession, the schematics and technical information for their new jet powered fighter, code named Schwalbe, *Swallow*."

"You want those plans"

"Yes, we do. However, we are not entirely sure he actually has them"

"You want me to find out"

"Yes, that is part of your objective"

"Part?"

"Hmm, the other part is quite different. If you ascertain that he does indeed have the genuine plans, you are to travel to Regensburg, and get his family to Switzerland"

"What?" I was stunned. "How?"

"We have false documentation for all of you. You will be traveling as an SS representative at the Reichsbank, to a meeting in Zurich, and taking your family along for a short holiday"

"That sounds fantastical" I said.

"We have done our research Joseph, these meetings happen all the time, and the SS has representation at all of them"

"Why would the SS attend Reichsbank meetings?" I knew the answer as soon as I'd finished saying that. "Because they bank all their stolen gold and currency in neutral Swiss banks"

"Correct" he said.

"The first part of my objective seems fairly straightforward, the second..."

"It's going to be dangerous, but it was the very reason you were recruited into our group"

"Regensburg is a long way from the Swiss border" I said.

"Yes, it is, but you have travel passes allowing travel on the Reichsbahn"

"I see. I assume I don't get to think it over?"

"No, you accept, or... well, let's just assume you're going to accept" he smiled.

"Yes, let's just do that shall we" I agreed. The alternative was obviously death. I wasn't ready to die.

"Fabulous. Now, once you have completed part one, you will receive a more in depth briefing on part two"

"I will arrange a meeting with Von Graeve tomorrow"

"Good. Play it carefully Joseph, don't lose him"

"I won't, he likes me remember?" I smiled.

"I'll leave the detail to you. Right. Questions?"

"Yes. What is a jet powered fighter?" I had never heard of such a thing.

"I'm not a technical man, let's just say it's an aircraft engine that uses thrust instead of propellers, and is twice as fast as any aircraft in existence."

"No propellers?"

"It appears not. I'm afraid I can't tell you any more about it, like I said, I'm not a technical man. Any more questions?"

"No, not for the moment"

"Ok, well, in that case I wish you goodnight Joseph, and good luck"

"Thank you, I have a feeling I may need it at some point"

He smiled, and left the room. A few seconds later, I heard his car start and dive off into the distance.

There was a deathly silence in my room.

I had my objective. And what an objective it was.

16. Bringer of Joy.

I woke up tired; I had not slept well at all. I was worried about the second part of my objective. It was extremely dangerous. I wasn't so much worried about myself, but for Von Graeve's family. If we got caught, we'd be shot as traitors.

After a shower, I dressed, and went for breakfast, apprehension still on my mind. The steward took my breakfast order, and I sat reading the papers to try take my mind off my worries. The Ersatz coffee did nothing to lift my mood. "Excuse me" I said to the steward.

"Yes sir?"

"Would it be possible to get a cup of tea instead?"

"Tea sir?"

"Yes, tea. Do you have any tea?"

"Well, yes, we do, but nobody ever asks for it"

"Ah, then I will be the first, delightful"

"As you say sir"

Ten minutes later, he returned with tea, in a coffee pot.

"Apologies sir, we don't seem to have any tea pots"

"This will do just fine" I assured him.

He left, looking rather bemused. I smelled the tea; it was rich and strong. I put some milk in my cup, and poured the tea into it. It tasted delicious. Why hadn't I thought of it before? All this time I'd been drinking that disgusting Ersatz coffee. But, I knew better now, which made me happy. My mood lifted somewhat, and I drank the whole pot. Small victories...

When I got to the office, I found Zielinge sitting anxiously behind his desk.

He jumped up out of his chair when he saw me "Oh thank god!" he exclaimed "Tell me it's done?"

"It's done" I smiled. "You have nothing to fear, they are both gone"

He collapsed back into his chair with sheer relief.

"Gone? Where?"

"Hell, more than likely"

"They're dead?" he smiled.

"Yes, they are. And here, is my thank you gift" I said, handing him a folded piece of paper.

He opened it up, and shouted out with pure joy "My transfer orders! Thank you sir"

"There's more" I said, handing him the large envelope.

He emptied the contents out onto the desk, picked up a collar flash, and read the promotion order. "Sergeant?"

"It was the least I could do for you"

"Thank you sir" he said "Thank you so, so much"

"My pleasure UnterScharführer Zielinge. I wish you all the best of luck in whatever posting you decide to take"

"Thank you sir"

"One last request"

"Sir?"

"Get me a blank leave pass would you?"

He produced said document from his drawer and handed it to me. I wrote it out, and signed it. "You have an office stamp?"

"Sir" he said, handing me the inked stamp. I stamped the slip of paper and handed it to him "Enjoy" I smiled.

"Two weeks leave?" he exclaimed.

"Go spend some time with your family before reporting to the base"

"I, I don't know what to say sir" he stammered.

"No need to say anything Sergeant" I held out my hand, and he shook it "Good luck to you"

"Thank you sir".

I left him staring in amazement at his leave pass. It felt good to make someone *that* happy.

Seeing Zielinge so happy lifted my mood even more, and the second part of my objective faded into deep memory. I had to focus on the first part, which wouldn't be too difficult to complete. I had Von Graeve's confidence, all I needed to do was nurture it a bit more, then start asking direct questions. Sadly, it would have to wait a few days, as I had the aftermath of losing my entire staff to deal with.

I would need to place a phone call to SS headquarters in Berlin to request replacements, or, recommend closure of the site, considering the SD headquarters were so close to the Fliegerhorst.

Something to think about.

Downstairs, I heard Zielinge packing up his belongings.

It wouldn't be long before he was gone also. Then I would be alone.
I picked up the phone, and asked the exchange to put me through to headquarters.
After spending twenty minutes on the phone to some SS bureaucrat, I got my replacements.
Apparently the SS office on the Fliegerhorst was deemed essential, and would not be closed down. I didn't mind either way.
My replacements would be sent out next week, and I was to run the operation from SD headquarters in Enschede in the meantime.
For obvious reasons, this suited me very well indeed. Zielinge had left some ten minutes ago, and the place was silent. I got up, and walked downstairs to have a look around the office. I found some empty boxes, and decided to clear out Mencke and Lohmann's desks. To my surprise, I found many packets of English cigarettes, bars of chocolate, and condoms in Mencke's personal locker, on which I'd had to pick the lock. My training had come in handy. In addition, there were also six bottles of French brandy. I kept everything but the condoms.
I would have no need for those.
Lohmann, had very little in the way of personal effects in his locker, and it all fitted in a small box. There were some photographs of his family, and of various men. Possibly friends, possibly not. It didn't matter. I filled four more boxes with stuff from their desks and filing cabinets.
I piled the boxes by the door; I'd have to take them one at a time over to the field at the rear of the building so I could burn them. I carried the first box out, and almost bumped in to a passing Luftwaffe Leutnant.
"Apologies Herr Leutnant" I said smiling "I did not see you"
"Not a problem sir" he responded "Do you need help?"
"If you could spare me five minutes, I would be grateful" I said.
"I can spare five minutes" he smiled.
"Excellent, thank you. There are more boxes inside"
He nodded, and went inside, picked up a box, and followed me.
Three trips later, we were done, and there was a pile of boxes, ready to be burned.
"Thank you Herr Leutnant" I said gratefully.
"Not a problem sir, is there anything else I can help with?"
"No thank you. Oh, wait, tell me, are you a smoker?"

"Yes sir"

"Excellent, come with me"

He followed me inside, and I handed him all of the packets of cigarettes I had found in Mencke's locker.

His eyes widened "Are you sure sir?" he said.

"Yes, please take them, I have no use for them"

"Thank you very much sir" he smiled, and walked off with his newly acquired treasure.

Again, it felt good making someone happy. And even more so knowing it was from Mencke's private hoard.

I went back inside and placed a telephone call to the base security officer, asking permission to burn the documents. He had no issues with it, as long as it was done during daylight hours. I thanked him, went out to the field, and burnt the lot.

Watching the last traces of the two traitors go up in smoke brought immense satisfaction. I knew for a fact that disgraced SS men would be buried in unmarked graves, so they were officially erased from existence.

Happy, I went back inside, and packed the chocolate and brandy in a box, which I placed in my vehicle. The office had been cleansed of all traces of badness. I hoped it was going to be a happier place from now on.

Checking my watch, I observed it was almost lunch time, so I decided to stay for lunch before setting off over to Enschede. I took two bottles of brandy from the box, and walked over to the mess.

After signing in, I made straight for the bar, and handed the two bottles to the barman. "Here, compliments of the SS" I smiled.

He examined the bottles, and gave me a broad smile "Thank you sir, this is very fine cognac. Are you sure?"

"Yes, absolutely. Please ensure each member gets a measure with their dinner tonight. And one for yourself of course"

"I will sir, and I'm sure they'll be most grateful. Thank you sir"

"I'm sure they will" I smiled.

A table by the window was free, so I made straight for it.

A steward appeared almost straight away, and took my lunch order.

I was careful to order tea instead of coffee this time. Lesson had been learned.

When lunch came, I took my time eating it, taking the opportunity to read a few newspapers as I did so.

It was just after one o'clock when I finally started up the car and got underway. The weather wasn't too bad, bit cloudy, but the sun peeked out every now and then. I was in the mood for a drive, so drove all around the Singel before parking up outside the villa. I went inside with a spring in my step.

"Ah Hauptsturmführer, the Obersturmbannführer has asked that you see him at once" Ecke's adjutant said as I walked in.

"At once?"

"Yes sir"

"Ok, I'd better go see him then" I smiled. "There's a box in my vehicle, would you be so good as to take it up to my office?"

"Of course sir"

"Thank you"

I knocked on Ecke's door.

"Come"

I entered, and saluted "Obersturmbannführer"

"Afternoon Hauptsturmführer, please close the door"

When I had done so, he smiled and said "Sit Joseph, sit"

I did as requested. "Afternoon sir"

"How did your meeting with the Commander go?" he asked eagerly.

"Rather well sir, I received my objective"

"Excellent. How do you feel about it?"

"Do you know what it is?" I asked.

"No, and I don't need to either. I just wanted to see how you felt about it"

"Mixed, I suppose. I'll tell you that it is in two parts, the first being relatively easy, and the second being extremely dangerous"

"You feel ready for the second part?"

"Yes, I do. I just hope it is as well organised as he thinks it is"

"I'm sure it is. He hasn't failed us before"

"That's comforting to know sir"

"I have something for you" he said, opening his desk drawer.

He handed me a medal case, with its certificate, and an envelope.

"A medal?" I queried.

"Nothing special, but the letter is"

I opened the medal case, it contained the Kriegsverdienstkreuz 2 Klasse (War Merit Cross, Second Class), with swords.

"For exposing Mencke and Lohmann" he explained.

"Ah, thank you sir"

"It's a token gesture" he said dismissively. "Read the letter"

I opened the envelope, and took out the letter. It was a personal commendation from Himmler himself, thanking me for routing out undesirables from the ranks of the SS.

"High praise indeed" I commented, putting the letter back in the envelope.

"Little things like that make us more secure in our positions Joseph, which is good for the group"

"Yes, I suppose that is right. I hadn't thought of it that way"

"As for the medal, the more decorations on your uniform, the better. It gives you more credibility, and less likely to be questioned if on a mission, if you see what I mean"

Again, he was right. The more bits of shiny metal on my uniform, the more credibility I would have when trying to cross the Swiss border. A distinguished officer was less likely to be challenged than a lowly Lieutenant without combat decorations.

The sound of bottles clinking together came from outside the door, causing Ecke to raise an eyebrow.

"Permit me one moment sir" I said, and popped out into the hall.

"One moment please Lieutenant"

The adjutant stopped "Sir?"

I opened the box in his hand and took out two bottles of the French brandy. I placed one on his desk "For you. Don't let the Obersturmbannführer see" I winked.

"Thank you sir" he said with a broad smile.

I went back inside and handed the other bottle to Ecke.

"From Mencke's personal collection" I said, smiling.

He examined the bottle "My god, where did he get his from?"

I shrugged "I don't know. I just know it's better off in the hands of those who will appreciate it"

"Indeed, indeed" he said gratefully.

More happiness spread, but I had one more act of kindness to carry out.

"I need to see Judith"

"For any particular reason?"

"I have some chocolate from Mencke's locker I wish to donate to the school children"

"It's like Christmas!" he chuckled. "I'll arrange it"

"Thank you"

He picked up the bottle and opened it "Let's celebrate" he smiled.

I was in no mood to turn him down.

The cognac proved to be of excellent quality, and I could still feel its effects as I sat at my desk a bit later. The stack of reports was growing steadily higher, so I decided to just get it over with.

Fortunately, an hour and a bit later, Ecke popped in and said he'd arranged a meeting with Judith. Could I find my own way to the lumber shack for five o'clock? Yes, I could.

Excellent, the day just got a whole lot better. If that was even possible.

My eagerness refreshed, I read through more of the reports, before finishing at half past four. I put the bars of chocolate in a leather satchel, and went down to the car.

I was in high spirits as I drove out to the location of our meeting. Hopefully she would take it well, and not go off on some tirade or other. She hadn't spoken to me for some time, and I was concerned as to why that was.

There was no sign of her as I parked up, so I got out, and repeated Ecke's knocking sequence on the door. To my surprise, the door opened, and there she was.

"What is so important that we have to meet?" she asked, full of anger.

This was not good.

I went inside, and closed the door "You are alone?" I asked, looking around.

"Yes, I am alone. Not that I want to be here at all"

"Sorry" I said

"Just get to the point. What is it you want?"

"I wanted to give you something" I said, offering her the satchel.

She rolled her eyes "What is it?"

"A gift" I replied "For the children"

She gave me a suspicious look, and opened the bag. "Oh my god, where did you get this?" she shrieked "There must be fifteen bars here"

"Twenty two" I corrected.

She sprang forward and embraced me "Thank you so much, the children will be so happy"

"My pleasure" I said "I couldn't think of a better place for them to go"

She let go and stepped back, gathering herself "Sorry"

"No need. I'm glad it will make someone happy"

"It will. It really will"

"I'..." but I didn't get to finish. She stepped forward and kissed me, cutting off my words.

We stood and kissed for what seemed like an eternity, but in reality was only a few seconds. She stepped back, and blushed. "I, erm, sorry, I don't know what came over me" she muttered.

"Don't be" I said.

"Ok, well, you should probably go now" she said flustered, then quickly added "You know, I have things to do, and I can't be hanging around here all evening"

"Yes, of course" I smiled "I understand. Well, I hope the children enjoy the chocolate" I said, and turned to leave.

"Wait" she said.

"What?" I asked, turning.

"Do you have a sweetheart?"

"Yes, I do. Her name is Gisela" I said.

"She is very lucky"

"It is I who am the lucky one"

Even though she tried not to let it show, I knew I was watching her heart breaking right in front of me.

"Thank you" she said quietly.

"For?"

"For not lying"

"I'll never lie to you Judith" I smiled, and left.

17. Unexpected Travel.

The meeting with Judith played on my mind for the rest of the evening. Her kiss even more so. I felt bad for not having stopped her, or not pulling back. But, did I have the time? I was taken completely by surprise, and it didn't last long enough for me to do anything about it. Still...

I felt bad for her. In her eyes, I could see her heart being torn in two, and it saddened me. I also felt bad for Gisela. I felt like I had been unfaithful to her somehow. Not only for the kiss, but for all my obsessive thoughts and behaviours towards Judith over the last week or so.

I sat in the mess, pushing my dinner around on my plate. I had long since lost my appetite. From behind me, I could hear the cheers of joy as my fellow officers received their measure of cognac. But it sounded kilometers away. Hands patted me on the back, but I did not feel them.

It wasn't until one of them sat down next to me that I snapped out of my depressive funk. It was the Major. I sat upright immediately "Herr Major"

"Easy Joseph, easy. What's on your mind? You look lost"

"I haven't seen my girlfriend for some time now. I miss her"

"Here" he said, handing me my measure "A toast to our loved ones, wherever they may be" He said it loud enough for all to hear, and they all responded in unison "To loved ones"

"You have done good work here Joseph, and have an empty office until next week. Take some leave, go see her if you can"

"Obersturmbannführer Ecke would never allow it" I said mournfully.

"You leave Ecke to me. Put in your request, I will see to it that he approves it. Nothing is more important than the ones we love Joseph"

"Thank you sir"

"The Reich will not collapse because you take a few days off" he winked "Cheers"

"Cheers" We drank the cognac, and talked a little more about the importance of family.

Later, after returning to my quarters, I placed a telephone call to Ecke.

"Yes?"

"It worked"

"Excellent"

"There is a cost"

"Oh?"

"Three days leave and a travel pass to Lychen"

"A small price to pay. You deserve some time off"

"Thank you sir"

"Goodnight Joseph"

"Good night sir"

I hung up. Our plan had worked. We had discussed how I could get closer to Von Graeve, as per Ecke's original request to me. The one thing Ecke wasn't aware of was that he was helping me with part one of my objective. Without knowing. He had suggested trying the Gisela angle, playing on his humanity, and it had worked perfectly.

Von Graeve had fallen for my play acting. Partial play acting. I really was in the dumps about the whole kiss thing, but not to the extent that I showed in the mess; that was for his benefit.

The unexpected leave pass was just the icing on the cake.

The following morning, I packed my suitcase, and ate my breakfast with gusto. I was in my car, on the way to the villa before nine.

I parked out front, and went inside to see Ecke. His adjutant informed me that the Obersturmbannführer was not in, but had left my leave pass and travel papers for me to collect. He handed me the envelope. I thanked him, and drove back to the Fliegerhorst. It saddened me a little that I didn't get to speak to Ecke before I left, but it couldn't be helped.

Von Graeve had arranged for me to fly to Berlin in the back of one of the older ME 110's that needed to return to Berlin to be added to the training school there.

The pilot packed my case into a stowage compartment in the tail section, and helped me up into the rear cockpit. There was a lot of room in the back, making it comfortable enough, and I enjoyed every second of the flight to Berlin.

The landing was smoother than my previous experience, and we taxied to the allocated stand for the aircraft.

I jumped out, and thanked the pilot for a fantastic experience.

He laughed, and retrieved my suitcase "Enjoy your leave sir" he said, handing it to me.

"Thank you, enjoy the flight back"

"Oh I will" he laughed.

I knew he would, as he was returning in a newer model ME 110, which was both faster, and more maneuverable.

The way out, I was informed by a young airman, was through the terminal building. Inside, I saw a row of Stuka dive-bombers being assembled on a makeshift production line.

Once outside the terminal, I considered flagging a ride with one of the Army transports, but decided to walk to the station instead, as it was a nice day and my leg was hurting a bit from being sat in the cockpit for so long.

Berlin looked as it had when I had left it, but there were more military vehicles on the roads this time. I got to the station, and took the next train to Lychen.

The journey to Lychen took almost four hours, as we had to stop repeatedly to allow transport trains to pass. As the trains passed by my window, I wondered if the cars contained human cargo.

It saddened me. I had not heard of many of the labour camps on the memo that Ecke had shown me, but I was sure they weren't a good place to go.

It was dark by the time we pulled into Lychen, and walked around the town, trying to find somewhere to stay for a few nights, as I didn't have a room at the hospital this time. I found a small inn near the place where Gisela and I had enjoyed lunch. The elderly woman that ran the place was extremely kind, and showed me to her best room. She apologised for the sparse furnishings, blaming the war. I told her that for someone who was used to military dormitories, it was like a palatial bedroom.

She chuckled, reminded me breakfast would be available from nine, and left me alone. I fell down on the bed; it was superbly comfortable.

It was too late to go to the hospital now, so I unpacked my things and went to bed. It was the best night sleep I'd had in a long time.

I woke the following morning to near total silence.

All I could hear was the sweet sounds of birdsong.

The sun was filtering in through the curtains. It took me a moment to remember where I was; Lychen. Full of sudden enthusiasm, I jumped out of bed, and washed in the basin. I dressed, and went downstairs to find my landlady. She was busy in the kitchen preparing breakfast, so I stepped outside and sat on the doorstep for a while, until she came up behind me and asked if I wanted any coffee.

"I'd prefer tea actually, if you have any" I said.

"Of course, I'll make you a nice pot of tea. Please make yourself at home in the dining room"

I thanked her, and followed her to the dining room. It was a beautiful, traditional German dining room, full of oak furniture.

I sat as close to the window as I could, and opened it a little to let some of the cool morning air in. The landlady came out a minute or so later, holding an old brown earthenware teapot. She set it on the table.

"Here, a nice pot of hot tea."

"Thank you, would you happen to have any milk at all?"

"You're in luck, I had a delivery from my brother yesterday. He has a farm not far from here"

"That is lucky" I smiled.

She shuffled off to fetch a jug of milk. I stirred the tea in the pot whilst staring out of the window. There wasn't much to see, just a street really, but it wasn't a military base.

"Here you go dear" she put the milk on the table, and shuffled away again.

I poured some milk in my cup, and added the hot tea. It looked strong. I liked it strong. My mum used to call it "builders tea". I liked the idea of that.

The landlady returned, holding a tray "I put some cheese and meats together for you, hope that suits" She put down the tray containing thick sliced bread, fresh butter, and the nicest selection of cheese and meats I had seen in a long while.

"More than" I smiled "It looks delicious, far better than what they feed us on the base"

This made her laugh, and she called me a sweetheart.

"You are very generous, thank you" I said, taking a sip of my tea.

"Our fighting men must be well fed and strong for the front" she smiled.

"They should all have a cook like yourself" I said "Then we'd win the war tomorrow"

This made her laugh, and she shuffled away, still laughing.

I ate like I hadn't eaten for weeks. It was all fantastically good. Fresh butter on bread! Heaven!

We had butter in the mess of course, but it was far from fresh.

I could stay here forever. But, Gisela awaited me.

Stuffed full of rich food and strong tea, I thanked my landlady again, and set off for the hospital. I didn't trust myself to get the correct bus, nor did I trust they were actually still running. It was sunny and dry, so I set off on foot.

The walk took about forty minutes, but it was forty minutes well spent. My bloating had subsided, and I had enjoyed the beautiful scenery along the way.

The hospital looked a bit busier than the last time I had been here, six ambulances were parked outside, and patients were walking around the garden. I had to stop two wounded men from trying to salute me.

At the reception desk was sat a receptionist I didn't recognise.

"Good morning" I said cheerfully.

She looked up from whatever she was doing "Good morning Hauptsturmführer, how can I help?" She sounded tired, fed up.

"I was hoping to find nurse Gisela" I said.

"Ah, yes, she's in ward two, just up there to your right"

"Thank you"

I walked up the corridor, and stood for a moment at the doors to the ward. This wasn't the ward I had laid in, but it was the same size. Through the window I could see the rows of beds, all full of wounded men.

My heart went out to them. There was a loud clatter, like someone had dropped something and a loud shout "Joseph!"

She had dropped whatever she was holding, and was sprinting down the ward towards the door. I opened it and she ran into my arms as I stepped through.

"Oh my god Joseph, is it really you?" she cried into my shoulder.

"My darling, yes it is me" I kissed her head, and held her close for a while.

"I missed you so much"

"I missed you too" I said "More than anything"

"Please tell me you don't have to rush off again?"

"No, I have three days leave"

"Three days? Oh thank god"

She held me at arm's length and looked me up and down.

"I'm not wounded" I said

"No, you're not. Good. But, you're a Captain now?"

"Yes, I got promoted just recently"

"You look so handsome in your uniform" she said, stroking my face.

"As do you in yours" I smiled.

"Where are you staying? Here?"

"No, I'm at a guest house in the village"

"That's good, I am staying in the village too" she smiled.

Her face fell a little "I'm afraid I won't be able to get any time off, as you can see we are completely run off our feet"

"It is fine. Any time at all spent with you fills my heart with joy" I said.

She kissed me, and we stood there holding each other, until a polite cough behind me broke the spell.

"I'm afraid I must insist you release my nurse Hauptsturmführer"

I turned "Apologies. Oh, doctor, hello again" I said, holding out my hand.

"Good to see you are still in one piece Herr Deckman" he smiled

"Keep it that way, for her sake"

"I will, thank you"

"Right nurse, we have work to do" he said to her.

"Of course" I said "What time do you finish?"

"I get away at five" she said

"I'll meet you outside at five then"

I kissed her, and walked back out into the fresh air. I felt good. No, I felt fantastic. I loved this woman. With all my heart.

It was only just after eleven, so I decided to go back to the village, and change into the walking clothes I had brought. It would be nice to get out of my uniform for a while.

After changing, and ensuring I had my identification and leave pass with me, I set off down the road to find the walking path my landlady had recommended. In a small knapsack I had a cheese sandwich and a small bottle of milk. The landscape was stunning, I walked along a river which snaked it's way down a long valley framed on either side by tall fir trees.

"You! Halt!"

The shout made me jump a little. Off to my left, on the other side of the river, a man stood beside a motorcycle. He wore the large gorget that identified him as Feldgendarmerie, military police.

"What do you want?" I shouted.

"Stay where you are" he shouted back, and jumped on his motorcycle. After a couple of attempts, the beast roared into life, and he set off down river. I reasoned there must be a bridge nearby. It was as good a time as any to stop for lunch, so I took off my jacket, sat on a rock, and started eating half of my sandwich.

Within a minute, I heard the roar of his machine speeding towards me. He came racing around the corner and came to a halt in a cloud of dust. He jumped off his bike and aimed his MP40 at me.

"Ausweis!"

"My papers?" I said "Of course" I went to pick up my jacket.

"Slowly"

I stared at him whilst retrieving my papers from my pocket.

"Who are you?" he asked

"Why don't you read and find out for yourself" I said, laying them in front of me on the rock.

He was unsure of what to do, and hesitated before finally stepping forward and snatching up my papers. He looked through my Soldbuch and frowned.

"What are you doing here Deckman?" he demanded.

"That's Hauptsturmführer to you" I said sternly.

He stood, staring at me, not sure what to do.

I sat, and continued eating my sandwich.

A few moments of silence passed before he said "What are you doing here Hauptsturmführer?"

"That is better. Can you not see? I am eating lunch"

He stiffened noticeably, unaccustomed at being spoken to in such a manner.

"You are on leave?" he asked, irritated.

"My papers say so, do they not?"

"Yes"

"Then why ask?"

That completely threw him. His face flushed, and he was about to shout something.

I held up a finger to stop him "Before you say anything else stupid"

He lowered his weapon in defeat.

"I would suggest you show a bit more respect in future....Corporal. You may leave, I wish to finish my lunch in silence" I waved him away.

He slung his machine pistol over his shoulder and went to get back on his motorcycle.

"Have you forgotten something Corporal?" I said angrily whilst standing up.

He looked at me confused. Oh, how I was enjoying this.

"I am a Captain of the SS, holder of the Ritterkreuz!" I yelled "You *will* salute a superior officer"

The shock on his face was worth it, and I almost laughed.

He stiffened and saluted me. I waited a few seconds and returned his salute. "Better. If you had the guts to join the real army rather than playing around on your little motorcycle, you might have learned some discipline and respect for those fighting on the front lines. Away with you" I dismissed him with a wave of my hand, and went back to eating my sandwich.

He tried desperately to make a quick exit, but his bike refused to start. He tried several times, but to no avail. Rather than stand there any longer, he pushed the bike at a running pace and disappeared back in the direction he had come from.

I laughed. Harder than I'd ever laughed before. I'm sure he would have been able to hear too. Pathetic little man. How I hated them. The Kettenhunde, Chain-dogs, so called because of the chain gorget they wore. They were the lowest of the low; self-important little men who were too scared to fight for their country, hiding behind police badges instead.

My sandwich eaten, I set off downstream again, looking to walk another half hour or so before turning back. This would get me back to my room at four, leaving me enough time to change and walk to the hospital.

There was no sign of the chain-dog on either side of the river, he must have run away with his tail between his legs. I walked past the bridge he must have used to cross, and carried on another kilometer or so before turning around and retracing my steps upstream.

When I returned to my lodgings, my landlady was sat out in front of her home in a rocking chair, knitting. "Ah, Captain, did you enjoy your walk?"

"Yes I did, thank you for the recommendation" I took the empty milk bottle from my knapsack and handed it to her "And for the milk, it was most refreshing"

"Ja, my brother has some of the best milk in the area"

"Certainly the best milk I have ever tasted"

She laughed "Will you be having dinner Captain?"

"No, I'm meeting someone for dinner" I said

"A lady friend, nicht?"

"It's obvious?" I chuckled

"Ja, I can see it in your eyes. Junge liebe!"

"I must go wash up now, thank you again"

"You are most welcome Captain"

"Please, call me Joseph, Captain sounds so formal"

"Enjoy your evening Joseph" she returned to her knitting.

"Thank you"

I went up to my room, washed up in the basin, then changed out of my walking clothes into plain civilian clothes. I was unaccustomed to wearing civilian clothing. Looking in the mirror, I hardly recognised myself. I'd never spent this much time out of uniform, it felt strange. It was time to go, or I'd be late. The old lady was still outside knitting, and I bade her a good evening as I left.

18. Gisela Becker.

I was a couple of minutes early in arriving at the hospital, so picked some flowers in the garden for Gisela. When she came out, she looked tired.

"Oh my love" I said "You look exhausted"

"I am, it's been a busy day. We received twenty more patients this afternoon. You should have seen them Joseph, they are so young"

I sighed "Poor lads, are they all from the eastern front?"

"Yes, they were all from the Leibstandarte, fighting for our Führer"

"Come, let me take you away from here" I took her hand, and we walked to the bus stop.

I gave her the flowers as we walked, which at least made her smile, if only for a second.

"The bus is no longer running" she said. "It stopped last month, I walk every day"

"After such exhausting work?"

"We all have to adapt, the war takes its toll on everyone in one way or other. But enough about that, tell me about your day"

I told her about my landlady, my hearty breakfast, and my walk along the river.

"I love walking along the river, but haven't been any further than the bridge" she said "I never have enough time to go further, or the strength"

I told her about the chain dog, which made her laugh. "Oh you! You should be more careful, they are nasty"

"Ach, I am a Captain in the SS, I have nothing to fear from those cowards"

"The Captain of my heart" she said, putting an arm around me.

"I like the sound of that" I said, smiling. Then gathered up all my courage, and said "I love you Gisela"

She stopped. "Say that again"

I looked deep into her eyes "I love you Gisela"

"I love you too Joseph" she said.

We stared into each other's eyes for a long moment, then kissed. My head span, and I felt all faint.

I never wanted to be apart from her again. This must be what it feels like to be in love, I thought.

"Hey"

"What?"

"Marry me" I said

"What?"

"Marry me"

She lowered her gaze "I cannot"

My heart felt like it was exploding in my chest "What? Why not?"

She looked up and said "You don't even know my name" then broke out in giggles.

"You have me there" I laughed. More of a nervous laughter than anything else. "What is your name, fair maiden?"

"Gisela Becker"

I knelt down on one knee "Gisela Becker, will you marry me?"

"Get up you fool" she said, looking around in case people were watching.

"Is that a yes?" I asked.

"Of course it is. Yes. Yes, I will marry you, Joseph Deckman. Now get up"

We embraced and kissed again. It was possibly the happiest moment of my life. I will always remember it.

The rest of the walk was a haze, I was caught up in the most intense happiness; I was to be wed to the most beautiful woman in the world. I couldn't imagine anything better, even in my wildest imaginations.

I walked her to her lodgings, which was a few streets away from my own. We arranged to meet in an hour, giving her time to freshen up and change. I floated back to my room on a cloud of the purest joy. A quick wedding was out of the question. As much as I wanted to do it right away, I could not. As an SS man, I had to get permission from Heinrich Himmler himself to marry Gisela.

I would have to fill out an application, which would have to go through a lengthy review and then signed by Himmler if it came back satisfactory. Only then would I receive a permit, allowing us to marry. It was all to do with keeping the German blood pure. I detested the very idea of it. However, Himmler knew my name, he had just decorated me after all, so this would likely be the best time to do it.

When I told Gisela this over dinner, she didn't seem concerned, but extremely positive in fact.

She had been as happy as I'd ever seen her, enthusiastically talking about the arrangements, but now, she wanted to know more about the forms.

"It won't take long to get the certificate" I promised. An empty promise, for I did not know how long it would take. "I will send in the forms as soon as I get back to Enschede"

It was a meagre consolation, but there wasn't much I could do about it. I was not permitted to marry without Himmler's approval.

"What is this form?" she asked.

"It contains all information regarding your bloodline, so they can verify it is pure Germanic"

"How horrific" she said.

"I know. I will need details of your parents, grandparents, and great grandparents."

"I will have to speak to my father to get that"

"Get it as soon as you can, I am in Himmler's good books at the moment"

"Ok. I shall telephone him when I get into work tomorrow morning"

"Thank you. I'm so sorry it has to be done this way. Believe me; I'd rather be stood in a church this very second promising my life to you"

"As would I"

"Soon Gisela Becker, soon."

"Gisela Deckman" she said with a smile.

"I like the sound of that"

"Me too. I'll proudly carry your name" she leaned over the table and kissed me "And hopefully your children"

Children? I hadn't thought that far ahead. But of course I wanted children with her, I just hadn't thought about it.

"I hope to give you many sons" she said, dreamily. Then, she sobered "You know it will take more than Himmler's permission for us to wed don't you?"

"Your father"

"Yes. You will have to ask his permission"

"We will travel to see your parents together, and I will beg for his permission" I said.

Her father was a doctor at a hospital somewhere in Bavaria, where he lived with her mother and younger sister Elsa.

"We could marry in Bavaria" I said "We would have to travel there anyway to see your parents. I could collect the certificate from SS headquarters, rather than wait on the Feldpost."

"I like the sound of that" she smiled "We would have to plan it carefully, as I won't be able to get much time away from work"

"I will plan everything so we can do it all in a couple of days, four at most."

"You sure you can do that?"

"Well, no. But I can only try" I smiled.

"Ugh, this war! When will this nightmare end?" she lamented.

"I do not know. Let us forget about the war. Tell me about your childhood" I said, desperate not to talk about the war.

We talked for another hour or so about her growing up in Garmisch-Partenkirchen in Bavaria. I hadn't ever been there, but had heard of it. The way she described it, it sounded like heaven on earth.

We could have chatted all night, but eventually, she said "Right, Hauptsturmführer Deckman, I think its time you took me back to my lodgings."

"Of course, it would be my pleasure"

We walked hand in hand back to the lodging house where she had a room.

"I'd ask you inside, but our landlady is a feisty old bat, and will probably chase you out with a broomstick"

"We wouldn't want that now would we?" I laughed. "Will I see you tomorrow?"

"Of course, come see me at the hospital, we can have lunch"

"I look forward to it" I went to kiss her hand, but she flung herself at me and kissed me fiercely.

I returned her embrace, and we stood for a long while, bodies entwined, lips locked in a desperate exchange of passion.

"I love you" she whispered in my ear

"I love you too"

I let her go, and she disappeared inside. Full of the joys of love, I returned to my own lodgings, and went to bed. Sleep did not come easy though, my thoughts were of Gisela, and the dangers of my upcoming mission.

19. Berlin.

I woke the next morning to incessant knocking on my room door.
"Just a moment" I wiped the sleep from my eyes, got up, and opened the door.
"Hauptsturmführer" A young Wehrmacht motorcycle messenger saluted me.
"Too early for such formality" I joked, but the young man seemed either not to hear, or not to react.
"What is it?" I said, shaking my head.
"A message for you sir" he said, and handed me an envelope.
I took it from him and examined it, it was from the office of the Reichsführer SS. "Thank you"
The lad stayed where he was "With respect sir, I am ordered to await a response"
What could possibly be so important that it needed an immediate response? "Very well, please go sit in the kitchen and get yourself some breakfast.
"I have already eaten sir"
Again, I shook my head "No, no. You really don't want to pass up the offer, believe me. There is fresh bread, eggs, cheese, butter, and real milk" His eyes widened. "Go, I'll be down in ten minutes or so"
"Yes sir" he smiled, and turned to leave.
"Oh, and Sergeant?"
"Yes sir?" he stopped and turned back to me
"Have the tea, it is most excellent"
"Yes sir" he smiled, and went downstairs, hungry for decent food.
Starting the day with a good favour made me feel better. The lad had probably left extremely early to get here at this hour, so he deserved a small reward of sorts.
A letter from Himmler? What could he possibly want? I washed, and changed into my uniform. Once ready, I opened the letter.
There wasn't much to it, just another demand for me to appear in his office.

From: Reichsführer SS
To: Hauptsturmführer Joseph Deckman.

Joseph,

Please report to my office at your earliest convenience, I have
important matters to discuss in person.
I will be departing for a tour of our concentration camps this
Thursday morning. I would appreciate seeing you before I leave.

Heil Hitler.

Signed: Himmler

Before Thursday? It was Wednesday today! I would have to leave
immediately to get there on time. How would I let Gisela know?
An idea came to me, and I wrote her a quick letter.
I checked myself in the mirror before going down to the kitchen; I
looked like everything I had admired in the SS as a child. It made my
heart both swell with pride and sink with dread. I shook off the feeling
and went to join the Sergeant for breakfast.

I found him tucking into a very hearty looking breakfast, looking
extremely happy.
"Hope you've left some for me!" I joked.
He swallowed whatever he was chewing "Yes sir, of course"
"Just kidding Sergeant, eat as much as you can, can't be often you get
the opportunity"
"No sir" he said, and continued eating. I poured myself a cup of tea,
and peeled a boiled egg.
"I have a small favour to ask you" I said.
"Of course sir"
"I have my response for the Reichsführer" I said, handing him an
envelope.
"But also ask if you could deliver this to the Hohenlychen Sanatorium
before you return to Berlin"
I handed him the letter for Gisela.

"I do not have time to go myself, and would appreciate if you could hand it to the receptionist"

"Absolutely sir" he said, taking the letter and placing it with the other in his satchel. He stood, ready to leave. I held up a hand to stop him.

"Please" I said "Make yourself a sandwich for lunch. There is far too much food here for just me"

"Are you sure sir?" he asked.

"Absolutely, please"

He thickly buttered two sliced of bread, and took a chunk of cheese, then wrapped them in some paper the landlady had left for me to wrap my own lunch in.

"Here" I stood, and poured milk into an empty flask. "Take this to quench your thirst"

"And these" I put four boiled eggs in his pocket.

"Thank you sir" he smiled "Thank you"

"Think nothing of it, ride careful"

"Yes sir" he saluted, and left.

I fell back down into my chair, and finished my tea. I quickly stuffed some eggs in my pockets, made a sandwich and wrapped it up before returning to my room and packing my case. I had to get to the station to catch the first available train to Berlin. Then all I needed to do was find my way to Himmler's office from the station. I knew the way of course, but it was some distance from the station, and I would rather get there by car than walk. I wanted to look fresh for my meeting.

I went downstairs and thanked my landlady for her excellent hospitality, paying her far more than I needed to. She told me I was welcome to return anytime, and to stay safe.

I made it to the station pretty quickly, but found that the next train to Berlin was not due in for another hour. Disappointed, I found a bench outside, and sat reading a book to pass the time.

I sat reading, but after a while, I looked up, with a feeling of being watched. I looked around but only saw a lady and her young son.

"Forgive me" she said "He was admiring your uniform. Young boys with their dreams" she smiled uneasy. She was obviously fearful of my reaction. What a reputation we had! I hated it.

I smiled "Not a problem madam. You want to be a soldier?" I asked the boy. He couldn't have been more than nine or ten years of age.

"Yes" he said proudly, and saluted.

I stood, and clicked my heels together sharply, returning his salute. The army salute thankfully, not the dreaded right armed salute.

"You will make a fine Wehrmacht soldier one day" I smiled at him. Silently, I prayed the war would be over before he was old enough to join.

"Thank you sir" he said loudly. His mother sat him back down next to her "That's enough now Hans, let the officer be. Apologies again" she offered.

"No need to apologise" I said "I was like him once, I know how it feels"

I opened my case and rummaged around for a moment before pulling out what I had been looking for; a field cap. "Here you go soldier" I said, offering it to the boy. "With your permission of course" I said to his mother.

"How very kind, thank you" she smiled. The child took his treasure and placed it on his head. It was far too large of course, but to him it didn't matter.

I smiled at my second good deed of the day, and returned to my book.

The train pulled in half an hour later, and I boarded, hoping to find a compartment. Unfortunately, the train was quite full, and it took me some time to find an available seat in a third class compartment.

It didn't matter to me where it was, I was just happy that I wouldn't have to stand all the way to Berlin.

During the journey, I made conversation with the seven young men sat around me, and discovered that the train was full of volunteers, heading to Berlin to enlist in the Kriegsmarine. I shared my lunch with them as fair as I could, the eggs in particular being received greatly. We talked for some time about where they were from, and what they hoped to do in the navy. When we eventually arrived in Berlin, I wished them the very best of luck, and bade them farewell.

Outside the station, I had to wait some fifteen minutes before I spotted a staff car dropping an SS Captain off. I ran over, gave him a friendly nod, and jumped in the car after he got out.

"SS Headquarters please"

The young driver was shocked, but wasn't about to argue with a Captain. "Yes sir" he said, and drove off.

We arrived at SS headquarters on the Prinz Albrecht Strasse some twenty minutes later. I thanked the driver, who sped away as soon as I got out. I looked up at the building, took a deep breath, and went inside. Firstly, I went to the administrative office and collected the forms required for our marriage permit. Once I had them, I went to the main reception area, where I spotted the staff officer.

I walked up to him. "I have an appointment with the Reichsführer" I showed him the letter from Himmler.

"Of course Hauptsturmführer, please follow me"

I followed him up stairs, down a long corridor, and to a large set of double doors. He knocked, and entered "Hauptsturmführer Deckman, Reichsführer"

"Ah, Joseph, please, come in" He rose from his desk and walked over to greet me.

The staff officer, left, closing the imposing doors behind him. Himmler's office was large, but sparsely decorated. There was little in the way of furniture in the room, and it struck me as the office of a soldier. Not a chicken farmer. Himmler himself was shorter than I had expected, and was wearing little wire glasses. His hair was slicked over, and gleamed with hair grease.

I saluted him sharply "Heil Hitler"

He half-heartedly stuck up his right arm "Heil Hitler", then shook my hand. "Come, sit with me" We walked over to the window, where two ornate sofas were set opposite each other. We both took a seat on opposing sofas.

"I apologise for summoning you here on such short notice, I am aware you were on leave"

Were on leave, meaning no longer.

"No problem sir"

"Ah, I see you carry the Luger pistol, excellent choice. An elegant weapon, much more so than the P38. I carry one myself."

"Yes sir, I prefer it"

"Good man, the professional choice"

"Yes sir" I smiled.

He fixed me with a hard to read look, then said "I don't have much time Captain, so I'll get straight to the point.

I have followed your career with great interest, and am aware you have received specialist field operations training"

More a statement than a question, but I said "Yes sir"

He continued "Can I trust you Joseph?"

"Sir?"

"Are you loyal to your Führer?"

"Of course sir, I swore an oath"

"Yes, yes, I know all that" he said, waving his hand dismissively "I mean, can I actually trust you? Can I take you into my confidence?"

"I would like to think so sir" I said. Where was this going?

He rose, walked over to a small table, and poured a drink from a decanter. "Irish whiskey, the best. Would you care for some?"

"No thank you sir" I said.

He sat back on the sofa, and continued.

"Reports I see from both the Fliegerhorst Commandant, and the SD Obersturmbannführer…"

"Ecke sir"

"Yes, Ecke. They speak highly of you Joseph, and your recent actions in revealing the undesirables in our ranks really add to your case."

"My case sir?"

"The case for me to trust you. Tell me, do you know Reinhard?"

"Obergruppenführer Heydrich sir?"

"Yes"

"No, I have never had the pleasure of meeting him sir"

"Good. That means he doesn't know your face."

"Sir?"

"The Obergruppenführer was recently appointed Reich Protector of Bohemia, and is now based in Prague"

"I didn't know that sir"

"Of course you didn't. Why would you?" he gave a nervous smile. "I need you to do something for me Joseph"

"Of course sir"

"I need you to kill him" He said it so matter-of-factly, I almost thought I'd misheard him.

"What?"

"I want you to go to Prague, and assassinate Reinhard"

"Why sir? Surely he's your closest ally and right hand man?"

"He is getting ideas above his station, and I fear that he will soon make a move to discredit me to Hitler, and take over the SS"

I took a moment to take all this in.

I couldn't believe what I was hearing. He wanted me to kill Heydrich?

"You want me to kill Obergruppenführer Heydrich?" I asked, incredulously.

"That is what I said, was it not?"

"Yes sir, I'm just struggling..."

"Of course, I understand. It's a big ask. I could order you to do it, however, this is something that needs to be between you and myself only"

"Of course sir"

"Like I said, I'm off to tour the concentration camps tomorrow, and will be back on Monday evening. Return here Tuesday morning with your answer"

"Yes sir"

"Needless to say you aren't to discuss this with anyone, are we clear?"

"Of course sir"

"Very well. Five days, Joseph. You have five days to convince yourself."

"Thank you sir"

"Now, is there anything I can do for you in the meantime?"

He meant as an incentive...

"Well, there is something sir"

"Yes?"

"I wish to marry" I said uneasily.

"Gisela Becker?"

I was astounded. "Yes sir, how..?"

"I am the Reichsführer SS Joseph, I know everything. I will consider your request. You have the forms?"

"I do sir, but they have not been filled out yet"

"I will get someone to fill them out by Tuesday" he said. I handed him the forms, which he put down on his desk.

"Thank you sir"

He opened his drawer and took out a few sheets of paper.

He scribbled on them, then handed them to me.

"Here, take your sweetheart to Bavaria for a few days"

I took the papers from him and read them. They were leave passes and travel orders for both of us to a villa in Garmisch-Partenkirchen.

"Maybe you can visit her parents to formally ask for her hand" he smiled, nervously.

"Yes sir, thank you sir"

"Relax and enjoy yourself Joseph, then come back to see me"

"Yes sir"

"And Joseph..."

"Yes sir?"

"If you do this for me, you will have nothing to fear. Your career will be long and successful, with me on your side. You have my word"

Another incentive... And an attempt so belay my fears of being killed afterwards.

"Thank you sir"

And with that, our meeting was over. He stood, I saluted him, and walked out of his office.

My head was spinning, and I thought for a moment that I might faint. What had just happened? The Reichsführer SS had just asked me to assassinate his protégé. If rumours were to be believed, the two were like brothers, or a rather nervous uncle with his favourite nephew. He wanted him dead?

How fragile was the man's confidence that he saw him as such a threat that he must be killed? By me???

I had never met Himmler before, and had always imagined him as a fierce, confident, arrogant type of man. That was his public persona at least. But I found him nervous, unsure, insecure. There was sweat on his brow, his hands were visibly shaking, and he kept adjusting his spectacles like some sort of nervous tic.

It could be that he was genuinely worried about approaching me like that, which I *could* understand. He had just asked me to kill an SS General after all. And it was to be kept between the two of us. Hmm. I didn't like the sound of that, it meant I could easily be made a scapegoat, and arrested. They would never believe me of course, and he would likely have me killed before I could be questioned.

None of this made sense, and none of this was good. I needed to talk to someone about it. But who?

Maybe I just needed to put it out of my mind, and take advantage of the opportunity to have a weekend away with Gisela. I could meet her parents... Wait. Parents. That's it! I could speak to my mother.

She was part of the 22, and could communicate with the rest of the group.

With a renewed confidence, I made for the general office where I could use a telephone. If they were listening, it wouldn't matter; I was just arranging to meet my parents. Perfectly natural.

I also needed to telephone Gisela to let her know of our leave and travel. Again, this would be expected of me, and perfectly natural.

I would really like to speak to Ecke. But, that was an impossibility. Or was it?

He was my superior officer, and I worked for him, so would it not be natural for me to speak to him? I needed to let him know I would not be back when expected because of my meeting Himmler on Tuesday.

Further convincing was not required. I placed the three telephone calls. My mother was happy that she would see me, Gisela was ecstatic with the prospect of us meeting her parents. One last call to make.

"Operator"

"Put me through to the office of Obersturmbannführer Ecke at SD headquarters, Enschede, the Netherlands"

"I will call back when connection has been established"

I hung up and waited. And waited. Some ten minutes later, the phone rang, and I was through to Ecke.

"Hauptsturmführer Deckman?"

"Obersturmbannführer, yes, I am here"

"This line is terrible. What is it you want Deckman?" He sounded agitated.

"I just wanted to let you know my plans have changed sir, I will now not be back in office until Thursday morning"

"What? I thought you were back on Monday?"

"I have a meeting with the Reichsführer SS on Tuesday sir, so that is not possible"

"Ah, ok, well, I'll see you Wednesday then Deckman"

"Yes sir"

He hung up. He played his part well, typical impatient SS officer.

I had gotten the message across though; something was wrong.

He wouldn't have expected me to be in Berlin, and hopefully they would monitor communications channels to see if they could pick up on anything.

I doubted it, but at least I had alerted him to a potential issue.

Right, that was all done, now I needed to get back to Lychen to pick up Gisela.

Suitcase and briefcase in hand, I made my way to the front desk to get the staff officer to arrange our flights for tomorrow afternoon, and to get me a car to the station.

21. Garmisch-Partenkirchen

Not surprisingly, the train heading back to Lychen was almost empty. I found a compartment, and dozed the entire way. We pulled into Lychen well after nightfall, as the train had to pull into sidings several times to allow other trains to pass. I went straight to my old lodgings, to see if my landlady had a room available. She was pleased to see me, and showed me up to my old room. Food was brought up, and I fell asleep happy.

I woke early the following morning, and enjoyed a full breakfast before walking over to the Hospital to pick up Gisela. She was waiting for me at reception, and we ran into each other's arms.

"Oh Joseph, I am so glad to see you"

"And I you" I said.

"How did you get us leave passes to Bavaria?"

"I didn't, the Reichsführer SS gave them to me and suggested I took the opportunity to ask your father for your hand"

"Himmler? Really?" she seemed excited.

"Yes, really"

"You met him? How was he?"

"Come, I'll tell you on the way to the station".

I carried our cases, and told her about my meeting with Himmler, omitting the killing of Heydrich part of course. She seemed impressed, saying it was extremely generous of him. I couldn't tell her it was a bribe, so just agreed.

We sat for a while on the platform, discussing what we would do with our short time in her home town. The train arrived on schedule, and was again, full of recruits heading for Berlin. We managed to find some seats after some of the recruits generously gave them up for us. Again, I made conversation with them, and was able to distribute some more boiled eggs I had liberated from my landlady's kitchen. We alighted in Berlin with only an hour to spare before our plane was to take off.

I desperately tried to secure us a ride to the airport, and was running out of hope until a truck carrying some of the recruits from the train stopped and asked if we needed a lift.

We gratefully accepted, and climbed up into the back of the truck with them. Fortunately, we made it to the airport in time. After several people checked our papers, we boarded the Junkers JU 52 that was taking us to a small airfield in Oberammergau.

From there, I was planning to commandeer a vehicle for our use. The flight was wonderful, only because Gisela was so full of wonder, having never traveled by air before. The plane itself was rather sparsely kitted out. It was noisy, and uncomfortable. I hated it.

I hated flying, and was relieved when we eventually landed in Bavaria. After collecting our cases, we made our way to the small command building, where I obtained the vehicle. The Luftwaffe staff were extremely accommodating, and after a quick visit to the officer's mess, we were on the road down to Garmisch.

It was unseasonably warm for the time of year, and the sun was out. I hoped it would be like this all weekend, but wasn't holding out much hope. The roof was down on our little kübelwagen, and Gisela let her hair down, allowing it to fly in the breeze. Life couldn't get better.

The drive to Garmisch took us fifty minutes, and Gisela directed us to her parents' home once we got to the town. The house was a typical Bavarian homestead, and looked lovely in the sunshine. Her mother waved enthusiastically from the balcony as we pulled up outside the house. "Mama!" she shouted, waving back.

She looked so happy. I was slightly nervous about meeting her parents. What if they didn't like me?

I was about to find out. Gisela had jumped from the vehicle and ran to the door to meet her mother. I took the cases from the back of the car and joined her. She was hugging her mother when I walked up.

"Mama, this is Joseph" she said.

"Pleased to meet you Frau Becker"

"I have heard so much about you, welcome Joseph"

"Where's papa?" Gisela asked.

"Your father is out at the moment, trying to get food from the shop. It has been getting more and more difficult"

That reminded me. "I have brought some supplies from the mess" I said, and went to get the box from the car.

"It's not much, but was all I could get" I said, opening the box for her to see.

I had managed to get a tray of eggs, some butter, cheese, a bag of flower, sugar, and a few chocolate bars.

"Oh my!" she exclaimed "Thank you. So many eggs!"

"I could go get more tomorrow if required" I offered.

"No, this should be more than enough, thank you"

Gisela smiled and mouthed "Thank you"

"Come inside, I shall make some coffee" Her mother said, leading us in. I picked up the cases and followed the two ladies inside. The house was tastefully decorated, and looked extremely homely.

"Would you prefer coffee or tea?" Her mother asked.

"Tea please if possible"

She smiled "I don't like that Ersatz coffee either"

We sat and drank tea at the kitchen table, and I did my best to answer all her mother's questions about my upbringing, my family, and my job.

"You are based in the Netherlands?"

"Yes, at an airbase just over the border"

"How exciting. Have you been to Amsterdam? It's so beautiful"

"I'm afraid I don't know that part of the country" I said.

With that, Gisela's father came through the front door, and Gisela bolted out to meet him "Papa!"

"Oh, hello my angel" he said, embracing his daughter "It is so good to see you. And this must be Joseph" he said, stepping forward to meet me. I stood, and bowed my head "Yes sir"

He held out his hand, and I shook it. He had the firm handshake of a man used to working with his hands. "Pleased to meet you Joseph"

"And you sir"

"Joseph brought us some supplies" her mother said.

"Oh that is fortunate. The shops these days aren't what they used to be"

He looked in the box on the sideboard "Oh my! What treasure is this?"

"I brought what I could" I said apologetically.

"Don't be apologetic" he said, shaking my hand again "This is marvelous, thank you"

"Joseph has just been telling us about his childhood" her mother said.

"I'm sorry I missed it" he said "Would it be a bother to go through it again?" he asked.

"Not at all sir". So I did. He then offered up some embarrassing stories about Gisela as a child. I could see by the glint in his eye when he spoke that he absolutely adored his daughter.

We sat, drank tea, and talked for some time. It was the perfect family setting. Gisela's sister Elsa was married, and currently living in Stuttgart with her husband and four sons.

"You have the Knights Cross. You have seen action?" He said suddenly.

"Yes sir, in Poland and the Netherlands"

"Must have been pretty special to earn such a prestigious award" he smiled.

"I did my duty" I said, embarrassed.

"You did far more than that" Gisela said, and told them all about the Captain visiting me in the hospital and reading out my commendation.

"Such bravery" her mother whispered.

"Well done my boy" her father said, shaking my hand again.

"You have served yourself?" I said, indicating a photograph on the wall showing him in his uniform.

"Yes, artillery regiment in the Great War" he said proudly.

"It must have been quite terrible" I said.

His face changed, becoming more reflective "Yes, yes it was".

"I think I'll go bake us a cake. Gisela, why don't you come help me?" her mother suggested.

Gisela hesitated, but I said "I haven't had cake in a long time" and she got the hint.

"You were wounded?" her father asked when we were alone.

"Yes sir, my shoulder in Poland, and leg in the Netherlands"

He nodded and tapped his left arm "Shrapnel shard"

We sat in silence for a moment, and I thought it wasn't going too well, when he suddenly said "I assume you are here to ask for my daughter's hand?"

"Yes sir, I am" I said with all my confidence.

He seemed to think for a moment "I hear bad things about the SS"

I hung my head. "Yes sir, so do I"

"You don't seem like a bad person Joseph, and I very much doubt my daughter would have brought you here if you were"

"I realise the SS has a reputation sir, and I can only offer you my word of honour that I am not part of that"

"I accept your word. And, I give my blessing to this union. Make her happy Joseph. I see that you do already. Don't make her a war widow"

"I have changed to a non-combat role, but, we are at war, and I can't promise anything"

"Understood. Just look after her please? She's the most precious thing in my life"

"As she is in mine sir. I promise I will look after her"

"Good" he said, and stood "Let us drink on it" He walked to a cupboard, and produced a bottle of whiskey. "Irish, I save this for very special occasions" he smiled "And I think this is one of those"

He poured us both a generous measure, and handed me a glass "To the happy couple, may you know nothing but happiness"

"Cheers to that sir" I said, we clinked our glasses together and took a sip. "Excellent whiskey sir" I said.

"Thank you. And please, call me Gerhardt"

We sat for a while, exchanging war stories, and sipping our liquor.

A huge wave of relief swept over me, and I relaxed. It had gone well, and I had been accepted. This was going to be a good weekend.

The following day was picture perfect; we ate well, shared stories, went for walks in the beautiful mountains, and explored the beautiful town. When we told her mother the news of our marriage, she was overjoyed "Oh I'm so happy. My little girl getting married."

"Yes mama" Gisela said hugging her mother.

"I'm so glad. You spoke to your uncle?"

"Yes I did" she said hastily.

"Good, good. I'm so happy for you both" She hugged me and gave me a big kiss on my cheek "Welcome to our family Joseph"

"Thank you Frau Becker"

I hadn't enjoyed myself so much in a long time, what a beautiful family, and place. I could see us living here after the war.

Before dinner, I drove to the airbase and secured two more boxes full of stores from the mess, one of which I kept back for my own parents. They also gave me two small chickens, and a small bag of potatoes, which were received with much gratitude.

Dinner that night was spectacular. All too soon however, it was time to say farewell to Gisela's parents, and drive across the border into Austria to meet mine. It was a tearful farewell, and Gisela had tears in her eyes for some time afterwards. I reassured her parents that I would take good care of their daughter.

I hoped I had made a good impression.

22. Salzburg.

The drive to Salzburg was uneventful except for the border crossing. I was questioned for a while on where I was going, and how long for. The Gestapo were really trying to catch me out as a deserter, but I managed to convince them otherwise by showing my passes, signed by Himmler. They soon backed down, and let us continue.

Four hours later, as darkness fell, we pulled up outside my family home.

I knocked loudly on the front door, and my father opened "Joseph! My boy!" he hugged me tightly "How we've missed you"

"I missed you too dad" I said falling back into English out of habit.

"And you must be Gisela" he said

Gisela looked at me, questioningly.

"German, dad"

"Entschuldigung" he said, switching back to German. "I'm so sorry my dear, old family habits die hard. You are far more charming than my son's letters suggest"

This made her blush. "Thank you"

"Come inside, your mother is dying to see you" He stepped aside and let us in. "Mary! Come, Joseph has arrived" he called out. I heard something banging to the floor upstairs, and footsteps hurrying down the stairs "Oh my beautiful boy!" she said, running towards me with her arms open wide "Come here" I hugged into my mother. "Let me look at you. Oh, how thin you look" she said stepping back. "What rubbish are they feeding you?"

"I'm fine mum. This is my verlobter, Gisela" I said, introducing my wife to be.

"My word. Aren't you beautiful" she smiled and hugged her

"Welcome my dear. Wait, did you say verlobter? Oh my god Joseph, why didn't you tell me?"

"Congratulations son" my dad said, shaking my hand, then hugged Gisela. "Welcome to the family my dear"

"That's fantastic news" my mum said excitedly "I can't wait to tell your aunt Penny"

My aunt Penny, my mother's sister, lived in England.

I was the apple of her eye, every time I saw her she showered me with love. "My little boy getting married. Oh! And to such a beautiful young woman too. Come, sit, tell me all about it" She ushered us through into the lounge, where she served tea.

She asked so many questions, and had so many ideas for the wedding. It was quite overwhelming. But, to her credit, Gisela took it all in her stride, and her and mum got on like old friends.

A bit later, Gisela went up to unpack and freshen up, and I found myself in the kitchen with mum. "She's beautiful"

"I know"

"Did you ask her father for her hand?"

"Yes mum, we've just come from there"

"Good boy"

"Mum?"

"Yes?"

"I need to talk to you about something"

"Your objective?" she said, matter-of-factly. So much so in fact that it stunned me into silence.

"Oh, I know all about that" she winked "What did you want to talk about?"

"Not about my objective" I said.

"Oh?"

"I got called into a meeting with the Reichsführer SS on Thursday"

"You met with Himmler?" she asked, lowering her voice.

"Yes, he sent for me"

"What did he want?"

"He wants me to kill Reinhard Heydrich"

She almost dropped the cup she was putting away "What?"

"He asked me to assassinate Obergruppenführer Heydrich"

"When? How? Why? I thought they were extremely close"

"Apparently, he sees him as a threat to his power"

"I don't understand, he's just been appointed protector of Bohemia"

"Yes, I know, he told me as much"

"Are you going to do it?"

"I have little choice"

"How so?"

"Mum, I'm SS, I can't marry without his authorisation. He won't give it to me until I've done as he asked"

"He said that?"

"No, he implied it. He gave us leave and travel passes to come here so I could see her parents"

"Slimy little bastard" she hissed. "Did he give you a deadline?"

"Yes. I have to go see him this Tuesday morning with my answer. Which will obviously be yes"

"There may be a problem" she said, furtively.

"A problem?"

"SOE are planning to assassinate Heydrich"

"SOE? Why?"

"The man is a monster"

"Many men are monsters. Whose idea is this?"

"The Czech resistance approached them with the plan"

"They have a plan?"

"Yes. I don't know what it is, but I do know SOE will not be involved on the ground. Support only"

"When?"

"Soon. June I believe" That was just over a month away.

"June??"

"Yes, that's what I hear"

"Ok. I need to know what comes first; this or my objective"

"I can't tell you that"

"But you can find out from Marcus"

The name made her smile. "You met with him?"

"Yes, I did. He gave me my objective"

"Did you remember him?"

"Yes. Once I saw his face, I remembered Uncle Marcus"

She smiled. "I won't be able to get you an answer before you leave"

"Write me a letter. Feldpost is still very reliable, so it should arrive at the Fliegerhorst before I get back"

"Very well, I'll write a letter, and will tell you the dog died if the Heydrich mission is more important"

"Sounds reasonable"

"You actually met Himmler? I can't believe it."

"Yes, I have, and he knows of me. He said he'd been following my career with interest. Any idea why?"

"No, why?"

"Just wondering"

"What is he like?"

"Creepy, and very ordinary. For a man who came up with the ideal Aryan; tall, blonde, blue eyes, he looks nothing like it himself. Makes you wonder. In fact, none of the top brass look anything like their picture perfect Aryan man."

"Except for Heydrich" she noted.

"Come to think of it, you're right. Except for Heydrich"

"Maybe that's why they want him gone"

"Maybe. Maybe he's just a pathetic, paranoid little chicken farmer hiding behind an army"

She laughed "True"

"I have to do it, you know that right?"

"Yes, I do"

"He'll have me killed"

"He'll have you killed either way"

"Unless..."

"Unless?" she asked.

"Unless I find a scapegoat"

"Who?"

"The Czech resistance. I mean, they're going to do it anyway"

"Yes...?"

"I just need to be there, to make sure he actually dies. Whether they do it, or I do it"

"Either way, they'll get the blame"

"Exactly"

"Have you thought of the consequences?"

"Consequences?"

"There will be reprisals. They will exact their revenge upon the Czech people"

"They will do that with or without my involvement"

"Could you live with that on your conscience?"

"No. But if the Czech resistance succeed in killing him, will they be able to live with the consequences?"

"I'm not sure they've even thought of it"

"Me neither. The way I see it, there are three scenarios. One; they, or I, kill him. Himmler will have to take revenge to protest his reputation. People will die, hundreds perhaps."

I paused, before continuiny.

"Two. They try, but fail. Heydrich lives, and kills thousands upon thousands of people in a mad rage."

"Three?"

"Three. No attempt is made, and Heydrich is left alone. How many people die?"

"Unknown"

"Yes, unknown"

"Which is the preferred option?"

"Three is a big gamble. Two is unthinkable. One makes the most sense."

"I need to be there"

 "I'm not sure that's a great idea"

"I need to be there to make sure it goes well"

"You don't trust them?" Typical mum question. She knows I don't.

"I'm sure they're perfectly capable, but there's no room for error here"

"I can speak to London and see what they say"

"Very well, thank you"

"Can we get back to family business now?" Smiles.

"Of course, sorry"

I went off to find Gisela, whilst mum unpacked the box of goodies I had brought with me.

"Oh there you are" she smiled as I walked into the bedroom "Your parents are just lovely"

"Now you see where I get it from" I joked.

"Oh, you. You're right though"

There was an awkward issue I had to discuss, and I wasn't sure how to do it.

"So, erm, I wanted to talk about something"

"The sleeping arrangements?" she smiled. Mind reader.

"Yeah, my mother just assumed that we would be sharing a room, and I obviously understand if that's not the case. I can sleep in the other spare room"

"Why would it be a problem?"

"I, erm…"

"Joseph, we are to be married. We can share a room, a bed. It's natural"

"Are you sure you're ok with that?"

"Of course. And before you ask; no, I haven't before"

"What? I hadn't even thought of that"

"Just to put your mind at ease, I'm a virgin"

"So am I" I said, truthfully. There had been girls of course, but it had never gone that far.

She smiled "That makes me very happy"

"Good. Want to go for a walk around the city tomorrow morning? There is lots to see"

"Sounds perfect. Is there anything I can do to help your mother? I feel like I should be doing something to help"

I chuckled "I'm not sure, you can ask her. I'm sure she would appreciate the help, and the opportunity to spend time with you. I'll go get our passes from the car before I forget"

"I'll be down in a moment" she said.

I went down and retrieved our papers from the vehicle, and sat chatting to mum whilst Gisela got ready.

"Thank you so much for all these provisions" mum smiled. "I can't remember the last time I saw so many eggs"

"One of the privileges of rank" I smiled.

"Look at you" she said "In your smart uniform. You look every inch the dapper officer"

"Thanks, not sure I deserve all these promotions though"

"Ach, we take what we can, whilst we can Joseph" she said.

I laughed.

"What's funny?"

"Ecke said exactly the same thing when I got promoted to Captain"

"He's a wise, and good man" She smiled.

"Amen to that" I agreed.

Gisela joined us a minute or so later "Hi"

"Hi" I smiled, taking her hand, then turned to mum "I'm going to show Gisela around the old town tomorrow morning, would you like to join us?"

"Ach, no, you don't want to be dragging me around with you. You two lovebirds go have a nice walk"

"Are you sure?" I asked.

"Yes. Do make sure you go to old man Holz's backerei on the Domplatz market. Tell him I said to give you real coffee, I know he has some saved back"

I liked the sound of that.

"Here" she said, handing me a small bag of eggs "Give him these"

"Are you sure?" I asked.

"He'll be overjoyed to get some real eggs, so will probably fill your plates with pastries"

Again, I liked the sound of that.

"Shame you can't go up to the castle anymore, out of bounds now" she lamented.

"We'll see about that" I winked. "I'm a Hauptsturmführer in the SD, I can get in most places"

She smiled "I'll go see what I can rustle up for dinner"

"Will you let me help?" Gisela asked

"Of course, come my dear"

I smiled as mum put her arm around Gisela and started chatting to her about cooking. In her own way, she was trying to see if Gisela would be able to cook and look after her son. Bless her.

Mum and Gisela had managed to scrounge together enough to make a mutton stew, which we all enjoyed. There was a lot of laughter and conversation around the dinner table. Gisela was fitting in perfectly, and I could tell my mother liked her. That was important to me.

Our conversation from earlier was playing on my mind though.

I needed to be there, needed to be part of the team when they planned the event. The consequences of it not going to plan were astronomical, and didn't bare thinking about. This needed to be done right, or not at all.

After clearing up, we all sat and enjoyed some schnapps together, talking about old times, and times to come. It was quite obvious to me that my parents were desperate for a grandchild, and I only hoped I could live up to their expectations.

Gisela made them both happy by promising them many grandsons. This was all going very well indeed. I sat and watched Gisela interact with mum and dad for a bit, she was a natural; laughing, smiling, listening intently. She'd completely won them over.

I couldn't wait to have a family with this beautiful woman.

But, there were things to be done before I could make that happen. Bad things. Dangerous things. I only hoped that I survived to marry my love and see my parents' dream come true.

Later, in bed, Gisela and I snuggled up to each other. It was the first time I had laid in bed with a woman, and it felt good. She felt good. The feeling of another person's warmth is quite something else. There was an unspoken agreement that we wouldn't get up to anything untoward, which suited me. We just slept, holding each other. I hadn't slept so well in my entire life. *This* is what I want for the rest of my life.

I opened my eyes. Sunlight was filtering in through gaps in the heavy curtains.

"Morning" a sweet voice beside me said. For a moment, I thought it an angel. I turned to face her.

"Morning" She was indeed an angel. How beautiful she looked, even first thing in the morning.

"Looks like it's a nice day outside, perfect for our walk" she smiled.

"We are fortunate" I said "It normally rains quite a lot at this time of year"

"I enjoyed sleeping with you" I told her "I've not slept so well in my entire life"

"Me neither," She said, and hugged into me "It feels like home"

"It does" I said and kissed her head. "Ich liebe dich"

"I love you to" she responded, and hugged even tighter.

We lay for a while longer, until sounds from downstairs indicated that my parents were both up and about.

"Come" I said "Let's get ready to go out, we can have breakfast at the bakery"

She stretched out and smiled "Sounds heavenly. Don't forget the eggs"

"I won't"

Father had already left for work when we went downstairs, mum was sat in the kitchen on her own, humming a tune that sounded vaguely familiar. Something from my childhood.

"Morning mum" I said, and kissed her cheek.

"Morning, isn't it a beautiful day?"

"Yes it is" Gisela said enthusiastically.

"Lovely day for a walk" I noted. "You sure you don't want to join us?"
"No, I have things to attend to" Contacting London probably.
"Very well, we're off out. I hoping this will get us a decent breakfast I said, holding up the bag of eggs.
"Don't forget to ask for the real coffee"
"Oh, I won't. Right, you ready?"
"Yes, I'm quite excited to see your hometown" Gisela said.
"It's beautiful" mum smiled.

The narrow streets of old Salzburg are indeed beautiful, but sadly not as full of life as they were before the war. Most of the shops were closed, and there were very few people to be seen. It saddened me to see it like that.
We eventually found ourselves in the Domplatz market, and found Holz's bakery in the far corner.
"Let's go see if he remembers me" I said "I haven't seen him in years"
We walked inside, but there was no sign of him. "Just a moment please" came a call from the back of the shop. He was likely out the back, doing most of the work himself.
When he walked through, there was an initial look of shock mixed with fear on his face, which slowly turned into a broad smile when he finally recognised me "Joseph!" he said, holding his arms out.
"Mr Holz" I smiled, and hugged him.
He clapped me on the back "It's good to see you my boy. Please tell me you're keeping yourself out of harm's way?"
"Yes sir I am. This is my fiancé Gisela"
He kissed her hand "What a beautiful young woman"
"Pleased to meet you" Gisela said.
"Mum said to give you these, and to make sure you serve us real coffee" I said, handing him the bag.
"Oh my life! Real eggs? And so many!" he seemed genuinely taken aback, and I thought I could see a tear in his eye. "Please, sit, I will make you the best coffee in Salzburg" he said, ushering us towards a table in the window.
"You wish to sit in or out?"
"Out please" Gisela said "It's such a beautiful day"
"Indeed it is. Please, make yourselves comfortable, I will return shortly"

We sat out in the sunshine, and waited for our coffee. I noticed some people walking past giving me looks. This didn't sit well with me. I didn't want Mr Holz to lose custom because of me.

"Come" I said to Gisela "Let's go sit inside"

"But is nice out here"

"Please" I said "I'm attracting unwanted attention"

She gave me a sympathetic look "Very well"

We went inside, and sat far away from the window, so as not to be seen.

Mr Holz came through a few minutes later, holding a tray with a coffee pot and some cups and saucers. "Why are you sitting all the way back there?" he asked.

"People were looking. I don't want any trouble for you"

"Ach, pay no attention to them"

"Please" I said to him "I really don't want any trouble for you, and we don't mind" I said, looking at Gisela to back me up.

"He's right, please" she said.

"It saddens me that this is what this country has come to" he said mournfully. He set the tray down "I'll get you some pastries, fresh from the oven" he smiled "Made with powdered egg sadly" he added, with a tinge of sadness.

"Thank you sir" I said gratefully.

"Poor man" Gisela said after he'd left "I feel bad for him. He's so happy to see you"

"I know, but you can't trust anyone, and I don't want anything bad happening to him"

"This war will be the end of us all"

"Let's hope not"

Mr Holz came back out with a plate full of fresh pastries, and we ate greedily. Memories of childhood flooded back. I had spent much time in here, and actually worked for Mr Holz for a while before enlisting. When we had our fill, we bade Mr Holz farewell. There was a lot of hugging, and he made me promise I would look after myself. "I will sir, please do the same"

We walked across the square, and I had a sudden impulse to go up to the castle. "Come" I said, taking Gisela's hand "Let's go up to the castle"

"Are you sure? Your mum said it was off limits"

"It's an NSDAP training facility, where they brainwash people" I said

"But, there's an officer's mess"

After a brief discussion with the guards, we got the small train cart up to the castle.

Up top, we alighted into a sort of reception centre, where we were met by an Unterscharführer. He saluted loudly "Heil Hitler" I returned his salute, then he asked "Can I be of some assistance Hauptsturmführer?"

"I wish to visit the mess" I said in my best aloof tones.

"This is most unusual Hauptsturmführer, you are not stationed here"

"Indeed I am not, but I am still an officer in the SS am I not?"

"Yes sir"

"In that case, show me to the officer's mess"

"Of course sir, follow me please"

He turned at led us to the mess at the other side of a large courtyard.

"If there is anything else I can help with, please let me know sir" he said formally.

"Relax Sergeant, we're just here to have a coffee and maybe read a paper. Nothing else"

"Yes sir" he saluted again. The clicking of his heels echoed loudly in the courtyard "Heil Hitler"

"He doesn't trust you" Gisela noted.

"No, he doesn't. I'm not overly familiar with what they do here, but whatever it is, they don't want anyone seeing it."

"It's uncomfortable"

"We won't stay long"

By contrast, the head steward couldn't have been nicer or more accommodating. "Welcome sir, madam. Please sign in here and make yourselves comfortable"

"Thank you sir" I said, and signed the ledger "Why don't you find a table dear" I said to Gisela "I have to talk business for a moment"

She gave me a puzzled look, but went off anyway "Of course dear"

"Yes sir?" the head steward said after she left. We had a brief discussion, and then I joined Gisela.

"What was that all about?"

"Oh, just formalities" I said. "Have you ordered?"

"I'm not really hungry" she said "We've only just eaten"

"I know. Let's just have a cup of tea, read a paper, and leave"

"The sooner the better. There's something about this place that just doesn't feel right"

"I know what you mean"

We had a nice cup of tea, read a couple of papers, and then made our way back to the train cart. The Sergeant was right there to see us off. But, he had company.

"Gestapo" I whispered to Gisela "Let me do the talking"

"Ah Sergeant, here to see us off I see" I smiled. He looked uneasy.

"And how can we help the Gestapo today?" I said, turning to the man dressed in standard black suit. How I despised these people.

"Papers" he said, holding out his hand.

"Newspapers? We left them in the mess"

"Your travel and identification documents"

"You want to see them?" I asked.

"Yes" he was growing impatient. The Sergeant was stood next to him, with a tight hold on his MP40 machine pistol.

"Why didn't you just say that?" I asked.

"What are you doing here Hauptsturmführer?" he asked, impatiently. I still didn't hand him my documents.

"I am on leave, and visiting the officer's mess, as is my right as an SS officer"

"Show me your leave papers" he said, again holding out his hands.

"Why?"

He looked puzzled "Because I asked" he said.

"But you didn't ask" I said "You demanded"

He stiffened noticeably, but gave in. "May I see your papers please Hauptsturmführer?"

"Of course you may" I said, and handed him our identification

He looked through our documents and handed them back "You are on leave? Here? On whose authority?" he demanded.

I handed him our leave papers "The Reichsführer SS"

He let out a small chuckle as if he thought I was making a bad joke, but blanched when he saw our papers.

"These papers, how do I know they are real?" he asked out of pure desperation.

"You could make a telephone call and ask him yourself" I said.

"That will not be necessary" he said, handing back our papers. "Enjoy your leave Hauptsturmführer"

"Thank you" I took the papers, and we got in the train.

"A word UnterScharführer" he said to the Sergeant, who was about to walk away.

Gisela chuckled as we went back down in the train, watching the arguing men slowly disappear from view.

"Well, that was exciting" she said "You're so clever"

"People like that need putting in their place, they all think they're so much better than the rest of us. It angers me"

"Well, you certainly did that" she smiled.

We spent a few more hours wandering the streets of Salzburg before returning to my parents' house.

Dad was sat smoking a pipe, reading the daily papers in the lounge.

"Good afternoon, did you have a pleasant walk? What did you think of our old city?"

"I loved it" Gisela said "And we got to go up the castle"

"Yes, I know" dad said. "Best go speak to your mother about that" he smiled.

"Are we in trouble?" Gisela asked as we went to the kitchen.

"No, quite the opposite, she's in quite a good mood" he chuckled.

"My goodness Joseph" she said when we walked in "Where on earth did you get all this from?"

Strewn around the kitchen were various bags of potatoes, some bunches of carrots, packs of butter, a large flask of milk, chocolate bars, 3 bottles of wine, two trays of eggs, sausages, and four chickens.

"Joseph!" Gisela exclaimed "How?"

"The head steward at the mess was very friendly" I commented.

"You got all this from the mess in the castle?" mum said incredulously.

"I asked if he could arrange a delivery of fresh supplies, I had no idea what it would be. He merely smiled and said he'd send whatever he could"

"Well it certainly looks like he did that" mum laughed "This is amazing" she hugged me tight. "Thank you"

"We take what we can, whilst we can mum" I said.

"Well said" she chuckled "We'll have a feast for dinner tonight!"

"It'll be just right for a farewell dinner" I said, kissing her cheek. "One request if I may though?"
"Of course"
"Could you keep a pack of butter and some eggs for Mr Holz?"
"You're a good person Joseph Deckman" she said, stroking my cheek.
A kiss on my cheek from Gisela "You certainly are"

Dinner was indeed a feast; roast chicken, potatoes, carrots, gravy.
I hadn't eaten so well in a long time; I missed mum's cooking.
After dinner, we all sat in the lounge, drinking wine, and talking about family, the war, and then family again. They were both content that the wedding would be held in Garmisch, as it wasn't too far away.
Today had been perfect, and I really wanted to spend more time with my parents. Sadly, I knew we had to leave the following morning, and I wished so badly that it wasn't so.
I wanted this war to be over, to get back to normal life, whatever that was. Raising a family with my love, in a beautiful setting. Gisela was first to go to bed, and dad wasn't far behind her. That left mum and I to sit and talk.
"Top up?" I asked.
"Just a little" We had swapped to English with the greatest of ease.
"I spoke to London" she said.
"Oh?"
"They don't want us involved, this is to be a Czech resistance operation. No outside interference."
"But I need to be there mum"
"I told them about the situation, and they eventually agreed for you to observe only"
"Observe?"
"Yes, they will tell you the time and location. You're to be there, but not interfere."
I thought this over. I really wanted to be involved. Did I trust them? No, not at all. This needed to be done properly. But, observing was the best I was going to get.
"Ok, observing only" I conceded. I had no intention of observing of course, and my mother knew that only too well.
"Observing only, of course" she repeated "I'll let them know. What are your movements after tomorrow?"

"I'll be going back to Berlin after taking Gisela back to the hospital. My meeting with the Reichsführer shouldn't take long. After that, I'll fly back to the Fliegerhorst and report to Ecke"

"Wednesday?"

"Should be sometime Wednesday, yes"

"Fine, I'll leave word with Ecke as soon as I hear anything"

"Thank you"

She regarded me for a moment. "Are you scared?"

"Of course I am. I'm scared of Himmler, scared of being caught, scared of dying"

"It's ok to be afraid, in fact, it's better to be afraid than not."

I'm sure I'd heard that somewhere before, but couldn't think of where or when. It didn't really matter of course, but it triggered a memory.

"I'm off to bed mum, early start tomorrow"

"You go, I'm going to tidy here and read a little"

"Goodnight" I kissed her cheek.

"Sleep well my boy"

Gisela was tucked up in bed, waiting for me. "Everything good?" she asked.

"Yes, of course" I smiled.

"Good, come to bed"

I undressed, and started to put my pyjamas on.

"No. Don't put those on" she said.

"What?"

"Don't put them on. Come to bed" She held up the blanket to reveal her nudity.

"Are you sure?"

"Shhhh. Just get in" she said.

I turned the light off, and got into bed with her. The sensation of her naked body against mine was unlike anything I had experienced before.

Her caresses were light, caring, sensual, and she encouraged my hands to do the same. I kissed her deep, evoking the deepest sense of lust in me. She lay on her back, and pulled me on top of her, wrapping her legs around me.

In a husky voice, she whispered in my ear "Please be gentle".
I was. It was both amazing and scary all at once. We started slow, and she let me know when she was ready for more, controlling the intensity. I was terrified of hurting her, but she seemed to be enjoying it, so I put it out of my mind and joined her in the sensuality of our coupling.
Like young lovers should, we did it several times during the night, each time feeling as good if not better than the last.
Eventually though, we fell asleep in each other's arms, completely exhausted.

23. Berlin.

"Good morning my love"
I woke to her kissing me.
"Good morning" I smiled "How are you feeling?"
"In general, or about last night?"
I laughed "Both I suppose"
"I feel fantastic, and ready to repeat last night right now" she traced her finger along my chest.
"We can't" I chuckled "As much as I want to, we can't. Busy day, and we have a flight at 11.00"
"Best get up then, its half past nine" she winked.
"What??" I fumbled to pick up my watch. She was right. "Sheiße!" I laughed "We have to get ready"
We jumped out of bed, washed, and dressed in a rush. Within a few minutes, we were downstairs, sat at the kitchen table. Mum was just pouring dad a cup of tea. "Morning love birds" she smiled as we came in. Gisela blushed hard. It was funny. "Morning" I said.
"Sit, I'll get you some breakfast"
"Not for me thank you, just a cup of tea will do"
"Are you sure? Surely you must eat?" mum said.
"I'll be fine mum, just a cup of tea will do"
"Gisela?" mum asked.
She followed my lead. "I'm happy with tea also, I'm not really hungry after last night"
This made dad chuckle, and Gisela blush again.
"I wish you didn't have to go" mum said. I could see tears forming already.
"I have to mum, or they'll come get me. Deserters are shot on sight"
"Oh, you know what I mean" mum said flustered "I didn't mean it like that"
"I know. We'll be back mum. Promise."
"You both just look after yourselves" dad said "We're really looking forward to this wedding"
"Of course dad" I said. "I have a few things to do first, but it will be soon"

I can't wait for you to meet my family" Gisela said to them.

"I am looking forward to it" mum said "We both are" She smiled, and gave Gisela a big hug.

We drank our tea and packed our case. It seemed like we'd only just gotten out of bed, when we were stood outside, ready to drive off. I hated leaving in a rush. Mum was crying, and dad was doing his best to comfort her. We said our tearful goodbyes, and then we were off, driving to the airbase. "We'll be back soon enough" Gisela said, placing her hand on mine. She could sense my sadness. "I know, it's always tough leaving them, you know? I never know when, or if, I'll see them again. This bloody war"

When we arrived at the airbase, I took Gisela for breakfast in the mess before our flight.

"You're a good man, you know that?" she said, as we ate buttered bread and boiled eggs.

"I am?"

"You know you are. You purposely told your mother that you didn't want breakfast so she wouldn't use more of their precious supplies on us"

I held my hands up in surrender "You got me"

"That's such a good thing to do" she smiled "I'm so glad you're mine"

"So am I. More tea?"

Our plane ride was noisy, uncomfortable, but thankfully uneventful. I was glad when we landed in Berlin some hours later. I collected our luggage and we managed to catch a transport truck to the train station. We were drained by the time the train pulled into Lychen station, and the walk back to Gisela's accommodation was a quiet one. We were both contemplating what we were coming back to. The realities of war were coming back to us after our little break to heaven. I left a teary, thoroughly sad Gisela behind as I walked back to the station. I wasn't sure when we'd see each other again, but I promised her it would be soon. The next train wasn't due for another hour, so I dozed on the platform to pass the time.

The station master woke me as the train approached. I thanked him, and found a quiet compartment on-board. The train was almost empty; I guessed the numbers of volunteers was dwindling somewhat. To be honest, I didn't care.

I lay down on the bench and fell asleep.

I struggled to do so at first, but the rhythmic clattering of the rails soon helped me to drift off.

It was dark by the time I alighted in Berlin, and it took some time for me to find a staff car to take me to the barrack rooms at headquarters. I signed in with the desk officer, and made my way to my allocated room. It was 3 floors up, and at the end of a long corridor.

I threw my stuff on the bed, and had a long shower. I felt tired, despite having slept for a few hours on the journey. Once I'd dressed and checked my appearance, I made my way to the mess hall to have some dinner. It was uneventful; soup, and bread with cheese.

I had a couple of glasses of terrible brandy, before finally retiring. As I left, the staff officer caught my attention and told me there was a message for me. He handed me an envelope. I thanked him, and walked up the stairs. At the top of the stairs, I stopped and opened the envelope with trembling hands.

It was from Himmler's secretary; my appointment with the Reichsführer SS was at 09.00 sharp. A feeling of dread hit me instantly, and my stomach dropped.

Consequently, my night was troubled. I lay awake for a long time thinking about what to say to Himmler the following morning.

My dreams were haunted by the usual images of falling comrades but also of everything going wrong with the resistance plan and me ending up dead.

When the steward came to wake me, I was in such a deep sleep that he took to banging loudly on the door. The sounds eventually penetrated my dreams, and I woke with a start. "Yes, I'm awake" "Apologies Hauptsturmführer"

"No, its fine, I was in a deep sleep. Thank you for your perseverance"

I stretched, and got up. Stumbling around the room, body still half asleep, I found my way to the wash basin and splashed cold water over my face.

That did the trick. The face staring back at me from the mirror shocked me.

I looked hollow, tired, unlike the carefree young man I had been two years ago. I suppose that is what combat exposure and the constant pressures of war do to you.

I dressed and went for breakfast. However, I found that my stomach was not up to food, so I just had tea. I would eat after my meeting, if I was up to it.

At the allotted time, I found myself standing in front of the imposing double doors of Himmler's office. His aide knocked, and led me inside. "Hauptsturmführer Deckman sir"

"Ah Joseph, come in" he didn't bother standing, but remained seated behind his desk, reading some document or other. His aide quietly closed the doors behind me. "Come, sit" he waved me over.

I sat, and instantly remembered that I hadn't saluted. I jumped back up to attention, and was about to salute, when he stopped me "Please, we don't need to bother with such formalities. Tell me, have you made your decision?"

"Yes sir, I have"

He put the document down, and looked me in the eye "So, what is it to be Joseph?"

He knew the answer before asking. He'd likely known since the time he'd originally asked the question. His eyes though, were daring me to say no. I didn't like it. I didn't like him. But, I couldn't let that show. "I will do as you ask Reichsführer"

His threatening demeanour vanished instantly "Splendid. Splendid. Now, I won't ask you for details, I only ask that you give me a few days' notice before it happens"

"Of course Reichsführer"

"I know I can count on you Joseph. Would you like some coffee?"

"I have just had some tea Reichsführer"

"Of course. Here" he opened his desk drawer and handed me two packets.

He saw the questioning look on my face "Ground coffee Joseph, not that Ersatz rubbish"

My eyes widened "Thank you sir"

"Ach, don't mention it. Now, don't forget to let me know when. I'm placing my trust in you Joseph. Don't let me down"

"Of course not Reichsführer"

"Good. I look forward to hearing from you" And with that, he opened his desk drawer and took out a file. He opened it, took out a document, flicked through it, and signed the last page. He held it up "Your marriage permit, authorised"

"Thank you sir" I said, holding out my hand to take it.

He shook his head "Come see me when your job is done. It will be waiting" he said, putting it back in the drawer.

Damn. "Yes sir"

"Good luck Joseph" He picked up the file he had been perusing when I came in, and started reading. The meeting was over. I stood, and left. No more words were spoken. As I closed the heavy double doors behind me, a wave of relief swept over me. With my heavy burden lifted, my stomach indicated it was ready for food. Obediently, I went to the mess and ate a large breakfast. Afterwards, I telephoned the airfield at Berlin to ask about a flight to the Fliegerhorst. I was told there would be a supply drop taking off in three hours. I reserved a seat, and hung up. Three hours. I ordered more tea, a sandwich for my trip, then read the papers.

I couldn't wait to get back to my office and talk to Ecke about all that had happened.

He was using my marriage to Gisela to get me to kill for him. I should have expected as much. I really didn't want to kill a General of the SS. But, what choice did I have?

24. Enschede.

The flight to Fliegerhorst Twente was as uncomfortable as expected, but I didn't care. My jump seat in the back of the shaky old transport plane was hard, and hurt my back, so I sat on some mail sacks instead.

Eventually, I felt the plane make an incredibly bumpy landing. There were no windows, so I couldn't actually see what was going on, but I didn't care; I was back. I jumped out of the plane, collected my belongings, and made my way to the accommodation block. There was a light drizzle in the air, but it didn't bother me. I was just happy to be back.

My case was heavy, and the walk to my block took a while, but I was enjoying the by now familiar sounds of the airfield; aircraft engines running, trucks driving about, automatic weapon fire from the range. I smiled. It felt good to be here. I signed in with the staff officer, and took my suitcase up to my room. He had handed me a couple of mail items, one from headquarters, one handwritten letter. My mother's handwriting! I opened it immediately. Decision made: the dog was dead. Heydrich was my priority. The other was from headquarters personnel division. Oh no! I had completely forgotten! I checked myself in the mirror, and headed out in a rush.

When I opened the door, three young men almost fell over themselves trying to stand to attention "Heil Hitler!"

"Gentlemen" I smiled "Relax. I am Hauptsturmführer Deckman. Good morning. Apologies for my absence, but I had business in Berlin. I trust you have settled in?" All three nodded. "Excellent. Now then, I have only one rule here; no saluting. We all know who we are, and what the chain of command is. I run a tight ship, but don't stand on formality if it's just the four of us. Is that understood?" More nodding. "Good. How about some introductions?"

The first lad to gather the courage stepped forward "Rottenführer Dietz sir". I shook his hand "Pleased to meet you Dietz".

"Rottenführer Altman" the second lad said, and I shook his hand.

"Rottenführer Schwartz" the last one offered. "Pleased to meet you Schwartz"

"Three Corporals eh? Interesting. Tell me, which of you is the senior?"
Schwartz and Altman both looked at Dietz "I am sir, I suppose"
"Excellent. Draw up your promotion papers to Scharführer, and have them on my desk for signature in the morning."
"Sir?" he looked shocked.
"I need a staff sergeant to run the place when I'm not here do I not?"
He smiled "Yes sir"
I turned to the other two "Have no fear gentlemen. Perform as expected, and promotion is guaranteed for you both by the end of summer"
"Thank you sir" they both said in unison, with broad smiles.
"I do have some bad news however"
"Sir?" Dietz said
"You will not see much of me I'm afraid. I have an office at SD headquarters in Enschede, where I will spend most of my time."
The relief was obvious. I smiled. "I'll try to keep out of your way, as long as the incoming reports are read, and the important issues passed up to me. I expect a summary report on my desk when I come in every Thursday morning. Do that one thing for me, and you'll find me extremely generous.
I don't intend to police your attendance, but I expect the work to be done. If not, I can always request replacements. Are we clear?"
"Crystal clear sir" Dietz said.
"Excellent. There are two vehicles out front. One is mine, the other is for your use. Please don't kill anyone or damage it. I'm off to Enschede now, and will return in the morning to sign those papers Dietz"
"Yes sir, I'll have them ready"
"See you in the morning gentlemen" I smiled, and left them to it.
I could hear excited, happy chatter as I left. Mission accomplished.

I jumped into the vehicle, and drove out of the base, handing a bar of chocolate to the gate guard as I went through. Leaving a trail of happiness behind me made me feel good. I parked up outside the villa, and went inside.
"Good morning Hauptsturmführer"
"Good morning Oskar" I said to Ecke's adjutant "Is the old man in today?"

He smiled "He will be in around lunchtime sir, would you like me to make an appointment for you?"

"Yes, that would be good thanks"

"No problem sir. I'll let you know once I've spoken to him"

"Thank you Oskar"

In my office, there was a stack of reports to get through. But, I was not in the mood. I'd take them with me and get my team to go through them on my behalf. There were a few mail items that needed responding to, so I wrote those out and went for a walk around the town centre.

The drizzle had stopped, but it was still grey and dull. My boots sounded stupidly loud on the brick roads as I walked around, making me feel self-conscious.

I wasn't sure what I was expecting to see or find, but I started to feel a bit depressed after a while. I found a small coffee house that was open, and was relieved to find a few German soldiers already inside. They went to stand and salute, but I stopped them "At ease lads, I'm just here for a hot drink" I smiled warmly.

They sat back down, and continued their conversation, which appeared to be about who could drink the most coffee.

I sat at a window table overlooking the market square. An old lady came over and asked for my order. "Thee alstublieft, een pot als het mogelijk is?" *Tea please, a pot if possible*. She smiled, nodded, and went off to the kitchen. She returned a few moments later with a small pot of tea and an ornate cup. "Dank u wel" I smiled. *Thank you*.

I sat sipping hot, strong tea whilst watching the world go by outside. The young men had finished their coffee drinking game, and left.

The place was empty, but for me.

Or so I thought.

"It is nice to see you again Joseph"

I turned. "Judith?" She stepped out of the kitchen. "How did you know I was here?"

"My grandmother owns this place. I was out back, having tea with her when I heard your voice."

"She seems nice"

"She said the same about you. Not bad. For a German pig"

I laughed. "Being here is not my idea remember, just going where I'm told to go. Though I can think of worse places to be"

"How was your time away?"

"It was nice" I said, unsure of what exactly I could say.

"It's ok to talk about her" she smiled.

"It was nice, I spent a day with Gisela in Lychen, and then we visited our parents in Bavaria and Austria"

"So when is the happy day?" she asked, pouring herself a bit of tea. She's a sharp one, I thought. "We don't know yet. I need approval from Himmler first"

"You do?"

"Yes, I do" I really didn't want to go into the reasoning behind it.

"Have you never questioned that fact that your state controls everything you do?"

"Every day"

Her turn to laugh. "Not what I was expecting to hear. You also seem to have made it through a week without being promoted I see"

"Yes, not sure why that is. I shall telephone headquarters when I get back to the office"

"Jullie hooren niet grappig te zijn weet je dat? Wat een leuke verassing" *You people aren't meant to be funny you know? It's a nice surprise.*

"I'll take that as a compliment, and also point out that I am only half German"

"Your best half isn't German" she said, and blushed slightly.

"Oh, erm, thank you..." There was a moment of uncomfortable silence.

"How are the children?" I asked on impulse.

"They were very happy with the chocolate" she smiled.

"I'm glad. The poor things probably don't even know what all this nonsense is about"

"It's the best way to be. Have you spoken to Ecke since you returned?"

I shook my head "I haven't had the chance, he was out when I arrived"

"He's been spending a lot of time with the Ortskommandant and the Police chief. The deportations are still happening"

"I'm sorry" I said, hanging my head.

"What is your problem with Jewish people?" she asked, with a flash of anger, which she seemed to regret instantly. "I'm sorry. I know it's not your fault"

"You're right to be angry. I'm ashamed of what is happening"

"Like I said, not your fault."

All the happiness had gone from the conversation, and it felt like we were strangers for a moment.

She placed her hand on mine "I know you're not a bad person Joseph, forgive me"

I should have pulled my hand away, but the feel of her touch was electrifying, and I could not.

She looked at me "You're staring" She was right. I was sat, staring at her hand on mine, not wanting this moment to end.

She pulled her hand away. No! "Apologies, I didn't mean to..." I said

"No, my fault, I should never have..."

It was awkward. "I, erm, should get back" I said.

"Yes, and I have to get back to, you know..."

"Of course, it was good to see you Judith" I said, putting my gloves on.

"And you Joseph" she said, and for a moment there was something in the way we looked at each other. I couldn't put my finger on it. Sadly, the spell was broken when she turned away and disappeared out to the back. I left a generous payment for my tea, and left.

Guilt. That's what I felt. I hadn't moved my hand, and hadn't wanted her to do so either. Why was that? From her perspective, it was clear; she liked me.

A lot. From my perspective? I liked her too. A lot. But, I wasn't supposed to, I had Gisela after all. And I loved her with all my heart. So what were these feelings? And why did I have them? I shouldn't have. But, I did. Meanwhile, I had returned to the office in the villa.

"Ah, Hauptsturmführer, the Obersturmbannführer has been waiting for you"

"He has? That's not good. I'll just get my briefcase, then will be ready"

I ran upstairs, picked up my briefcase, and ran straight back down. Oskar knocked on the door "Come!"

"Hauptsturmführer Deckman sir"

Ecke looked up at me and roared "Hauptsturmführer Deckman, I do not like being kept waiting. Oskar, get me some lunch from that place in town"

"Yes sir" Oskar winced, and backed out, quietly closing the door behind him.

"Sit Hauptsturmführer" he said angrily. I was hoping it was all for show.

He stood, walked to the window, and peered out. "Ah, we're safe now. Joseph, how are you" he said kindly.

"I am good sir, how are you?"

"Not too well I'm afraid. These deportations are really getting to me."

"Yes, I heard as much"

"You did?" he asked.

"I saw Judith this morning"

"You did?" he repeated.

"I went for a walk, and stopped for some tea"

"Ah, her grandmother's tea room"

"Yes. She came out to see me when I was sat on my own"

"She's a beautiful girl"

"Yes she is" I blurted before I was able to stop myself.

He chuckled "Love is a minefield Joseph. Can a man have feelings for more than one woman? Who knows?"

"Yes sir"

"Just be mindful"

"I will sir"

"Now, tell me about your business in Berlin"

"Well, I was in Lychen to visit Gisela, when a motorcycle messenger came to see me in my rooms with a message from Himmler. I was to report at once, and I did as ordered, naturally."

"What did he want?"

"He wants me to kill Obergruppenführer Heydrich"

"What??" Ecke exclaimed, and immediately got up. He opened the office door and checked outside. Satisfied we were still alone, he came back in. "He wants you to kill Heydrich?"

"Yes sir"

"But why? They're like father and son"

"That may well be, but he fears Heydrich, sees him as competition"

"It makes no sense. Heydrich is the Führer's favourite"

"Maybe that's why" I noted

"You may be right. Have you accepted?"

"I had no choice. I want to marry Gisela, and he won't grant permission until it's done."

"Sneaky little bastard. You know he'll have you killed afterwards?"

"Yes, but I have a plan"

"The Czech's?"

"Indeed. They have a plan, and I intend to sacrifice them"

"Will Himmler let you live, even if you do?"

"As long as they actually kill him, I believe so. Why would I tell anyone?"

"He doesn't really need a reason, just to tie up loose ends"

"He promised me a long and successful career, and gave me his word that I would not be touched"

"He actually said that?"

"He did"

"You believe him?"

"Of course not"

"Just watch yourself"

"I will"

"How is your mother?"

Turning to slightly happier subject matter, we had a nice chat, both glad for the escapism it offered.

I told him about my daring trip up to the castle, to which he responded "You were lucky, they don't admit strangers up there. It's all a bit hush-hush"

"I almost forgot sir" I said, opening my briefcase. "I have a small gift for you"

I handed him one of the packages Himmler gave me, he looked at me quizzically.

"Coffee. Real coffee, from the Reichsführer SS himself"

He opened the pack and inhaled the smell of the coffee grounds

"Oh, that smells like heaven"

"Yes sir, it does"

"He gave you these?"

"Yes sir, he handed them to me on my way out"

"Did I ever tell you how highly I regard the man?" he smiled.

"I find him a despicable, horrid, jumped up little chicken farmer" I responded.

We both laughed at this.

On a more serious note, I had a lot to consider. I needed a fool proof plan to keep Himmler from killing me. But first, I needed to know how much time I had.

"Do you know when they plan on carrying out the assassination?" I asked him. He shook his head.

"I don't. I only know it's going to be soon."

"Soon? This month? Next month? Mum mentioned June"

"Soon can be anytime Joseph. Patience"

"Patience? I want to marry Gisela in July, it's almost the end of April already"

"Have you heard from the Commander yet?" he asked.

"Yes. I had a letter from my mother; Heydrich is my priority"

"In that case, I suspect the attempt is imminent" he noted.

"If that is so, then I need to get to Prague. I'll telephone Himmler and request I be attached to the Prague SD headquarters temporarily."

"You think he'll be able to do that?"

"He's the Reichsführer SS, I'm sure he can"

There was a knock on the door. Oskar entered "Your lunch sir" he said, and gave me a sympathetic look.

"Thank you Oskar" Ecke said "One more task for you"

"Sir?"

He handed him the pack of coffee "Brew up a pot of coffee would you?"

"Real coffee?" he asked, stupefied.

"Yes, not too strong please"

"Of course sir" he said, and went off to do as ordered.

He returned a few minutes later, and the smell of fresh coffee filled the room.

When he set the tray down, and made to leave, Ecke stopped him.

"Oskar, something is missing"

"There is sir?" He looked at the tray, confused.

"There are only two cups here"

"Sir?"

"Get one for yourself Oskar" He said kindly.

"Sir?"

"Forget about the sir for a moment, enjoy a cup of coffee with us"
"Yes sir" he smiled, and went off to fetch another cup.
When he returned, we all sat drinking delicious coffee, all ranks
forgotten; just three men chatting about life before the war.

25. Judith Rietveld.

The following morning, I found myself running across to the mess through the pouring rain.
"Horrible day out there sir" the head steward noted as I ran in, dripping water onto the floor.
"Apologies, I don't have a raincoat or an umbrella"
He handed me a hand towel from behind his desk "Here you are sir"
"Thank you" I smiled, and dried myself as best I could.
After yesterday, I couldn't bring myself to order coffee, so had tea again. For breakfast, I asked for scrambled eggs and toast. A peculiar request for a German, but the steward was very accommodating. He soon returned wuth my meal.
"The cook sends his apologies sir, and asked for any comments that could help him improve"
The eggs were a bit rubbery, but perfectly edible. I asked for a couple more slices of toast to take to the reading room. Again, the fellow was very obliging.
I sat for a while, drinking tea and reading the papers. There was an article about the allied bombing of Lübeck, and our revenge bombing on the cities of Exeter, Bath, and York. It boasted how far into enemy territory our bombers could fly. Not for a moment did they discuss how enemy bombers could reach as far as Lübeck without our "Superior" Luftwaffe intercepting them.
After breakfast, I had a quick chat with the cook. The chap was extremely passionate about his craft, and was desperate to get this new challenge right. I told him how my mother usually made them, and he was extremely thankful for this new information.

"Morning gentlemen" I said, walking into the office.
"Morning sir" they all said in unison.
"Terrible weather out there today" I commented and went up to my office. On my desk, as expected, were the promotion papers for Corporal Dietz. I took out my pen and signed them, then went back downstairs.

"Here you go Sergeant" I said to him, handing him the documents and the stack of reports from my office in Enschede.

"Go to the quartermaster and get your new rank badges. I expect see you in the correct uniform, and a summary report on my desk tomorrow morning. Oh, and get me a raincoat and umbrella please"

"Yes sir" he said

"Have a good day gentlemen, I'm off" I smiled, and left. The roof was up on the kübelwagen thankfully, so it was mostly dry inside.

I say mostly, as the roof on these cars was never perfectly waterproof. There were small leaks here and there, but fortunately not over the driver seat in this particular one.

I drove slowly, as the brakes were not the strongest in the world, and the tyres were pretty worn. I was angry with myself for not taking it to vehicle maintenance before now. I made a note to get the lads to do it. I would take their vehicle in the meantime.

There wasn't space to park outside the villa, so I had to park up the road, and run to the office through the rain.

"Morning Oskar" I said, bursting through the door, dripping all over the floor.

He laughed "Morning sir. You don't have a coat or umbrella?"

"I don't sadly, but will have tomorrow"

"Ah, good. If you need one in the meantime" he said, gesturing towards an umbrella in the corner by the door.

"Excellent, thank you"

"Message for you sir" he handed me an envelope.

I opened it, it was from Ecke: *Go for tea at ten this morning*.

Go for tea? Where? Did he mean the old lady's tea room? I assumed so as it was the only place I knew.

I checked my watch; it was almost half past nine already.

"I'll take you up on your kind offer Oskar" I said "I will be heading out again shortly it appears. Would you do me one favour before I go?"

"Of course sir"

"I need to speak to the office of the Reichsführer SS, could you place a call?"

"Yes sir, I'll let you know when I am connected"

"Thank you"

I went upstairs, where there was only one report waiting for me.

I flicked through whilst I waited. A minute or so later, my phone rang
"Deckman"
"Office of the Reichsführer for you sir" he clicked off, and connected
me. "Office of the Reichsführer SS"
"Hauptsturmführer Deckman speaking"
"How can I help you sir?"
"I have a priority message for the Reichsführer, could you make sure
he gets it as soon as possible please?"
"I'll make sure he gets it this morning sir"
"Excellent. Message start. Hauptsturmführer Deckman requesting
immediate temporary transfer to SD Headquarters Prague. Stop."
"That it sir?"
"Yes thank you, response to Obersturmbannführer Ecke, SD
Headquarters, Enschede, Netherlands."
"I should hopefully have a response for you today sir"
"Thank you"
I hung up, and reluctantly went back out into the rain, though armed
with an umbrella this time.
The clock tower of the old church in the market square was halfway
through ringing out the tenth hour as I walked into the tearoom.
It was empty. Had I come to the right place?
"Hello?" I called out.
"Sit at the back"
Judith.
I sat at the table on the back wall, away from the window. Judith
walked out from the back, turned the sign on the door to "Gesloten"
Closed, and locked the door.
"What's going on?" I asked.
"Nothing, I just wanted to spend time with you"
I was confused. "Why?"
"You need to ask?"
No, I didn't. I knew exactly why.
"Would you like some tea?"
"Yes please"
She went out back to make a pot of tea, leaving me alone for a
moment.
Alone with my thoughts, which were telling me to leave.
There was no reason for me to be here.

Before I could convince myself to leave, she returned with a tray.

"Why am I here?" I asked.

She sat, and poured tea for us both. Without milk, in the traditional Dutch fashion.

"Only you would know the answer to that. Why are you here?"

"I received a note, asking me to be here at ten"

"Then you know why you're here" she smiled.

"Very well. Why am I here with you?"

"I told you, I wanted to spend time with you"

"Is this some kind of test?"

"Test? Why would you think that?"

"I thought it may be some kind of resistance thing"

She laughed "You're funny"

"I wasn't making a joke" I said evenly.

"You like me" she said, looking into my eyes.

"Yes"

"I like you"

"I know"

"So, if we like each other, we should be able to spend time together"

"True. And I am happy to spend time with a friend"

"A friend"

"Yes, a friend"

"Hmm" The word had fallen hard upon her.

"Are we not friends? I mean, I know we met not long ago, and know little about each other, but I thought we were friends"

"What if I want to be more than friends?"

"You know I can't"

 "Do you not find me attractive?"

"That's not fair"

"How so?"

"Because you know I do"

"Find me attractive?"

"Yes"

"Hmm"

"You're enjoying this"

"Maybe" She started unbuttoning her blouse

"What are you doing?" I asked, alarmed.

"It's warm in here" She pulled her blouse open slightly to reveal the swell of her bosom.

"Button up your shirt Judith"

"You don't like what you see?"

"You know I do"

"So what is the problem?"

I sighed. "Thank you for the tea" I stood up and unlocked the door.

"Don't leave" she said.

I turned to look at her. "I really hope this was some kind of test, and not just some cruel joke" I said, then left without looking back.

I walked the streets for a while trying to make sense of what had just happened, but couldn't. It must be a test surely, it was totally out of character for her. Or was it? I didn't really know her at all, so maybe it was what she was really like.

If it was a test, then for what? To what end? To prove I was loyal to Gisela? Why would anyone care?

A man appeared at my side "Joseph, do you have a moment?"

It was Marcus.

"What do you want?"

"A moment of your time"

I sighed. "Look Marcus, I've had it up to here with you lot today. I'm not really in the mood"

"I can understand that. Come, Judith and I need to talk to you,"

"Judith?"

He walked through some back streets, which led us to the bar I'd been to with Ecke; Judith's father's bar.

"Why here?" I asked before he went inside.

"It's the only safe place in town" he said, and disappeared inside.

I stood outside, staring at the door. I didn't really want to go inside, but what choice did I have? Reluctantly, I followed him in.

Inside, Marcus had sat down at a table with Judith.

"Please, sit Joseph" Judith said.

"So you can play with me some more?"

She looked genuinely hurt at the accusation. "Please just sit"

I pulled out a chair, and sat down. "What do you want?"

She held out her hand for me to shake. I stared at it for a long moment, then shook it.

It was like being struck by a bolt of lightning. Her hand was soft, and warm.

"Judith Rietveld, pleased to meet you"

"Ok, now what?" I pulled back my hand.

"You're angry" she said.

"You think?" I said with more than a hint of anger.

"I understand"

"Well, how nice for you"

"You were right, you know? About the test"

"I don't really care anymore. Just say whatever it is you want to say so I can get away from you people"

"It was necessary" Marcus said "It's not her fault"

"You see, Marcus, I don't really give a damn whose fault it is. I'm sick of being played with like some kind of laboratory rat"

"It was necessary for us to see if you were able to be turned"

"By her?"

"By any female" she said, clearly hurt. I felt bad. But knew I shouldn't; they were toying with my emotions after all. I had every right to be angry.

"Well, I guess you have your answer now" I said, standing up, then looked her in the eye "Hope it was worth it".

I left before they could protest. I was sick of them all, sick of this game. I needed a break. I needed Gisela. I walked back to the car, and drove at speed back to the Fliegerhorst.

How dare they mess with me like that? How dare she lead me on like that? She knows exactly how I feel about her, which just made it worse.

I wanted to shout out, scream; let out all the anger. The only way I could think of to do that was through physical exercise, so I went to the gymnasium to do some weight lifting. Afterwards, I sat on the floor under the shower for almost half an hour. I still felt angry, but the feeling was by then abating somewhat.

I gathered myself, and went back to my room where I dried and dressed, then had lunch in the mess. I was hungry. And still angry.

"Mind if I join you?" It was Major Von Graeve.

"Off course not Herr Major" I said, standing up. "Please"

He took a seat opposite me, and I sat back down.

"How are you doing Joseph? You look a bit flustered"

"I am fine sir, just work getting to me I guess"

"Gets to us all in the end, whether we like it or not."

"It's been a tough week"

"You have new personnel I see, better than the last bunch I hope?"

"So far so good sir" I smiled "We'll see how they get on"

"I'm sure they'll be fine under your command"

"Nice of you to say so sir"

"It is true. You are a good officer Deckman; fair but strict, and you have compassion. The rarest sort"

"I have met a few good officers since I've been here sir"

"I hope I'm among them?"

"Absolutely sir"

"Kind of you to say" he smiled. "Right, I'll leave you to your lunch Joseph, I just wanted to see how you were. May I make a suggestion?"

"Of course sir"

"Go to the range and get some practice in, works for me every time" I smiled "I might just do that sir"

He stood to leave, then bent down to pick something up.

"You dropped this"

"Oh, I don't think so sir" I said, not recognising the envelope in his hands.

"I believe you did" he said, looking earnestly.

"Oh, yes, of course. Thank you sir"

He smiled "Good day to you Captain"

"And you Herr Major"

And with that he was gone, and I had a mystery envelope in my hand. This game never ends.

He was right about one thing though; the range sounded like a great idea. I finished up and headed over. The envelope could wait a while longer.

"Ah good afternoon Hauptsturmführer, back for more?"

It was the same Sergeant I had met the first time I'd come to the range.

"Good afternoon Scharführer, yes, I have some frustration to vent"

"Ah, in that case may I suggest 200 rounds?"

"An excellent suggestion". He went out to the back, and returned with two boxes of 9mm ammunition.

"Enjoy sir"

"Thank you, I will" I smiled.

I emptied the first magazine within seconds, and unsurprisingly, none of the 9 rounds hit the target. It wasn't important, I just wanted to shoot. I reloaded, and shot the next magazine with more care. By the time I'd gotten to the fifth magazine, I'd gotten the frustration out of my system, and was ready to shoot properly.

By the time I'd worked my way through both boxes of rounds, I was tired. My arm ached, and the smell of cordite was getting to me. I let the Scharführer know I was done, and asked for a cleaning kit. I sat at one of the workbenches in silence, stripping and cleaning my weapon.

"That was some shooting sir, feel better now?" the Sergeant asked as I signed out of the range.

"Yes, I feel great, thank you. Would it be possible to get some new magazines for my pistol?"

"Of course sir. I'll have them delivered to the officer's mess for you in the morning"

"Thank you Sergeant"

"My pleasure sir" he said, and went off to clear up my spent casings.

I checked my watch; it was almost seven o'clock. I'd been in the range for over three hours! My eyes stung from the acrid smoke. I was ready for bed.

However, instead of going to my room, I headed straight to the bar and ordered a double brandy. I drank it down in one.

It was disgusting, but I didn't care. I just needed something to help me sleep. I didn't want my night haunted by bad dreams again. I had another, then went to my room where sleep came quickly.

26. Prague.

The following morning, in a better mood, I walked over to the mess for breakfast.

"Good morning Hauptsturmführer" the head steward said.

"Good morning Hans, has a parcel been left for me?"

"I'll just check sir, one moment" He went out back to the office, and came back holding a small parcel "Yes sir"

I took the parcel from him "Thank you Hans. What do we have for breakfast this morning?"

"Well, the cook has been practising his scrambled eggs sir, and is keen for you to try them"

"That sounds marvelous"

He led me to my usual table in the window "I'll get you some tea sir, and tell the cook you're here"

I opened the parcel, and the Sergeant had been true to his word. Inside were two brand new magazines for my Luger. I put them in my pocket. Pocket. Damn! The envelope! I'd completely forgotten about it. I waited for Hans to serve my tea, then opened it.

Inside was a short note, and what looked like a piece of microfiche film. The note said; *A token of my good faith.* Without a light and magnifier, I couldn't make out what was on the fragment of film. I put it and the note back in the envelope, then put the envelope in my brief case. I would show it to Obersturmbannführer Ecke later.

He would likely know what to do with it.

"With the cook's compliments sir" a steward appeared with a plate of scrambled eggs and toast.

"Thank you" They looked far better than his first attempt, and tasted better too. They were delicious in fact. When I'd finished eating, I asked the steward to bring out the cook.

He appeared moments later with the cook I'd spoken to the previous morning. "Yes sir? How were they?" he asked eagerly.

"They were absolutely delicious Stefan, my compliments. Almost as good as my mother's" I winked.

"Thank you Hauptsturmführer, you are too kind" He smiled broadly, and went back to his kitchen a happy man.

I was dreading going into Enschede today, I really didn't want anything to do with the Group for a while.

But, there was no avoiding work, I had duties to perform. Before I drove into Enschede to face the music, I needed to see my own team, and to pick up my summary report. Hopefully.

The men were all hard at work, clacking away at typewriters when I entered. "Good morning gentlemen"

"Good morning Hauptsturmführer" The Sergeant said, and came over.

"You have my report?"

"Yes sir, it is on your desk as requested"

"Excellent, thank you Oberscharführer"

"Is there anything I can do for you today sir?"

"No, thank you. I shall take the report with me to my office in Enschede"

"Of course sir. Let me get it for you"

"No need, I'll get it. You carry on Sergeant"

"As you wish sir" he said, and went back to his desk.

I went up to my office, and picked up the report; it looked impressive enough. I put it in my briefcase, and went back downstairs.

"Gentlemen, thank you for the report, Make sure you finish a bit earlier today, have a few drinks on me at the mess bar." I placed some kantinegeld (canteen money) on the table, enough for a couple of rounds or drinks.

"Thank you sir" they almost said in unison. I smiled "Oh, one more thing, could you please have my vehicle checked over at the motor pool today? The tyres are completely worn out"

"Yes sir, not a problem. Leave it here, and take the other vehicle. I will get it looked at today" Dietz said, and we swapped keys. I thanked him, and left them to their typing.

I drove the little kübelwagen at speed down the roads towards the town. Not because I was desperate to get to the office, but because I craved the sensation of danger.

It was preferable to the sensation of dread. I wondered when I would have to face Judith again. It was not something I was looking forward to. I tried to put it out of my mnd as I parked up outside the villa.

"Morning Oskar, is the old man in?"

"Morning Hauptsturmführer, yes, he is upstairs."

"Thank you"

I went on up, and let myself in without knocking.

"Joseph" Ecke said, looking up from a file he was reading.

"Morning sir. Forgive the lack of formality and manners, but I appear to have run out of both"

He sighed. "What is it Joseph?"

"Well, whatever that stunt was yesterday, it left a sour taste in my mouth"

"What stunt?"

"Judith and Marcus?"

"You met with Marcus yesterday?" he asked. He seemed genuinely surprised. Had he not known?

"Yes sir. You didn't know?"

He shook his head "I'm afraid not"

"How did you not know?" I asked. It seemed unlikely, but his reaction genuine.

"I'm not aware of all activities in the Group Joseph, surely you can see that?"

"Possibly"

"Why don't you tell me what happened?"

I relaxed in my chair, and told him all about the note, my meeting with Judith, and her behaviour, and the subsequent meeting with Marcus.

"That's not good. I'm sorry Joseph. I had no part in it"

"I can see that now" I said apologetically. "Why would they do something like that?"

He took a deep breath. "They do have a point, you know. The Group needs to be sure you can't be tempted, and maybe compromised"

I knew he was right, I just wasn't ready to admit it. I told him as much.

"You are entitled to your anger, maybe Prague would be a good place to cool your heels" he said, handing me a small bundle of papers.

"Your transfer orders and travel authorisations"

"It came through" I said, taking the papers.

"Yes, you leave this evening. No flight this time sadly. Train all the way"

"I don't mind that at all, it will give me time to think"

"I'll miss you Joseph. Make sure you come back won't you?"

I stood and shook his hand "I will sir"

As I was opening the door, I had the feeling something wasn't right, or I was forgetting something.

The note.

"Sir?"

"Hmm?"

"I almost forgot, I got this from Major Von Grave this morning. It contains a fragment of microfiche film. I couldn't make out what it was"

I handed him the envelope. He took out the contents, and stared at the microfiche fragment for a moment.

"I have a magnifier, let's see if we can make out what it is"

He took a magnifying glass from his drawer, and held the fragment over a light. "Hmm, I can't be sure with my old eyes, but it looks like part of an engine schematic wouldn't you say?"

He handed me the glass, and I took a look for myself. "It looks like something, I'm no expert, but it has fan blades doesn't it?"

"Yes, I thought I could see something like that also"

"Seems legitimate" I said, handing the glass back.

"He's letting us know he has the real deal Joseph. We need this business with Heydrich over with quickly so we can get him and his family out. The information he holds is crucial"

"Understood sir, I'll do what I can"

"I know you will. In the meantime, I'll pass this on to Marcus, he will know how to get it to London"

Back at the Fliegerhorst later that day, I was sat on my bed thinking about the day's events. A few days ago, I had been desperate to get back here, now I couldn't wait to get away. I *needed* to get away. What Judith had done was completely underhand, and had eroded my trust in her completely. Maybe time would heal that, I wasn't sure. The train was leaving Enschede station at 18.30, and I had asked Sergeant Dietz to drop me off. That meant I needed to have an early dinner, and there was packing to do before that.

I enjoyed a nice dinner in the mess, and was picked up outside by Dietz at 18.00 on the dot.

"Good evening sir"

"Evening Dietz, thank you for driving me"

"Pleasure sir. Am I to assume I am to provide the weekly summary report to Obersturmbannführer Ecke's office in your absence?"

"You assume correct, thank you"

He nodded, and we drove off.

When we arrived, he carried my case up to the platform. "Have a nice trip sir"

"Thank you Dietz. Look after the team won't you? I'm relying on you"

"I will sir, don't worry"

"Good man. Go, get back, the bar is open" I handed him a handful of kantinegeld "Treat yourself"

He smiled "Thank you sir" and saluted. I returned his salute, and he marched off back to the vehicle.

The train was due in about ten minutes. I took out my travel papers and checked my route. What a journey.

Enschede – Osnabruck
Osnabruck –Hanover
Hanover – Berlin
Berlin – Dresden
Dresden – Prague

It would take almost two days. I planned to stay overnight in Berlin and Dresden. I had a budget review meeting to attend in headquarters, and I had always wanted to visit Dresden.

The train was on time, as expected, and I found an empty compartment as the train was not busy.

It had two flatbed carts with AA guns, one at either end of the train. Something I had not seen before. A clear indication that our glorious Luftwaffe was completely outgunned by the enemy. So much for that fat swine Göering promising us air superiority over all of Europe.

There was a loud whistle, followed by being rocked back and forth in my seat gently, indicating the train was setting off.

I had not seen this part of the town before; more factories, textiles likely, and then we were in the open country, on our way to the Fatherland.

There were flak battalions all along the route, another indication that the enemy could now penetrate well into our territory. To me, it was an indication that we were already losing this war.

We didn't arrive into Osnabruck until almost nine because we had to stop various times to allow military trains to pass.

Fortunately, the connecting train to Hanover was already waiting to depart. I jumped on board just as it was setting off. After a tedious journey, we pulled into Hanover at a few minutes past midnight.

I decided to get off and overnight here. Going on to Berlin would take another 3 to 4 hours, and I wasn't in the mood. I found a small guest house not far from the station, and they graciously gave me a room for the night.

The following morning, I was on the train pulling out of Hanover station at six in the morning. The train was quite full, and I was fortunate to find a seat, even at that early hour. I was wedged in between two burly Wehrmacht soldiers. We struck up a conversation, and I discovered that they were being transferred to the eastern front from France. I wished them well. I knew most of those brave boys wouldn't survive. This war. Ugh.

The journey took almost six hours. By the time we pulled into Berlin, I was starving. My connecting train to Dresden left in four hours. That gave me time to go to the mess at headquarters for lunch. The budget meeting woould have to be postponed.

I flagged down a staff car before it was able to drive off. The driver took me to headquarters, and I had a large lunch. I asked the steward to make me a few sandwiches, and to get me some chocolate bars if he could. He was very obliging, and a while later, I was stood on the platform handing out chocolate bars to the men I'd met on the train. They were still sat out waiting for their connecting train into Poland. I felt sorry for them, but it warmed my heart to bring them some joy.

The Reichsbahn conductor informed me that the journey to Dresden should take about four hours.

In fact, we made it in just over three and a half.

A minor miracle! It was early enough for me to find lodgings, and then walk around this beautiful city.

It felt good to stretch my legs. There was a hostel not far from the station that Ecke had recommended to me.

I found it quite easily, using the directions he had given me. After freshening up in my room, I went out for a walk. I crossed the Adolf Hitler Platz, and walked down to the river. Up ahead, there was the old Catholic Church and castle. I decided to follow the river, as I wasn't in the mood for Gothic architecture. There were a lot of people walking along the river; lovers taking a romantic stroll, parents with laughing children. I wondered if any of them knew of the horrors their sons, grandsons, husbands, fathers were facing at the front? Probably not. Probably best they didn't.

I found a café that was still serving, so I sat outside and ordered a glass of water. I was hungry, but that could wait until I got back to my room. I still had the sandwich from the mess. My stomach must have overheard my thoughts, as it growled loudly in protest. I sat for a little while longer, then made my way back to my lodgings. I wrote a letter to Gisela, telling her how much I loved and missed her. It made me feel sad and homesick. I wondered how she was getting on at the hospital. The wards were likely full of injured men, keeping her extremely busy. I couldn't tell her where I was going of course, but she would be able to tell from the Feldpost mark where I was. Tiredness overtook me eventually, and I fell asleep on the bed in my uniform.

My train wasn't until 09.30 the next morning, so when I had changed and packed, I made my way to the station. There was a small tea house outside the station building, so I sat inside and had a cup of tea. Sadly, they did not have any food available. I would have to wait until I got to Prague. As I still had half an hour until my train departed, I drank my tea slowly, and read through some old newspapers.

The train journey itself was uneventful, and I dozed for a short while. As the train wound its way southward, I noticed how little the Czech landscape differed from the German one.

If I hadn't known, I would swear we were still in Germany.

Prague itself looked beautiful as the train made its way through the suburbs towards the central station. As with the Dutch, I was sure the people here hated us, we were invaders after all.

Here though, I was on unfamiliar turf, and I'd need to be on guard as I found my way to the SD headquarters.

I had no idea where it was, and was hoping to find a transport or staff car outside the station. Sadly, I did not. I looked around; there was a park opposite the station and rows of official looking buildings on the other side of it. I decided to try my luck. The park was pleasant enough, and I soon found what I was looking for; a large building with swastika flags and guards outside.

"Pardon me Corporal, is this the SD headquarters?"

He gave me a strange look "No sir, this is the Gestapo office. The SD headquarters are in Prague Castle, across the river" He gave me some general directions, and I thanked him.

It wasn't difficult to find once I got to the river; it was clearly visible. I hastily made my way towards it, keen not to spend too much time alone on the streets. When I got there, the guards directed me to the administration's office, where I reported for duty.

"Hauptsturmführer Deckman?" The girl said as she read through my papers. "We were expecting you a bit later today"

"The train got through without stopping, a minor miracle"

She smiled "You have an appointment with Obergruppenführer Heydrich at ten"

"I do?" What? I do? I was shocked. What would Heydrich want with me? I had never met the man, and I was convinced that he didn't know of me either.

"You do" she chuckled.

"His office..?"

She pointed up. "Just come back here and I'll show you up" she smiled.

"Of course. Could you point me in the direction of the accommodation block and the officers mess please?"

She handed me a small map of the castle "This makes it easier" she smiled.

"Thank you"

"Have a good day Hauptsturmführer"

"And you" I smiled, picked up my case, and followed the map to the accommodation block. The desk officer was short and angry looking and, as expected, his attitude was suitably brusque. "Sign here Hauptsturmführer, your room is on the third floor, 316."

"Thank you Corporal" I said evenly, then went off to find my room.

27. Reinhard Heydrich.

The room was small, but comfortably furnished. It looked like a cell of some sort, with a small window looking out over the city. The bed was comfortable enough, which was good. I wasn't sure how long I would be staying here, and had no idea how to contact either the Group or the resistance. I felt terribly alone suddenly. The Group. Is that what I was calling them now? I didn't know if they had a specific name. The Group would have to do.

I unpacked, and went off to the laundry room to have my shirts pressed. I paid a little extra to have them done straight away. If I had an appointment with Heydrich, I wanted to look my best.

Half an hour later, I was back at the administration office, reporting to the same girl as earlier.

"Ah Hauptsturmführer, back again. He is a stickler for punctuality, so you have a few minutes to spare. Please take a seat and I'll take you up when he expects you" she smiled.

"Of course" I said, a little uneasy. "What's he like?"

She looked around, then whispered "A monster"

I was looking for traces of a smile or humour, but there weren't any; she was serious.

"I see" I said.

I sat for a few minutes, the eerie silence broken only by the ringing of telephones deep inside the building.

"Are you ready?" she said, standing up.

I shot up "Yes, of course"

"Relax Captain, he only hates the Jews, you'll be fine"

I wasn't sure what that meant, and it did little to ease my nerves.

She walked ahead of me, up two floors to a small door at the end of a long corridor lined with various suits of armour.

After checking her watch, she knocked three times, took a breath, and entered.

"Hauptsturmführer Deckman sir"

He was on the telephone, and just waved me in. She gave me an encouraging look, and walked out, closing the door behind her.

I was trapped. By the very man I was here to kill. Would he be able to tell? Read my mind somehow? I was petrified.

I remained standing at attention until he looked at me and gestured for me to sit. I sat watching him for a moment.

He was a handsome man, the incarnation of the perfect Aryan man; blonde hair, physically fit, tall, efficient. It felt wrong to think it, but the man seemed inspirational, I admired him instantly.

He put the phone down and regarded me with cold blue eyes.

"Deckman, Joseph Deckman. Twenty four years of age, German father, English mother. Wounded twice in combat; Poland and the Netherlands. Awarded the Knights Cross for valour in the Netherlands. Currently posted to Fliegerhorst Twente, under Obersturmbannführer Ecke. To be married to Gisela Becker. Nurse at Hohenlychen Sanatorium. You were posted here by the Reichsführer SS personally."

He sounded like a machine, rattling off stored information. He had clearly done his homework.

"Yes Obergruppenführer" I said. I wasn't sure what else I could say.

"Your progression through the ranks has been even faster than my own" he said evenly. No hint of emotion.

"Yes sir, I'm not sure how either to be honest"

"Hmm. Let's see. First promotion to Rottenführer by order of Himmler" he raised an eyebrow. "You seem to have caught the eye of the Reichsführer, Deckman."

"Yes sir"

"Second promotion to Untersturmführer upon graduating Bad Tolz academy. Third promotion to Obersturmführer by Standartenführer Von Harten. This was because?"

"He didn't want to send an UnterScharführer into the field sir. And I was to command the local SD office at Fliegerhorst Twente. He felt I should outrank the personnel already there. He also mentioned I could at least go to my death as a full Lieutenant, sir."

Was that a hint of a smile? "Makes sense. Fourth promotion to Hauptsturmführer by Obersturmbannführer Ecke?"

"Yes sir, following a recommendation by Major Von Graeve"

"The Fliegerhorst Kommandant?"

"Yes sir."

"Tell me, Deckman... Listening to what I just said, does it sound plausible to you?"

Oh no. "Sir?"

"The only promotion that doesn't make sense to me was your promotion to Captain. Explain to me, how you impressed the Kommandant of a Fliegerhorst, a Major in the Luftwaffe, so much in such a very short period of time, that he felt compelled to recommend you for promotion."

It made sense. It was suspicious. Verdammt. This man was good.

"I exposed two undesirables in my office sir, and solved a murder by doing so"

"Ah, yes. The homosexuals" he sounded disgusted just speaking the words. "Tell me how"

"Sir?"

"Tell me how you exposed them?"

"There was something off in the office sir. I noticed it as soon as I met the men."

"In what way?"

"Mencke outranked the other two men, but there was something more. They feared him. I don't know how to explain it"

"Hmm. Carry on"

"The train track to the Fliegerhorst had been sabotaged, and I asked Mencke to investigate. He concluded, quite naturally, that it was the work of the local resistance"

"That seems obvious. But then you ordered fourteen men to be rounded up and deported to Mauthausen?" He looked at me in surprise. Or was it a look of admiration?

"Yes sir. We had to send a clear message to the resistance that this would not be tolerated"

"Why fourteen?

"Sir?"

"Why fourteen men? Why not ten? Or twenty?"

What an odd thing to ask.

"I don't know sir, it was the first number that came to mind"

"How did Mencke react?"

"He seemed surprised"

"Why?"

"I run my command in a more relaxed fashion than most sir, I suppose he saw that as a sign of weakness"

"It is though, is it not?"

"I don't think so sir. I feel that men will never trust someone who rules by fear and intimidation."

"You know this how?" he seemed genuinely interested.

"I have experienced both on the battlefield sir. Successful combat units are run by men that the troops respect. Those run by tyrants do not do so well"

"Interesting theory" he thought for a moment. "You promoted one of your new Corporals to Staff Sergeant without knowing him. Why?"

"Two reasons sir. One, I needed a Staff Sergeant to run the office. Two, it bought me respect"

"You think respect can be bought?"

"No sir, but I felt it was required in order to establish myself as a fair, rewarding commander. I informed the other two Corporals that I reward good work, and they could expect promotion themselves if they worked well for me."

"You think this strategy works?"

"For me? Yes sir. I have three faithful, loyal men under my command"

"Interesting Deckman. Interesting."

"It's not a strategy I use lightly sir. I like to think I am a good judge of character"

"Really?" he raised his eyebrows. I didn't like the sound of this.

"Tell me, what is your opinion of the Reichsführer SS?"

And there it was. Damn.

"Sir?" I looked suitably uneasy.

"The Reichsführer SS, tell me your opinion of him."

The Reichsführer SS. How to describe him? Do I go ahead and refer to him as the horrid little chicken farmer? Do I lie? Tell the truth?

He must have sensed my unease.

"To put you at ease, I'll tell you my opinion. He's a pathetic little man. A chicken farmer no less! I have little respect for the man. He preaches of Aryan men, when he himself looks nothing like one!"

I was shocked.

"Yes sir" It was all I could think of saying. What was the point of this exercise? I wasn't sure, but decided to speak the truth. I had the feeling he'd know if I was lying.

"The Reichsführer scares me. He hides behind his power. A weak man, using an army as his muscle."

"Excellent. I knew you wouldn't lie to me. Now, tell me, what is his opinion of me?"

"He fears you sir"

"He does?"

"Yes sir. You are, or were, very close. The public perception is very much of a father and son type of relationship"

This made him laugh "It is?"

"Yes sir."

"He fears me?"

"Yes sir. He fears you will take over the SS, and his position."

"He is right"

I looked surprised. "It is?"

"Of course it is. It is the natural order of things Joseph. The young cub taking over from the old lion"

"Yes sir" Made sense.

"So, we get to the crux of the meeting"

"Sir?"

He leaned forward, and his eyes bored into mine. It was terrifying "Why are you here?"

"I'm here to kill you" The words spilled out before I could stop myself. He sat back in his seat, and assumed a pensive pose. "Thank you"

"Sir?"

"For not lying. I would have known if you had. It would not have ended well for you. But, I something told me you wouldn't lie to me Joseph"

I could feel my body shaking, what had I done? He'd have me killed. If he didn't, Himmler definitely would. Oh my God. Gisela.

"I would request you only punish me sir, my family and fiancée have no knowledge of why I am here"

"I have no interest in killing you Joseph. Or your family."

"Sir?"

"I respect you. I respect a man who faces death, and doesn't try to cheat his way out of it. You faced it like a man Joseph."

I didn't know what to say, so didn't say anything. I just stared at the man. Had I misjudged him? Had everyone? Or, was he exactly the calculating monster everyone thought he was? I was confused.

"You are a keen fencer?"

"Sir?"

"You fenced at Bad Tolz. You are good?"

"I, erm... I like to think I can hold my own sir"

"What foil do you have?"

"My parents presented me with a Leon Paul foil at my graduation sir"

"A fine weapon!" he beamed "I have the same"

"It is indeed a good weapon sir, perfectly balanced"

"My thoughts exactly. This evening. You and I, we will fence. See what you are made of"

"Sir?"

"Meet me here at seven. Bring your foil"

"Yes sir" I sensed the meeting was over, so stood, and saluted.

"No need for such formality Joseph" he smiled "See you at seven. Sharp"

"Yes sir"

I walked back downstairs to the reception, and collapsed onto the bench with a loud sigh.

"That went well I assume" the girl said.

"Yes, I rather think it did" I said with relief.

The telephone rang and she picked it up "Yes sir. Of course sir. I'll let him know sir"

I stood, and was about to leave when she stopped me "Captain? A moment if you please"

"Yes?"

"You must have made quite the impression"

"How so?"

"I am to draw up your promotion papers, congratulations Sturmbannführer Deckman"

"What?" What was happening?

"He wants me to inform you that you are now appointed his official personal Adjutant."

I couldn't believe what I was hearing. I was a Major? And Heydrich's personal assistant? My head spun, and I felt faint.

"He expects you in correct uniform this evening, Major. The quartermaster's office is on your map. I suggest you go there straight away."

"Of course. Tell me, where can I get a fencing uniform?"

"The quartermaster can help, he has a range of sizes. The Obergruppenführer is an avid swordsman, so he has to have them available for guests"

"That doesn't surprise me. Thank you"

"You are welcome Major Deckman"

"Joseph, please. Deckman sounds so formal"

She blushed "Maria"

"Pleased to meet you Maria. Thank you for your kindness" I smiled, and made my way to the quartermaster's office.

After trying on various sizes, I finally managed to put together a uniform for fencing. The breeches were a little big, but the next smaller size he had were too small. A compromise had to be made. He was rather reluctant to issue me with the Major insignia for my uniform without the requisite paperwork.

"It is rather unusual sir, I cannot issue rank badges without paperwork"

"I completely understand your position. I have, however, been ordered by Obergruppenführer Heydrich to meet him this evening in the correct uniform"

"No paperwork?" he asked.

"No, I don't have it yet, his secretary is currently filling it out for him to sign"

"Maria? Ah, one moment please sir, I'll telephone her" He picked up the receiver and dialed a number. After speaking to the exchange, he was put through to Maria. They spoke briefly, and he seemed satisfied.

"My apologies Major. I will get them for you now. You understand my predicament I hope?"

"Completely, I would do exactly the same in your position"

"Thank you sir" He went out back, and came back a few minutes later with my new shoulder and collar patches.

"I am indebted to you, many thanks" I said. "I hate to think how he would have reacted had I shown up not wearing them"

"If you need anything else, please let me know sir" he smiled

"Thank you, I will"

I collected my bundle of clothing, and made my way back to my room where I spent the next twenty or so minutes changing my insignia.

Farewell Hauptsturmführer Deckman, I thought as I threw the Captain patches into the bin. I checked myself in the mirror. "Pleased to meet you, Sturmbannführer Deckman" I smiled. I laughed. Major Deckman. Who'd have thought it possible? And Heydrich's personal assistant. It was highly unusual for a Major to be an adjutant, but this was Reinhard Heydrich; he could have a General as an assistant if it pleased him.

28. Dancing with the Devil.

At seven sharp, Maria showed me into Heydrich's office.
"Sturmbannführer Deckman sir" she said, and winked at me on her way out.
"Joseph, come, sit." He was sat on a sofa in the window, checking over his foil.
I set down my bag, and joined him.
"You have your foil? May I see?"
"Of course sir" I opened the case, and removed the foil for him to inspect.
He held the foil in his hand, testing the weight and balance. "A fine weapon Joseph" he smiled. "Your parents have exquisite taste"
He handed me back the foil, and I returned it to its case.
"Thank you sir"
"I hear good things about your fencing game, have you practised recently?"
"No sir, I haven't had the opportunity since Bad Tolz sadly"
"I'm sure you're quite the swordsman" he smiled.
"Likely not as accomplished as yourself sir" I said, complimenting him.
He waved his hand "Ach, I dabble" He did more than that. He was an extremely accomplished fencer, with many championship titles.
It was going to be tough, but I wasn't going to make it easy for him.
He finished cleaning his foil, and returned it to its case. "Come, we shall see how good you are" he winked. I followed him out of his office, and to the gymnasium. Fortunately, he led the way as I would never have found it on my own.

After changing into our fencing uniforms, we both spent a few minutes warming up. I had my own established routine, as did he.
After finishing his warm up, he stopped and looked at me, I nodded; I was ready.
We walked over to the piste, and took our positions on the En Garde lines. He lowered his mask "En Garde" I lowered my own, and assumed the starting position.
He started aggressively, with a lunge.

I was ready however, and parried his attack.

I went straight in with my Riposte, and he easily parried my attack.

We again took our En Garde positions. "En Garde" I said.

After ensuring I was balanced, I did a double lunge, which he parried, but I then hit him with my third lunge, which he obviously wasn't expecting. Score one for me. I doubted I would score another point, but I had made my mark.

"Excellent fake Joseph" he smiled, obviously impressed. A triple lunge is unusual, and I had worked hard to fit it into my routine.

We once again took up our positions. I didn't stand a chance; he started straight off with a Balestra, and the following lunge was so powerful, that my parry was easily beaten. One all. He had caught me completely off guard. I bowed, and returned to the start position.

He came at me again with a strong lunge, but I deflected his blade and lunged at him "Allez!" I scored my point. He lifted his mask "Superb attack au fer Joseph"

And so it went on for an hour or so. In the end, I managed to score three more points, but he had me beaten by almost twenty points.

"Your technique is strong, but I think you could do with a few more hours of practice. You're a worthy opponent" he held out his hand, and I shook it.

"Thank you sir, though I didn't really stand much of a chance against such a superb swordsman as yourself."

He shrugged "We are only as good as our last engagement"

Very true. I felt exhilarated. We showered afterwards, and he took me to the mess for a Schnapps.

"To your good health Joseph"

I raised my glass "To yours sir" We both sipped our drink, and set them down.

"I can only stay a short time I'm afraid, I have to get back to my family" He said.

"I understand sir. I will not be long for bed anyway"

"Tell me about your mother" he said out of the blue.

Completely off guard, I had to think quickly. "My mother?
Well, she was born in England sir, as you know.

She was an English lecturer in Stratford upon Avon before meeting my father. They married, and moved to Austria. She took German citizenship after their marriage. She now works as his assistant"

"And you speak fluent English?" he asked in English.

"Yes sir, I do. I spent a few years in an English school"

"You speak without a trace of a German accent"

"Yes sir, I speak English with my parents at home"

"Most curious" he smiled. "And tell me, how is your Dutch?"

"I can speak Dutch without an accent also. I attended school in Leiden for two years"

"Fascinating. No wonder Ecke wanted you"

"Sir?"

"He was quite insistent on your posting to the Fliegerhorst, which I found very puzzling"

"How so sir?"

"He doesn't know you, so why would he be so insistent that you be posted there?"

"He knows my mother sir, they were friends before the war, when he visited England"

"Ah, of course. It makes sense to me now." he finished his drink.

"I'll see you in the morning Joseph. Thank you for a pleasant evening" He stood, and picked up his briefcase.

I stood to attention. "Good evening Obergruppenführer"

"Good evening Joseph".

And then he was gone. I fell back down into my seat. What had that been about? He had a habit of catching you completely off guard.

I made a mental note to be more prepared for such conversations in future. Had I just given him what he needed? A link between Ecke and my Mother.

I let out a loud sigh, and finished my drink. I had fenced with the devil and lost. I only hoped I wouldn't lose the entire match. I had a mission to accomplish.

In the meantime, I needed a brandy. I held up my hand, and a steward came over.

"Sir?"

"A large brandy please".

I sat in silence, and enjoyed the surprisingly fine brandy. I had a lot to think over. With unprecedented access to my target, I could strike at any moment and complete my mission.

But he knew my intentions. He knew, and *still* took me into his inner circle.

What was his plan? What was my plan?

I didn't have one that covered this particular set of circumstances.

I couldn't stop asking myself what his intentions were. Would he want me to strike at Himmler? That would be impossible. If it was difficult to get at Heydrich, Himmler was on a whole different level.

This was doing me no good. I went back to my room and wrote to Gisela. I needed to take my mind off the Heydrich problem.

I told her how much I desperately wanted to see her, and hoped that we could be wed soon. It killed me that I couldn't tell her all about what was happening. But, Feldpost letters were very much likely read by the Gestapo, and I didn't want to give them anything to investigate.

I kept it perfectly innocent, and asked her to write at her earliest convenience as I was desperate for word from her. It had worked somewhat; Heydrich was at the back of my mind by the time I went to bed.

Fortunately, I didn't have an early start; Heydrich wanted me in his office at ten, ready for him to arrive at 10.30. It was a late start, which was unusual. But, from what Maria had told me, he did work until late at night.

I had requested a nine o'clock wakeup, and it was already past midnight. I needed to sleep. I turned off the light and lay down.

It took some time to fall asleep, and when I did, my dreams were dominated by a devil like creature chasing me around a labyrinth with a fencing foil. I slept badly as a result.

When the steward knocked on my door, it was like I hadn't slept at all. "Thank you" I said, and he left. I sat up, and breathed deeply. I was exhausted after a terrible night's sleep. But, I needed to be fresh and full of energy when I reported for duty. This new routine was going to be tough, especially if he kept me busy until late in the evenings.

The next week was spent reporting for duty at ten o'clock sharp every morning, and liaising with the various departments within the local SD area.

It took me a few days to get to grips with who was whom in the hierarchy, but I got there eventually.

The man himself was a machine.

He turned up for work at 10.30 exactly each morning, and often didn't go home until after nine or ten.

We fenced almost every other day, and although he beat me every time, the scores were getting closer and closer. Soon, I'd have him. Today, we'd been for a meeting at the mayor's office, and it was getting close to dinner time when we finally returned to our office. It had been some time since I'd had the opportunity to talk to him alone, and thought today might be my chance. Sadly, it was not to be. He called for his car; a large open top Mercedes staff car. I had mentioned on several occasions that I would like to increase security when he drove to and from his home. But he would always respond with "Ach, Joseph. If I increase security, it shows fear. They should fear me, not the other way around"

I didn't agree of course, but he ignored my protests. Today, I was too tired to argue, so I let him go without comment. I was tired. It was almost eight, and I hadn't eaten since breakfast. Exhausted, I made my way to the mess for a quick dinner. After that; bed.

The following day, Heydrich called me to his office, just before five in the evening. I picked up my diary, and went to his office. He was sat on the sofa by the window, looking though some photographs.

"Yes Obergruppenführer?"

"Come, Joseph, sit with me"

I went over, and sat on the opposite end of the sofa.

"You recall our conversation on the first day you came here?"

"Yes sir"

"Good. Your fifth promotion. Tell me about it" Was he serious?

I couldn't read his face, and wasn't about to question him, so told him about my fifth promotion.

"My fifth promotion to Sturmbannführer, by Obergruppenführer Heydrich."

"Yes. Interesting. Why do you think he promoted somebody he barely knew?"

Was this a trick of sorts?

"In my opinion sir, the Obergruppenführer promoted me and made me his adjutant to keep me close. If I was close, he could keep an eye on me. I was to be his assassin after all, something which fascinated him. He wanted to get a measure of the man, and to do that, I'd need to be in his life on a daily basis. What better way to do that than to make me his adjutant."

"Excellent reasoning" he smiled. It was a cold smile. "My would-be assassin. Tell me, do you still have plans to carry out your mission?"

"If I did, I would have had ample opportunity to have done so by now"

"Quite so. That doesn't say much about my personal safety"

"I wish you would increase your security detail" I said.

"Don't be a broken record Joseph, you know I won't"

"I hope my protests are duly noted"

"They are. Are you available this evening? Come to the theatre, meet my family, have a few drinks. You can stay overnight in the guest room. And, if it sets your mind at ease, you can drive the car and be my security detail"

"I'd love to sir" I said. He picked up on my tone.

"But...?"

"But I am exhausted sir, and just want to get to bed. You work me like a slave"

He laughed "Very well Joseph, go to your bed. Maybe tomorrow night? I'll get the cook to source some beef"

"Tomorrow night would be a pleasure sir, I look forward to it"

He smiled, and picked up his telephone "Maria, please tell Klein to bring the car around"

I closed the door behind me, and walked back to my room.

He was off to the theatre to watch a performance of his father's opera Amen. I was not a fan of the opera, and was glad he'd excused me from going. We'd have another of our fencing duels tomorrow night, and I wanted to practice a new move I'd been developing. After leaving his office, I went straight to the gymnasium and practiced until I had the move perfected.

Tomorrow, I'd beat him. But, for now, it was late and I was tired. Wearily, I showered and changed.

Once safely back in my room, tiredness overcame me, and I fell asleep in my clothes.

29. Prague, 27 May 1942.

The following morning, I reported for duty at ten, as always. After sorting through the mail and various reports, I went in and prepared his office, ordered coffee, and laid out the daily newspapers.

I checked the clock; 10.04. All was ready, and I had some time to spare, so I went down to see Maria.

"Maria, have you heard from Heydrich?" Informally, between the two of us, we referred to him as Heydrich. Never when anyone else was around of course.

"Yes, well no, but I heard from Johannes. He telephoned earlier and said they were about to leave, and will arrive at the usual time."

Despite having worked with him for a while, I continued to be filled with nervousness and dread anticipating his arrival. I had perfected my routine, and he seemed happy with it. Yet I was still afraid I'd do something wrong, and for him to turn on me as a result. He just seemed like that kind of person; nice, but with the ability to turn on you in an instant. I did not want to be on the receiving end of his wrath.

"Very well, let me know when you hear the car"

"I will" she smiled. If she heard the car, it meant I had enough time to run downstairs and meet him at the main entrance. I sat down at my desk, and went through some reports, sorting them in order of importance. The sun was shining in through the window, and I thought of Heydrich driving here with the roof down on the car, enjoying the sunny morning.

I was just reading the last report, when Maria came crashing into my office "There's been an attack!" she shouted.

"What?"

"An attack! The car was attacked on its way here!"

I shot up, and looked from the window. Down below, I saw several trucks parked up with armed soldiers running towards them. Officers were busy shouting orders, and the whole scene seemed slightly chaotic. An attack? Was he hurt?

"Is he alive?" I turned to Maria.

"I don't know" she sobbed.

"Hey, I'm sure it will all be fine. I'll go and find out"

I left her crying in my office and ran out into the busy courtyard.

I spotted Gruppenführer Mansfeld, and ran over to him.

"Sir, what has happened? Is the Obergruppenführer alive?"

"Deckman. Yes, he's badly wounded, and was taken to Bulovka Hospital"

"What happened?"

"I am unsure, but it appears the Czech resistance tried to assassinate him"

Oh no. They carried out the assassination attempt without telling me.

"I'm going to the hospital" I said, and turned to leave.

"You're staying here Deckman" He barked.

I turned back to face him "I need to see how he is" I said.

"No, you do not. You will remain here, that's an order. Get on a telephone and inform to the Reichsführer, he is yet to be told. I'm leading the search for the resistance men"

I had no choice. Mansfeld hated me; he did not agree with my promotion, and was jealous of my closeness to the Obergruppenführer. Damn.

Dejected, I went back inside and up to Heydrich's office. Maria had calmed herself somewhat, and was back at her desk.

"Maria, get me the Reichsführer SS on the telephone, immediately"

I went inside, and sat heavily in his chair. What was going on? I was supposed to be there! Was he dead? Alive? Why hadn't they contacted me to let me know what the plan was? I was incredibly angry. The phone rang, I picked up the receiver and barked "Yes?"

Maria whimpered "The Reichsführer SS sir" There was a click, and then I heard his voice.

"Joseph?"

"Sir. There's been an assassination attempt on Heydrich"

"What? By whom? Is he dead?"

"I don't know sir. It appears it was the Czech resistance, details are vague. Heydrich is alive, but badly wounded, and being treated in hospital."

There was silence. "Sir?"

"I'll send down my personal physician, and talk to the Führer at once"

"Sir...?" but the line was dead.

I put the receiver down, and sat back in the chair. This was not good.

Heydrich wounded, god alone knows how badly, and Himmler angry that the attempt had failed. He had not said as much over the phone; he was too careful to do that.

There was a knock on the door, and Maria entered.

"Forgive me, but is there any news?" she asked quietly.

"Nothing, I am as much in the dark as you are. They won't let me see him"

"Has there been any news about Johannes?"

Klein. The driver. I hadn't even thought about him.

"Can you put me through to Bulovka hospital?" I asked her.

"I can try" she said, and went out to her telephone. A moment later, my phone rang. I picked up "Hospital reception for you sir" There was you usual click, and I was connected.

"Main reception desk"

"This is Sturmbannführer Deckman, do you have an Oberscharführer Johannes Klein there?"

"One moment please Sturmbannführer". There was a long pause, then "Hello? Yes, we do. He is being treated for gunshot wounds"

"Gunshot wounds?"

"Yes sir, it says here he arrived with two gunshot wounds to his leg. He is currently in surgery"

"Any idea when he will be out of surgery?"

"I'm afraid not sir, it could be five minutes or four hours"

"I understand. I shall telephone again in an hour"

"Very well sir"

I hung up. "He's in surgery, shot twice in the leg"

"Oh no" she put her hands to her mouth. "Will he survive?"

"They don't know. I will call again in an hour to see if there is any news"

She didn't look convinced. "Hey, it will all be fine. If it was really serious they would have told me"

They wouldn't have of course, but saying it made her feel slightly better. She and Johannes were an item, something I'd only recently discovered.

"What do we do now?" she said "There's nobody here to run the office"

"We will run it as best we can until he returns" I said confidently.
What if he doesn't" she asked.

"He will. But, if he doesn't, I'm sure a replacement will be put in place sharply. Best thing we can do right now is return to our duties"

She wiped her eyes, nodded, and went out to her desk.

We telephoned the hospital a few more times during the day, and finally got the news that Klein was out of surgery, and he would be fine. It was a relief to us both.

The following days passed slowly for us. I was still denied access to Heydrich, but we at least now knew he was still alive. I had taken up station at his desk in order to run the department in the absence of a replacement. It was there, that on 30 May I received a telephone call. I was sat reading a depressing report on labour camp deportation numbers, when the telephone rang. I picked up "Hello?"

"Reichsführer SS for you sir" Maria said. There was the usual click, and Himmler spoke.

"Joseph, how are things going?"

"As well as can be expected sir"

"These are difficult times for us all. I will be traveling down tonight, and will be visiting the Obergruppenführer in hospital tomorrow"

"I'm sure he would appreciate seeing you sir"

"Have you been in to see him?"

Odd question. "No sir, I have been prevented from visiting him"

"Hmm. We'll see about that. I will come to see you in the Obergruppenführer's office after my visit to the hospital at ten tomorrow morning"

"Yes sir" there was a click, and he was gone. Did he mean he'd be here at ten, or seeing Heydrich at ten? Didn't matter. He was coming here. I wasn't sure what I could tell him, and that scared me.

There was no point worrying over it, it would only keep me awake all night, and I needed my wits about me tomorrow.

I finished early, and did a couple of hours of fencing practice, followed by dinner with Maria. The poor girl was in a bit of a state, but the good news about Johannes should improve that somewhat. He would have a permanent limp, but was otherwise fine

We had a nice meal in the officer's mess, and enjoyed a nice brandy after. I escorted her back to her quarters, and then made my way back to my own.

I wrote to Gisela, frustrated that I couldn't tell her about what had happened. Still, it eased my mind. In my imagination, I was talking to her. I was imagining responses to my questions, but found that I was already starting to forget the sound of her voice.

I feared a bad night; my mind would not stop. And I was right.

My night was tormented by dreams of Himmler, and a fully recuperated Heydrich killing people at random with an insatiable bloodlust.

I woke the following morning after perhaps a couple of hours sleep. Groggily, I made my way to the shower room and stood under a lukewarm stream of water for a good ten minutes. Slowly but surely, my body woke up. After dressing, I made my way to the mess for breakfast, and plenty of strong tea. What I really craved was coffee, but that was back at the Fliegerhorst. Strong tea did the job though.

30. Bulovka Hospital.

Later that morning I was sat in the office, nervously awaiting Himmler's arrival. I had managed to work out that he was visiting Heydrich at ten, so would be here any time after that. I checked my watch for the twentieth time that morning. It was almost twelve. Perhaps I should go for lunch? Would I have time? I sighed, and sank back into the chair. As soon as I did, I heard vehicles pull into the courtyard below. I got up and looked through the window onto the courtyard below. A procession of vehicles and motorcycle guards had just parked up. I saw Himmler alight from the middle vehicle and walk inside. I stood, checked my uniform, and made ready to meet him. There was a knock on the door and Maria led Himmler inside.

"Thank you Maria" I said, and she quietly closed the door on her way out.

"Good morning Joseph" Himmler said, taking off his peaked cap and gloves.

"Good morning sir" I stood aside to let him sit behind the desk, but he surprised me by sitting in the chair opposite instead. "Sit, Joseph" I sat. "How is the Obergruppenführer sir?"

"He seems in good spirits" he said evenly. In other words, he was disappointed he was still alive.

"They failed" I said.

"Yes, they failed. However, you will not." he reached inside his jacket pocket and placed a vial on the desk in front of me. Inside the vial was a colourless liquid.

"Poison?" I asked.

"Of sorts. Leaves no trace."

I took the vial, and put it in my pocket.

"Does it need to be ingested in a certain way?" I asked.

"No, can be added to any drink, or just ingested on its own."

How would I get him to do that? Poison? Too many ways for it to go wrong.

"I know what you're thinking; poison, unreliable. But, I have faith in you Joseph"

"Yes sir"

"You are cleared to visit any time. Might I suggest you go immediately?"

"Yes sir"

"Very good. I look forward to hearing the good news" he said, and picked up his cap "Don't let me down"

"I won't sir"

He nodded, and left.

Just like that. Poison an SS General. And hopefully get away with it. No problem...

But I was permitted to visit. I waited for the motorcade to leave, then ran down to my vehicle and drove to the hospital.

I checked in with reception, and went up to what apparently used to be a Doctor's office, but had temporarily been turned into a private room for Heydrich. After I got past the guards in the adjacent room, I knocked on the open door. He was sat up in bed, looking out of the window, his Luger pistol on the bedside table. He turned, and looked at me evenly.

"Joseph" he said "Come in. Close the door behind you"

I entered, closed the door, and joined him at his bedside.

"Please, sit" I did as ordered.

"How are you feeling sir?" He waved my question away.

"Before we talk, I need to know if you were involved" He looked at me, daring me to lie.

I met his gaze. "I was not involved"

He regarded me for a moment, then smiled. "I believe you"

My relief was immense. I had feared he wouldn't believe me, and my life was to end, right here in this hospital room.

"I feel fine" he said.

"Sir?"

"You asked, I replied. Simple"

"Ah, good. That is good to hear sir"

"Can't wait to get out of here though, I tell you. If I have to kill a thousand Czechs, I will find who did this to me"

His words hit like daggers. Thousands? Any hopes of him being reasonable had been wiped out with that one sentence.

He coughed. "Be a good man and get me some water would you, I'm parched"

"Of course" I went to the small sink in the corner and filled a glass with water from the tap. Without thinking, I emptied the vial into it. I then filled another glass, and went back to his bedside.

"Here sir" I said, handing him the poisoned water. "To your good health" I raised my glass.

"Thank you" he said and raised his. He drank the whole glass in one go, as did I. He grimaced "Ugh, even the water is foul in this place!"

I faked a grimace "Yes sir, it is quite horrid" My heart was pounding in my chest.

We sat and talked for a while about work. He was keen to get back and to start his now investigation into the assassination attempt.

He asked if I had been keeping up with my fencing practice, and I told him that I had, and was looking forward to finally beating him when he was well enough. He laughed heartily. "You would take advantage of a weakened man?"

"Yes sir, I would, if it allowed me to finally beat him" We both laughed.

His doctor entered, and said "That's enough excitement for one day I'm afraid. You need to rest"

Heydrich held up his hands in defeat, and looked at me. "Doctors' orders" he said apologetically.

"Its fine sir, I have work to get back to"

"Good man, go find them for me Joseph"

"I will sir" I lied. We shook hands, and I turned to leave.

"Joseph, one more thing"

"Sir?" I turned back to face him.

He looked at the doctor who reluctantly said "Very well. I shall wait outside" and walked out, closing the door behind him.

"Joseph" he looked serious "In the event of my death, I need you to do something for me"

"Sir?"

He handed me a small key "Behind the painting on the wall of my office is a small safe. The contents are yours to do with as you please."

"What is in it?"

"That doesn't matter right now, I just need you to promise you will not leave it behind"

I looked at the key in my hand. "I promise"

"Good man" he said smiling. "Tell the doctor he can come back in"
I walked out, and told the doctor we were finished.
As I walked down the corridor, I checked my hands; they were shaking badly. Had he noticed?
I had no idea what was in the vial, or how long it would take to affect him. But, it was done. There was no turning back. And what exactly was in this safe? What could be so important that I *had* to take it?
My heart was pounding as I descended the stairs and made my way back to my vehicle. I got in the car and closed the door.
Only then did I let my emotions out. I didn't cry, but was close to it. Not because of his condition, but because out of absolute fear.
After a couple of minutes, I gathered myself, and was ready to drive back. As I drove away from the hospital, I had a sudden urge to see where it happened. It took a while to find, as I wasn't familiar with Prague at all.
But, when I got there, it was fairly obvious as the place was roped off for investigation. I parked up, and walked over. I found the spot where the car had stood, and saw the damage to the roadway where the grenade had detonated. I looked around. Why would he order Klein to stop? Surely the best course of action was to accelerate away? An error in judgement, or just plain arrogance? The grenade had blown a hole in the rear side of the vehicle, sending shrapnel and parts of the interior padding into his body. His spleen had been pierced, his lung deflated, and he had a broken rib. The pain must have been incredible, yet he managed to get out of the car, and give chase to one of the attackers, even managing to get some shots off. It was a testament to the man's physical fitness. Incredible.

Some three days later, Maria came to find me in my office. She was crying. "Maria, whatever is the matter?"
"He's gone" she said.
"Gone? Who?"
"He died this morning"
"Oh my God" I said. "Oh my God. He'd seemed fine, I don't understand" I did, but couldn't admit to it, not even to Maria.
"I heard he had recovered, and was doing fine, but suddenly doubled over in pain" she continued.
"I was going to visit with him this afternoon. When did it happen?"

"He fell ill around lunchtime yesterday, and passed away in the early hours of this morning"

"I can't believe it. He seemed fine" I repeated. Mostly for effect though, as on the inside, I was glad it had worked. Relieved more than anything.

Maria was crying. I took her in my arms "Go home Maria, be with Johannes"

She thanked me, and went back to her quarters. Good. I wanted to be alone. There would be no need for me to inform Himmler; he likely already knew. He had been stationed in Heydrich's office for the last few days, personally coordinating the investigation.

I carried on with my work, sifting through the letters and reports that had piled up on my desk. There were many of them, and I was making good headway when my telephone rang.

"Deckman"

"Joseph, come see me"

"Yes sir" I hung up. Himmler.

I went up the stairs and stood outside the door for a long moment. I took a deep breath, knocked, and entered.

"Joseph, enter" I went in and closed the door behind me. "Come" He indicated for me to sit. I walked to the desk and sat. "You have done me a great service" He smiled.

"Thank you sir"

"The autopsy was clear of poison, as expected." he added.

"That's' good sir" I said, relieved. Autopsy? So soon? He was in a hurry.

He looked at me with a curiously comical look on his face "Do you know what his last words were?" he chuckled.

"No" Hopefully not *"Joseph Deckman poisoned me"* I thought.

"The water was foul" he said. "Can you believe that?"

"What?" I asked, incredulously.

"He whispered that the water was foul. That was all"

"He knew"

"Yes, it would appear so, wouldn't it?"

"His last act was to protect me" I couldn't believe it.

"You must have made quite the impression on him"

I didn't respond.

I was too busy processing what I'd just heard. He knew it was me. He'd probably known when he drank it. He'd probably known before then, which is why he asked for water. To protect me. I looked up at the wall behind Himmler; there was the painting. How was I going to get into the safe? I'd have to wait for him to leave and sneak in this evening.

"I am generous to those who help me Joseph, and I am a man of my word" He handed me an envelope. I opened it, it was my signed marriage permit. "And here" he said, passing me some keys and some documents. "My wedding gift"

"Sir?"

"A nice home in Garmisch" He smiled. "It is where you want to live is it not?"

"Yes, yes I suppose so sir" I looked at the documents, they were the ownership deeds to a house. I didn't recognise the address, but had no doubt that it was something special.

"Thank you sir, I don't know what to say"

"Say nothing Joseph, it is not necessary"

"Yes sir"

"One more thing" he opened his drawer and took put a small package. "Stand please"

I did as ordered. He rose, and walked around the desk.

"Sturmbannführer Joseph Deckman, it is with great delight that I present on behalf of the Führer, the Oak Leaves to the Knights Cross. He pinned the Oak Leaves to my medal.

"Thank you sir" On behalf of the Führer? I doubted that Hitler knew anything about this award. It was yet another part of his generosity.

"Quite. Now Joseph" he said, sitting back behind his desk "You will return immediately to your duties in the Netherlands, and marry your young bride when Obersturmbannführer Ecke sees fit to grant you leave"

"A request, sir. If I may?"

"Yes?" he raised an eyebrow.

"I would very much like to attend the state funeral, pay my respects" He thought for a long moment. "Out of the question"

"To be honest sir, if I may?"

He nodded.

"I don't care if it's a good idea or not. I considered him a friend of sorts, and he thought enough of me to protect me even when he knew he was dying by my hand"

Silence.

"Very well. I will arrange it"

"Thank you sir" There was nothing else; our meeting was over. I stood and saluted him. "Heil Hitler" He limply returned my salute without looking up, and I left.

The administration office issued me with my travel documents and transfer orders. I booked the first available flight to Berlin, which fortunately wasn't until early tomorrow morning. After spending some time in the gymnasium, I went back up to my office, and gathered my belongings. Himmler had long since left, so I had my opportunity to retrieve the contents of the safe. The whole building was quiet, so I walked over to Heydrich's office and opened the safe. Inside were some photographs of his family, his passport, Soldbuch, a Luger, some money, a couple of small gold bars, and a sealed folder. I didn't have time to sort through it, so I took out everything and put it in my briefcase. Once done, I locked the safe, re-hung the painting, and left. As I was walking down the stairs, I had a sudden thought. I turned back and ran back upstairs and into the office. Heydrich's prized statue of The Fencer was stood on the desk. I picked it up and left.

I had a quiet dinner in the mess, and then went to bed early. I was tired; not physically, but mentally. It had been a tough day.
I slept through the night for the first time in a long while. In fact, I slept so well that I barely made it to the airfield in time for my flight. Looking down at the world below, it seemed peaceful, like there was no war at all. How I longed for the day when it was true. Sadly, the spell was broken when we came in to land in Berlin and I saw the fighter aircraft, flak batteries, and barrage balloons.
I was tired, and longing for a bed. It took a while to find transport to headquarters, but I eventually managed to find a friendly Standartedführer who offered me a lift in his staff car.
After staying overnight at headquarters, I took the earliest possible train back to Enschede.

31. Fliegerhorst Twente.

The train pulled into the station just before lunch time, and I went straight to the office to collect my vehicle. Ecke was out. That was good, as I was not in the mood to talk to anyone. I was hungry, and needed a drink. More than anything, I needed a drink. My nerves were shot, I needed a break.

Seeing Gisela would heal me. I would speak to Ecke tomorrow to request leave.

As I drove to the Fliegerhorst, I took my time, enjoying the fresh air in my face. The guard at the gate recognised me "Welcome back Hauptsturmführer" he smiled as I stopped to let him check my papers. "Apologies sir. Welcome back Sturmbannführer"

I smiled "Thank you Stefan"

He smiled broadly, delighted that I had remembered his name.

He had told me when I had given him the chocolate when I had departed.

I parked the kübelwagen outside the mess, and went inside. It was well after lunch time by now, and the place was deserted. I spoke to the head steward, and begged for something to eat. He had buttered bread and some soup left over.

"Thank you, that would be great, I am starving"

I sat in the window, looking out over the farmers' fields, and enjoyed my lunch.

"Mind if I join you?"

I stood to attention "Herr Major, of course, please, sit"

Von Graeve sat opposite me. "No need to be so formal Joseph, we are of equal rank now I see" he smiled "Congratulations. And the Oak Leaves no less. You *have* had a successful posting"

"Not really sir, I am glad to be back" I said dejected. He sensed my desperation for solitude.

"I won't ask. I just wanted to say it's good to have you back"

"Thank you. I will be meeting with Ecke tomorrow, and will come see you after if that suits?"

"I will be in my office all afternoon, drop by any time"

He smiled, and left. I sat alone once more, lost in thought. Thoughts of how he must have felt when he realised it was me. Did he feel betrayal?

I like to think his sense of duty was such that he understood I had to do it. If I didn't someone else would.

After lunch, I unpacked, and put my laundry in. I took the opportunity to order some new shirts, as I was running low. Once I'd squared away my kit, I walked to the office, ensuring I had my briefcase safely with me.

I stood at the door for a moment and listened. Inside, I could hear the clacking of typewriters, and some jovial conversation. Smiling to myself, I opened the door and walked in.

"Afternoon gentlemen"

All three hurried to their feet and stood to attention.

"Welcome back sir" Dietz said, then noted my new rank and said "Welcome back Sturmbannführer"

"Thank you Dietz. How's things been here?"

"All good sir, report submitted promptly every Thursday morning"

"Excellent Dietz, excellent."

"There is an urgent message for you sir" he went to his desk and picked up a telegram.

"This came this morning" he handed me the envelope.

I opened it and read.

From: Office of Reichsführer SS
To: Sturmbannführer Joseph Deckman

Joseph,

Your name added to access list for Berlin funeral ceremony 09 June
We are now even.

Signed: Himmler.

I was going to the funeral. Thank heaven for small mercies. We were even; I couldn't care less. I had killed one man, in return I had received promotion, honour, a home, and a wife. A fair trade?

I still wasn't sure. The guilt I felt weighed heavy on my mind. Would it ever go away?

"Bad news sir?" I heard Dietz asking from what seemed kilometers away.

"Hmm? No. No, not at all. It would appear that I'll be leaving for Berlin today"

"But you only just returned from Berlin?" he said, confused.

"I am attending Obergruppenführer Heydrich's funeral"

"A great honour sir" he said reverently.

"Yes, I suppose it is" I said absently. I'd have to go back to my lodgings immediately to pack.

"Call flight control and find out if there are any flights headed to Berlin today"

"Yes sir" he went off to telephone the flight control office. Hopefully there would be something. Anything would be better than the train. Dietz had a brief conversation with whomever was on the other end of the line, then asked "A plane is leaving in forty minutes sir"

"Excellent, I'll take it" Forty minutes! I'd barely have time. Dietz spoke some more on the telephone, then hung up.

"All arranged sir. If you pack, I'll drive you to the airfield"

"Thanks Dietz" I said, and ran up to my office. I took all the items from Heydrich's safe from my briefcase and locked them securely in my own safe. I put the statue on my desk, then went back to my room to pack. I carefully placed my parade uniform and boots in the case, along with a couple of clean shirts and whatever else I'd need for the brief journey. Outside, Dietz was waiting for me in the car, engine running. I jumped in, and we sped off.

32. The Funeral.

The old ME 110 that was to take me to Berlin was already idling on the field. The pilot waved, and I went over. After placing my case in the hold, I put on my parachute, and with great difficulty climbed up into the back-seat. I strapped in, put on the head set, and indicated to the pilot that I was ready. He responded by increasing engine power. We taxied slowly to the end of the runway, and turned into the wind. We stood for a moment whilst he made his final checks. The engines went into full power, and we accelerated down the bumpy runway until we gained sufficient lift to let us take off. We climbed steadily up into the clouds, and turned onto our target bearing. The cloud level was way below us, so I couldn't see any land at all, just white cloud. What seemed like an eternity later, we started our descent into Berlin. As we broke through the cloud, I could see the funeral procession at the Reichs Chancellery. The streets were lines with thousands of people. The pilot flew over a couple of times, so we got a good look. The line of people waiting to pay their respects snaked back for what looked like kilometers.

Walking through the airport terminal half an hour later, it was equally busy with people arriving from far and wide for the funeral. Ahead of me, there was a bit of a stir. I strained to see what it was, and saw Goebbels with his family walking out to waiting cars. His wife Magda, looked very glamorous, dressed all in black, with a black veil. They waved to the ecstatic onlookers, then the family climbed into their waiting vehicles and disappeared.

Walking to headquarters was not an option; thousands of people blocked every street. Fortunately, an SS staff car pulled up, and two Captains jumped out. I ran over, and threw my case onto the back-seat before the driver could speed away. "You are returning to headquarters?" I asked.

"Yes sir" he said, and drove off. The going was slow, as some streets had been closed off for the funeral procession.

We eventually made it after almost forty minutes. I thanked the driver, pushed my way through the crowds, and went inside.

I joined the queue for the front desk. It was busy, and I held out little hope of securing a room. After fifteen minutes, the staff officer stood on his desk and shouted "There are only two rooms left, given out in rank order"

I think he meant highest ranking officers in the queue got the rooms, so I stuck up my hand.

He pointed at me "Sturmbannführer"

Someone else stuck up their hand "Obersturmbannführer" He was invited to come forward and register. One left. No other hands went up, meaning it was mine, much to the disappointment of the many remaining men standing in line.

I was glad to finally be alone in the silence of my room. I lay out my parade uniform, and ensured my boots and belt buckle were polished. When I went down for an early dinner, I found the mess packed to capacity. The head steward looked at me apologetically.

"Sorry Sturmbannführer, we're full"

"I'm happy to eat in my room if I can secure a plate of food, and perhaps some tea?"

He looked relieved. "Of course sir, one moment" he went out to the kitchen and returned a few minutes later with a large tray containing cheese, meats, a couple of eggs, bread, butter, and a pot of tea.

"Excellent, thank you very much" I took the tray and went back to my room.

I ate my dinner hastily, as I had little time left to change into my parade uniform and make my way to the Chancellery where the funeral ceremony was being held.

The funeral was something I would never forget, great pomp and circumstance, Nazi propaganda at its best. I was far away from the front, but was at least allowed to attend after my plea to Himmler. The ceremony moved me. Not the fakery of the speeches, though I thought that Hitler himself was no doubt completely genuine and sincere. He was not aware of Himmler's involvement in his Aryan hero's death.

It was the first time I'd laid eyes on our Führer. He looked smaller and frailer that I had expected. It was altogether anticlimactic.

Himmler's speech was pathetic. Only because I knew it was all false. I had no respect left for the man.

He called Heydrich a truly great SS man, and thanked him for his unwavering loyalty and wonderful friendship. Hypocritical bastard. After the ceremony ended, I caught Himmler's eye. He nodded. I nodded back.

Needing to get away, I started walking away when a woman's voice stopped me.

"Excuse me, Major?"

I turned to find a woman waving at me and making her way towards me through the crowd. It was Lina Heydrich, I recognised her from the photograph on Heydrich's desk.

"Frau Heydrich" I said, bowing my head in respect "My deepest condolences"

"Thank you Joseph. You are Joseph are you not?" She asked kindly.

"Yes Frau Heydrich"

"He spoke so very fondly of you, you know? He enjoyed your company immensely"

"Thank you"

She smiled. "He'd want you to have this" she said, handing me his foil case. "I had so hoped you would come today, so I could give it to you, and let you know how fond of you he was"

I took the case "Thank you. I, I don't know what to say" A tear ran down my cheek. She took out her handkerchief and wiped it away.

"There are times" she said "When words are not necessary, we speak through our actions"

"Thank you Frau Heydrich, I shall treasure this forever"

She smiled, turned, and was lost in the crowd.

I walked away feeling deeply sad. He had been every inch the monster that people said he was. He had been a truly evil man. But, I liked him. I liked the small part of him that wasn't evil. I couldn't help it, there was just something about him.

Inside the case I found a photograph of the two of us, he had insisted on it one evening after fencing. We were both in our fencing uniforms, smiling like the best of friends. On the back, in his handwriting, it said "Prague 1942. To my friend Joseph, one day you'll beat me!" underneath was his signature. Sadly, I would never get the chance. In fact, I rarely fenced again.

It was a photograph I would treasure for the rest of my life.

The flight back to the Fliegerhorst was uneventful. We made a bumpy landing on the grass runway, and came to a halt. Wearily, I got up, and climbed out. I retrieved my case from the hold, and made my way to the accommodation block. It was late, and I was tired. I closed the door, and sat on the bed. What a day. I opened the case and took out the foil.

It was a beautiful weapon, with the same Italian grip as my own. It had the initials RTH engraved in elegant script on the guard. I placed it back in the case and stared for a moment at the photograph. He'd known. He knew it was me who had poisoned him. "I'm sorry" I said, and dropped the photo back in the case. I closed it, and slid it under my bed. Then I lay down. I felt terrible sadness. And also something else; Guilt.

That was what I was feeling. I thought it had been grief, but it was guilt.

He was my friend, and I had killed him.

I needed to talk to someone about it, I needed someone to tell me that he was a murderous bastard and deserved to die. That someone was Gisela. How I longed to see her!

Sleep came rapidly, and I was glad when it did; I was exhausted.

33. Ecke and Reality.

The following morning, I slept until almost nine. I had needed it, and could probably have slept longer, but I really needed to see Ecke. Reluctantly, I got up and showered. I looked in the mirror, then looked away; I did not want to face myself today. As I dressed, I wondered if Ecke had managed to get the section of microfiche film to the British. Only one way to find out.

I went down to the mess, and although I was late, the cook made me scrambled eggs to celebrate my return. I was extremely grateful as I needed a good start to my day. After drinking my tea, I drove to Enschede.

If I was being honest to myself, I was dreading going into work today. It had been a long time since I'd seen or heard from Ecke, not to mention the resistance, or the other Group members. Being removed from it all had done me good, and I wasn't sure I was ready to dive back into that world right now. I was mentally tired, and desperately needed a break. But, duty calls. I parked up outside, and walked in.

"Morning Oskar, is the old man in?"

"Good morning... Sturmbannführer. Good to see you again. Yes, the Obersturmbannführer is upstairs in his office. Shall I announce you?"

"No, it's fine, I'll surprise him" I smiled.

"Very well sir" he said.

I went up and knocked on the door. "Come" came from within.

"Oskar, you really don't have to...." he looked up and stopped.

"Joseph! My god. Is it really you?" He got up and rushed over to shake my hand.

"Yes sir, I believe it is really me" We shook hands vigorously.

He opened the door, and shouted "Oskar! Coffee, the real stuff".

He closed the door and asked me to sit.

"It is good to see you Joseph, we've all been very worried about you"

"Thank you sir, I was worried about myself also"

"Tell me all about your time spent with that monster Heydrich. Was he really as evil as they say?"

Silence. The Heydrich in my life wasn't the evil monster part, it was the tiny part of him that was still decently human.

"I erm… I'm going to be honest sir. I'm struggling with his death."

"Yes, we can't quite believe it either, the world is a far better place without him eh Joseph?"

"That's just the problem sir, I have mixed feelings. I'm sad that he's gone."

"But how? Surely not? The man was an animal"

"Did you know him sir?"

"No, I did not"

"See, I did. And he was someone I considered a friend"

"A friend? You are joking of course?"

"No sir, I don't think I am"

He was silent for a moment. "What happened Joseph?"

Oskar knocked, and placed the tray on the desk. He gauged the mood in the room, and quietly left.

I poured coffee for us both, and, like a sinner at a confessional, I told my confessor all about my time spent with the Devil.

When I'd finished, we sat in silence for what seemed like an eternity. I had long since finished my coffee, as had Ecke. Finally, he broke the silence letting out a loud sigh.

"My god Joseph, that's some tale"

"Can you see my reasoning?"

"Yes, I think I can"

I exhaled sharply "Thank you" I hoped he couldn't sense my anguish. "Thank you"

"I'm going to be perfectly honest with you here Joseph" he continued "You can't tell anyone else this story"

"Why not?"

"I have a certain ability to see things from other people's perspectives, a sympathetic soul if you like. I would not expect other people to react the same."

"People?" I asked.

"People here. The Group, the resistance. Keep it to yourself"

I could see how that made sense.

"Of course sir. I think I just needed to get it out to somebody, does that make sense? I spent all that time without anyone to talk to, or to confide in. It was tough. I was so desperate to talk to someone"

"I can imagine. It takes a strong man to go through what you endured Joseph"

"Thank you sir"

"You should be proud of yourself. Proud of what you achieved under the most challenging circumstances"

"I did what I needed to do to marry Gisela" I said quietly.

"Ah yes, the beautiful mysterious Gisela. I should like to meet her one day"

"I hope that day comes soon sir"

He smiled "Me too. Tell me one thing"

"Yes?"

"What happened to Maria? Did you just leave her there to fend for herself?"

I chuckled "No sir. Klein was promoted to Untersturmführer and re-assigned. He now administers the SS Driving School in Iseghem. Maria went with him as his personal assistant"

"A happy ending"

"I suppose. Though the poor man has the horrid memories and a permanent limp as a constant reminder"

"But is out of harm's way, and has a good job"

"Yes, I suppose that's true" I smiled. "I have a question, if I may?"

"Of course"

"The microfiche fragment"

I poured us both more coffee.

"Ah, yes, the film! Nice change of subject Joseph" he smiled "It is the genuine article, London has confirmed as much. We have the go-ahead to for you to complete your Objective."

"The adventure never ends"

"Afraid not. There is a war on, don't know if you'd noticed" he winked.

"Yes sir, I just about have" I smiled. "No time for leave?"

He shook his head "Afraid not. You are to leave for Regensburg with Judith as soon as possible"

I almost spat out my coffee "Judith??"

"Problem?"

"You know it is" I said, my voice tinged with anger.

"You need to put all that aside Joseph, the mission is more important"

"I don't want to spend any time with that woman" I said vehemently.

"You have no choice Sturmbannführer" he said sternly.

He sighed, and continued "This isn't a game Joseph. We need that family smuggled into Switzerland as soon as possible.

Every day wasted is a day we don't have the plans for this new fighter. And I'm sure I don't need to spell out what that means"

"No sir"

"Very well" he paused, and softened his tone. "Go back to the mess Joseph, have a few drinks, enjoy yourself. Tomorrow, you leave for Bavaria."

I did as suggested, and drove back to the Fliegerhorst. I let Dietz know I would be leaving tomorrow, and that I wasn't sure when I'd be back. He wished me luck in whatever I was doing. Yeah, I thought, I'm going to need it.

Before I spent the evening in the bar, I went back to my room and packed my case. Yet again.

Fortunately, my new shirts and laundry were hanging in my room when I got back, so I had sufficient clothing at least. All I need now is the willpower and courage to spend time with her. And that's where the drink came in handy. Six brandies later, I was warming to the idea. After two more I thought it was actually half decent. That was enough. Half decent was as good as this situation was going to get. Besides, I still had to walk back to my room, and the room was already spinning somewhat.

34. Travels with Her.

The following morning I woke with two things in my head; a splitting headache, and Judith.

I really didn't want anything to do with her anymore, and this was just going to be torture. She would likely be all smug and aloof, knowing I'd been forced into the situation. I needed to get my focus back.

I needed a long, hot shower and to drink some water. The first was bliss. I let the hot water rain down on the back of my head, and soon the pain in my head abated somewhat. Somewhat. After dressing and checking I'd packed everything, I went down to the mess for breakfast, and a large glass of water. I ate with some of my pilot friends, who regaled me with tales of daring against formations of heavily armoured allied bombers. I had always envied them; the ability to fly up into the sky and experience complete freedom.

But upon hearing about the comrades they had lost, I became slightly less envious. There was danger everywhere, even close to heaven.

I obtained some sandwiches for my journey, and also some bars of chocolate for bargaining. And I was sure Von Graeve's children would appreciate a sweet treat.

My office had been chosen as our briefing location, and I had half an hour until they all arrived. I chatted with my team for a little while, getting to know them better. Dietz was just telling us a funny story from his basic training when the door opened and Ecke came in, followed by Judith. We all snapped to attention and saluted.

"Good morning Obersturmbannführer"

"Good morning Joseph, at ease gentlemen"

The men relaxed, and returned to their duties. I, meanwhile, did my best to ignore Judith.

"Shall we go upstairs?" I suggested to Ecke.

Judith gave me a suggestive look "Shall we?"

I shot her an angry glare. Ecke stepped in before I could say anything "Excellent idea. Sergeant, would you be able to get us some coffee?"

"Yes sir, of course" Dietz said, and made for the mess.

"Come now children" Ecke said quietly "Let's try keep this civilised"

Still angry at her suggestive comment, I led the way upstairs, and we all sat down in my office.

I gave Ecke the chair behind the desk as he would be the one presenting to us.

"Right" he said, leaning forward "I want to make one thing perfectly clear. You two *will* work together. You need to in order to complete this mission. Are we clear?"

"Yes sir" I said, Judith just nodded.

He turned to her and said "Maybe refrain from making inflammatory comments going forward"

She blushed hard. Serves you right.

"Now that we have that out of the way, let's get down to the matter at hand. He opened his briefcase and handed us both a passport and various other documentation we would need.

"These are your cover documents, memorise them, this is basically who you are until you get Von Graeve's family to the safe house in Switzerland. Among the documents are your travel papers, and a letter from the Reichsbank detailing the meeting you are attending"

"Have Von Graeve's family been briefed?" I asked.

"No, we are not in a position to do that. We will require you to brief them when you get there. You will have a week to bond as a family unit before you cross the border into Switzerland"

"And my role?" Judith asked.

"You are Joseph's assistant. You will wear the uniform of an SS secretary"

"SS uniform?" she asked.

"You are both representing the WVHA for this mission"

"The WVHA?"

"It is our main economic and administrative branch" I explained.

"Indeed" Ecke confirmed "These trips are commonplace. Judith will have the uniform of the newly created SS Helferinnenkorps"

"Sir?" I asked. I had never heard of it.

"It is a newly established corps, mainly to provide administrative support to the SS"

Made sense.

"Your uniforms are in my vehicle, I hope the sizing is correct."

Judith nodded and went off to fetch them.

"Is it commonplace for an entire family to travel?" I asked after she'd left.

"Our sources say it has been known, but isn't the norm"

"Will our papers pass scrutiny?"

"Absolutely, they are all genuine, so there is no reason why they wouldn't. And we have a man in the WVHA, so your background will check out"

"Judith?" He knew what I meant.

"She will stand up to scrutiny. Her German is perfect"

"Does she drive?"

"Yes, she drives. I had an SS license made for her"

I nodded.

"I need to know you two being together isn't going to be a problem"

"Not on my part" I assured him.

"Good. She is a good operative Joseph, and will help you"

"I'm sure she will sir"

Judith appeared a few moments later, wearing her new uniform.

"Perfect fit" Ecke said, pleased with himself.

I didn't comment. She looked amazing in uniform. It was a plain grey skirt and jacket. The only identifying mark was a large round SS patch sewn onto the left side of the jacket.

"Yes it is" she agreed, and winked at me. She knew she looked fantastic, and knew that I thought the same. We stared at each other for a while. I tried my hardest not to show any kind of emotion, especially attraction.

"Hate to interrupt this private moment" Ecke said "But your plane leaves in half an hour"

"Of course sir" I said, gathering up my documents, and those for the Von Graeve family.

"Good luck Joseph" he said, and shook my hand.

"Thank you sir"

I left the two of them to have a private conversation whilst I collected my case from my room.

Dietz was waiting with the engine idling outside the office. There was still no sign of Judith.

I put my case in the back of the car, and chatted to him whilst we waited.

As she came out, I jumped into the back seat so she could have the front seat. To my dismay, she put her case in the front, and squeezed onto the back seat next to me, leaving no space for me to move away from her.

"I left you the front seat" I said evenly.

"I wanted to sit next to you. You are my boss after all."

I rolled my eyes, but was secretly enjoying the feeling of her body against mine. We drove to the airstrip where our plane was waiting with idling engines.

The car pulled up next to it, and she got out of the car, purposely pressing herself against me as she did so. I wasn't going to complain. Besides, to mention it would only provide her with the satisfaction she sought.

Fortunately, the Junkers Ju-52 had two rows of single seats, so she couldn't sit next to me.

This particular plane was more luxuriously appointed than the previous one I'd flown in, with soundproofing and leather seats.

It made the trip to Regensburg extremely comfortable and enjoyable. Judith sat on the seat across from me, and was busy looking out of the window. I leaned over and picked up my briefcase from the seat in front of me. I opened it up, and took out my sandwiches. The bread was thickly buttered and had equally thick slices of cheese on them.

I picked one up and took a big bite. Out of the corner of my eye, I saw her looking over, but I ignored her. Instead, I looked out of the window at Germany below. There was a lot of cloud, so visibility of the ground was intermittent. I finished my sandwich and looked over at her. She was staring at the other sandwich on my lap.

"You hungry?" I asked.

She nodded.

"Did you bring lunch?"

She narrowed her eyes "And where would I have gotten it from?"

I shrugged "Wherever you would usually get it from"

"Don't be an arsch"

I sighed and handed her the other sandwich.

I had brought it for her anyway, but just wanted to make her work for it. Now she owed me, which was the idea.

She ate greedily. It looked like she probably hadn't eaten anything like it for a long time.

"Thank you" she said reluctantly after she'd finished.

"Welcome"

Leaning back, I made myself comfortable in my seat to have a doze. I wasn't interested in any further conversation with her, and she seemed engrossed in whatever book she was reading.

The gentle vibration of the plane's engines soon had me drifting off to sleep.

I was woken by a violent shaking sensation, and I woke with a start, thinking the plane was in trouble. It was just her, trying to wake me.

"What is it?" I said, worried.

"We're coming in to land" she said.

I looked out of the window, and saw the landscape below us slowly getting nearer as we descended.

Moments later, we landed with a bump, and slowed gently on the grass airstrip.

We came to a halt outside a small building with a wooden control tower. The co-pilot came through and opened the door to let us out.

"Welcome to Nuremberg" he smiled.

"Ladies first" I said.

She gingerly climbed down the short ladder onto the ground, much to the delight of the ground staff stood watching behind her. I chuckled, and followed her out. We collected our cases, and went off in search of transport to the SS barracks.

A Luftwaffe Lieutenant kindly offered to drive us to the barracks after we failed to spot any other mode of transport.

After a short drive, he dropped us at the main gate of an incredibly grand looking building. It was new, and supposedly the largest SS barrack in the country. We walked through the imposing archway topped by a large eagle, and headed to the reception.

"Good afternoon Sturmbannführer" the receptionist smiled "You would like a room?"

"Two rooms please"

"Of course. Have you made a reservation?"

"No, we are just passing through on our way to Regensburg"

"Ah, no problem. If I could just ask you to fill out the ledger whilst I check your papers"

"Of course" I said, handing him my Soldbuch. Judith handed over her identification also.

I filled out the ledger for both of us, and returned it to the clerk.

"Thank you Sturmbannführer" He smiled and handed back our documents. After checking the ledger, he turned to the large key board on the wall behind him and picked out two keys.

"Adjoining rooms on the first floor, room 114 and 115, right hand block sir, over that way" he pointed to a staircase to our right.

"Excellent, thank you"

We walked up the marble stairway to the first floor, and found our rooms just down the corridor.

I handed Judith the key to 115 "We'll meet for dinner in fifteen minutes?"

She nodded, took her key, and disappeared into her room. I went into my own room, and threw my case on the bed. The window looked out onto the rear of the barracks, which had a very large parade ground. Down below, soldiers were receiving instruction on the maintenance of the MG39. I remembered when I myself had received the same training. It seemed like a lifetime ago now.

I washed my face in the small sink, and went out into the hall to wait for Judith. She came out a minute or so later.

"Did you bring your Soldbuch?" I asked.

"Yes, I have it in my pocket"

"Good. Shall we go find the mess?"

We walked back downstairs, and I asked the clerk at reception the whereabouts of the mess.

"Officers' mess is at the end of the hall to your left sir, general mess is in the same location on the first floor"

"Thank you" I said, and we walked off.

"I don't suppose I'm allowed in the Officers' mess?" she asked

"Sadly no. And I'm not allowed in the general mess" I said apologetically.

"I have to go in there on my own?" she asked, clearly alarmed.

"Yes, there is nothing I can do about it"

"But... On my own?"

I shrugged.

"You're enjoying this" she said.

"Me? Not at all. I'd love your company for dinner. But, rules are rules"

"Hmm. I'm pretty sure you knew this was going to happen all along"

"I'll meet you outside our rooms at seven thirty in the morning"

I smiled and walked off to the mess.

She huffed, and stomped off towards the stairs.

I chuckled to myself as I found a quiet table in a window. It felt good to have the upper hand for a change. A steward came over and took my order for dinner, and I wondered what was on the menu in the general mess. From experience I knew it was nowhere near as fine as the officer's mess.

I had survived day one of my travels with her.

35. Regensburg.

The following morning, we met outside our rooms at the agreed time.
"How was dinner last night?" I asked.
"It was fine thank you" she said tersely.
"Mine also, the beef was particularly nice"
"How nice for you. I suppose we have to breakfast separately also?"
"No, I arranged last night to bring you in as a guest"
She whipped her head around "I'm pretty sure you could have done that for dinner also"
"I wasn't sure it was possible" I said "Shall we?"
"You can be a bastard, you know that?" she hissed.
"No worse than you" I responded.
She was quiet for a moment, then sighed. "Can we call a truce now?"
I thought it over "Hmm, I guess so"
"Good. This would have been a long trip otherwise"
We arrived at the mess, and I signed us in. Her face was one of wonder and awe as we made our way to a table. We sat, and a steward asked what we wanted.
I ordered boiled eggs, toast, and a pot of tea.
"You have eggs?" she asked the steward. He looked confused.
"Yes, of course"
"I'll have the same as him"
He looked at me and raised an eyebrow. "She'll have the same as me"
"Very good sir" Still slightly confused, he walked away to the kitchen.
"What was so funny?" she asked.
"Nothing"
"You like to see women struggle Deckman? Is that it?"
"Just you" I chuckled.
"You're a kraut bastard" she whispered.
"That may well be true" I smiled.
The steward returned, and set our food and drink on the table.
"So many eggs" she said in wonder. "You eat like this every day?"
"Not always boiled eggs, I prefer them scrambled"
"In future, order extra and bring me a couple of boiled eggs to the tea room" she smiled.

"Was that a smile?"

"Don't be an arse"

"Fine. I have commandeered a staff car, the drive to Regensburg is approximately two hours, depending on traffic"

"Excellent, we should make it there by noon"

After we'd finished our breakfast, I asked the steward for two packed lunches, and perhaps a box of supplies for our stay in Regensburg.

"It is a highly unusual request sir, but I will see what I can do"

"Thank you" I said, and handed him a chocolate bar. His eyes widened and he quickly slipped it under his jacket.

We saw him again on our way out, and he had two paper bags with lunch, and a box.

"It's the best I could do sir" he said apologetically.

I checked inside "This is perfect, thank you"

"Come Judith, you can carry the lunch bags" I picked up the box, and we walked to the courtyard where the vehicle was parked. The license plate was SS-33. I don't know why, but it reminded me of Heydrich for a moment. His license plate had been SS-3.

We placed the bags and box in the vehicle and went back for our cases.

Ten minutes later, we were driving towards Regensburg.

The drive was surprisingly pleasant; the road was decent, and the landscape was beautiful. Judith sat in the passenger seat, her hair catching the breeze. She looked amazing.

When we eventually made it to the city, we stopped and asked the first person we saw for directions to the address Ecke had given us. It took some time to locate the road, but we managed eventually.

"This is it, Luitpold Straße 12" I said, as we drove past the house.

"You're not stopping?" she asked.

"Just checking the neighbourhood, making sure they're not being watched or something"

She nodded and looked around as we drove to the end of the road.

"I can't see anything suspicious. You?"

"No, nothing" she said.

I turned the vehicle around, and parked up outside number 12. It was a beautiful old home on the corner of the road. It had a wrought iron balcony and a small tower room.

"Lovely house" Judith said.

"Yes, it is"

I got out, and walked up to the front door. Judith waited in the car.

"Come" I said "I will appear slightly less menacing with you by my side"

"I'll take that as a compliment" she smiled, and stood next to me.

I knocked loudly and we waited. A few seconds later, the door opened and Von Graeve's wife looked out at us with fear in her eyes.

"Yes?"

"Mrs Von Graeve?" I asked.

"Yes, how can I help?" She asked, her voice trembling.

"I recognise you from the photograph on your husband's desk" I smiled.

"Joseph?" she asked, still unsure.

"Yes Frau Von Graeve, Joseph Deckman. Your husband Adolf sends his regards" I pulled a note out of my pocket and handed it to her. I didn't know what it said, Von Graeve had given it to me to pass to his wife.

She read it and smiled. "You'd better come inside"

She took us into a beautifully decorated sitting room, and asked us to sit on a sofa.

"Are you really here to take us to Switzerland?" she asked hopeful.

"Yes Frau Von Graeve, we are. Are your daughters at home?"

"No, they are all at school. They won't be home for a few hours yet"

"Are we able to stay here for a week or so?"

"Of course, I'll make up a spare room for you"

"Two rooms if possible" I said.

"Apologies, I didn't mean to infer anything"

"It is fine Frau von Graeve"

"Please, call me Hilde. I must apologise, but I only have a single spare bedroom, the rest of the rooms are empty. We have had to sell some of the furniture and art work"

"I understand. One room is just fine, thank you Hilde" One room was *not* just fine, but what choice did I have? She smiled hesitantly. Selling her belongings must have hurt her pride. But, we all have to make sacrifices.

"Can I offer you some tea or coffee?"

"Tea would be perfect thank you" I said.

"I apologise, I cannot offer you anything to eat; supplies are scarce these days"

"I can help a little" I said "One moment. Judith?" We got up and went out to the car, and returned holding the box, and lunch bags.

"I hope these may be of some use. Apologies, it is not much"

I placed the box on the table, and she opened it. She let out a large gasp, and tears welled in her eyes.

Inside were four trays of eggs, two pounds of butter, two bags of flour, four large sausages, three chickens, a large block of cheese, and a bag of sugar.

"Where did you get all this?" she asked, wiping tears from her eyes.

"Let's just say the SS won't miss it" I winked. "We also have lunch we can share with you"

Judith emptied the contents of the bags; Ham sandwiches and four boiled eggs.

Tears of joy ran down her face. "I'll make the tea"

We left her to make the tea, and went out to get our cases.

"You have a happy soul Joseph Deckman" Judith said. I wanted to correct her and tell her its good soul, not happy, but decided against it. Happy soul sounded better.

"Ach, it is but a small gesture"

"To you maybe. You saw the tears, she probably hasn't seen so much food in a long time"

"I like making people happy" I said

"You do a good job" she smiled, and placed her hand on mine.

"If only you could make everybody happy" The feel of her touching me sent shivers down my spine.

"Let's get back inside" I said picking up my case, avoiding further discussion.

She smiled, and followed me in.

"I have no milk I'm afraid, so you'll have to take your tea black"

"Oh, I almost forgot" I said, and opened my case "Here" I handed her a bottle of milk.

"Oh dear me!" she exclaimed "It is like Christmas"

Judith nudged me under the table. I looked at her and she smiled warmly. "Happy soul"

Hilde poured the tea, and we ate our lunch whilst talking about their life since Adolf had left. It had not been good.

Even though he sent home most of his salary, they were still desperately short of money, and had to sell their belongings as a result.

She asked how her husband was, and I told her he was fine, and that we had become good friends in the short time that I'd known him. Then she asked what the plan was. I looked at Judith, who explained that we would be traveling to Zurich as a family on a business trio. From there was a choice; they could remain in Switzerland, or fly to Lisbon, and then onwards to London.

"And Adolf?" she asked.

"Getting him out is another matter altogether, and slightly more complicated. But, we'll deal with that after we get you and your daughters to safety" I said.

"How will we pass as a family? I am older than you are" Hilde said.

"We will make it work. How old are your daughters?"

"6, 7, and 9"

"That matches with the passports at least"

"The gentleman that came to take the photographs, he said I would be in good hands. I hope he was correct"

"Marcus?" I asked Judith.

"Yes, he was here a few weeks ago to take the pictures for the passports"

"I will do my best to get you out safe Hilde" I said "I can't promise anything more"

She nodded.

"We are going to stay here for a few days to get to know your girls better, and they must get used to calling me papa" I said "It is crucial"

"They are smart girls" she smiled "They will be fine"

The girls came home a few hours later, and were introduced to Judith and myself. Martha, Liesl, and Lina. Hilde told the girls my name was Papa, which they all thought very funny. I told them it was true, and that my parents were both very silly. More laughter. Hilde divided up the ham sandwich she had saved for the girls, and gave them all a small glass of milk each. Shrieks of excitement filled the kitchen as the three girls feasted on this unexpected surprise.

Hilde looked at her happy girls, then at me "Thank you" she said.

I smiled and nodded. There was nothing to say.

When they'd finished, Hilde made them go into the parlour to do their homework. There were a few complaints, but eventually, they all gave in.

"They're lovely" Judith said.

"Thank you, they're hard work sometimes though"

"I bet"

After they'd all finished their homework, we sat in the lounge, and they sang some songs whilst Hilde played on the piano. It was a picture perfect family scene. Von Graeve was a lucky man.

"Bravo ladies" I clapped when they'd finished "That deserves a reward" I went out to my case and got a bar of chocolate. I held it behind my back so they couldn't see.

"Let's play a game" I said "Can you guess what I'm holding behind my back?"

"A puppy!" Martha said excitedly.

"No" I laughed "Not a puppy"

"A flower?" asked Lina.

"No, not a flower"

"A pancake!" Liesl shouted.

We all laughed "No, not a pancake! Give up?"

They all nodded. "It's a.....bar of chocolate!" I said, making a grand reveal.

Loud shouts and shrieks of joy filled my ears. The girls were jumping up and down with excitement.

"Joseph! You're spoiling them" Hilde shouted over the noise.

"Ach, let them be happy" I said, handing them their prize.

"Share please Martha" Hilde warned.

Still shouting with joy, the girls ran off upstairs with their precious loot.

"You have any more surprises?" Hilde asked.

"No, sorry, that's all I have"

"Don't be sorry. I haven't seen them so happy in a long time"

Judith looked at me "Happy soul"

I smiled. "Yes, I guess I am"

36. Uncomfortably Comfortable.

The rest of the evening was just wonderful. The girls went to bed extremely happy, and full of promises of drawings they were going to make for me in school the next day. We spoke some more with Hilde about the plan, and how we needed to decide on the best day to take the girls out of school. In the end, we settled on Saturday, as taking the girls out of school would arouse suspicion. By the time we'd decided that, it had gotten quite late, and Hilde bade us goodnight.

"Right" said Judith yawning "I think it's time we went to bed too"

Oh, damn. I'd forgotten; we were sharing a room. Reluctantly, I took my case and followed her up to our room. The room was at the back of the house, and just big enough for the bed and wardrobe that were in it. I sighed loudly.

"Hey, it's not that bad" she said "The bed is big enough at least"

"Small mercies" I muttered. "I can sleep on the sofa"

"Ach, and what would the girls think of that? No, you'll sleep right here"

"With you? But…"

"No protests. I don't know what kind of girl you think I am Deckman, but I can assure you I am not like *that*"

"I didn't mean to imply…"

"Shush! Now turn around so I can dress for bed"

I did as ordered. I turned to face away from her only to find myself staring into a small mirror over the sink. In it, I could see her undressing. Her naked body seemed to glow in the light of the small lightbulb that hung from the ceiling. She pulled a nightdress over her head, and slowly slid it down over her bare breasts until she was fully covered.

"I'm ready"

She jumped into the bed "Your turn"

"Turn away" I said.

"Ach, you're such a prude" she chuckled, but turned around anyway. I hastily changed into my pyjamas, turned out the light, and got into bed.

The bed was extremely comfortable, and the blankets luxurious compared to the military bunks and harsh woolen blankets I was used to. I lay back into my soft pillow and closed my eyes contentedly.

"Hey" Judith whispered from the darkness.

"What?"

"I saw you looking" she chuckled happily. Then she ruffled my hair, rolled over, and went to sleep.

I, on the other hand, lay awake for a long time, absolutely mortified.

Sunlight shining through a gap in the curtains woke me the following morning. Slowly I became aware that something didn't feel right. I pulled up the blanket, and saw that Judith had put her arm around me in the night. Mildly irritated, I gently lifted it off me. I thought I had managed to do so without waking her, but I was wrong.

"Morning" she said.

"This isn't going to work"

"What Isn't?"

"This. Us. Sleeping together. It's not right"

"Joseph, we're just sleeping together. Actually sleeping"

"It's not right" I protested.

She propped herself up on one elbow. "Do you know what it's like?"

"What?" Where was she going with this?

"Do you know what it's like to have never been held by anyone, and knowing that any day could be your last? I don't want to die without knowing what it feels like to be held by someone"

What she said was confusing, but I kind of understood the point she was trying to make.

"But you, and me, it's not right. Gisela..."

"Lucky Gisela" she snapped "Every day I live in fear of being beaten, attacked, raped by German soldiers. I've seen the way they look at me. It's only a matter of time before I'm found naked in an alleyway somewhere, and don't you dare tell me that it doesn't happen, because it does. Three of my friends have been raped and murdered since the Germans invaded"

I was stunned into silence.

"I just want to be held" she said sadly.

I turned onto my side and held my arm up.

Without speaking, she snuggled into me and held me tighter than I've ever been held before. The feeling was unlike anything I'd experienced.

My senses were completely overwhelmed; the feeling of her body against mine, the sweet smell of her hair, her fingernails digging into my back. It felt like she was holding on for fear of dying.

A wave of arousal swept through me like wildfire. "Ok, ok, I think that's enough" I said, letting go and pulling away. I hoped to god that she hadn't noticed.

If she had, she didn't say anything. She just looked at me and said "Thank you".

I lay on my back for a bit, thinking over what had just happened. I was angry with myself for getting aroused. But then, could I really be blamed?

Yes, of course I could; I shouldn't be here, in bed with her. What would Gisela say if she found out? I was suddenly filled with guilt. Guilt for something that was nothing. Was it nothing though? I had been aroused, and I was sure she had felt it. Ugh, I was confused. Three more nights of this!

By the time we'd managed to dress without incident, we went downstairs. Hilde was in the kitchen, drinking a cup of tea. "Good morning, I trust you slept well? The girls are away to school" she smiled. Was that a knowing smile? Or just a smile? She offered us breakfast, but I declined. I wasn't hungry.

Judith accepted happily, and sat at the table.

"Why don't you two take a walk around the town, see the sights. I'm going to drive back to Nuremberg to get some more supplies"

"Are you sure?" Judith said "I could come with you"

"No, it's fine. You stay here, enjoy your day. I'll be back after lunch sometime"

"If you're sure?"

"Yep, all good" I said "Enjoy your day" I picked up the keys and left. Getting supplies was one of the reasons why I wanted to leave, but more so than that I just needed to get away from Judith for a while. For my own sanity. Gisela was my fiancée, and I would never betray her trust. But... I wanted this woman. Badly.

The long drive to Nuremberg did my mind the world of good.

I'd gotten lost three times, and by the time I got there it was almost lunch time.
I parked up and headed straight for the mess.

37. Three Nights Left.

My stomach was growling by the time I walked into the dining hall, so I ordered a large lunch. Afterwards, I spoke to the head steward in his office, and was able to secure a supply of potatoes, vegetables, butter, loaves of bread, flour, and milk in return for signing a leave pass. It was for three days, and I was happy to sign. I wasn't sure if it would work for him as I wasn't his commanding officer, but that wasn't my problem. I had what I needed.

I sat for a while, eating slowly, and enjoying a pot of tea afterwards. Judith had drifted back into my thoughts. The whole situation was dangerous. I couldn't continue to share a bed with her, it wouldn't end well. On the other hand, she had made a good point this morning. I was confused!

Very well, I thought, I can be strong for three nights.

My stomach and mind feeling content, I drove back to Regensburg.

With difficulty, I carried the supplies through into the kitchen.

Hilde was beside herself with joy at the sight of all this bounty on her table. Judith reminded me again about my happy soul, but I tried my best to keep a healthy distance from her. She gave me a strange look, then told me all about their walk around the old city. It sounded like they'd had a pleasant day, and I was keen to explore the beautiful medieval city myself.

The rest of the afternoon was spent in the kitchen, preparing a proper old fashioned dinner. Hilde looked radiant in her happiness, and I wondered if she knew she was about to leave behind all her belongings, her home, and her life. I decided I would speak to her after dinner to make sure she was fully aware of her situation. She seemed awfully happy, and I didn't want to ruin her mood.

The girls returned home, and once again the house was filled with joy and noise. How I adored them. It made me crave children of my own, and Gisela had already mentioned an interest.

I collected all my drawings from the girls, as my reward for producing the goods yesterday. The drawings were all perfectly innocent; a unicorn, a family drawing, and what looked like a portrait of me.

I loved them, and kept them close for the rest of my life.

Our meal was superb; roast chicken with potatoes and vegetables. Although I was used to the occasional good meal in the mess, for the ladies at the table, including Judith, it was a novelty and they were enjoying every little bit of it. Afterwards, Judith and the girls cleared up and washed the dishes whilst I took Hilde off into the lounge for a chat.

"Thank you very much for the meal" I said "It was delicious"

"The thanks should go to you for providing the food" she said.

"We'll call it a draw then" I smiled.

"What did you want to talk about Joseph?"

I took a breath. "You know what you're giving up on Friday?"

"Yes, I do. I am trying my hardest not to think about leaving behind my home and all my belongings"

"I understand, and we needn't discuss it any further. I just wanted to ensure you were fully aware"

"I would prefer not to talk about it, it's too upsetting."

"Are the girls aware?"

She shook her head vigorously "No, and they don't need to be. They think we're going on a holiday"

"Very well. I'm sorry to raise it, but I had to be sure"

She placed her hand on my shoulder "I'm grateful for all you have done, and all you are still to do"

"You can thank me after you're all safely in Switzerland"

"May I ask a question?" she said.

"Of course, anything"

"You and Judith?"

I shook my head. She looked shocked.

"Oh dear. I'm so sorry. I just assumed you were, which is why I put you in the same room"

"It's fine. We're both grownups, we can manage"

"Are you sure?"

"It's only for a couple more nights, so yes, it's fine"

"I'm still a little embarrassed. But, if you say its fine, then its fine."

"Thank you"

"Was there anything else you needed to talk about?"

I smiled "No, we can talk about the trip on Thursday evening"

"Very well. I am out most of tomorrow, visiting with friends. It may be nice for you and Judith to walk around the city. She can show you the sights, spend some time together"

"I would like that very much"

"She would enjoy your company. Now, I have to put the girls to bed, I'll leave you two to talk"

We re-joined the girls in the kitchen. "Right girls, say goodnight to Judith and Papa"

Hugs and kisses for both of us. It made me stupidly happy to see the children well fed and so full of happiness. They ran off upstairs, Hilde following close behind.

"They're so lovely" I said.

"You would make a good father" she smiled.

"Well, I certainly hope so"

"You will. How was your day?"

"Well, there was a lot of driving, but I did have a nice large lunch"

"I did also today, thanks to you. You are a very thoughtful and kind person Joseph"

"Not the best credentials for an SS officer" I smiled.

"It's what set's you apart from the monsters, it's a good thing"

"Thanks. So, Hilde is out visiting friends most of tomorrow, how about you show me around the city?"

Her face lit up "I would love to"

"Good. Do you drink Schnapps?"

"I've never tried it. Is it like Jenever?"

I laughed "Jenever is like petrol compared to Schnapps"

"It is stronger?"

"No, no, it is weak, but actually has flavour"

"Ach, Jenever has plenty of flavour, you're just not man enough to appreciate it" she winked.

"You're absolutely right. Maybe one day, after this is over, you can teach me"

Hilde came back down, and joined us in the kitchen.

"Hilde, would you like to enjoy a few Schnapps with us?" I said.

"You have Schnapps?" she asked.

"Yes, I bought a bottle from the bar in the mess" I opened my briefcase and took out the bottle I had bought.

"It's Kirsch, all they had available."
"You say that like it's a bad thing" Hilde laughed.
The rest of the evening was spent sat around the kitchen table, playing cards and drinking schnapps.
It was an extremely pleasant evening; I really enjoyed Hilde's company.

All too soon, it was time for bed. Hilde thanked us for an extremely pleasant evening, and went off to bed.
"So" Judith said "Bed, or another drink?" The bottle was still a quarter full.
"Drink" I said. She poured us both a small measure.
"Small measure?" I asked.
"I don't want to get drunk" she winked.
Good point.
"Cheers" we raised our glasses and took a sip each.
"Tell me about Heydrich" she said.
"Curious. Why?"
She shrugged "He was one of Hitler's top men, and you spent time with him"
"I did"
"Tell me about him"
"He was an evil, cold hearted bastard"
"Ach, dat weet ik toch" *I know that*
"So what then?"
"Tell me about him. What was he like with you?"
"He was my friend"
She almost dropped her glass. "What?" she whispered incredulously.
"Allow me to explain"
"Please do"
"Imagine a person, like him; evil, cold-hearted, sadistic, monstrous"
"Yes, all of those"
"Would you agree that even a person so evil has a glimmer, no matter how small, of goodness and humanity?"
"It would be a tiny glimmer, if anything" she said sarcastically.
"Let's just agree that it's possible" I said.
"Yes, very well"

"That part of him, however small you want to imagine it, was my friend. I know all the badness about him, and don't deny that he was a monster. But, there was a part of him that was likeable. He was a doting father, and treated me like a son. We fenced a lot"

"You fence? Like with swords?"

"It's called a foil, but yes, I do."

"Were you sad when he died?"

"You want me to say no, that I was happy"

"Of course"

"I can't. I grieved for that tiny part of him"

"At least the Czech resistance did a good job" she said proudly.

"No they didn't, they completely messed it up" I said.

She looked shocked. "But, they assassinated him"

I nodded "Yes, but he survived"

She looked confused "Then how?"

I hung my head.

"You" she said "It was you"

"Yes"

"How?"

"Poison. Himmler gave it to me"

"Himmler? You know him too?"

"Yes, I've met him on a few occasions"

"Wow, you move around in high places"

"Not by choice"

"Did you go to the funeral?"

"Yes, I went to Berlin"

"What was it like?"

"It was ridiculous"

"Was Hitler there?"

"Yes"

"What is he like?"

"I have no idea, I've never met him. Though he looked shorter than I expected"

She laughed. "I bet he was missing his little monster" she mocked.

"I guess so. I met his wife"

"Hitler has a wife?"

"No, Heydrich's wife, Lina"

"What was she like?"

"She seemed nice enough. She wiped a tear from my eye and presented me with his foil"

"You cried?"

"A little tear, for my friend"

"You should be proud of what you did"

"Oh, I am. And I was fine with it, until Himmler told me what his last words were"

"What were they?"

"The water was foul"

"That's what he said?" she asked "What a weird thing to say"

"Not really"

"How so?"

"It meant he knew it was me"

"He knew you poisoned him?"

"Yes. He complained that the water I gave him tasted foul"

"He knew it was you, but didn't tell anyone?"

"He knew before I gave him the water."

"How?"

"I told him the day I met him"

"You *told* him?"

"It's how I won his confidence; I told him the truth. I'd been sent by Himmler to kill him."

"Why would you kill him for Himmler? I don't understand"

"Himmler refused to sign my marriage permit until I had killed Heydrich"

"He has to sign a permit for you to marry?"

"Yes, all SS men that want to marry, have to have it approved by Himmler personally. A thorough check is conducted on the bride's family to ensure racial purity"

"That must take months to do! How ridiculous. You believe in all that nonsense?"

"No, I don't. It's disgusting"

"Hmm. So, Heydrich allowed you to kill him?" she asked, changing the subject.

"He knew he was dying, regardless. The injuries had caused an infection."

"But, that means..."

"It means he helped me. He sacrificed his life so I could marry Gisela, and he took the secret to his grave"

"That was a kind thing to do"

"Yes it was. That didn't change the fact that he was pure evil though. If he survived, thousands would have died."

"People did die" she protested "A whole village"

"Hundreds compared to thousands"

We finished our drinks in silence.

"Let's go to bed" she said "it's late"

We repeated the process for changing into our nightclothes, but no mirror this time.

She kept her distance in bed, respecting my wishes. After a simple "Goodnight", she turned and fell asleep almost instantly.

38. Breaking a Happy Soul.

I couldn't sleep. Something she had said had triggered an alarm in my mind. I tried, but couldn't think of what it was. Eventually, exhaustion took over, and I fell asleep. My dreams were haunted by memories of Heydrich, and I woke with a start, filled with guilt.

I had no idea what time it was, but it must have been extremely early as it was still dark outside.

Judith had turned and put her arm around me in the night. I decided to just leave it, rather than risk waking her up by moving it.

I tried to get back to sleep, but my mind was racing. Then, like a flash of lightning, it came to me; I remembered what it was she had said.

I shook her.

"Hmmm? What?"

"Wake up, I need to talk to you"

"What? What time is it?"

"I don't know"

"It's still dark. Can't it wait till the morning?"

"No, it can't."

She huffed, and sat up. "Fine. What is it?"

"Earlier on, when I told you about the marriage permit, you said it would take months"

"Yes?"

"Why?"

"Why?"

"Yes, why would it take months?"

"A racial purity check? I assume you had to provide family background on this form of yours?"

"Yes"

"How long do you think it would take them to research the validity of the information, and ascertain the purity of the family line?"

She was right. "Probably months"

"Exactly"

"But I only gave him the form 5 days before..."

"What?"

My heart sank. "Oh no..."

"What is it?"

"Gisela"

"What about her?"

"She's Himmler's niece"

"What!?" she jumped out of bed, and stumbled her way to the light switch. She fumbled for a moment, and then the tiny lightbulb glowed into life. She looked at me angrily, and repeated her question. "What?"

"She's Himmler's niece. There's no other explanation for it"

"You're marrying Himmler's niece?"

"What? No. Well, yes. But, ach, I don't know"

"I don't understand"

"When you said it would take months, it triggered something in my mind"

"What?"

"I didn't know, I couldn't think what it was"

"Until just now"

"Yes"

"What is it?"

"He signed and gave me the completed forms only five days after I gave them to him"

"They must have rushed them through the system, he is the Reichsführer after all."

"No, you don't understand"

"What?"

"The forms I gave him were blank"

"Blank?"

"Yes, I'd only just collected them from the administrative office"

"But how? Unless..."

"Unless he knew exactly what her family line was."

"Jesus Christ. Her father?"

"No, her mother. She wouldn't have the surname Becker if it was her father"

"Are you absolutely sure? There could be a perfectly innocent explanation"

"I didn't have to tell him her name, he already knew. There were other signs too"

Dammit. I had missed them all.

"There were?"

"Yes. When I first met Himmler, he complimented me on my choice of pistol, saying it was an elegant weapon, the professional choice"

"Odd words to use"

"Indeed. The first time Gisela saw me in uniform, she commented on my pistol, saying it was old fashioned, and that her uncle said it was worn by professional officers"

"Too strange to be coincidental"

"Yes it is. Also, Himmler offered me whiskey, Irish whiskey. He called it the best kind of whiskey"

"Ugh, it all tastes like dirt"

"Agree to disagree. When I asked her father for her hand in marriage, we celebrated with whiskey he kept for special occasions. Irish whiskey"

"Could be a coincidence"

"When I first went to Lychen to see her, the receptionist told me she was in Berlin, visiting her uncle. After we told her mother the good news, she asked Gisela if she'd spoken to her uncle. She said she had"

"That does sound suspicious"

"And, he gave me a house. A house! Who gives a house as a wedding present to someone he barely knows? It's in Garmisch, where her parents live. He actually said; *It is where you want to live is it not?* He wrote out the leave and travel passes for us to go to Garmisch when I was there with him. How would he know that her parents lived there? I hadn't mentioned it"

"It all sounds very damning when you add it up, but, you'll never know for sure until you ask her"

"I know" I needed to look her in the eye when I asked, only then would I know for sure. There was no doubt in my mind. But, I needed to hear it from her.

"Turn out the light" I said quietly.

"What? Why?" A tear rolled down my cheek. "Oh" she got up and turned out the light. It was the cue for my tears to start in earnest. My heart was broken. We were to be married, to have kids, to have a future together. All gone.

Judith turned over and took me in her arms, no words were necessary; I cried like a child.

She comforted me until I fell asleep. A broken man.

When I woke, Judith was not in the bed with me. I checked my watch; it was almost ten o'clock. "Sheiße!" I cried, and jumped out of bed. I washed and dressed, then went downstairs to see where she was. I found her sitting in the lounge, reading a book. "Good morning" she said, putting the book down "How are you feeling?"

"Broken, but otherwise fine" I smiled.

"I'm sorry" she said.

I shrugged "It's not your fault"

"Still..."

I smiled "Thank you by the way, for, you know..."

"Oh, yes, sure...you're welcome"

"I don't know what happened"

"Your heart broke, that's what happened"

She got up and hugged me "Let's get out of here, get some fresh air"

"I'd like that" I said.

As we walked the old streets of Regensburg, Judith talked excitedly about all the sights. She was in her element, and she looked fantastic. The sun made her red hair shine like it was on fire, and she insisted on holding onto me the whole time. We both wore our uniforms, and were catching admiring glances from the people around us. I was completely spellbound.

We took a stroll along the Danube, and sat under a tree, staring out at the beautiful river scene.

"How are you feeling?" She asked.

"Better, thank you"

"Hey"

"What?" I turned my head towards her, only to be met by her lips on mine. My instinct was to pull away, but she put her hand on the back of my head. Instinct lasted but a split second, and then I gave in, and was lost in the warmth of her mouth.

The kiss was only brief, and I wished it had gone on forever. She let me go and pulled away. "Sorry" she said "I shouldn't have..."

I stared into her eyes for a second, and was afraid I'd get lost in a shiny green emerald sea.

"What?" she said "I apologised. What more do you...?"

"Stop talking" I said, and pulled her towards me "Just stop talking"

And then my lips were on hers again. She didn't hold back.

My need was so great, I thought I was going to lose my mind.

It took all my willpower just to let her go. We were both breathing heavily.

"We should probably…" she said.

"Yes, we should definitely…" I said. We jumped up and ran all the way back to the house.

After checking nobody was home, we rushed upstairs to our little room, where the passion took over. We pulled the clothes off each other, and fell onto the bed, our naked bodies entwined.

The sex was spectacular, she was fiery and commanding, which just made it all the better.

Sometime later, we lay naked in each other's arms, exhausted from the ferociousness of our love making.

"How are you feeling?" she asked again.

"On the mend"

"Good" she snuggled into me and kissed my neck "Good"

39. Two Nights Left.

The sound of kids running around downstairs woke us from our afternoon slumber.

"We should go downstairs" Judith said.

"Yes, I suppose we should. Though I'd be quite happy to stay here"

"Me too"

We washed and dressed, then went down to see the kids.

There was much excitement when we appeared in the kitchen, and they crowded around us, telling us all about their day in school.

Hilde did her best to calm them down, but they were too excited.

"How about a walk down to the river?" Hilde said "Hopefully expend some of this excess energy"

"We'll take them" I said "Give you a bit of a break"

"Oh, are you sure? They can be a bit of a handful"

"I'm a Major in the SS, I think I can handle three little girls" I chuckled.

"If you're sure" Hilde said.

"Absolutely"

"Very well, I'll prepare dinner whilst you're out. Those chickens need to be eaten"

"I look forward to it"

And so Judith and I took the kids down to the river, where we played hide and seek for a long time in the slowly diminishing sunlight. It was time well spent, moments of pure, innocent joy. Sadly, there was an element of melancholy to the whole experience; the thought that my future with Gisela was over, and we would never have a family. But, I pushed that to the back of my mind for the time being. Instead, I watched Judith running around in the golden sunlight, her fiery hair flying in the air as she went. She looked beautiful. Should I feel guilty about what happened today? Absolutely not. There was no turning back, and my relationship with Gisela was over, even if she didn't know it yet.

I had no intention of marrying into Himmler's family, and her betrayal was too great to ever be recovered.

Did I have a future with Judith?

I wasn't sure.

I'd like to resign my commission and live in Enschede with her, perhaps work in her father's bar. But, we were at war, and resigning was not an option. We could run away to England, and start again. Would she leave her family behind?

Too many questions. For another time. Right now, it was my turn to find the little devils.

"One, two, three, four..."

After a delicious dinner, we sang songs at the piano, put the kids to bed, and played cards until bed time.

And for the first time since we'd arrived, I wasn't dreading bedtime; I was looking forward to it.

Alone in our small room, I stood watching her undress for bed.

"See something you like?" she said.

"Yes, I do" I said. I picked her up and threw her onto the bed.

"Be gentle with me sir" she pleaded whilst fluttering her eyelashes.

I stripped off, and stood at the end of the bed.

"Oh my" she said, looking at my arousal "You'd better come here and let me see to that for you"

We laughed, and I jumped onto the bed with her. Whilst our lovemaking was intense, we tried our best not to make too much noise. I think we tried, but failed.

Needless to say, we slept well that night.

40. The Day Before Tomorrow.

We woke in each other's arms, and I lay staring at her for a while before she woke.
"Morning"
"Morning" she said "See something you like?"
I should have known she knew I was staring.
We had a big day ahead of us, lots of planning and checking to be done. Hilde was going to drop the kids to school, and then carefully select what she would be taking with her in two suitcases. Any more would arouse suspicion. She didn't know about this yet, but that's the way it was going to be.

We had breakfast of boiled eggs and buttered bread, then Hilde went off to take the kids to school. Judith and I sat drinking our tea.
"We should probably go to the mess and get some packed lunches, the bread is all gone"
"Good idea" she said "You want to go do that first?"
"Yes, let's go and get that over with. We also need to commandeer a second vehicle. You have your license?"
She nodded.
"After that I want to go through the paperwork and make sure it's all good"
"Good idea"
The drive to Nuremberg was pleasant, the weather was lovely, and I had put the roof down on the car. I parked up in the carpark, and we went inside. Our footsteps echoed loudly in the marble interior as we walked to the head steward's office.
"Good morning Sturmbannführer, how can I be of assistance?"
"I am traveling to Switzerland with my family tomorrow" I showed him the travel documents "And wanted to see if I could obtain some provisions for our journey"
He perused the documents, then handed them back "Of course sir, would you like some tea whilst you wait?"
"That would be splendid, thank you"

We followed him into the dining hall, and sat at a table. He returned a few minutes later with a tray, and set it down on the table.

"Would you like me to pour sir?"

"That will not be necessary, thank you"

He nodded, and left us to our tea.

Judith chuckled "It must be fantastic being an officer. Yes sir, no sir, would you like me to pour sir?"

"It has its perks" I smiled.

The steward came over holding a box "Your provisions sir"

I looked inside, and was pleased to see bread, cheese, ham, milk, and apples.

"Excellent, thank you very much"

He nodded and went off to his office.

"Drink up, let's get out of here" I said to Judith.

After signing out the second vehicle, we drove back to Regensburg in convoy.

We parked up and took the box inside. Hilde was sat in the parlour, reading a magazine.

"I have some provisions for the journey" I said, setting down the box.

"We still have so much left" she said, meaning the stuff in the kitchen.

"Are you able to distribute it to close friends? Friends you trust?"

"I shall give it to my sister, she has Jews hiding in her attic"

I laughed. "I couldn't think of a more apt place for SS provisions to go"

We placed all the items for her sister in a box, and left it on the side for her to collect in the morning, after we had left.

"Now. Packing" I said "Two cases only"

Her face fell "Two cases only?"

"Our cover is that we are vacationing in Zurich for one week. If we take more, they will question it. Take only what you need"

She started crying "I knew it was coming, but still, I haven't yet resigned myself to the fact that I'm leaving behind everything I have spent a lifetime collecting"

"I understand, and I am sorry, but you can't take much."

"What will you do with the house?" Judith asked.

"I hadn't thought of it" she admitted.

"Your sister?" Judith suggested.

"A good idea" I added "She could look after it for you until you return"

Content, she went off to pack for the journey.

"That was a great suggestion" I said to Judith.

"Not just a pretty face" she winked.

"Apparently not" I smiled. "Let's go through the travel documents and re-confirm our plan"

I fetched my briefcase, and we spread the various documents out on the kitchen table.

"Right. Passports on one pile"

"Check" she said, having checked them.

"Letter from the Reichsbank confirming the meeting for both of us to attend"

"Check"

"Our travel permits, one for you, one for the rest of us"

She read through the forms "Check. Anything else?"

"No, I think that's it. That's all the documents we need"

"You have any concerns?"

"The children. I hope they don't do or say anything to arouse suspicion"

"I'm sure they'll be fine"

Hilde came down, holding two heavy cases.

"You should have said, I would have carried them" I said.

"Ach, I can manage"

"How are you holding up?" Judith asked.

"I am better, knowing that my home will be looked after"

"That must be a relief" I said.

"It is. Tell me, do you have any concerns about tomorrow?" she asked.

"The whole thing scares me" I admitted "It only takes one slip up and we're all dead"

"Dead?" She hadn't realised the possible consequences of what we were about to do.

"Apologies, I didn't mean to..."

"No, its ok" she said evenly "I should have thought about that, I just never imagined it going wrong"

"It won't" Judith said. "Joseph is extremely good at this"

"Thank you" she said "I'll be fine tomorrow, I promise"
"We'll all be fine tomorrow" Judith assured her. "This time Sunday you'll be drinking real coffee and eating strudel with fresh cream in Zurich"
This made her smile "I hope so"
"Let's put the cases in your vehicle" I said to Judith, I'll have Hilde and the girls in with me"
"Good idea"

With the cases all packed away in Judith's vehicle, we all sat around the table in the kitchen.
We sat in silence for a minute or so, lost in our own thoughts.
Hilde took in a sharp breath "I'm so scared. The girls" she started crying.
I went over and put an arm around her "It's going to be fine, trust me"
"You can't be certain of that"
"Not completely, no. But we have the correct papers, and they are all legitimate, no forgeries"
She gathered herself "You're right. I know you're right. I just can't help worrying"
"I understand. I need you to think positively though. Positivity will get us across the border"
"For you, I will be positive" she smiled, and kissed my cheek.
"Thank you."
"Now, I must collect the girls from school."
"I'll start making us some dinner" Judith said.
"Are you sure? I can do that when I return"
"No, its fine. I don't mind"
"Take the girls to the park on the way home, let them enjoy their familiar surroundings for a while" I added.
"Very well." she rose "Thank you both for being so patient with me"
"Not a problem, we're all scared" I said "We just can't let it show"
She smiled, and went out to get her girls.
I turned to Judith "You can cook?"
"Of course I can" she smiled "I'm a girl of many talents"
"Yes, you are..." I said, taking her into my arms.

"Not now Deckman, I have work to do" she said, and pushed me away.

I sighed. "What am I to do?"

"You can sit there, watch, and just look pretty" she winked.

Dinner was delicious. Judith had made a traditional Dutch stamppot, which was carrot and potato mashed together roughly with some butter, sausages on the side, and served with gravy. For such a simple meal, it tasted fantastic. The kids agreed, as evidenced by the second serving they had.

After Hilde had gotten the girls into bed, I went up and read them a story from their fairy-tale book, which they enjoyed immensely, begging for more. I would have loved to, but I told them we had a long day tomorrow and that there would be chocolate when we got there. That sealed the deal, and I left them to their excited whispering.

Afterwards, we cleared up made sure everything was packed up and ready, went through the plan again, and finally went to our beds.

"You're very good with those girls" Judith said as we lay in bed.

"It was just a story" I said.

"Ach, I mean in general, not just the reading. They adore you"

"Well, that's good for the mission right?"

"Is that the only reason?"

"Of course not, I've completely fallen for them"

"As they have for you" she smiled "You'll be a fantastic father one day"

I sighed "One day maybe"

"Hey, don't let that get to you, we have a mission to focus on"

"I know, it just plays on my mind, you know?"

"I do, but I also know how to cure that" she said, and disappeared under the covers.

And cure it she did.

41. Lindau.

"Joseph"

"Hmmmm?"

"Joseph, wake up"

I sat up with a shock "What? What is it? The girls?"

"No dummy, it's nine o'clock, time to wake up. We should get going soon"

"Ach! You had me worried" I said.

"Sorry, I thought I'd let you sleep in a bit. Come on, I'll make you breakfast"

"I'll be down shortly" I said, and fell back onto my pillow. Big day today. The Von Graeve family were about to leave their lives behind and start another in a strange country. I got up, and washed my face in the sink. After drying off, I looked at myself in the mirror. "It's all on you Deckman. Don't let them down"

There was hot tea and toast waiting for me when I came down.

"Papa! There you are!" the three girls were super excited "We're going on holiday today!"

"I know! Isn't it exciting?" I laughed "Remember, if you're all good, there will be chocolate when we get there"

"Yeay!" they all shrieked and ran off chasing each other.

"They're very excited" Hilde said.

"As long as they're happy" I smiled. "Don't worry too much, today is pretty easy, we just have to drive down to our overnight destination." She nodded.

"Right" I said loud enough for everyone to hear "We should go"

Judith had just finished making the packed lunches. "Oh, already?"

"It's a long drive to Lindau" I said. Lindau is where I had chosen to stay overnight. There were plenty of guest houses, and it was only a short drive from there to the border.

We gathered the rest of our stuff, and went out to the cars. After ensuring the girls were safely sat in the back she said "Would you mind if I just go around the house once more? Just to say farewell?"

"Of course not, we'll wait"

She went off to say goodbye to her house and all her possessions.

I wondered if they would actually ever see the house again.
Likely not, but I didn't want to tell her that. Best that she had faith.

The drive down to Lindau was long, and we'd had to pull over several times to allow convoys of troop trucks go past on their way to Munich. Once we got past Munich, the roads were clear, and we made good time.
We drove into the town of Lindau at just after three in the afternoon. There were many guest houses to choose from, but I thought the girls would appreciate being on the lake. We crossed the small road bridge into the old town, which was located on a small island, and found a very nice guest house overlooking the lake. Whilst Hilde and the girls settled in the rooms, Judith and I drove to the Wehrmacht barracks to hopefully find some fuel for the vehicles. We were in luck, and it only cost me two chocolate bars to have both vehicles topped up.

When we got back to the guest house, Hilde and the girls were nowhere to be found.
"Where are they??" I said in a panic.
"Relax, they've probably just gone outside, it's difficult to keep three kids locked up in a room"
I went to the window and looked up and down the shoreline.
There they were, about 200 meters up the road, sitting on a small beach.
"There they are" I said relieved. Greatly relieved.
"Hey" Judith said.
"What?"
"Don't get angry, she's just looking after the kids and trying to act like normal holiday makers"
I sighed. "You're right. Thanks" I relaxed. She was absolutely right. What they were doing was perfectly natural.
"Come on, let's go join them" she said.
"Good idea" I smiled, and followed her out of the room.
We retrieved the lunches from the car, and then walked down the path that followed the shoreline and were soon surrounded by screaming girls.

I took off my shoes and socks, pulled up my trouser legs, and went into the water with them. "Look papa, there are many tiny little fishes" Lina said pointing at the various schools of infant fish.

Try as they did, they didn't manage to catch any, much to their frustration. We sat for a while, just passing the time. The view was beautiful, the weather was nice, and we were close to freedom.

I sat next to Hilde and pointed out across the lake "Over there is Switzerland"

"We're so close" she said "But we have the most dangerous part of our journey ahead of us"

I nodded "Yes we do. But, we should just concentrate on having a bit of fun today"

"Look at them" she said "They're so happy. They have no idea"

"Best way to be" I said, then added "We'll be fine. Have faith"

She patted my arm "I do"

We found some benches in a small park and had our lunch. It was late in the day for lunch, but we'd all had a big breakfast. After, I took Judith for a walk along the lake shore whilst the girls played on a swing in the park.

"It's beautiful here" Judith said "It would be nice to just stay here"

"It is just as beautiful across the lake" I said "And far less dangerous"

"You think we are going to get across the border without issues?"

"Well, one can only hope"

"Yes sir, one can"

"Ah, I see you have finally learned your place" I said sarcastically.

"You cheeky sod" she laughed.

Out of sight of prying eyes, I pulled her to me and kissed her.

"We're going to be fine. Tomorrow night we'll be safely tucked up in our hotel room in Zurich"

"That sounds heavenly" she said.

"Sadly, we can only stay a few days. We have to cross back over before our permits run out"

"Or, we could just stay there forever"

"You know I have to get back" I said.

"Yes, I know. I have to get back too. It was a nice thought though wasn't it?"

I hugged her "It was"

We made our way back to the park and re-joined the happy Von Graeve family.

The girls insisted we play games, so we ended up playing hide and seek for a while, followed by tag.

It was almost seven o'clock by the time we returned to our rooms. The girls were tired, so Hilde made them wash up and change into their nightdresses. When they were tucked up in the large bed, I went in and read them the story of Jack and the Beanstalk.

After they were safely asleep, I suggested we go downstairs to the tavern and have a schnapps or two, but Hilde said she was tired and just wanted to go to bed.

Judith and I went down and sat at the bar, drinking some very nice local schnapps. There was a small band playing in a corner, and the whole place seemed very festive. A far cry from the front lines, I thought.

We went to bed at around ten as we'd have to be up early in the morning.

"How are you feeling?" Judith asked as she lay in my arms in bed.

"Nervous I suppose"

"It will be fine"

"I know, but I won't be happy until we've crossed the barriers"

She kissed me "I can make you forget…"

"No, the walls, they're paper thin. I don't want the girls hearing"

She chuckled "They're fast asleep"

"Very well then, but gently"

"I promise to be gentle" she winked.

42. The Crossing.

I had slept badly, and it was no surprise to me that I was awake at six the following morning. Judith was still sound asleep next to me, so I got out of bed carefully and went out onto the balcony.
"Good morning"
Hilde was sat out on her own balcony, adjacent to ours.
"Trouble sleeping?" I asked.
"Yes, I'm too nervous. I assume you have the same problem?"
I nodded. "Judith is still asleep"
"You two are an item now?" she asked.
"I don't know"
"You don't know?"
"It's complicated"
"The girl loves you, it's obvious"
"It is?"
"Are you telling me you can't see it?" she asked.
"I suppose I can" I admitted "But, like I said, it's complicated"
"I won't ask, but you should know that the girl is besotted"
I knew that already, I just didn't want to admit it. My relationship with Gisela was dead, even if she was unaware. What was going to happen after I confronted her? Would I run back to Enschede and straight into Judith's arms? Would she be waiting? I wasn't sure.
I looked back over to say something to Hilde, but she'd disappeared. Wide awake, but craving intimacy, I went back to bed and hugged into Judith's warm body.

I lay thinking about how difficult it would be for us to be together in the Netherlands. If she was seen with me, she'd likely be beaten, or worse. And I could understand that. She'd be classed as a collaborator, and that wasn't something I wanted for her. That left us two choices; we either had a secret relationship, or left the country. The last option seemed like the best one, but I'd be taking her away from her family. I'm not sure how my own parents would fare. Would the SS machine extract its revenge upon them? Something to worry about later.

I kissed her forehead "Wake up"

She opened her eyes "Is it time to go?"

"Not yet, but we should probably get ready"

"Ok, give me five more minutes" she cuddled up to me.

"We should really get ready. I want to get to the border by eight"

"Ugh, that's so early" she complained.

"I know, but we need to"

She sighed "Ugh, fine" and sat up "What time is it anyway?"

"Just before seven"

"What? Ugh, that's so early"

"I know, I'm sorry my love"

"Love?"

"What?"

"Nothing" She rolled over and got out of bed. I watched as her naked form stretched out, and walked to the bathroom.

Arousal stirred, but I jumped out of bed. No, not going to happen.

We took turns in the bathroom, and were packed, ready to go at half past seven.

"Should we wake Hilde?" Judith asked.

"She's awake. I spoke to her earlier.

"You did?"

"Yes, she was out on the balcony"

"Ah, I see"

"Besides, I think I hear excited little people next door"

She chuckled "Bless them, I hope this goes well, for their sakes.

"It will. For all our sakes"

We had breakfast down in the dining room, where our landlady lavished us with fresh baked rolls and honey. The girls had milk, and the adults drank tea.

After, they packed and met up with us outside the guest house. The girls were jumping up and down with the excitement of holidays.

"They seem pretty excited" I said to Hilde.

"Is that going to cause problems?"

"No, it would cause problems if they weren't. Kids are supposed to be excited to go on holiday"

"He's right" Judith added "The border guards would find it odd if they weren't"

She held up her hands "You're right, you're right. I'm sorry, I'm just nervous"

"It's fine to be nervous" I reassured her "I'm nervous too"

As Hilde put the girls in the back of our vehicle, I took Judith aside.

"You need to keep an eye on her, make sure she doesn't say anything stupid"

"How am I supposed to stop her from doing that?"

"I don't know. If you think she's about to, adjust your stocking or something. Anything to distract the guards' attention away from Hilde"

"Very well, I'll keep a close eye on her"

Hilde came over to join us "Isn't it a bit early to travel?"

"The earlier we get there, the busier it will be. They'll be more likely to wave us through if it's busy" I reasoned.

"That makes sense" she said.

"Have faith, It's all going to be fine. Come, let's get going"

I walked her to the vehicle, and held the door open for her. She sat in the passenger seat, and I closed the door. "Relax Hilde."

She nodded. I went around to the driver side and jumped in. "Ready girls?"

"Yeay!" they shouted from the back. I started the engine and we drove the short distance to the border post.

There was a small queue of vehicles when we pulled up to the crossing. To my dismay, the guards seemed to be doing thorough checks of both documents and vehicles.

"Don't worry" I assured Hilde. I could feel her nervousness.

When it was our turn, the guard walked over to my side.

"Papers" Terse. To the point. I offered up our passports and travel documents.

"One moment" he said, and walked over to the border station.

"This isn't going to work" Hilde whispered desperately.

"Shhhh! It'll be fine. Just relax"

The guard reappeared a moment later with a Gestapo officer. Oh no.

"What is your business in Switzerland Sturmbannführer?" He said whilst looking through our passports.

"I am attending a meeting on behalf of the WVHA, as my papers quite clearly state" I said evenly, trying to project calm.

"And these people?"

I raised my voice "*These people* are my family, they are joining me for a short holiday"

"So your papers say" he said.

"Yes, I thought that was quite obvious, even to the Gestapo" I said angrily.

He handed back our documents to the border guard and walked away.

"Where are you going Sturmbannführer?" he asked.

"Zurich, I have a meeting there"

Suddenly, Lina spoke up from the back seat "Will we see papa when we get there mummy?"

The guard looked at me "What does she mean? You are not her father?"

Damn. Think quick….

"I will be in meetings most of the time, so will not be able to spend much time with them. That's what she means."

He regarded me with suspicion, his hand moving slowly towards his weapon. For a moment I thought he was going to prevent us crossing.

"Can we go now papa?" Liesl asked.

Suddenly, he smiled broadly and said "Enjoy your trip Sturmbannführer, I hope you find time to spend with your children, they look adorable"

"Thank you, that's very kind of you"

The barrier opened, and we drove through. My heart was pounding in my chest.

What if they stopped Judith? Keep driving, don't look back. The drive to the Swiss border station was only about 50 meters, but might as well have been 50 kilometers.

In the rear view mirror I saw him have a brief conversation with Judith, and then her vehicle drove up behind us. The relief was overpowering.

The Swiss border guards checked our documents and let us through without question. We were free! We'd done it!

We drove a few hundred meters up the road, then stopped and jumped out of the vehicles.

"Oh my god" Hilde said "We made it! Thank you so much!" Crying with joy, she flew into my arms. I hugged her tight.

"You are welcome Frau von Graeve"

We *had* made it. It had been close, but we had made it. All we had to do now is drive to the hotel in Zurich. I could place a telephone call to Ecke from there.

43. Zurich.

The drive to Zurich took an hour or so, and we passed through some of the most beautiful scenery I had ever seen. My relief at having made the crossing without issues was so immense, I thought for a moment that I may throw up. The girls were singing in the back, and Hilde looked more relaxed.

"You did well" I said to her.

"Really? I was a bag of nerves! I thought I may be sick"

"I know the feeling" I smiled "But, we made it, you're free"

"Free. We were free before. I'm not sure what we are now"

"It's going to be a difficult time for you and the girls"

"I need to speak to my husband. Can you arrange that?"

"I'll see what I can do"

"I haven't heard his voice in such a long time" she lamented.

"I'll do my best to remedy that" I assured her.

"Where are we to stay in Zurich?" she asked "I have little money"

"Don't worry about that. You have rooms in the Metropole Hotel, British Government is paying"

"That's a relief. How long will we be there for?"

"I haven't a clue I'm afraid. My mission was to get you to the Hotel, what happens from there is out of my control."

"Oh, I see" she said sadly.

"I can tell you one thing though"

"What?"

"I will miss you all."

"We will miss you too Joseph"

An hour later, we were safely in our hotel rooms. The telephone operator was routing a call through to Ecke for me, and I was sat out on the balcony waiting for the telephone to ring.

"How does it feel?" Judith asked, brushing her hair from her face.

"How does what feel?"

"How does it feel, knowing you have saved their lives?"

"Did we though?"

"You don't think so?"

"I'm not sure. They were perfectly safe in Regensburg"

"I suppose that's true"

"If it wasn't for this war, and the British government being so desperate for the plans that Von Grave has, they'd still be perfectly happy where they were."

"Do you know what Von Graeve has agreed with them in return for these plans?"

"No, I'm not privy to that"

"I am" she said.

"You are?"

"It's part of my Objective to seal the deal"

"Why didn't you tell me that earlier?"

"I didn't want you distracted from your mission, besides, it was irrelevant"

"Irrelevant?"

"Of course. What difference would it make to what we've done this week if you knew what the deal was?"

Cold, hard logic. She was right. It wouldn't have made any difference at all.

"Very well. You are right. Would you care to tell me what it is now that we're here?"

"Yes"

"Well...?"

"After you speak to Ecke" she winked.

Just then, as if planned by the gods, the telephone rang.

I walked over, picked it up "Deckman"

"Obersturmbannführer Ecke for you Herr Deckman" the receptionist said, and put me through.

"Joseph?" The line was faint.

"Obersturmbannführer Ecke? Can you hear me?"

"Yes, a little faint, but I can hear you"

"Excellent"

"How is your assignment?"

"Completed sir, awaiting further instructions"

"That is good news. Return here immediately Sturmbannführer"

"Yes sir"

And then he was gone. Just like that. He told me nothing.

"That was short" Judith said.

"Yes, rather."

"Did he tell you anything?"

"Just to return immediately"

"I see"

"He is probably fearful that the Gestapo are listening in"

"Possibly. I guess it's down to me to tell you then" she smiled.

"I guess it is"

"Right. So, the deal. Von Graeve has arranged for his family to live here in Switzerland for the remainder of the war."

"In this hotel?"

"No, they have secured a house for them in a place called Lachen. It is a little south of here on the lake"

"On the lake? They'll like that"

"I've not seen it, but am assured it is a nice family home."

"What will they do for money?"

"I'm assured that employment will be found for Hilde, and the kids can attend school. Passports have already been issued for them"

"These plans must be critical to the war effort" I said.

"They are. Imagine an aircraft that flies twice as fast as anything in the skies today"

"Surely that is impossible?"

"This is a revolutionary design, using engines that don't have propellers"

"How do you know all this?" I asked. She seemed to know more about it than I did.

"I have had a low level briefing from Ecke, it was important in order to get across the importance of the mission. It was not detailed, that was all he told me"

"Twice as fast as an ME 109 even? I can hardly believe it"

"You saw the fragment of film?"

"Yes, it was part of a complicated looking engine"

"An evolution in engine design"

"Hmm?"

"That's what Ecke called it"

"Ah. Well, I suppose we have to get the Von Graeve's to their new home. When do we do that?"

"We don't. We travel back to Enschede immediately" she said.

"Pardon? We've come all this way with them, it would be cruel to leave them at this juncture"

"We have no choice. SOE will take it from here. Our job is done"

It didn't sit well with me, but what choice did we have? Besides, Ecke had said as much to me on the telephone. It would be sad to say farewell to the girls; I would miss them badly. She must have sensed my sadness.

"We will see them again" she assured me.

"When?"

"I can't say. Whenever this war is over I suppose"

"That could be forever"

"Or not. Missions like this help to shorten the war"

"Then we'd best get back to work"

"Yes" she smiled "We'd best"

"In the meantime, we have this room..."

"You're insatiable" she said, unbuttoning her blouse.

44. A Tearful Farewell.

The following morning, we met up with Hilde and the girls for breakfast.

"How are they coping?" I asked Hilde.

"They're fine, it's all a big adventure to them"

"I'm glad they're happy"

"Am I able to speak with my husband?"

"I'm afraid the risk is too great at the moment. The Gestapo listens to most telephone traffic in Germany"

She looked deflated.

"I'm so sorry" I said.

"It's not your fault Joseph" She placed her hand on mine "I am grateful for all you have done for us"

"It was a pleasure. I will miss you all so much"

"What is to become of us now?" she asked.

I turned to Judith "It's probably best that you debrief her on that"

"You are staying in Switzerland" she said.

"Oh, thank God" Hilde said with relief "I was afraid we'd have to travel onwards to God alone knows where"

"You have a new home, a short drive from here, on the lakeside"

"Oh, the girls will love that. When do we leave?"

We don't I'm afraid. This is as far as Joseph and I go. SOE agents will take you to Lachen from here. We are to return to the Netherlands immediately."

"SOE agents?"

"British agents" I explained "They have Swiss passports for you, and the girls will go to school here"

"I am so very grateful" she said "It is beautiful here, and close to my homeland"

I knew what she meant; it was stunning here, I wouldn't mind settling here myself.

"It will be sad to say goodbye" Hilde said "The girls will miss you both like crazy"

"We will miss them too" Judith said.

"When will the agents get here?" Hilde asked.

"Around midday" Judith said.

"Oh no, that's not long. Will you be able to spend some time with the girls before you go?"

"Of course" I said "I wouldn't think of leaving without doing so"

"We have to handover to the British anyway, so we won't be leaving until that is done"

Tears filled her eyes "We will miss you so much"

"Ach, stop" Judith said "You have me crying now too"

I could easily have cried myself; walking away from them filled my heart with sadness. My desire to have children of my own had been growing steadily since we had met them. But, all hopes of that were currently dashed.

We were to return to Enschede, but I needed to be in Lychen. I would have to speak to Ecke about that when I got back.

After breakfast, we went for a walk around Zurich. It was so nice to see so many people going about their daily business, completely free of the fear of war. It reminded me of my life before the war, when everything had been so innocent. Innocence had truly been lost now. The girls ran around without a care in the world. We found a park, where we played hide and seek until it was sadly time to head back to the hotel.

We spotted the British agents as soon as we entered the lobby. They were sat on a bench, dressed in business suits, pretending to read newspapers. A Gestapo agent on his first day of training would have picked them out. Amateurs.

We exchanged a nod, and they waited for us to go upstairs before following us up.

Once safely in our room, we handed over the passports, and debriefed them on the crossing. Then, sadly, it was time to say goodbye.

We asked the agents to wait in our room whilst we went to see Hilde and the girls in their room.

"Papa!" Lina called out as we walked in "Are we going to the park again?"

I picked her up and held her close "I'm afraid not my little angel. Judith and I have to go"

"Where are we going?" Martha asked.

"I'm sorry girls, but you won't be coming with us. You're going home"
"We're going back to Regensburg already?" Martha asked. She was a sharp little thing, I thought with pride.
"No, you're going to a new home, it's on the lake, so you can go swimming every day"
"Yeay!" Liesl and Lina shouted.
"But" Martha said sadly "You're not coming with us?"
"I'm sorry angel, I can't. Judith and I have to go home now"
She started crying "But I want you to stay"
"I want to stay too Martha" I said "But we have to get back to our own family"
"You have children?" she asked.
"No, I don't" I said "But my parents are waiting for me at home" I lied. It was a good lie.
"Come here, all of you" I said, and took all three of them in my arms "I will miss you devils so very much. But I promise we will come back"
"When" Lina asked.
"I don't know, but we will be back, I promise."
I couldn't help it, I started crying. I hugged them tight "I love you girls. You look after your mother for me ok?"
They nodded. "Good girls" I kissed each of them on the head, then went over and hugged Hilde.
"I promise you will see your husband soon" I told her "Look after these angels for me in the meantime"
"I will" she said, tears rolling down her cheeks "Tell him I love him?"
"I will" I said.
Judith said her goodbyes to the girls and Hilde, and we both left the room with tears in our eyes.
We went back into our rooms to see the British agents.
"All done" I said to one of them "Make sure you look after them won't you"
"I promise sir" he said "You have my word"
I nodded, and they both walked out, leaving Judith and I behind.
We sat in the room, listening to the Von Graeve family next door until their door slammed shut for the final time. The girls' voices faded as they walked down the stairs, until they couldn't be heard at all anymore. They were gone. It felt like a piece of me had vanished with them.

We sat for a while I silence, each of us lost in our own private misery.
"We should do something" Judith said finally.
"What can we do?" I asked.
"We still have this room until tomorrow, seems a shame to waste it"
Each of us tried hard to banish our sadness through the act of love making. It worked. When we were worn out, we lay in bed in each other's arms.
"Better?" she asked.
"Better" I said.
"Good"
"Better?" I asked.
"Better" she said.
"Good"

After spending the rest of the day wandering the streets of Zurich, we had dinner at the hotel.
The menu was unlike anything I'd seen before. We both ordered schnitzel.
Needless to say, it was delicious. I ordered us some brandy afterwards, and we sat in the hotel bar, surrounded by business men.
"So, where are we crossing back over?"
"I've been thinking about that. We can't cross at the same place we came in, as the risk of being recognised is too high"
"Where then?"
"There's a Luftwaffe base in Neuhausen ob Eck"
"Where is that?"
"Its north of here. We would have to cross the border at Neuhausen"
"And then hope there is an aircraft to take us home?"
"I guess so, yes"
"Why can't we just go by train?"
"All the way back?"
"We could get the train back to Nuremberg, and arrange a flight from there"
The idea had merit. The chances of us getting transport in Neuhausen were slim, but from Nuremberg? Easily arranged.
"Very well. We leave tomorrow morning. By train"

The journey to Nuremberg would take us through Stuttgart, and would take 9 hours. However, I anticipated several stops along the way where we'd have to make way for military trains. My estimation was closer to 12 hours.

"We'll have to make sure we take provisions" I said "It's going to be a long journey"

"I'm sure we can purchase some food from the restaurant" she said.

"I'm sure we can. How much money do we have left?"

She checked her purse "Enough"

"Good. Right, let's get to bed. I want to get the earliest possible train"

We asked the receptionist for a train timetable, and took it up to our room. After weighing up the various options, we settled on the 08.15 train.

It was the best option, as it would get us there with enough time to get to the SS barracks before sunset. We'd have to explain away the cars, but I was confident it wouldn't be an issue. And if it was, it was their issue to deal with.

Tiredness overcame both of us as soon as we got into bed, as we fell asleep fairly quickly just cuddled up together.

45. Journey Home.

We made it to the train station just before the train was due to depart. The ticket seller told us we'd have to run to make it. And so we ran through the terminal to track four, where our train was just about to depart. We made it with seconds to spare.

The journey itself passed without incident. The border crossing was straightforward, as we were entering Germany, not trying to leave. There were a few instances where we had to pull into a siding to allow trains to pass. I thought they would be troop transports, but they all looked like cattle carts.

We had no difficulties getting rooms at the barrack as there were hundreds of them. We were on the third floor this time, rooms 316 and 325. Sadly, the beds were too small for us to spend the night together, so we slept in our own rooms. It felt strange sleeping alone, I couldn't get settled at all. As a result, I had a terrible night's sleep.

In the morning, we tried to arrange a flight to the Fliegerhorst, but it proved to be more difficult than I thought. The closest I'd managed to get was a flight to Osnabruck. From there we'd have to get a train to Enschede. Not ideal, but the only way it was going to happen.

The cars caused a minor stir in the administration office, and for a moment I thought they were going to make a big deal out of it. However, they worked out a plan to get them back. A few telephone calls were made, and I was off the hook.

Our flight would depart in three hours, so we had time for a leisurely breakfast. I booked us both into the officer's mess, so we could eat together.

"My goodness" Judith said, yawning deeply "This is turning out to be an incredible journey"

"Yes, it is. It's going to take a long time to get there tomorrow. Almost makes me think we would have been better off driving, but, there was no way I was going to ask them for another vehicle!"

She laughed. "I don't mind the train, there's no stress, and we can just relax"

"True. It just take such a long time with all the stops"

"But what other choice do we have?"

"You're right" I said "Come on, we'd better pack and get to the airfield"

As expected, the flight to Osnabruck was the best, and quickest leg of our journey. The train ride to Enschede took 5 hours due to frequent stops we had to make to allow transport trains to pass

As a result, it was almost midnight by the time we pulled into Enschede station.

"I'll say goodbye here" she said "I can't be seen with you"

"Understood" We hugged, and I gave her a long kiss before she stepped off the train and disappeared into the night. I waited a few minutes, then left the train myself. The walk to the office on the Rembrandtlaan was only about ten minutes, but unfortunately, the front door was locked. There was a light on inside, so I knocked on the door. After speaking to the night-watchman, I went up to my office, where I fell asleep in my chair.

"Joseph"

A voice from a million kilometers away, gradually getting closer, until I opened my eyes. "Obersturmbannführer" I said, and jumped up from my chair "Apologies. The train didn't get in until midnight, and it was too late to go back to the Fliegerhorst"

"Calm down Joseph, its fine. How are you doing?"

"I'm fine sir, just tired I suppose"

"I'm not surprised. You deserve a rest after all that hard work"

"I could certainly use a rest sir"

"Fine, you can take a few days leave. Catch up on some sleep"

"Thank you sir"

"Don't thank me yet, I want a full debrief before I let you go"

"Of course sir"

"First though, let's get you some coffee. I have a little left, should be just enough"

"That would be fantastic" I said, rubbing my tired eyes.

I followed him through to his office, and we sat whilst Oskar made us some coffee.

"You look tired" he said.

"I am exhausted. Physically and emotionally"

"How was everything with Judith? I hope there weren't too many issues"

"No sir, we are getting along extremely well"

"Ah, that's good to hear. Now, tell me all about it"

"Well, there isn't much to tell really. We met the family, spent time with them, and got them over the border safely"

"I suppose when you put it like that..." he laughed.

"It was a tough mission sir, and I have grown rather fond of those little girls. I miss them dearly"

"Well, it's a good thing you're to be married then, you can start a family of your own"

"I'm not so sure of that anymore sir"

"How so? Something happened?"

"Where do I begin?" I sighed.

"Well, a good place to begin would be a nice cup of coffee" he said as Oskar brought the tray in. He set it down on the desk and discretely closed the door on his way out.

"I may as well just tell you"

"Tell me what?" he asked, pouring the coffee.

"I'm certain that Gisela is Himmler's niece"

"What?" he almost dropped the coffee.

I told him about all the little clues I'd discussed with Judith a few days before, and he came to the same conclusion.

"Well, it does all seem to be a bit too much to be coincidental"

"Yes sir, my thoughts exactly"

"You'll be wanting to ask her in person I assume?"

"Yes sir, as soon as possible"

"Very well. I'll write up your leave and travel papers, and you can leave tomorrow morning. But for now, let's enjoy the coffee. Tell me about Switzerland"

We sat talking and drinking the coffee Himmler had given me. I didn't tell him about Judith, and our blossoming relationship. I didn't want to tell anyone. I wanted to deal with Gisela first.

I left Ecke's office a little before lunch time, and drove over to the Fliegerhorst. A shower was top of my priorities list, followed by a laundry run.

When I'd finished all my chores, I telephoned Von Graeve's office to see if he was there.

His adjutant told me he would be in office in about an hour, he was attending a security briefing.

I thanked him, and hung up. An hour; that gave me time to have a relaxed lunch in the mess.

I knocked on Von Graeve's door just over an hour later.
"Come" came the command from within. I opened the door and went through.
"Joseph!" he stood up and walked over to greet me. "How the devil are you?"
"I am fine thank you sir"
"Good, good. Tell me, how did it go? How is my family? Are they safe?"
"They are just fine sir. You have a wonderful family"
"That is good to hear. Are they safely in Switzerland?"
"Yes, they are at their, apologies, *your* new home. Hilde asked me to tell you that she loves you"
"I owe you a great debt Joseph" he said.
"Spending time with those little girls was reward enough; they are very special. I miss them so much"
"That is kind of you to say. I miss them more than I could possibly put into words" he said sadly.
"You will be with them soon"
"Yes, I suppose I will. Do you know how this transaction is going to happen?"
"The handover of the Schwalbe plans? No idea, that is up to Ecke"
"The sooner the better. I hear talk of being transferred to France, so I'd like to get this done before that happens"
"Understood. I would suggest meeting with Ecke as soon as possible"
"Can I not just hand over the plans to you?"
"I'm afraid I'm going up to Berlin tomorrow, you'll be in safe hands with Ecke"
"You trust him?"
"With my life"
He nodded "Very well. Let me take you to the mess bar for a drink before you go"
"I would like that very much" I smiled.

After spending a few hours in the bar with Von Graeve, I went back to my room to pack.

Fresh laundry had been delivered, so I had clean clothes for traveling. Small things make all the difference.

I closed the clasps on my suitcase and lay back on the bed. I thought of Heydrich, and our fencing matches. It made me smile. Heydrich. Wait. The file! I would need to go to my office in Enschede to retrieve it before my flight tomorrow morning. Damn! How could I have forgotten it! I cursed myself loudly. I would get up an hour earlier that planned and drive straight over to get it. No problem. I took a deep breath to calm myself, then went to bed.

46. The Second Reckoning.

As planned, I got up early the following morning and dressed hastily, then ran down to my vehicle and drove into Enschede. It was just before seven when I arrived at the villa, and I ran straight up to my office. I unlocked my safe, and retrieved the file and the pistol. I held the pistol in my hand for a moment, wondering if I should take it with me or not. I decided against it, and placed it back in the safe.

When I got back to the Fliegerhorst, I checked myself in the mirror and went down for breakfast. I was relieved I'd remembered the file, I had the feeling I was going to need it. My flight was at 08.30, so I had to have a quick breakfast before making my way to the airstrip.

My pilot was walking around the ME 110, making sure everything was in order before we took off. The plane looked in a sorry state, and the look of worry must have been obvious

"Don't worry sir, this trusty bird will get us there without problems. She may look worn out, but she's got lots of life left in her yet"

"I'll take your word for it" I smiled uneasily. He took my case and placed it in the hold for me. One of the ground staff helped me into my parachute, and then I climbed up into the rear of the cockpit.

I clipped in my safety belts, double checked that I had my briefcase, and sat back. Relax Joseph, it's going to be fine.

The engines started up, and a comforting hum of the engines vibrated through the old airframe. We sat for a moment whilst the engines warmed up, then accelerated down the grass strip until we finally lifted off into the air. The pilot climbed rapidly, and before I knew it, we were above the clouds, on our way to Berlin. I was nervous, and it wasn't just the flight. I was nervous about confronting Gisela.

We touched down in Berlin a few hours later, and taxied to a halt by the terminal building. I unclipped my harness and climbed out holding my briefcase.

After struggling out of my parachute, I collected my case and thanked the pilot for a smooth flight.

I checked again that I had my briefcase, and went off to find transport to the train station.

The train journey to Lychen took almost two hours due to yet more stops for freight trains. Because of that, it was almost lunch time when we came to a halt in Lychen station.

I went straight to the lodgings I had used previously, and was met by the overly generous landlady who welcomed me with open arms. After taking my case up to my room, I joined her in the kitchen for a sandwich and some milk.

She served a delicious lunch, and we had an amiable chat. I thanked her for her hospitality and generosity, then set off for the hospital on foot. I wasn't sure she was going to be there, but I had no choice but to take a chance.

I didn't know the girl sat behind the reception desk, which gave me an idea.

"Good afternoon Sturmbannführer, are you here for an appointment?"

"Good afternoon, no I am here to see Nurse Becker. Do you know her?"

"I'm afraid not, I am new, I only started a few days ago. I can check if she's in if you like?"

"That would be perfect, but one more question before that, if I may?" She smiled "Of course"

"Would you be able to check in your files when Nurse Becker started working at this hospital?"

"Well, I'm not sure..." she said

"I'm Siecherheitsdienst" I said, showing my warrant card "It is of vital importance that I know when she started working here"

"Is she in trouble?" she said, worried.

"No, I just need to check for our records"

She eyed me suspiciously, but conceded "Very well, I will check. One moment"

She stood and walked over to a row of filing cabinets, and started going through the drawers.

"Ah, here it is" she pulled out a file and opened it "5 July 1941"

"Thank you" I pretended to write it down in my notebook. "You've been most helpful"

"You are welcome sir. Shall I go see if she's on duty?"

"If it's not inconvenient"

"Of course not" she smiled and went off down the corridor to the wards.

Fifth of July! That was only a few days before I had been admitted. Another convenience.

She returned a few minutes later "I'm sorry sir, she's not here; she's not on duty until five o'clock this evening"

"Ach, what a pity. Oh well, thank you very much for your help"

"Glad to be of assistance sir" she smiled.

I walked out. Damn. Five? It was only one o'clock. I had four hours to kill. I weighed up my options; I could either wait to meet her here at five, or go and see if she was at her lodgings back in the village.

I decided on the latter, and started walking back.

Half an hour later, I was stood outside her room, working up the courage to knock on the door. How was I going to handle this? I wasn't at all sure. No point delaying any further; I knocked on the door.

Seconds later she opened it "Joseph! Oh my god what are you doing here??" she threw her arms around me and kissed me. I held her loosely, and didn't kiss her back. She pulled away "Are you well? Why didn't you tell me you were coming?"

"I wanted to surprise you"

"Oh, what a great surprise. Come in"

I went inside, and she sat on my lap "I have missed you my love" she said.

"And I you" I said.

"I have news" she said excitedly

"I also have news" I said evenly.

She looked at me quizzically "Why don't you go first"

I took a breath. "I know"

"You know? How? I haven't told anyone"

"What?"

"I haven't told anyone yet, I wanted you to be the first"

"Tell me what?"

"You tell me your news first" she said excitedly.

"You're Himmler's niece"

He face dropped, all excitement was gone in an instant.

"What? Don't be silly Joseph, you're playing games"

"It's no game Gisela"

"That's crazy"

"Is it?"

"Of course it is. Stop playing games Joseph"

"Lots of little signs that all add up to one, horrifying truth; Heinrich Himmler is your uncle"

"No. But, if he was, what difference would it make?" she asked, trying to smile.

"What? What *difference* would it make?"

"Yes"

"It means you lied to me. And if you lied about that, what else have you lied about? Besides that, I have a feeling that us meeting wasn't coincidence"

She looked down at her feet.

"You started at the hospital a few days before I arrived there, and you took an immediate interest in me, almost like I'd been chosen"

"Chosen? For what? Don't be silly" she said, again, trying to smile, but failing.

"I'm not sure. Why don't you tell me?"

"What does it matter Joseph? We're in love, and I'm going to..."

I cut her off. "What does it matter? Are you insane? What am I? Some kind of sick experiment?"

"It's not an experiment" she said angrily.

"Oh really, then please enlighten me"

"You were chosen by my uncle as my ideal mate"

"Mate?"

"Yes, we will have many pure Aryan children Joseph"

"No, we won't"

"What do you mean?"

"I mean that this is over Gisela, your experiment has failed"

"Failed? No, I'm..."

"You're what? Sorry? I don't want to hear it"

"But we're to be married, it's all been arranged"

"Married? Good god no, that isn't happening" I said.

"What do you mean? We'll be happy together"

"No Gisela, we won't"

"But the Führer says we must produce many children to help Germany grow stronger and to ensure the survival of the thousand year Reich" she actually sounded like she meant it.

I laughed "Thousand year Reich? This war will be over soon, and we will not win it"

"How can you say that? The Führer tells us victory is imminent"

"He's lying"

"No. I don't believe it" she said vehemently. "We will win this war, and our pure Aryan civilisation will live on for a thousand years"

"He is lying Gisela"

"No" she was adamant. "You and I were joined to create a family of strong German warriors" she said. My God, I thought, she's actually serious. This is worse than I thought.

"Gisela, it's not true. None of it is true. Me? I'm not true"

"What do you mean?"

"I'm no war hero Gisela. I work for British intelligence"

"What? No, it's not true" she was shaking her head vigorously.

"It is true. I killed Reinhard Heydrich"

"What?" she cried "No! It's not true. Why are you saying these things?"

"Because they're true."

"They can't be. You're not a traitor"

"I am. But, I was acting under orders"

"Orders? From who?"

"Heinrich Himmler"

Her whole world came crashing down. "No! Lies! It's not true!" she was shaking her head madly, with her hands over her ears.

"Gisela" I said calmly "It's true. I killed him on your uncle's orders"

"No, I refuse to believe it"

"It's true" I opened my briefcase and showed her a document

"What is this?" she read through "A house?"

"Part of my reward for killing Heydrich; a house for you and me in Garmisch"

"Nonsense!"

"Look at the signature"

She looked at the end of the document "Oh my god"

"It's all true. I'm no National Socialist" I said "and I am ashamed to wear this uniform"

"No! You can't say that! You swore loyalty to our Führer!"

"Gisela, it's over"

"No! It's not over. We can still be together. We can live here" she was waving the house deeds around "We'll be close to our parents, it will all be fine. Nobody would know. It will be fine"

I shook my head "No, it wouldn't. We're over Gisela. I'm sorry"

I expected her to break down in tears, but she went off on a crazed rant about how we had to further the Aryan race, that we owed it to our Führer. It was pure insanity.

"He's not my Führer" I said evenly.

"He is, you swore allegiance to him, until death"

"Have you seen him?"

"The Führer?"

"Yes"

"No, I haven't had the honour"

"Well, I have. At Heydrich's funeral. And let me tell you, he is no Aryan. And neither is your uncle. Or Göering, of Goebbels. None of them fit their own ideal of an Aryan male. Do you not find that odd?"

She was silent.

"The only one of them who fit the Aryan profile was Heydrich. And they killed him for it"

"Why?" She was crying.

"Because they felt threatened by him. He was the perfect Aryan and they couldn't control him"

"It doesn't matter" she said defiantly "We owe the Führer our loyalty"

"We owe him nothing!" I shouted.

"You're a traitor!" she shouted back, pulled out a pistol, and pointed it at me.

"Gisela, wait. Don't do anything foolish" I said, holding my hands up. She started crying "My life is ruined" she shouted "You have ruined everything! Everything!"

"You can still have a life without me"

"No, I cannot. Don't you see? We were destined to be together"

"No we weren't Gisela, it is all fake, based on lies"

"No more lies!" she shouted "I love you" she paused "But you're a traitor" the gun was pointed in my face, and her hand was shaking like mad.

"Gisela, put the gun down" I pleaded.

"I can't do it" she said, shaking her head. "I can't do it. I can't do it"

"Do what?"

"Have your child. A *traitor's* child!" she shouted.

"What are you talking about?"

"I'm pregnant Joseph"

"What?"

"I'm pregnant with your *traitor baby*" She said the last two words with incredible venom.

"You're pregnant?" I couldn't believe it.

"Yes, but you know I can't go through with it. I can't bring your traitor baby into the world"

"What? No, of course you can"

"You're right, you know" she said "It *is* over. I can't let this go on."
She was frighteningly calm.

"I've failed my Führer, and I can't let it go on. I can't let *this* go on" she started punching her stomach.

"Stop it! What are you...?"

Before I could finish, she put the gun in her mouth "No! No! Please Gisela no!"

She closed her eyes and pulled the trigger. There was a loud explosion, and her lifeless body dropped to the ground.

"No!!!!" I ran over and picked her up to check her pulse, but there was no point; she was gone.

"No!! Please god no!!" There was nothing I could do. She was gone. She was gone, and she had taken our child with her. I sat holding her, crying, until someone ran into the room.

47. Berlin.

The following morning, I was sat on the train to Berlin. I was dead inside, staring unfocused at the blur through the window. Images of Gisela's last moments haunted me every time I closed my eyes.

The overwhelming tiredness didn't help; I had spent the previous night at the police station, with very little sleep. The interrogations had gone on for some hours, but I had finally managed to persuade them that she had killed herself out of guilt because she had fallen pregnant out of wedlock. They had accepted my story and released me.

Sitting on the train, I thought my life no longer had meaning. She had killed my child. My child. Our future. It wasn't something I could fully understand. Why had she done it? Had she been so far gone that she couldn't see common sense? Or even reality?

I looked down at my shaking hands. They still had her blood on them. My uniform was also still covered in her blood as I had no fresh clothes to change into.

I needed to get back to Enschede, to see Judith, to feel her healing arms around me.

However, she would have to wait until tomorrow, because today I had an appointment with someone else.

Once at headquarters, I went straight upstairs and saw his adjutant.

"Can I help you sir?" he said.

"I want to see him, now"

"I'm afraid he's busy this morning sir, I can make you an appointment for later?"

"Just tell him Joseph Deckman is here"

He looked at me, my uniform covered in blood, unsure what to do.

"Now!"I shouted.

He shot up and walked over to the double doors where he knocked urgently, and entered.

A few moments later, he came back out, leaving the door open.

"He will see you immediately sir" he said.

"Thank you" I walked in, and closed the door behind me. He was sat behind his desk, busy reading something.

"Sturmbannführer Deckman. I was under the impression that our business had been concluded" he said without looking up from whatever it was he was reading.

"I'm here because of Gisela" I said.

"Who? Oh, the nurse"

"Yes, the nurse. Or, to be more precise, your niece"

He stopped reading, and slowly raised his head to meet my eyes.

"How do you know that?"

"So it's true? Thank you for confirming"

"Is that blood on your uniform?" He asked with a look of disgust on his face.

"Yes"

He blanched. "Gisela?"

"Yes"

He went to draw his pistol, but I was faster "By her own hand" I said, pointing my pistol at him.

"Absurd" he said, waving the allegation away with his hand.

"She didn't want to bring my traitor baby into the world. She said she'd failed her Führer, then shot herself"

He fell back into his chair. "Traitor baby? She was pregnant?"

"Yes, she was pregnant. And I told her about Heydrich, about how you'd blackmailed me into killing him for you"

"What? Why would you do that? Surely you must have known it would upset her?"

"That was before she'd told me she was pregnant!" I shouted.

I checked myself, and continued calmly "I tried to persuade her it was all over, and it would all be fine, but she didn't listen. Instead, she put a gun in her mouth and pulled the trigger"

He was silent.

"What happens now?" he said eventually, without even the slightest hint of emotion. Like nothing had happened. Like her life hadn't mattered. Like my child's life hadn't mattered. I wanted to kill him. It would have been easy; I could just squeeze my trigger finger ever so slightly, and shoot him like the cowardly dog he is. Naturally, I would be killed moments later by his guards, so I pushed the thought from my mind.

"Now, you get to do some things for me" I said, putting my pistol back in the holster.

"What things?" he sneered.

I opened my brief case and handed him a form. "First, you'll sign this" He took it from me, read it and laughed, saying "I'm not signing this" In disgust, he threw the document back at me.

"You *are* signing it" I said "Or *this* will be made public" I pulled the large file out of the briefcase.

"What is that?" he laughed.

"Heydrich's file on *you*. Telephone transcripts, documents, photographs. It's all in here"

His smile disappeared. "Where did you get that?"

"He gave it to me before he died"

"What? Why would he do that?"

"To help me" I said "I told you, he was my friend" There were many other reasons why, but I wasn't in the mood to get into a long discussion here. "It was right there behind you in his office safe the whole time"

He looked down at the file. "That could be anything" he said "How do I know it is what you claim it to be?"

I pulled out a photograph, and showed it to him. "Look familiar?" It was a photograph of him, tied, gagged and blindfolded with a man pleasuring him. The colour drained from his face.

"Where did you get this filth?" he spat, and tried to take the photograph.

I pulled back my hand "Tut tut Reichsführer, looks like you've been partaking in illicit activities with other men"

"What do you want?" He had a look of total resignation on his pathetic little face.

"Sign" I handed back the document.

He gave me long hard stare, then signed it.

"And the stamp" I said.

Reluctantly, he stamped the document with his official seal and handed it to me.

"And now?" he said. "Promotion? Medals? Money?"

I shook my head "I don't want your medals or promotion, and money is of no use to me. No, what I want is an assurance that if I give this file to you, you'll leave me alone. Forget all about Joseph Deckman"

"You're out of your mind" he laughed.

"Not at all. It's simple; I give you the file, you leave me alone"

"How can I be sure you've given me everything, or don't have copies?" He sneered.

"You don't" I smiled. "You are familiar with the stories of Sherlock Holmes? A Scandal in Bohemia? The possibility of copies is my safety net"

"How can I trust you won't use them against me?"

"You have my word of honour" I said.

"Pah! And why should I accept that?" he laughed.

"Because my loyalty is my honour" I said, and threw the pack of photographs on his desk.

"Loyalty to *whom* exactly?" He asked "Certainly not your Führer"

"I am loyal to the German people, and will do whatever it takes to bring this war to an end"

He stared at me for a long moment, then just nodded.

"One last thing…." I said.

48. Enschede.

"Good morning Sturmbannführer" Dietz said as I walked into the office the following morning.

"Morning Dietz" I said. I wasn't in the mood for conversation; I just wanted to lock myself in my office and stay there all day, wallowing in my own personal misery. Alternatively, I could drink until I forgot in the mess. Sadly, I couldn't of course, I had duties to perform.

"You look tired sir" he said.

"I am tired, and fed up Dietz, I've had it up to here with this war"

"I'm sorry sir. Can I get you some tea?"

I smiled "That would be fantastic thank you"

"I'll bring it up to your office"

I went upstairs, and read through the summary report waiting on my desk. Low level resistance activity, however, I did note that the telephone lines had been cut again. I'd have to get word to them to stop, otherwise the reprisals would be catastrophic. I'd speak to Ecke later today.

Dietz knocked, and came in with a tray "Your tea sir"

"Thank you Dietz. How have things been here? I apologise for my prolonged absences"

"Pretty quiet to be honest sir, not a lot going on for us. There has been another instance of the telephone lines being cut in Enschede. I don't see what it is they hope to achieve by doing so. It only enrages the Ortskommandant, and more people get deported to the labour camps"

"I completely agree" I said. The gain versus loss was insignificant. Waste of human lives.

"Other than that, we are up to date with our administration"

"How are the other two performing? You will have to forgive me, I have forgotten their names" I said wearily.

"Understandable sir. Corporals Altman and Schwartz are performing their duties with excellence sir"

"You have done well" I said, pouring my tea. "Would you care for some tea?"

"I have never tried tea before sir" he said.

"Ah! What better time than now" I smiled "Take a seat"

He sat at the desk with me, and I poured him a cup of tea with milk.

"To your good health Dietz" I said, raising my cup.

"And to yours sir" he said. He tasted the tea and pulled a face.

I laughed "What do you think?"

"Better than the coffee, but not quite my thing" he said.

"It's not to everybody's liking, that's for sure"

"No sir, I suppose it isn't"

I liked Dietz, he was a conscientious soldier, with a great sense of duty. He had run this office perfectly.

"Dietz, you know what I think?" I said.

"No sir, what?"

"I think you'd make a fine officer"

"Sir?"

"You've run this department exemplary in my absence, and you have the respect of the others"

"I suppose that's true, if you say so sir"

"How would you like to go to Tolz?"

"Me? I am a Sergeant, sir"

"Ach, I'll promote you to Oberscharführer, and write a letter of recommendation for the school"

"Why sir, if you don't mind me asking?"

"Someone else did the same for me not long ago. I owe it to myself to return the favour"

"I don't really know what to say sir" he said.

"You could just say yes"

He smiled "It would be an honour sir, my parents would be so proud. So, yes. Thank you"

"Excellent. Draw up the paperwork, and I'll sign it. I'll write the letter of recommendation now"

He stood up to leave, and a thought came to me. "Dietz, one more thing. Write up the other two, I'll promote them to Scharführer"

"Yes sir" he smiled "Of course"

I typed out Dietz's letter, and signed it. It felt good to do something positive, something that would make lives better. And, why not?

I had no idea how long this war was going to last, and I had the power to promote my men, so why wouldn't I?

We could all be dead tomorrow.

Ugh. This was a struggle. I needed a break from all this, some time to recharge.

There was a knock at the door, and Dietz came in. "Sorry to disturb you sir, but I have the paperwork you requested"

"Not a problem" I said wearily. He placed the documents in front of me, and I signed them all.

"Stamp them and get them off to headquarters as soon as possible. Then get yourselves to the quartermasters office, I expect to see you all in the correct uniform tomorrow morning"

"Yes sir" he smiled, and walked out with the papers.

I was starting to feel better. What would make me feel normal again would be Judith. I needed to see her. I grabbed my cap and gloves, and went downstairs.

"I'll be over in Enschede for the rest of the day. See you tomorrow gentlemen. And remember; correct uniform please"

"Yes sir" they all said, looking extremely pleased.

The drive was pleasant, as was the weather. It was sunny, with only a few clouds in the sky. True to his word, Dietz had the car serviced for me, and it had four new tyres. The fresh air in my face helped somewhat to lift my depressive mood.

I parked up outside the office in the Rembrandtlaan, and sat in the vehicle for a while, staring at the steering wheel. I couldn't face anyone just yet, so I decided to go for a walk rather than go inside.

I strolled into the old town centre, and walked along the bricked streets. There were children playing all around, meaning it must be the school summer holidays. That meant Judith wouldn't be at the school. Disappointed, I made my way to her grandmother's tea room in the hope that she might be there. I looked through the window, but didn't see her.

There was a small table set up outside, so I sat out in the sunshine and ordered some tea. Her grandmother came out to take my order, and she was very polite, even friendly towards me. In general, I found the local people to be friendly enough, but there was always the undercurrent of distrust and hatred. And I couldn't blame them.

We had invaded their country. If that wasn't bad enough, they saw the SS uniform and immediately thought the worst.

The old lady came outside without my tea, and said "It's a bit cold out here, why don't you come inside?"

This confused me for a second "No, I am fine out here in the sun thank you"

"It is warmer inside" she insisted. Why would she want me to go inside? Then I realised that Judith was probably inside. I stood up, gathered my things, and went in.

Straight away Judith flew into my arms "Oh Joseph, I've missed you" she kissed me passionately.

"I've missed you too" I held her tight, it felt so good to be in her arms. Her grandmother smiled, locked the shop door, and disappeared out to the back.

The warmth of Judith#s body against mine was like a wonder drug. Everything felt better when I was with her, and my depression seemed to lift almost instantly. There must have been some trace left though, because she looked at me and said "Something is wrong. What happened?"

"Gisela is dead"

"Oh my God, how?"

"She took her own life"

I told her the whole story about Gisela turning out to be a fanatical Nazi, totally devoted to the Führer, and that she thought she'd failed him. I chose to leave out the part about our child; I wasn't sure I was ready to talk about it yet.

She looked at me intently for a moment "There's something else"

I nodded "Ask me some other time, not right now"

"Very well. I'm just happy you're here" she smiled.

"As am I" I said "Things are better when I'm with you, I knew it from the first time I saw you. There was just something about you, I didn't know what it was back then. But now, I do"

"What?" she asked.

"I belong with you" I said. "I love you Judith"

A tear ran down her cheek "I love you too" she leaned over and kissed me.

She sat back, with a look of sadness on her face.

"What is it?" I asked.

"Us, being together is impossible" she said "It's not safe for either of us"

"I know" I said quietly.

I knew it wasn't the time to tell her about the marriage permit I got Himmler to sign, so I chose to keep that for a better time. I knew one thing though; if we were ever in Germany together, I would take her straight to a church and marry her.

"We can't be together here" I said "But I am due some leave. Come away with me"

"Where would we go?"

I pulled the house deeds from my briefcase "I know a nice place in Bavaria"

The End.

Outro.

I hope you enjoyed this first outing of Joseph Deckman. A total departure from my normal writing style, it was an absolute joy to write, and I managed it in just over two months.
I hope you enjoyed.

Just to re-iterate:
I make no apologies for historical inaccuracies; it's fiction for a reason.

Stay tuned, Sturmbannführer Joseph Deckman will return in the second part of this series:

The Second Objective.

Acknowledgements.

Thank you to my proof reader Sarah; your patience is infinite, and skill with the red font/pen is by now legendary. Thanks to you, I publish coherent stories, not nonsensical garbage.

Also, a big thank you to my dad, who took time to read through the draft copy and make corrections.

SS Ranks.

Schutze - Private

Oberschutze - Private First Class

SS-Sturmann - Lance Corporal

SS-Rottenfuhrer - Corporal

SS-Unterscharfuhrer - Sergeant

SS-Scharfuhrer - Staff Sergeant

SS-Oberscharfuhrer - Sergeant First Class

SS-Hauptscharfuhrer - Master Sergeant

SS-Sturmscharfuhrer - Sergeant Major

SS-Untersturmfuhrer - 2nd Lieutenant

SS-Obersturmfuhrer - 1st Lieutenant

SS-Hauptsturmfuhrer - Captain

SS-Sturmbannfuhrer - Major

SS-Obersturmbannfuhrer - Lieutenant Colonel

SS-Standartenfuhrer - Colonel

SS-Brigadefuhrer - Brigadier-General

SS-Gruppenfuhrer - Major-General

SS-Obergruppenfuhrer - Lieutenant-General

SS-Oberstgruppenfuhrer - General

Reichfuhrer-SS - Heinrich Himmler

Printed in Great Britain
by Amazon